P9-BYW-696

*It's the
sound
every killer
craves...*

A Killer's Trap

Tucking the Salems in the pocket of her windbreaker, Wendy approached the minivan. The little girl had been struggling with one of three bags. But now she stopped to stare at Wendy. The child kept shaking her head over and over. Tears slid down her cheeks. She seemed to be mouthing something to her.

"It looks like you could use an extra hand," Wendy said.

Propped up on his crutches, the father smiled. "I really appreciate this. If you could just slide those bags into the backseat, we can take it from there."

"No problem." Wendy hoisted one of the bags into the back. The young girl stood by the open door. She whispered something, and Wendy turned to her. "What did you say, honey?"

"*Run*," the child whispered.

Bewildered, Wendy stopped to stare at her.

The father cleared his throat. "If you could get in there and slide the bag to the driver's side. Just climb right in there . . ."

Wendy hesitated.

"*Run*," the young girl repeated, under her breath.

For a second, Wendy was paralyzed. She squinted at the child, who began to back away from her. Wendy wasn't looking at the man.

She didn't see him coming toward her with one of his crutches in the air.

"Run!" the child screamed at her. "No—"

It was the last thing Wendy heard before the crutch cracked against her skull. . . .

Books by Kevin O'Brien

ONLY SON

THE NEXT TO DIE

MAKE THEM CRY

WATCH THEM DIE

LEFT FOR DEAD

THE LAST VICTIM

KILLING SPREE

ONE LAST SCREAM

Published by Kensington Publishing Corporation

ONE LAST SCREAM

KEVIN O'BRIEN

PINNACLE BOOKS
Kensington Publishing Corp.
www.kensingtonbooks.com

PINNACLE BOOKS are published by

Kensington Publishing Corp.
850 Third Avenue
New York, NY 10022

All Kensington titles, imprints, and distributed lines are available at special quantity discounts for bulk purchases for sales promotions, premiums, fund-raising, educational, or institutional use. Special book excerpts or customized printings can also be created to fit specific needs. For details, write or phone the office of the Kensington special sales manager: Kensington Publishing Corp., 850 Third Avenue, New York, NY 10022, attn: Special Sales Department; phone: 1-800-221-2647.

PUBLISHER'S NOTE
This book is a work of fiction. Names, characters, businesses, organizations, places, events, and incidents either are the product of the author's imagination or are used fictitiously. Any resemblance to actual persons, living or dead, or events, or locales is entirely coincidental.

PINNACLE BOOKS and the Pinnacle logo are Reg. U.S. Pat. & TM Off.

ISBN-13: 978-0-7860-1776-8
ISBN-10: 0-7860-1776-7

First printing: January 2008

10 9 8 7 6 5 4 3 2 1

Printed in the United States of America

This book is for my friend Doug Mendini.

ACKNOWLEDGMENTS

My thanks to my editor and good friend, John Scognamiglio, who always knows just when I need a pat on the back or a kick in the butt. I couldn't have written this book—or any of my others—without him. I'm grateful to everyone else at Kensington, especially the wonderful Doug Mendini. About time I dedicated a book to this classy man!

A great big thank-you also goes to my agents extraordinaire, Meg Ruley, Christina Hogrebe, and the terrific people at Jane Rotrosen Agency.

I owe another big thank-you to Tommy Dreiling, for his support, encouragement, and friendship.

As usual, my talented writer-friends were incredibly helpful with their suggestions on how to make early drafts of this book better. Thank you to Cate Goethals and David Massengill; and to my Writers Group pals, Soyon Im and Garth Stein.

Thanks also to Lori, at Open Adoption & Family Services, for answering so many of my questions about adoption and foster care.

I'd also like to thank the following friends for their support and encouragement: Lloyd Adalist, Dan Annear & Chuck Rank, Marlys Bourm, Terry & Judine Brooks, Kyle Bryan & Dan Monda, George Camper, Jim & Barbara Church, Anna Cottle & Mary Alice Kier, Paul Dwoskin, Tom Goodwin, Cathy Johnson, Ed & Sue Kelly, David Korabik, Jim Munchel, Eva Marie Saint, John Saul & Michael Sack, Bill, JB, Tammy & Fran at The Seattle Mystery Bookshop, Dan, Doug and Ann Stutesman, George & Sheila Stydahar, Mark Von Borstel, Michael Wells, and the gang at Bailey/Coy Books.

Finally, thanks to my wonderful family, Adele, Mary Lou, Cathy, Bill, and Joan.

Chapter One

She turned the key in the ignition, and nothing happened, just a hollow *click, click, click.*

"Oh, shit," Kristen murmured. She felt a little pang of dread in her stomach.

The battery wasn't dead, because the inside dome light had gone on when she'd climbed into her Ford Probe a minute ago.

Biting her lip, Kristen gave the key another twist. *Click, click, click.* Nothing.

It was 11:20 on a chilly October night. Hers was the only car in the restaurant lot. Kristen had just finished a seven-hour shift waiting tables at The Friendly Fajita. She'd closed up the place with Rafael, the perpetually horny 19-year-old busboy, and he'd just taken off on his rusty old Harley. Kristen could still hear its engine roaring as he sailed down Broadway. It was the only sound she heard.

There was a phone in the restaurant, and she had a key. But she and Rafael had already set the alarm. It would go off if she went back inside, and she could never remember the code, especially while that shrill incessant alarm was sounding. She'd have to go look for a phone someplace else, and then call a tow company or a cab. Her boyfriend, Brian, was out of town at a golf tournament down in San Diego.

"Please, please, please," she whispered, trying the ignition once again. The car didn't respond except for that hollow *click, click, click.*

"Damn it to hell," she grumbled. Grabbing her purse and a windbreaker from the passenger seat, Kristen climbed out of the car and shut the door. She didn't bother locking it.

She took a long look down the street. Most of the other businesses along this main drag were closed for the night. There were a couple of taverns farther down Broadway. Kristen loathed the idea of hoofing it several blocks along the roadside. The waist-length windbreaker didn't quite cover her stupid waitress uniform. The Friendly Fajita's owner, Stan Munch, who was about as Mexican as she was, made her wear this señorita getup with a white, off-the-shoulder peasant blouse and a gaudy purple, green, and yellow billowy skirt over a petticoat, for God's sake. With her short, blond hair, green eyes, and pale complexion, she looked like an idiot in the outfit. But, hell, anyone would appear ridiculous in it. The thing looked like a Halloween costume.

The Friendly Fajita had been open for four months, and it was floundering. Moses Lake didn't need another Mexican restaurant. Besides, the food was mediocre and overpriced. And if that wasn't enough to drive customers away, Stan had the same two Herb Alpert CDs on a continuous loop for background *authenticity.* If Kristen never heard "The Lonely Bull" again in her life, it would be too soon.

Maybe she could flag down a cop car, or a good Samaritan. Kristen ducked back into the Probe just long enough to pop the hood and switch on the hazard lights. She figured that would make it easier for passersby to see that she needed help. Of course, she was also making it easier for the wrong person to see that she was stranded.

It suddenly occurred to Kristen that someone might have sabotaged her car. Just a little sugar in the gas tank—that was all it took. She'd read that before he started killing, the young Ted Bundy liked to screw with women's cars, so he could later watch them when they were stranded and vulnerable.

He just watched them. It turned him on.

Kristen wondered if someone was looking at her right now as she stood beside her broken-down car in front of the darkened restaurant. Maybe he was across the street by the flower shop. He could be hiding in the shadows behind those bushes, studying her through a pair of binoculars.

Or maybe he was even closer than that.

She shuddered and rubbed her arms. "Stop it," Kristen muttered to herself. "You're perfectly safe. There aren't any serial killers in Moses Lake."

Still, she reached inside her purse and felt around for the pepper spray. She wondered if it even worked any more. She'd bought the little canister over two years ago while a junior at Eastern Washington University in Cheney. She'd majored in graphic design, and planned to move to Seattle. But Brian got a job as the golf pro at one of Moses Lake's courses. It was a big resort town. Kristen had decided to put Seattle on hold, and stick with Brian for a while. There wasn't much need for a graphic artist in Moses Lake. So, here she was, dressed up like a Mexican peasant girl and stranded outside The Friendly Fajita at 11:30 on a cold Wednesday night.

Kristen kept the pepper spray clutched in her fist.

One car passed the restaurant, and didn't even slow down. She waited, and then gave a tentative wave to an approaching pickup, but it just whooshed by. Kristen glanced at her wristwatch—only two cars in almost five minutes. Not a good sign.

She noticed a pair of headlights down the road in the distance. Kristen stepped toward the parking lot entrance, and started waving again, more urgently this time. As the vehicle came closer, she noticed it was an old, beat-up station wagon with just one person inside. It looked like a man at the wheel. He got closer, and she could see him now. He was smiling, almost as if he'd been expecting to find her there.

A chill raced through her. Kristen stopped waving and automatically stepped back.

The station wagon turned in to the restaurant parking lot. Warily, Kristen eyed the man in the car. He was in his late thirties and might have been very handsome once, but he'd obviously gone to seed. His face looked a bit bloated and jowly. The thin brown hair was receding. But his eyes sparkled, and she might have found his smile sexy if only she weren't so stranded and vulnerable. Right now, she didn't need anyone leering at her.

He rolled down his window. "Looks like you could use some help." The way he spoke, it was almost a come-on.

Kristen shook her head and backed away from the station wagon. "Um, I already called someone and they should be here any minute, but thanks anyway."

"You sure?" the man asked, his smirk waning.

"Positive, I—" Kristen hesitated as she noticed the beautiful little girl sitting beside him in the passenger seat. She had a book and a doll in her lap. The child smiled at her.

"Wish I knew more about car engines," the man said. "I'd get out and take a look for you, but it wouldn't do any good. Want us to stick around in case this person you called doesn't show up?" He turned to the child. "You don't mind waiting, do you, Annie?"

The little girl shook her head, then started sucking her thumb. She glanced down at her picture book.

The father gently stroked her hair. And when he smiled

up at Kristen again, there was nothing flirtatious about it. "Would you like us to wait?" he asked.

Kristen felt silly. She shrugged. "Actually, it's been a while since I called these people. Maybe I should phone them again." She nodded toward the center of town. "I think there's a pay phone at this tavern just down Broadway. Would you mind giving me a lift?"

"Well, if you live around here, we can take you home." He turned to his daughter again. "Should we give the nice lady a ride to her house, honey?"

Breaking into a smile, the girl nodded emphatically. "Yes!" She even bounced in the passenger seat a little.

Kristen let out a tiny laugh. "I don't want to take you out of your way."

"Nonsense," the man said, stepping out of the car. He left the motor running. "We've taken a vote and it's unanimous. We're driving you home."

He touched Kristen's shoulder on his way to the passenger door. He opened it, then helped the girl out of the front seat. "This is my daughter, Annabelle," he said. "And her dolly, Gertrude."

"This isn't Gertrude!" the girl protested. "This is Daisy! Gertrude is home with—"

"Oops, sorry, sorry," her father cut in. He gave Kristen a wink. "I've committed a major faux pas, getting the names of her dollies mixed up." He opened the back door for his daughter. "C'mon, sweetheart, climb in back and buckle up. And hold on to Daisy. Let's hurry up now. This nice lady is tired, and wants to go home."

Kristen hurried back to her car, switched off the blinkers, locked the doors, and shut the hood. Then she returned to the station wagon. "I live on West Peninsula Drive," she said, climbing into the front passenger seat. The man closed the door for her.

The car was warm, and smelled a little bit like French fries. She noticed an empty Coke can and a crumpled-up Arby's bag on the floor by her feet.

The man walked around the front of the car, then got behind the wheel. He pulled out of the parking lot.

Kristen looked back at her broken-down Ford Probe. She'd call the tow company in the morning. Right now, she just wanted to get home and take a shower. She turned to the man and smiled. "I really appreciate this."

Eyes on the road, he just nodded. He seemed very intent on his driving.

Kristen glanced over her shoulder at the little girl. "Thank you for giving me your seat, Annabelle."

"You're welcome," the child said, her nose in the book.

"So, how old are you, Annabelle?"

The girl looked up at her and smiled. She really was beautiful—a little girl with an adult face. Kristin had seen photos of Jackie Kennedy and Elizabeth Taylor when they were around this child's age, and they had that same haunting mature beauty to them.

"I'm four years old," she announced proudly.

"My, you're almost a young lady!" Kristen turned forward again. "She's gorgeous," she said to the man.

But he didn't reply. Another car sped toward them in the oncoming lane. Its headlights swept across his face. He had the same strange, cryptic smile Kristen had noticed when she first spotted him.

She squirmed a bit in the passenger seat. Moses Lake was an oasis. Just three minutes outside of the bright, busy resort town, it became dark desert, with a smattering of homes. Kristen and Brian's town house was in the dark outskirts.

"Um, you need to take a left up here," she said, pointing ahead. But he wasn't slowing down. "It's a left here," she repeated. "Sir . . ."

He sped past the access road. "Oh, brother, I can't believe

I missed that," he said, slowing down to about fifteen miles per hour. "I'm sorry. I'll find a place to turn around here. I must be more tired than I thought. My reaction time is off."

Biting her lip, Kristen wondered why he didn't just make a U-turn. There was hardly any traffic.

"Here we go," he announced, turning right onto a street marked DEAD END. They crawled past a few houses along the narrow road. Kristen counted six driveways he could have used to turn his car around. They inched by the last streetlight, and the darkened road became gravelly. Kristen noticed a house under construction on her right.

"I think there's a turnaround coming up," he said, squinting at the road ahead.

Kristen swallowed hard, and didn't say anything. The car was barely moving. Its headlights pierced the unknown darkness ahead of them. "Can't we—can't we just back up and turn around?" she asked.

"I'm beginning to think you're right," he said. He shot a look in the rearview mirror. "How are you doing back there, honey? You tired?"

"Kind of," the child replied with a whimper.

"She's up way past her bedtime," the man said. "But I *needed* her tonight. She's Daddy's little helper."

The car came to a stop. The headlights illuminated the end of the road and a long barricade, painted with black-and-white diagonal stripes. Beyond that, it was just blackness.

Puzzled, Kristen stared at the man. "Why did you need your daughter tonight?"

He smiled at her—that same cryptic smirk. "If she weren't here, you never would have climbed into this car with me."

Daddy's little helper.

All at once, Kristen realized what he was telling her. She quickly reached into her purse for the pepper spray. She didn't see his fist coming toward her face.

She just heard the little girl give out a startled yelp. "Oh!"

That was the last thing Kristen heard before the man knocked her unconscious.

"God, please! Somebody help me!"

An hour had passed and they'd driven thirty-five miles.

The little girl sat alone in the front passenger seat of the old station wagon. With a tiny flashlight that had a picture of Barbie on it, she looked at her picture book.

"Please, no! Wait . . . wait . . . no . . ."

The woman's shrieks seemed to echo through the forest, where the car was parked along a crude trail. But the child paid little attention. She turned the page of her book, and tapped at the dashboard with her toes. Cold and tired, she wanted to go home. She wondered when her daddy would be finished with his "work."

When the screaming stops, that's usually when he's almost done.

She told herself it would be soon.

Seattle, Washington—*fifteen years later*

Someone had a Barenaked Ladies CD blasting. The music drifted out to the backyard—along with all the talking, laughing, and screaming from the party inside the townhouse. The place was a cheesy, slightly run-down rental down the street from the University of Washington's fraternity row. Amelia wasn't sure who was giving the party. A bunch of guys lived in the townhouse, sophomores like herself. One of them—a total stranger—had stopped her this morning when she'd been on her way to philosophy class, and he'd invited her. That happened to Amelia all the time. She was constantly getting asked to parties. It had something to do with the way she looked.

Amelia Faraday was tall, with a beautiful face and a gorgeous, buxom figure. She had shoulder-length, wavy black hair, and blue eyes. She also had a drinking problem, and knew it. So she'd declined many invitations to drink-till-you-drop campus bashes. Her boyfriend, Shane, didn't like the idea of strange guys inviting Amelia to parties, anyway. Among their friends, they were nicknamed the Perrier Twins, because they always asked for bottled water at get-togethers.

But tonight, Amelia wanted a beer—several beers, in fact, whatever it took to get drunk.

A few people had staggered out to the small backyard where Amelia stood with a beer in one hand, and the other clutching together the edges of her bulky cardigan sweater. She gazed up at the stars. It was a beautiful, crisp October Friday night.

She had a little buzz. This was only her second beer and, already, results. It happened quickly, because she'd been booze-free for the last seven weeks.

Shane didn't understand why she needed alcohol tonight. "Before you drink that beer," he'd whispered to her a few minutes ago in the corner of the jam-packed living room, "maybe you should call your therapist. Explain to her why you need it so badly."

In response, Amelia had narrowed her eyes at him, and then she'd chugged half the plastic cup full of Coors. She'd refilled the cup from the keg in the kitchen and wandered outside alone.

The truth was she hated herself right now. She was lucky to have a boyfriend like Shane. He was cute, with perpetually messy, light brown hair, blue eyes, and a well-maintained five o'clock shadow. He was sweet, and he cared about her. And his advice, patronizing as it seemed, had been practical. She'd tried to call her therapist this afternoon. But Karen had gone for the day.

So Amelia was left with these awful thoughts, and no one to help her sort them out. That was why she needed to get drunk right now.

Amelia's parents and her aunt were spending the weekend at the family cabin by Lake Wenatchee in central Washington. Ever since this afternoon, she'd been overwhelmed with a sudden, inexplicable contempt for them. She imagined driving to the cabin and killing all three of them. She even started formulating a plan, though she had no intention of carrying it out. Her parents had mentioned there was construction this weekend on their usual route, Highway 2. The cabin would be a three-hour drive from Seattle, if she took Interstate 90 and Route 97, and didn't stop. Her parents and aunt would be asleep when she arrived. She knew how to sneak into the cabin; she'd done it before. She saw herself shooting them at close range. As much as the notion bewildered and horrified her, it also made Amelia's heart race with excitement.

If only Karen were around, Amelia could have asked her therapist about this hideous daydream. How could she have these terrible thoughts? Amelia loved her parents, and Aunt Ina was like her older sister, practically her best friend.

The only way to get these poisonous feelings out of her system was to flush them out with another kind of poison. In this case, it was another cupful of Coors from the keg in the kitchen.

Amelia was heading back in there when a young woman—a pretty Asian American with a red streak in her long black hair—blocked her path through the doorway. "Hey, do you have a cig? A menthol?" she asked, shouting over the noise. "I can't find another person at this stupid party who smokes menthols."

"No, but there's a minimart about six blocks from here." Amelia had to lean close to the girl and practically yell in her ear. "If you want, I can go get some for you. I have my boyfriend's car, and I'm looking for an excuse to bolt out of here for a while." She drained the last few drops of Coors from her plastic cup. "Just let me get the car keys from my boyfriend, and then we can go."

Weaving through the crowd, Amelia made her way to Shane, who was still standing in the corner of the living room. Apparently, he'd decided that if she could fall off the wagon, so could he. He was passing a joint back and forth with some guy she didn't know.

"Are you drunk yet?" he asked, gazing at her with half-closed eyes.

"No," she lied, speaking up over the party noise. "In fact, I want to get out of here for a few minutes. Give me the car keys, will you?" With her thumb, she pointed to the other girl, who was behind her. "I'm driving my friend to the mini-mart for cigarettes. We'll be right back. Okay?"

But she was lying. She had no intention of going to the minimart. She just needed his car.

Shane dug the keys out of his jeans pocket. He plopped them in her hand. "Do whatever you want to do," he grumbled. "I don't care."

Amelia gave him a quick kiss. "Please, don't be mad at me," she whispered.

Shane started to put his arm around her, but she broke away and fled. She could hear the other girl behind her, saying something about her boyfriend being cute and that he looked like Justin Timberlake. Amelia didn't really hear her. Threading through the mob of partygoers, she made her way back to the kitchen.

"Hey, wait up!" the girl yelled. "Hey, wait a minute!" But Amelia kept moving. She spotted a half-full bottle of tequila on the kitchen counter amid an assortment of empty bottles and beer cans. She swiped it up, and then tucked it inside the flap of her cardigan sweater. Heading out the kitchen door, Amelia found a walkway to the front of the house. As she hurried toward Shane's beat-up VW Golf, she heard the girl screaming at her from the side of the townhouse. "Hey, don't forget the cigs! I'll pay you back! I need menthols! All right? Did you hear me?"

Amelia waved without looking back at her, and then she ducked inside Shane's car. Starting up the engine, she stashed the tequila bottle under her seat, and then peeled out of the parking spot. She didn't look in her rearview mirror as she sped down the street.

Four minutes later, she saw Marty's MiniMart on the corner. Only a couple of cars were in the lot in front of the tacky little store; there was plenty of available parking.

But Amelia kept going, and headed for the interstate. If she didn't make any stops along the way, she'd reach Lake Wenatchee by about two in the morning. The gas tank was three-quarters full.

Amelia pressed harder on the accelerator, and kept telling herself that she loved her parents and her Aunt Ina. She'd never do anything to harm them.

Never.

Chapter Two

Ina McMillan hated these sinks with separate spouts for the hot and cold water. Washing her face, she had to cup her hands under the cold, and then switch over to the hot water. It was either scalding or freezing when Ina finally splashed her face. Water ran down her arms to her elbows, dampening the sleeves of her robe. What a pain in the ass. It was a major undertaking just to wash her face here.

She didn't like Jenna and Mark's cabin, and she hated the country. Ina was a city girl.

Actually, her sister and brother-in-law's "weekend get-away" spot wasn't a *cabin*. It was a slightly dilapidated little two-story Cape Cod–style house built in the fifties. There was a fallout shelter in the basement, along with a furnace that manufactured more noise than heat. Ina's bedroom, with its cute dormer windows, slanted ceiling, and creaky twin beds, had a space heater that might as well have had FIRE HAZARD stenciled all over it. She'd been instructed not to leave the heater on overnight. Fine. Whatever. Either way, the room still felt damp, cold, and drafty.

The house was just off the lake, and cut off from the rest of civilization by rolling wooded hills that wreaked havoc on cell phone service. There wasn't a landline phone either. For emergencies, they were supposed to run a half mile around the lake to this old lesbian neighbor's house and use her phone. There was also a pay phone at a diner about three miles away at the mountain road junction.

Just what her sister and Mark saw in this godforsaken shack was a mystery to Ina. For a spot that was supposed to be so relaxing, everything was an ordeal. They couldn't even drive up to the place. Mark had had to park the car by a turn-around on a bluff, and then they'd trekked down a steep trail through the forest, lugging their suitcases all the way. And, of course, Ina had overpacked.

She felt like an idiot for bringing along her lacy burgundy nightgown and the matching silk robe. Flannel pajamas would have been more appropriate.

The sexy nightwear had been a Christmas present from George last year, back when he'd thought it possible to rekindle some romance in their marriage. He was home with the kids right now. They'd agreed this weekend away from each other might do them some good—a time-out from all the tension.

She was silly to think it would be any less tense here, with Mark and her sister.

Ina dried off her face and stared at her reflection in the bathroom mirror. Even with her wild, wavy, shoulder-length auburn hair pulled back in a ponytail, and no makeup, she was still pretty. How often did other 38-year-olds get mistaken for college girls? Well, that still happened to her sometimes. She had clear, creamy skin and blue eyes. And right now, the burgundy nightgown showed off her willowy figure to good advantage.

Padding down the hall to her room, Ina glanced over her

shoulder at the partially open bedroom door. Mark and Jenna still had the light on. She half expected, half hoped Mark would come to the door and see her.

He was the reason she'd packed the burgundy nightgown ensemble. Ina wanted to look sexy for her sister's husband.

But Mark wasn't looking at her in the hallway. He was where he belonged, in bed with her sister.

Ina retreated into her damp, drafty little bedroom and, once again, wished she'd packed her flannel pj's. With a sigh, she bent down and switched off the space heater. She turned down her bedcovers. She was about to take off her robe, but hesitated. She heard a noise outside, and suddenly stopped moving.

She listened to what sounded like footsteps. A hand over her heart, she crept to one of the dormer windows and looked down. Ina gasped.

Just below her, a dark figure darted between some bushes.

Reeling back from the window, she turned and raced down the hall. "Mark!" she called, but the word barely came out. She couldn't get a breath. Ina burst into their bedroom. "There's someone outside!" she whispered.

Mark and Jenna were sitting up in bed. "Are you sure?" he asked, putting his book aside.

She nodded urgently. "I saw someone—something—in the bushes right below my window."

"Some*one* or some*thing*?" he asked.

Flustered, Ina gave a helpless shrug. "I—I'm not sure—"

"It was probably just a bear," Jenna said, a copy of *Vanity Fair* in her hands. She was wearing her glasses and one of Mark's T-shirts. "They come around all the time looking for food scraps in the garbage. They're harmless."

Ina hated the way her sister was talking to her as if she were a scared little girl. "Well, whatever it is," she replied, still shaking, "this *thing* is right below my window, and it scared the shit out of me. What, do you expect me to go back in there and just fall asleep now? It looked like a *person*, Jenna."

"I better check it out," Mark grumbled, getting to his feet. "Could be our uninvited houseguest is back."

Biting her lip, Ina watched him throw a robe over his T-shirt and boxer shorts. Mark was balding and a bit out of shape, but he still had a certain masculine sexiness. He slipped his bare feet into a pair of slippers. The *uninvited houseguest* was another reason she didn't like this damn cabin.

When they'd arrived there earlier tonight, Mark and Jenna had noticed several things out of place. Someone had tracked mud onto the kitchen and living room floors. A few empty beer bottles, some cigarette butts, and a crumpled-up potato chip bag littered the pathway from the front porch to the lake. The intruder had even built a fire in the fireplace. Jenna wondered out loud if their daughter, Amelia, had stayed there on the sly with her boyfriend. But Mark, trusting soul that he was, insisted Amelia hadn't touched a drop in weeks, and neither had Shane. Both were nonsmokers, too. So the empty beer bottles and cigarette butts couldn't have been theirs.

Rolling her eyes, Jenna said he shouldn't believe everything Amelia told him. Their daughter had a good heart, but she wasn't exactly reliable—or honest. That was why Amelia was seeing a therapist once a week, to the tune of eighty bucks a pop.

Ina had tagged behind Jenna and Mark. They'd continued to bicker while searching the house for further signs of this uninvited guest. "Well, whoever was here, they're long gone," Mark had said, at last. He'd assured Ina that the culprit probably wouldn't be back. "If it'll make you feel any better, I keep a hunting rifle in the bedroom closet. We'll be okay."

Now, Ina watched him reach into the closet for that rifle. Cocking the handle, he checked the chamber to make sure it was loaded.

"Better bag this *prowler* on the first shot, Mark," Jenna said, still sitting up in bed. She tossed her sister a droll look, then went back to her *Vanity Fair*. "The great white hunter only keeps one bullet in that stupid gun. The rest are in the kitchen drawer downstairs. He hasn't fired that thing since—"

"Oh, would you just give it a rest?" Mark hissed. "Can't you see she's scared?"

"All I see is a lot of *drama*," Jenna remarked, eyes on her magazine.

Mark ignored her, then brushed past Ina and started down the hall.

Frowning at her older sister, Ina lingered in the bedroom doorway for a moment. Finally, she retreated down the corridor and caught up with Mark on the stairs.

Like a soldier going into a sniper zone, Mark held the rifle in front of him, barrel end up. He paused near the bottom step. Ina hovered behind him. She was trembling. She looked at the front door and then the darkened living room. Logs still smouldered in the fireplace, their red embers glowing. The cushy old rocking chair beside the hearth was perfectly still. Ina didn't see any sign of a break-in. Nothing was disturbed.

Mark crept to the front door and twisted the handle. "Locked," he said.

Ina put her hand on his shoulder and sighed with relief.

He squinted at her. "Did you *really* see something outside?"

Ina scowled at him. "Of course. Why would I make that up?"

"All right, all right, take it easy," he murmured.

Heading toward the kitchen, Mark stopped to switch on a lamp. Ina stayed on his heels. He checked the kitchen door. "We're okay here, too," he announced. Then he unlocked the door and opened it. "Stay put. I'll look outside."

"No, don't leave me here alone!" she whispered.

"Relax. I'll be two minutes at the most. Lock up after me if you're so nervous." He ducked outside.

Shivering, Ina stayed at the threshold for a moment, then she closed and locked the door. What was she supposed to do if he didn't come back? She imagined hearing that gun go off, and then nothing. She couldn't call the police; she couldn't call anyone, because they had no phone service in this god-damn place.

Ina gazed out the kitchen window. She didn't see Mark, and didn't hear anything outside. The refrigerator hummed. It was an old thing from the sixties. The avocado color matched the stove. Gingerbread trim adorned the pantry shelves. The framed "Food Is Cooked With Butter and Love" sign—along with the worn, yellow dinette set—had been in Ina and Jenna's kitchen when they were growing up. But these familiar things gave her no comfort right now.

And it wasn't much help knowing Jenna was upstairs—if she should need her. What could Jenna do?

Her sister was being a real pill tonight. Maybe Jenna knew what had happened between Mark and her. Had Mark said something? This was their first weekend together since she and Mark had "slipped." That was how Mark described it, like they'd had an accident, a little catastrophe. "It was a mistake. It never should have happened. It never would have happened if we weren't going through this awful time right now. We just—slipped, Ina."

It had been a rough summer. Mark and Jenna's 17-year-old son, Collin, had drowned in May, and his death had sent the family into a tailspin. Collin's sister, Amelia, became un-hinged and almost unmanageable. They had put her on some kind of medication, and that helped. But there weren't any pills Mark and Jenna could take to remedy their confusion, anger, and hurt. In their pain, they lashed out at each other.

One afternoon in early August, Mark came down to Seattle from their home in Bellingham, and he met Ina for a drink at the Alexis Hotel. He'd come to her for consolation. But they ended up talking about her problems with George. They also ended up in a room on the fifth floor—and in bed together.

She couldn't believe it. Mark, her brother-in-law, of all people. She'd known him for eighteen years and, yes, when he'd first started dating Jenna, she'd had a bit of a crush on him. In his late twenties, he'd been a cute guy, but he'd gained a lot of weight and lost a lot of hair since then. Appearances were very important to Ina, and she'd married the right guy for that. She loved hearing her girlfriends describe George as a hunk. He taught history at the University of Washington, and she relished walking in on his classes from time to time. Whenever George introduced her to the class as his wife, Ina could tell which ones had crushes on him. She'd get these dagger looks from several girls (and often a guy or two) sitting in the front row. She knew they wanted what she had. Her husband was six foot two and kept in shape with visits to the gym three times a week. Sure, his thick black hair had started to gray at the temples, and his pale-green eyes now needed glasses for reading, but those specs made him look distinguished—and even sexier. Mark couldn't hold a candle to George in the looks department. Yet her slightly chubby, balding brother-in-law had made her feel incredibly desirable in bed that afternoon at the Alexis. She'd never felt so sexy and attractive, so validated.

Still, as they were leaving the hotel, Mark started saying it had been a horrible mistake. They'd slipped. They were nice people—and married to nice people. This shouldn't have happened. He blamed it on his grief and the number of drinks he'd had. (Only two scotches; she'd counted.) But Ina knew better. He'd always been attracted to her, and what had happened in the Alexis that afternoon had been long overdue.

She, too, regretted "slipping," but a part of Ina still wanted Mark to find her desirable. Even if nothing ever happened again, she wanted to be desired. And for that she deserved her sister's snippy attitude tonight.

She took another look out the window. The trees and bushes swayed slightly in the wind. On a quiet night like this, she thought she should have been able to hear Mark's footsteps. But there wasn't a sound.

A chill raced through her, and Ina rubbed her arms. She glanced at the doorway to the cellar, open just an inch, and beyond that, darkness. They should have checked down there—in the furnace room and the fallout shelter. Mark and Jenna used it for storage. It was a perfect hiding place.

Moving over to the sink, Ina grabbed a steak knife from the drain rack. She checked the cellar door again. The opening seemed wider than before. Or was it just her imagination? She told herself that if someone was on those rickety old basement steps, she'd have heard the boards creaking. Still, she studied the murky shadows past that cellar doorway. With the knife clutched in her hand, Ina hurried to the basement door and shut it.

The clock on the stove read 12:20. Mark had been gone at least five minutes. How long did it take to circle around this little house? Something was wrong. "C'mon, Mark, c'mon," she murmured, looking out the window again.

She thought about calling upstairs to her sister. Why should she be the only one worried? But Jenna was probably asleep already.

Ina unlocked the kitchen door, opened it, and glanced outside. The cold air swept against her bare legs and her robe fluttered. Shivering, she held on to the knife. "Mark?" she called softly. "Mark? Where are you? Can you hear me?"

She waited for a moment, and listened.

Then she heard it—a rustling sound, and twigs snapping underfoot. "Mark?" she called out again, more shrill this time. "Mark, please, answer me . . ."

"Yeah, I'm here," he replied, emerging from the shadows of an evergreen beside the house. He carried the hunting rifle at his side, and seemed frazzled. "You were right," he said, out of breath. "Something was out there. I don't know if it was two-legged or four-legged, but I chased it halfway up the trail."

Dumbfounded, Ina stepped back as he ducked inside.

"We're okay now," he said, shutting the door and locking it. "Whatever it was, it's not coming back." He set the rifle on the breakfast table, then reached into one of the cupboards. "Jesus, it's cold as a polar bear's pecker out there. I think we could both use a shot of Jack."

Ina set the knife down beside the gun. She watched him pull a bottle of Jack Daniel's from the cupboard. He retrieved two jelly glasses with the Flintstones on them and poured a shot of the bourbon into each one.

"Has this kind of thing ever happened here before?" she asked warily.

Shaking his head, Mark handed her a glass. "Not quite. We've had bears come up to the house, like Jenna was saying. But I don't think this was a bear." He took a swig of bourbon.

Ina sipped hers. "What makes you so sure this . . . *creature* isn't coming back?"

"Because it was running so fast. The damn thing must be in another zip code by now. But to be on the safe side, I'll pull guard duty down here for another hour or so."

"I'll keep you company," she offered.

"I don't think that's such a good idea, Ina."

She let out an awkward, little laugh. "Why? Are you afraid we might 'slip' again?"

Mark sighed. "I told you before. It won't happen a second time. And it sure as hell ain't gonna happen with Jenna sitting in bed upstairs. God, Ina, what's wrong with you?"

Glaring at him, she gulped down the rest of her bourbon, and then firmly set the glass on the kitchen counter. "I was just asking a simple question. That wasn't a come-on, you asshole."

She started to head out of the kitchen, but he grabbed her arm. "Listen . . ." But he didn't say anything for a moment. Finally, he sighed and let go of her arm. "We're both tired and on edge, saying things we don't mean. Just—just let's call it a night, okay?"

Ina didn't say anything to him, but she nodded.

"I'm going upstairs to say goodnight to Jenna. Then I'll come back down here to keep watch. You should head up and try to get some sleep." He poured some more Jack Daniel's into her Flintstones glass. "Here. Have another blast of this. It'll help you doze off."

"Thanks," Ina said, taking the glass, and moving toward the sink. She still wasn't looking at him. But she could see his reflection in the darkened window as he stepped out of the kitchen.

Ina took a gulp of the bourbon. It was warming and took a bit of the edge off.

She listened to the staircase floorboards creaking. She just assumed it was Mark on his way up to the second floor.

Ina didn't consider the possibility that the sound might be coming from the cellar steps.

The toilet flushing woke her.

Ina had nodded off for only a few minutes. She'd come up to bed about an hour ago, leaving Mark down in the living room with his hunting rifle. As Ina had reached the top of the stairs, she'd heard Jenna calling to her. She'd poked her head into the master bedroom.

Her sister was lying in bed with the light on. "Listen, I'm sorry I've been such an unbearable shrew today," Jenna said, not lifting her head from the pillow. "You must want to clobber me."

"Oh, don't be silly," Ina said. "Go to sleep."

Jenna gazed up at the ceiling. Ina noticed, in this light, her sister was looking old and a bit careworn, and it made her sad. Neither one of them was young anymore.

"I think Mark has been with someone," Jenna said.

Ina let out a skittish laugh. "What are you talking about?"

"He's having an affair, or at least, he's *had* one. I can tell. By any chance, did he say something to George? He's close with George."

Ina shook her head.

"You'd tell me if you knew, wouldn't you? If George said something to you about it?"

"Of course, I'd tell you," Ina said. She sat down on the edge of the bed, on Mark's side. "Jenna, Mark loves you. He's not seeing anyone else. That's just nonsense. You're worrying about nothing."

"Maybe," Jenna allowed, sighing. "Jesus, I'm so messed up. Nothing's been right since Collin died. I feel like a zombie half the time. It's as if I were walking around with a piece of my insides cut out. It hurts, Ina. It's not just emotional either. It's a—a true physical pain."

"Oh Jen, I'm so sorry," Ina whispered. "There now . . . there now . . ." She couldn't think of anything else to say. She hugged her sister.

Jenna rested her head on her shoulder and wept. Ina felt her sister's tears through the silk burgundy robe.

After a while, they'd said goodnight, and Ina had slinked off to her room. Crawling into the creaky twin-size bed, she felt awful. Instead of supporting her sister during this terrible time, she'd slept with Mark. How could she do that to Jenna? And how could she do that to George?

She would be a better sister, a better wife, better mother, better person . . .

Ina had been telling herself that when she'd dozed off.

Now, she was awake again, listening to the toilet tank re-filling. The master bedroom door let out a yawn as Mark closed it. He would be asleep soon, and she'd be the only one awake in the house—this creepy little house in the middle of nowhere.

Ina heard a rustling noise outside, and told herself to ig-nore it. They were practically surrounded by a forest, and it was full of creatures making noises. Or was it that *thing* Mark had chased halfway up the trail? Maybe it had come back. Maybe it had been watching the house, waiting for him to go to bed.

Ina, quit doing this to yourself.

There it was again, the rustling sound.

Ina tossed back the covers and climbed out of bed. Padding over to the dormer window, she peered outside. She didn't see anything. But she heard those strange rustling sounds again. Was it coming from *inside* the house? Downstairs?

Standing very still, Ina listened. Floorboards creaked, more rustling. It wasn't Mark; she would have heard the master bedroom door squeak open again. Way down the hall and farther from the stairs than her, Mark couldn't hear what she was hearing, not even if he was still awake. She was the only one who heard it, the only one who knew something was ter-ribly wrong.

You're blowing this out of proportion. You got spooked earlier by that bear or whatever it was, and now you're imag-ining the worst.

That much was true. She was thinking about the type of killer who might lurk within these woods, someone resource-ful and clever, and yet savagely brutal. Someone deranged.

Stop it! She'd grown up listening to too many urban leg-ends: the killer with the hook for a hand; the babysitter men-aced by a maniac in an upstairs bedroom; and now, her own wild imaginings about this woodland killer.

She heard the noise again, and realized how silly she was. It was just the sound of logs in the fireplace popping and settling. That was all.

Ina crawled back into bed, and pulled the covers up to her neck. As much as she tried to convince herself everything was fine, she lay there tense and rigid, listening for the next sound.

She didn't have to wait long. It came from downstairs again, in the living room, and she could tell exactly what it was: the legs of a chair scraping across the floor. Someone must have bumped into it.

The noise was loud enough that Mark must have heard it, too, because the master bedroom door creaked open again. Then there were footsteps in the upstairs hallway.

Ina climbed out of bed and started toward the door. Her heart was racing. At least she wasn't the only one hearing the noises. And Mark was investigating it. She could hear him on the stairs. "Oh, thank God it's you," he murmured. "Jesus, what are you doing here? You scared the hell out of me. . . ."

A hand on the doorknob, Ina pressed her ear to the door. She could hear undecipherable whispering. But one thing she could make out was Mark saying. "Okay, okay, I'm sitting down. . . ." Obviously, he knew the person who was downstairs. There was more murmuring, and then Mark raised his voice. "Hey, no! Wait a minute, no—"

A loud gunshot went off.

Ina reeled back from the door.

She heard her sister's footsteps along the hallway. Someone else was charging up the stairs. "Oh, God, no, no!" Jenna screamed.

Ina's stomach lurched at the sound of a second blast. She heard someone collapse right outside her bedroom door.

God, please. This isn't happening, this isn't happening.

Ducking into her closet, she closed the door and curled up on the floor. She was shaking uncontrollably. She heard footsteps. She couldn't tell if they were coming toward her bedroom or moving away from it. She felt dizzy, and couldn't breathe. The dark closet seemed to be shrinking in around her. Ina's whole body started to shut down.

She wasn't sure what had happened, if she'd fainted or gone into a kind of shock, but Ina suddenly realized some time had elapsed. The house was still, and a very faint light sliced through the crack under the closet door. Dawn was breaking.

Was it all a nightmare? As she tried to move, every joint inside her ached. She felt as if she'd been beaten up. Her body was reacting to the trauma. This was no nightmare. It was real.

Ina managed to get to her feet and open the closet door. But she was shaking. The bedroom was still dark with only a murky, early dawn light seeping through the dormer windows. Nothing had been disturbed in the room. The door was still closed.

Ina swallowed hard, and then reached for the doorknob. As she opened the door, she saw the blood and bits of brain on the hallway wall. Only a few feet in front of her, Jenna lay dead on the floor facing that blood-splattered wall.

Ina let out a gasp. Tears stung her eyes, but she didn't stare at her dead sister for too long. She staggered back toward the stairs. She shook so violently she could barely make it down the steps. She clutched the banister to keep from falling—or fainting.

In the dim light she could see only certain areas of the living room. Other spots were still shrouded in darkness. She glimpsed Mark in his robe, sitting in the rocker by the fireplace. But his face was swallowed up in the shadows, and he wasn't moving at all. As Ina warily approached him, she saw that his wavy brown hair was matted down with blood on one side. He stared back at her with open dead eyes and a bewildered expression. The top left side of his head had been blown off.

"Oh, no," Ina whispered, a hand over her mouth. "No, no, no . . ."

Someone emerged from the darkness beyond the kitchen door.

Ina gasped again. She saw Mark's hunting rifle—aimed at her.

Tears streamed down Ina's face as she gazed at the person who was about to kill her. "Oh, my God, honey," she whispered, shaking her head. "What have you done?"

The shotgun went off.

Chapter Three

Her aunt was staring at her, and asking, "What have you done?" And that was when Amelia shot her in the chest.

All at once, she bolted up and accidentally banged her knee against the steering wheel of Shane's Volkswagen Golf. Amelia barely noticed the pain. She was just glad to be awake—and out of that nightmare. It seemed so horribly real. She'd even felt the blood splattering on her face as she'd shot her parents and Aunt Ina at close range.

Now Amelia anxiously checked her reflection in the rearview mirror. She touched her hair. Not a drop of blood anywhere. If she'd washed it off, she certainly would remember. It was a dream—vivid and frightening, but still just a dream.

Shivering from the cold, Amelia looked around. It took her a moment to realize she'd fallen asleep in the front seat of the VW. She'd parked in the small, desolate lot of a boarded-up hot dog stand. The unlit, cracked sign had a cartoon of a smiling dachshund. It read: WIENER WORLD! HOT DOG EMPORIUM—WIENERS, FRIES, & COLD DRINKS!

Amelia wasn't sure where she was, but she could hear cars zooming along on the other side of some evergreen trees across the street from Wiener World. She had to be somewhere close to a highway. She squinted at her wristwatch: 11:15 A.M.

Her head was throbbing and she felt so thirsty she could hardly swallow. She hadn't had a hangover in several weeks, and this was a painful reminder of what it had been like during her drinking days. Now Amelia remembered the party last night, and how she'd treated Shane so shabbily. She remembered grabbing that bottle of tequila and driving off toward Wenatchee. She'd had this sudden urge to get to the family cabin, and make certain her parents and her Aunt Ina were all right. She'd been convinced some harm would come to them.

Amelia felt around under the car seat for that bottle of tequila. There was still some left, and she took a swig from the bottle. But even the jolt of alcohol didn't erase the violent images lingering from that nightmare. Something had happened at the Lake Wenatchee house; she was sure of it.

Amelia wished she could remember, but everything was a blank from the time she'd sped away from that party on fraternity row to when she'd woken up here just moments ago. She suffered from occasional blackouts—lost time. It usually happened when she was drinking, but she'd experienced these memory lapses other times, too. On several occasions, people claimed they'd seen her here or there, and Amelia didn't remember it at all. It was almost as if she were sleepwalking some of the time.

Had she killed her parents and her aunt during one of these sleepwalking episodes? Was it possible?

Amelia put down the tequila bottle, then dug her cell phone from her purse. Squinting at it, she dialed her mother's cell number. But if they were still at the cabin, the call wouldn't get through. Sure enough, just as she thought, no luck. Biting her lip, Amelia dialed her Aunt Ina and Uncle George's house in Seattle. Her Uncle George had stayed home with her cousins this weekend. If something had really happened, he might know about it.

"Could you please make that announcement again?" George McMillan asked the woman at the concierge desk in the Pacific Place Shopping Center.

Nodding, the pretty concierge with curly auburn hair and cocoa-colored skin gave him a pained, sympathetic smile. She picked up her phone and pushed a couple of numbers.

"Stephanie McMillan, attention, Stephanie McMillan." Her voice interrupted the music on the public address system. "Please meet your father by the first-floor escalators." She repeated the announcement.

"Thank you," George said, nervously tapping his fingers on the edge of the desk. He gazed up at the people passing by the railings on all four shopping levels of the vast skylit atrium. No sign of Steffie. He scanned the faces of the shoppers lined up on the escalators. He still didn't see her. His stomach felt as tight as a fist.

His daughter had wandered off about fifteen minutes ago. Already, George had sweated through his shirt. He imagined every horrifying scenario of what might have happened to her. He saw Stephanie's face on milk cartons. He thought about the call from the police, asking him to come identify the corpse of a pretty, freckled-faced, auburn-haired five-year-old. He imagined looking for the little strawberry mark on her arm— just to make sure it wasn't Stephanie's double. As if there was another like her.

His son, Jody, eleven, was supposed to have been keeping an eye on her. George had taken the kids to Old Navy in downtown Seattle this morning. His wife, Ina, had made out a shopping list that included the kids' clothes and some other

things she wanted him to get. After Old Navy, he'd stopped
by Pottery Barn in the Pacific Place Shopping Center to pick
up candles—specifically, "eight-inch pillars in fig." George
had had a big bag from Old Navy weighing down one arm
and Steffie hanging on the other. He wasn't sure if fig was
tan, brown, or green. Or maybe it was purple—no, that was
plum. He had unloaded Stephanie on her brother, then went
in search of a saleslady.

At the time, he kept wondering why the hell Ina needed
these stupid candles *now*. She wasn't entertaining any time
soon. Why didn't she just buy them herself when she got
back from Lake Wenatchee? Considering the company and
their *situation*, George hadn't been up for the trip this weekend. Besides, someone had to look after the kids. Jenna and
Mark had volunteered Amelia's services as a babysitter, but
George didn't have much confidence his niece could handle
the task, at least not for the entire weekend.

The last few months had been pretty rough for everyone.
The drowning of his nephew, Collin, had hit George awfully
hard. Collin had had a special bond with his Uncle George,
and he'd been like a big brother to Jody. His death had devastated *two* families, not just one. George walked around in
a dark stupor for weeks afterward. Maybe that explained
why he couldn't see what was happening between Ina and
his brother-in-law.

Once George discovered the letter Ina had started to Mark,
he realized his wife must have *wanted* him to see what was
happening.

In fact, it had already happened—in the Hotel Alexis.
"Dear Mark," she'd scribbled on the hotel's stationery.

*As I write this, you're in the shower. I still feel you all
over me, and inside me. I know what we did was
wrong. I'm not arguing with you about that. But we're
two good people, who are hurting. We've found some-*

thing with each other, something that made our pain and loneliness go away. I'm not sure if it's love. But I do know I've always felt a connection with you. You haven't—

That was as far as she'd gotten before she'd half crumpled up the note and thrown it away—*in their master bathroom*, for God's sake. It lingered there at the top of the trash in the silver wastebasket from Restoration Hardware. George noticed the note while sitting on the toilet. She'd obviously wanted him to see it. Otherwise, she would have tossed the letter away in the hotel room, or torn it up and flushed it down the toilet, or at the very least, *buried* the damn thing under some used Kleenex in the trash.

Ina didn't deny her indiscretion.

"You left that *love letter* in plain sight," George pointed out. "God, what were you thinking? What if Jody had found it? Hell, I know what you were thinking. . . ." He kept his voice low. They were in their bedroom, and he didn't want Jody and Stephanie, downstairs, to hear. "It's pretty obvious you wanted me to find out about you and Mark."

"Now, why in the world would I want that?" she asked, shaking her head.

"I don't know. Why *did* you want it, Ina?"

George wondered if she'd been dropping any more clues about her infidelity. The note—with its cringe-worthy prose—mentioned Mark was taking a shower. Had she bothered to bathe at the Alexis that evening, or did she want her addle-brained husband to detect the scent of another man on her?

"I can't understand how this happened," he said finally. "You don't love him. Did you think screwing Mark and letting me find out about it would make me want a divorce? Is this your way of trying to end it for us? You haven't said you're sorry."

Flicking back her long, curly auburn hair, she turned and

headed for the door. "I have to get dinner started," she murmured.

"Do you love him?" George asked pointedly. The question made Ina stop in her tracks. "Or did you just use him to sabotage us? For chrissakes, he's your sister's husband, Ina. Tell me the truth, do you love him?"

Facing the door, she shrugged awkwardly. "I don't really know," she whispered. She started to cry, but kept her back to him. "I'm so sorry, honey. Do you hear that? I'm apologizing. I've screwed everything up but good. Maybe I *did* want you to know. You're probably right about that. God, I feel so shitty about this. You're a good man, George, and a good husband. You deserve better . . ."

He stared at her back, and wondered if this was a variation of the It's Not You, It's Me speech. "I'll be honest. Right now, I'm so furious at you, and so hurt, I'm not sure I have it in me to be forgiving. I need to know if it's worth a try. Do you want to stay in this marriage?"

"I—I can't say for sure," she whispered. "I'm not certain about anything right now."

"Hey, Dad!" Jody called from downstairs. "Dad?"

George brushed past her on his way to the bedroom door. "Goddamn you for doing this," he growled. Then he went downstairs to their son.

Ina wasn't the only one feeling uncertain. In the weeks that followed, it got so that George wasn't sure if he wanted to stay married to her, either. They'd been having problems for at least two years. They'd seen a counselor—six counselors, in fact—until she found one she liked: a "feelings physician" (at least that's what it had said on her shingle) with gobs of turquoise jewelry and green-tinted glasses. George hadn't noticed any medical degrees hanging on her wall, but she'd insisted on being called "Doctor." After twenty minutes of stroking a mangy cat in her lap and listening only to Ina, she'd suggested a trial separation. George had walked out on the session. Ina still went to her once every two weeks on her own. All too often Ina quoted her: "Dr. Racine says I should assert myself. Dr. Racine says I need to be more selfish. Dr. Racine says I need to take time to focus on myself."

He really had to hold his tongue when Ina came out with lulus like that. Ina was beautiful, funny, and intelligent, but as Ina's sister, Jenna, often said, "Ina's only really happy when it's all about Ina."

George had already known that about her. But he'd been in love. He used to feel so lucky. He was just a history professor with a modest income and, somehow, he'd landed this gorgeous woman who had so much class and style. Plus, she and her sister were loaded. The money part never really mattered to him. But Ina could have easily paired off with some hot-shot millionaire who played polo and drove a Porsche. George hadn't even owned a car when he'd met her, and his idea of a terrific time was sitting on the beach, gobbling up a new biography of FDR. And yet he was the one she wanted.

Somewhere in the back of his mind, he'd always been afraid she would get bored with him. And now that she had, it broke his heart.

Just recently, he'd started imagining his life without her. He thought about a divorce—after fourteen years together. She would get the house, of course. They'd bought it with her money—a four-bedroom split-level in West Seattle. She'd gone nuts decorating it. He wouldn't miss it. He'd do just fine in an apartment somewhere near the University District, so he could be close to school. But the place would need at least two bedrooms for when Jody and Steffie visited. *Visits* with his kids, *allotted time* with them; the notion made him sick.

He wanted to keep the marriage going for the kids. Yet Ina wasn't exactly the most nurturing mother around; at least, it seemed that way lately. All of Ina's shortcomings had become glaringly obvious once he knew about her and

Mark. He studied the way she treated Jody and Stephanie, and noticed when she ignored them, or was curt with them, or when she had them fetching things because she was too lazy to get off her ass. "Jody, honey, get me my purse . . .").

Then again, maybe he was just hypercritical of Ina because somewhere along the line, while wrestling with all his hurt, confusion and anger, he'd fallen out of love with her.

He had to be fair. She wasn't a bad mother. And he was in no position to criticize Ina's parenting skills right now. At least Ina had never lost one of the children while shopping.

It had happened so quickly. George had gotten a saleswoman in Pottery Barn to help him, and together they'd found the stupid eight-inch pillars *in fig*. She'd been ringing up his sale when Jody had come up to the counter and squinted at his father. "Where's Steffie?" Jody had asked, scouting out the general vicinity. "Didn't she come back to you, Dad? She said she was gonna . . ."

"But I left her with you," George had murmured.

She'd been missing for almost twenty minutes now. In his jacket pocket, George felt her inhaler. Stephanie had asthma. What if she was having an attack right now?

He couldn't get past the awful feeling that he'd never see his daughter again. *God, please, if I can find Stephanie, I'll work things out with Ina. I'll do whatever she wants. I'll even go see that stupid Dr. Racine with her. Just please bring Steffie back to me.*

Jody had been peeking into different shops on the shopping mall's main level. Now he hurried back to George at the concierge desk. Shaking his head, Jody looked so forlorn. "Dad, I'm sorry," he said, his lip quivering. "It's all my fault—"

George mussed his son's unruly, brown hair. "It's all right, Jody. We'll find her."

He asked the concierge to make the announcement again. Then he put down his shopping bags and turned to Jody.

"You stay here and keep your eyes peeled," he said. "I'll start on the top floor and work my way down. Have the woman call my cell if Steffie shows up. Okay, sport?"

Jody nodded. George kissed his forehead, then hurried toward the escalator. "Stephanie! Steffie?" he called, loudly. People stopped to stare at him, several of them scowling. He didn't care. He brushed past shoppers on the escalator, saying, "Excuse me," over and over again. He yelled out Stephanie's name a few more times. He kept looking around as he moved from each shopping level, stepping off one escalator and starting up a new one.

As George reached the top floor, where the restaurants and movie theaters were, he felt his cell phone vibrating. He stopped in his tracks. He quickly snatched the phone out of his jacket pocket, then switched it on. "Yes, hello?" he asked anxiously.

"Uncle George?"

"Amelia?" he asked.

"Yeah, hi, listen," she said. "Has Aunt Ina called you from the cabin today?"

Flustered, he shook his head. "Not yet," he said into the phone. "She's supposed to call from that diner near the cabin when they go to breakfast. I'm sorry, Amelia, but I—"

"Uncle George, it's past noon. She should have called by now—"

"Amelia, honey, I'm sorry, but I'm in the middle of something. I need to call you back."

"No! Don't hang up, please! Uncle George, something happened at the Lake Wenatchee house, something horrible."

He stood by the entrance of a fifties diner with the cell phone to one ear and a finger in the other to block out all the noise. "What are you talking about?" he asked, trying not to sound impatient.

"Remember how when Collin died, I knew before everyone else? Remember that premonition I had? Well, this is the same thing. I *feel* it. I know something happened at the cabin. You probably think I'm crazy. But I'm scared, Uncle George. My gut instinct tells me they're all dead—Mom, Dad, and Ina. I hope to God I'm wrong—"

"Amelia, I'm sorry, but I'm in the middle of something right now. It's an emergency. Let me call you back—"

"This is an emergency too, Uncle George! I'm serious—"

"Honey, I'm going to hang up, okay? I—I'll call you back just as soon as I can, all right?" Wincing, George clicked off the line. He felt awful hanging up on her, but he just didn't have time for Amelia's dramatics right now.

He hadn't even gotten the cell phone back into his pocket when it vibrated again. "Oh, Jesus, please, Amelia, leave me alone," he muttered. He clicked on the phone, and sighed. "Yes?"

"Mr. McMillan, this is Jennifer, the concierge. Your daughter's okay. She hadn't wandered too far. She heard the last announcement, and came right to us. She's here at the desk, waiting for you. . . ."

"Oh, thank God," he whispered. "Thank you, Jennifer. Thank you very much."

Fifteen minutes later, he was walking with the children toward the Pine Street lot where he'd parked the car. George gripped Stephanie's little hand. He felt as if he'd just dodged a bullet. He'd thanked the concierge, stopped by Pottery Barn to tell the saleswoman all was well, and he'd assured Jody that he wasn't mad at him for letting Stephanie wander off. But he still had some unfinished business.

He needed to call back Amelia, and he didn't want to. She'd been babbling on about some *premonition* she'd had that her parents and Ina were all dead.

"Okay, watch your fingers and feet, pumpkin," he said, helping Stephanie into the backseat. He shut the car door and made sure she was locked in. While Jody climbed into the front passenger side, George stashed the Old Navy and Pottery Barn bags in the trunk. He closed it, and then glanced at his wristwatch: 12:35.

Ina definitely should have phoned by now.

He checked his cell to see if he might have missed a call. There were no messages. The only call had been the one from Amelia.

Pulling at her leash, the eleven-year-old collie led the way. Abby knew exactly where her owner was headed. She had that sixth sense some dogs had. When they came to a split in the forest's crude path, Abby sniffed at the ground and quickly veered onto the trail that went along the lake's edge—toward the Faradays' house.

"That's a good girl," Helene Sumner said, holding the leash tightly. A chilly autumn wind whipped across the lake, and she turned up the collar to her windbreaker. Helene was sixty-seven and thin, with close-cropped gray hair. She was an artist, working with silk screens. She had a studio in her house, about a half mile down the lake from the Faradays' place.

Helene had hardly gotten any sleep last night. When those shots had gone off at 2:30 this morning, Abby had started barking. She leapt up from her little comforter in the corner of the bedroom and onto Helene's bed. The poor thing was trembling. So was Helene. She wasn't accustomed to being woken up in the middle of the night like that.

Hunting was prohibited in the area, and even if it were allowed, what in God's name were they hunting at that hour? The tall trees surrounding the lake played with the acoustics, and sounds traveled across the water. Those shots rang out so clearly, they could have been fired in Helene's backyard. But she knew where they'd come from.

She'd just started to doze off again when another loud

bang went off around five o'clock. Helene dragged herself out of bed and threw on her windbreaker. Grabbing a pair of field glasses, she walked with Abby to the lake's edge, and then peered over at the Faradays' house. No activity, no lights on, nothing.

She retreated to the house, crawled back into bed and nodded off until 10:30—very unlike her.

An hour ago, while having her breakfast—coffee and the last of her homemade biscuits—Helene had figured out who must have encroached on her sanctuary. Those three loud shots in the early morning hours must have been some kind of fireworks—bottle rockets or firecrackers.

Now, walking with Abby along the lakeside path, Helene gazed at the Faraday place and thought about the daughter, Amelia. She used to be such a polite, considerate girl—and so beautiful. But there was an underlying sadness about her, too. And talk about sad, it was such a tragedy when the Faradays' son drowned. It had been around that time, maybe even before, when Amelia and her lowlife boyfriend had started showing up at the weekend house without her parents. They were so obnoxious. Helene didn't care about the skinny-dipping, but did they have to be so loud? She heard their screaming and laughing until all hours of the night, and sometimes it was punctuated by bottles smashing. They trashed the lake, too. Helene would find food wrappers, cigarette butts, and beer cans washed up on her shore after each one of their clandestine visits. Those kids were making a cesspool out of her lake.

About a month ago, when the Faradays had come for a weekend, Helene stopped by with a Bundt cake and offered her belated condolences about Collin. Then, privately, she talked to Amelia about her secret trips there with her boyfriend. "It's none of my business what you do with him, Amelia," she told her, walking along the trail beside the water. "But I wish you'd be a little less noisy about it. And so help me God, I'm going to say something to your parents if I see one more piece of garbage in that lake. It's my lake, too, and I won't let you and your boyfriend pollute it."

Amelia stopped and gaped at her with those big, beautiful eyes and a put-on innocent expression. "Oh, Ms. Sumner, I—I don't know what you're talking about," she murmured. "I haven't come here with my boyfriend. I swear. Shane's *never* been here. You must be mistaken."

Helene shook her head. "You can deny it all you want. I know what I saw, Amelia. I'm really disappointed in you. . . ."

Now, as she approached the Faradays' front porch, Helene figured she'd get the same Little Miss Innocent routine from Amelia as last time. She would probably wake her up—along with her boyfriend—since they'd been lighting off firecrackers until the wee hours of the morning.

But something suddenly occurred to Helene that made her hesitate at the Faradays' front stoop. Why didn't she hear any laughing or screaming? People always laughed, yelled, or cheered when they let off fireworks. But there hadn't been a human sound—just those shots.

Abby sniffed at the front door to the Faradays' old Cape Cod–style house. She started whining and barking. The collie backed away. She had that sixth sense.

Something was wrong inside that house.

Although Abby tried to pull her in the other direction, Helene stepped up to the door and knocked. Abby wouldn't stop yelping. "Quiet, girl," Helene hissed. She tried to listen for some activity inside the house. Nothing. Helene knocked again, and waited. She wondered if she should take a cue from Abby and get out of there. But she knocked once more, and then tried the doorknob. It wasn't locked.

Abby let out another loud bark, a warning. But it was too late. Helene was already opening the door. From the threshold, she could see up the stairs to the second floor hallway, where a messy brownish-red stain marred the pale blue wall.

Baffled, Helene started up the stairs, having to tug at Abby's leash. Only a few steps from the landing, Helene stopped dead. She realized now that the large stain on the wall was dried blood. Beneath it, Jenna Faraday lay on the floor, her face turned to the wall. The oversized T-shirt she wore was soaked crimson. Her bare legs looked so swollen and pale—almost gray.

Helene gasped. She and Abby retreated down the stairs, and then she noticed what was in the living room. Helene stopped in her tracks. A second dead woman lay sprawled on the floor—a few feet from the kitchen door. She had beautiful, curly auburn hair, but her face was frozen in a horrified grimace. Her burgundy-colored robe and nightgown almost matched the puddle of blood on the floor beneath her. The shotgun blast had ripped open the front of that lacy nightgown. Helene could see the fatal, gaping wound in her chest.

Not far from the second woman's body, Mark Faraday's corpse sat upright in a rocker. At least, Helene thought it was him. Blood covered the robe he wore. The butt of the hunting rifle was wedged between Mark Faraday's lifeless legs, with the long barrel slightly askew and tilted away from his mutilated, swollen face.

One hand remained draped over the gun, his finger caught in the trigger.

Chapter Four

"What about that woman who lives down the lake from the cabin?" George asked. "Your dad told me they've used her phone in the past for emergencies. Do you know her number?"

"Oh, God, Ms. Sumner," Amelia murmured on the other end of the line. She sounded as if she were in a daze. "I forgot all about her. We have her number written down someplace, but I think it's shoved in a desk at home in Bellingham."

"Do you know her first name?"

"Hold on for a second, Uncle George. I'm about to go through a tunnel."

"I thought you'd pulled over. You shouldn't be on your cell while driving—"

"God, you sound just like Dad. It's okay. I have friends who text-message while driving."

"Well, then they're idiots," George said to dead air. She must have entered the tunnel.

Holding the cordless phone to his ear, he glanced toward the living room windows. From this spot in the kitchen, he

could see through the sheer curtains to the front yard. He'd
sent Jody and Stephanie outside so he could phone Amelia
and talk to her without the kids hearing. They didn't need to
know he was worried about their mother.

While driving home from downtown, George had gotten
more and more concerned. Ina had *promised* to call and
check in with him this morning.

There were no messages on the answering machine when
he'd gotten home with the kids, except two from a panic-
stricken Amelia, both within the last hour. Her premonition
that Ina, Mark, and Jenna had all been killed seemed prepos-
terous, but unnerving, too.

"Remember how when Collin died, I knew before everyone else?" she'd asked. What George remembered was Amelia
claiming after the drowning that she'd *seen* it all—in her
mind. She didn't think Collin had accidentally fallen off the
dock and hit his head on those pilings. She insisted there
was more to it than that. She had a feeling.

George remembered when Amelia had made all those
wild claims. He and Ina figured their sweet-but-screwed-up
niece was looking for some attention. Amelia must have felt
like an also-ran alongside her winning younger brother. Back
in 1992, Mark and Jenna had been trying to have a child. Finally, after weeks of foster parenting, they adopted beautiful
four-year-old Amelia. They didn't think anyone could eclipse
her—until two months later, when Jenna learned she was
pregnant.

Amelia adored her little brother. But apparently she became a handful. Mark and Jenna lost more sleep on account
of Amelia's nightmares than the baby's feedings. And even
when Collin was supposed to sleep through the night, Amelia
always woke him up when she jumped out of bed shrieking.
The nightmares hadn't yet subsided when Amelia started de-
veloping phantom pains and faked illnesses. "It feels like
someone's twisting my arm off, Uncle George!" he remem-

bered her screaming during a family Thanksgiving at his and Ina's house. It took several minutes for her to stop crying. According to Jenna, two days later, Amelia claimed her arm was still sore, though she didn't have a mark on her. Other times, she said it felt as if someone were hitting her or kicking her. There were several trips to the doctor and the hospital emergency room for absolutely no reason. By early high school, certain phantom aches and ailments prompted Jenna to rush Amelia to a gynecologist. Jenna had confided to Ina that she thought someone might have been molesting Amelia. But the doctors found no physical evidence of this whatsoever.

Amelia started drinking in high school, too. Despite all her problems, she was a near-A student, and extremely sweet. She had a good heart. If someone sneezed in the next aisle at the supermarket, Amelia would call out, "God bless you." George guessed that her eagerness to please, along with peer pressure, must have started her drinking. She'd been to several therapists, but none of them really worked out until she recently started seeing this one, Karen Somebody. Amelia liked her a lot, but George wasn't sure if this Karen person was doing any good.

The one who seemed to get through to Amelia best was Ina. Since Amelia had started school at UW, they'd seen a lot more of her. Ina relished the admiration of this college girl. They had their Girls' Nights Out together at trendy restaurants and college bars. They also teamed up for shopping expeditions and the occasional pedicure/manicure at Ina's favorite day spa. She got to be Amelia's fun aunt and confidante.

George wondered if Ina was better at being a fun aunt than a serious wife and mother. It was a terrible thought to have. And just an hour ago, he'd made a deal with God that he would try once again to make it work with Ina.

George continued to listen to the dead air on the phone,

and he stared out the window. One of the neighbor kids—Jody's friend, Brad Reece—joined the children on the front lawn. And now the boys were tossing around a Frisbee and ignoring Stephanie.

"Uncle George, are you still there?"

"Yes," he said into the phone. "I thought I might have lost you."

"The old lady's name is Helene," she said. "Helene Sumner in Lake Wenatchee. I'll call directory assistance and get the number—"

"No, let me." He grabbed a pen and scribbled down the name. "I don't want you making all these calls while you're driving. By the way, where are you? Where's this tunnel?"

She hesitated.

"Amelia?"

"I just got off the I-90 bridge. I was—I was visiting a friend in Bellevue."

"Well, listen, if you have nothing else going on, you're welcome to come over—"

"Um, I can't right now, Uncle George. I'm going to see my therapist. Maybe later tonight, huh?"

"Okay. I'll call this Helene Sumner and see if she'll check on the house for us. I'll phone you the minute I hear anything."

"My cell's running out of juice. Let me give you Karen's number in case you can't reach me. Karen Carlisle, she's my therapist. Got a pencil?"

"I'm ready." George scribbled down the Seattle phone number as she read it off to him. "I'll call you. And stop worrying. I'm sure everything's fine."

Speeding along I-90 in her boyfriend's car, Amelia clicked off the cell phone and tossed it onto the passenger seat. She clutched the steering wheel with both hands, and started to cry.

Uncle George had said everything would be fine. But he didn't know what she knew. Amelia hadn't told him the whole story. She'd failed to mention that, in all likelihood, she'd killed her parents and Ina.

Amelia had also lied about where she had been. After waking up at the deserted Wiener World parking lot, she'd driven around for ten minutes until she'd found the freeway entrance. Then she finally saw a sign telling her where she was: Easton, Washington—a little city ninety miles east of Seattle. It was also about halfway to Wenatchee—and *from* Wenatchee. Had she been there last night? Had Easton been a stopover so she could sleep a few hours on her way back from murdering her parents and aunt?

Shane had left three messages on her cell, wanting to know where she'd taken his car. Amelia was driving past Snoqualmie when she called him back. She lied and said she'd had a sudden urge to see the Snoqualmie Falls last night. Yes, she'd gotten a *little* drunk, and decided to sleep it off in the car in the Snoqualmie Lodge parking lot. Yes, she was all right. She just felt awful for taking his car and for the way she'd acted at the party last night.

She couldn't tell Shane the truth. The only person she could really talk to was her therapist, Karen.

Funny, the two people in whom she confided the most were both women in their thirties. They weren't alike at all. Karen, with her wavy, shoulder-length chestnut hair and brown eyes, had the kind of natural beauty other women admired, but only the most discerning men noticed. She was very down to earth, but still had a certain class to her. She could look elegant in just a pair of jeans and a black long-sleeved T-shirt. Meanwhile, Amelia's Aunt Ina was very flashy and fun, sometimes even over the top. All eyes went to her whenever she walked into a room. She was Prada to Karen's Banana Republic.

Amelia remembered how lucky she'd felt when her cool Aunt Ina had decided to spend more time with her. They went to art galleries, the theater, and all these terrific, hip restaurants. But then Amelia had started seeing Karen, who was so compassionate and kind. After a while, she stopped confiding in Ina, who wasn't a very good listener, anyway. Amelia realized her favorite aunt could be pretty selfish. Sometimes she felt like Ina's pet—just this silly, admiring college girl who tagged along in her frivolous aunt's shadow.

Selfish, manipulative bitch, Amelia remembered thinking last night as she'd aimed the hunting rifle at her Aunt Ina. Amelia's not your fucking pet.

It was as if someone else were speaking for her—and killing for her. Yet Amelia remembered pulling the trigger. She remembered the jolt from the gun—and the loud blast.

God, please, please, don't let me have done that. Make it not be true. Let them be all right.

She pressed harder on the accelerator.

Watching the road ahead, Amelia wiped her eyes, and then reached for the cell phone on the passenger seat.

She had Karen on speed dial.

"Frank, you need to put down the knife," Karen said in a firm, unruffled tone.

Everyone else around her was going berserk, but she tried to remain calm and keep eye contact with the 73-year-old Alzheimer's patient. The unshaven man had greasy, long gray hair and a ruddy complexion. His T-shirt was inside out, with food stains down the front. The pale green pajama bottoms were filthy, too. In his shaky hand he held a butcher's knife. He looked more terrified than anyone else in the nursing home cafeteria. Just moments ago, he'd accidentally knocked over a stack of dirty trays from the bus table. He'd bumped into the table, backing away from an overly aggressive kitchen worker.

"Drop the goddamn knife," growled the short, thirty-something man. He wore a T-shirt and chinos under his apron. Tattoos covered his skinny arms. He kept inching toward the desperately confused patient. "C'mon, drop it! I don't have all day here!" He kicked a chair and it toppled across the floor, just missing the old man. "You hear me, Pops? Drop it!"

"Get away from him!" Karen barked. "For God's sake, can't you see he's scared?"

Two orderlies hovered behind her, along with a few elderly residents wanting to see what all the fuss was about. The rest home's manager, a handsome, white-haired woman in her sixties named Roseann, had managed to herd everyone else out of the cafeteria. She stood at Karen's side. "Did you hear her, Earl?" Roseann yelled at the kitchen worker. "Let Karen handle this. She knows what she's doing!"

But Earl wasn't listening. He closed in on the man, looking ready to pounce. "You shouldn't steal knives out of my kitchen, Pops. . . ."

"No—no . . . get!" the Alzheimer's patient cried, waving the knife at him.

Wincing, Karen watched the frightened old man shrink back toward the pile of trays. He was barefoot, and there were shards of broken glass on the floor.

Roseann gasped. "Earl, don't—"

He lunged at the man, who reeled back. But the knife grazed Earl's tattooed arm. A few of the residents behind Karen gasped.

The little man let out a howl, and recoiled. "Son of a bitch!"

One of the orderlies rushed to his aid. Grumbling obscenities, Earl held on to his arm, as the blood oozed between his fingers.

"No . . . get!" the old man repeated.

"It's okay!" the orderly called, checking Earl's wound, and pulling him toward the cafeteria exit. "Doesn't look too deep. . . ."

"Fuck you 'it's okay'," he shot back. "I'm bleeding here."

Shushing him, the orderly quickly led Earl out the door.

Karen was still looking into the old man's eyes. "That was an accident, Frank," she said steadily. "We all saw it. No one's mad at you. But you should put down the knife, okay?"

Wide-eyed, he kept shaking his head at her. He took another step back toward the glass on the floor.

"Frank, how do you think the Cubs are going to do this season?" Karen suddenly asked.

She remembered how during her last visit with him, he'd chatted nonstop about the Chicago Cubs. But he'd talked as if it were 1968, back when he'd been a hotshot, 33-year-old attorney in Arlington Heights, Illinois with a beautiful wife, Elaine, and two children, Frank Junior and Sheila. The old man in the stained T-shirt and pajama bottoms used to dress in Brooks Brothers suits. The family moved to Seattle in 1971, where they added a third child to the brood, a baby girl. Frank started his own law firm, and did quite well in Mariner town. But he'd always remained a Cubs fan.

Though she knew it was typical of Alzheimer's patients, Karen still thought it was kind of funny that Frank often couldn't remember the name of his dead wife or the names of his three children and seven grandchildren. But he still recalled the Cubs' star lineup from 1968.

"How do you think Ernie Banks is going to do, Frank?" she asked.

He stopped, and his milky blue eyes narrowed at her for a moment. "Um . . . you need—you need to keep your eye on Ron Santo. This is—this is going to be his year." He lowered the knife. He suddenly seemed to forget he was holding it.

"I thought you were an Ernie Banks fan, Frank," she said.

"You know, there's some glass on the floor behind you. Be careful."

He turned and glanced down at the floor. "Yeah, you got to love Ernie. Who doesn't?"

Karen felt her cell phone vibrate in the back pocket of her jeans, but she ignored it. She took a few steps toward him. "You know, you ought to put down that knife. Should we get some ice cream?"

He frowned at the knife in his hand, and then set it on one of the cafeteria tables.

"Does ice cream sound good to you, Frank?" Roseann piped in. "I think Karen has a good idea there. You recognize Karen, don't you?"

The second orderly carefully reached for the knife and took it away. A few of the residents behind Karen sighed, and one elderly man clapped.

Karen put her arm around Frank. Between his breath and his body odor, he smelled awful. But she smiled at him. "You recognize me, don't you, Poppy?"

A smile flickered across his face, and for a second he was her dad again. "Of course," he whispered. "You're my little girl."

She gave his shoulder a squeeze. "That's right, Poppy. Let's get you cleaned up, okay?" She led her father toward the cafeteria doors.

Later, while the orderly got Mr. Carlisle changed and back in bed, Karen ducked into the employee lounge to check her phone messages. She'd been volunteering once a week at the Sandpoint View Convalescent Home for half a year now, and knew all the staff. It was one way to ensure her dad got special treatment, one way to keep from feeling so horrible for giving up on him and putting him in there.

In addition to her volunteer day, Karen saw her father at Sandpoint View about twice a week. She'd been driving over to visit him this afternoon when the call had come from

Roseann, saying her dad was having an "episode." Frank had slipped out of his room and under their radar a few times in the past; he'd even wandered off the grounds once. But this was the first incident in which he'd posed a threat to anyone.

Karen knew Roseann would have to take some measures after what had just happened in the cafeteria. They'd probably start him on a new medication, which would make him even more dopey and unreachable. Or maybe they'd move him into Ward E with the severe cases.

Karen didn't want to think about that right now.

She nodded hello to a nurse, sitting at the table with her iPod and a sandwich. The small lounge had one window with the blinds lowered, and yellow-painted cinderblock walls that someone had decorated with these sappy, inspirational posters entitled Achievement, Friendship, and Tranquility. The photos of people watching the sunset, goldfish in a bowl, and kites flying against a blue sky were fuzzy and the poetic sentiments were written in script. Someone had scribbled BLOW ME in the top corner of the sunset Tranquility poster. There was also a slightly tattered brown sofa, a mini-refrigerator, and a vending machine, along with a coffee-maker on the counter, not far from the sink.

Karen poured herself a cup of their rotgut coffee. She leaned against the counter and checked her cell phone. Amelia Faraday had called.

She had thirty-one clients, and Amelia was the one she cared about the most. At first, Amelia had reminded Karen of someone else, someone she'd lost. Karen figured that maybe by helping Amelia solve her problems, she could help herself. It wouldn't raise the dead, but maybe she could make some of her own pain go away.

She pushed a couple of buttons on the cell and played the voice mail. Amelia's slightly shrill, panic-filled voice was like an assault: "Karen? Karen, I left you a couple of messages at home . . ." She let out a little gasp, then started to cry. "God, Karen, I'm in trouble. Something terrible has happened. I really need to talk with you. Please . . . please, call me back . . ."

She was about to hit the last call return button when Earl swaggered into the lounge. A gauze bandage was wrapped around his wounded arm.

"You!" the creepy little man growled. He stabbed a finger in the air at her. "You're just lucky I don't need stitches. . . ."

Karen put down the phone. "Earl, I'm sorry about your arm—"

" 'Sorry' doesn't begin to cover it," he said, cutting her off.

The nurse took off her iPod headset, sat forward in her chair, and watched them.

"I'm gonna make sure your old man gets some bed restraints. They ought to keep him tied up twenty-four seven." Earl inched closer to Karen until he was almost screaming in her face. "Better yet, they should stick that crazy old fuck in Ward E with the rest of the lunatics before he kills someone. I don't need this shit. That crazy old fuck, I'm gonna see to it they lock him up—"

"No," Karen said resolutely. "No, Earl. You're going to see to it the kitchen knives are locked up. Over a third of the residents here have Alzheimer's or some other form of dementia, and you're leaving knives out where anyone can get at them. My father isn't responsible for his actions, but *you are*. What's more, you wouldn't have that cut on your arm if you'd let me handle him."

His mouth open, he glared at her and shook his head.

"And one last thing, Earl, if you call my father a 'crazy old fuck' again, I swear, I'll punch your lights out—or I'll pay one of the attendants here to do it for me."

The nurse watching them let out an abrupt laugh.

Earl kept shaking his head. "Listen, don't you threaten me—"

"Earl?"

He swiveled around.

Her arms folded, Roseann stood in the doorway of the employee lounge. "Karen's right about locking up the kitchen utensils. I've talked to you about that before. It better not happen again. Now, don't you have some potatoes to peel or something?"

With a defiant grunt, he turned to glare one more time at Karen, then stomped out of the room.

Roseann raised an eyebrow at the nurse. "Show's over, Michelle. So was your break, as of ten minutes ago."

Nodding, the nurse took one last bite of her sandwich, gathered up her things, and ducked out of the lounge.

"Thanks for running interference," Karen said, giving Roseann a weary smile. "How's my dad?"

"Sedated." Roseann plopped down at the table. "We'll give him a rain check on the ice cream. Listen, you and I need to talk about making some adjustments to Frank's routine."

Karen nodded. "I've seen that coming for a while now." She looked down into her coffee cup. Yes, she'd seen it coming, but hadn't wanted to acknowledge the inevitable. It meant giving up on him a little more.

"Do yourself a favor," she heard Roseann say. "Talk to a counselor or join a family of Alzheimer's support group. In all this time, you haven't gotten any help at all. And it's not just about what's going on with your dad. This last year has been pretty awful for you from what you told me about your breakup and what happened with that poor girl. What was her name again?"

"Haley Lombard," Karen said quietly.

"Such a shame," Roseann sighed. "Anyway, you'd be the first one to recommend counseling to somebody in your shoes."

"I know, I know, 'Physician, heal thyself,' " Karen replied.

Roseann was right, of course. But Karen made her living listening to people's problems all day long. And it seemed like the rest of her time lately was dedicated to her father. She didn't want to spend what little time remained in therapy or talking about Alzheimer's. A DVD of a familiar classic was her therapy; it was like having an old friend over. An evening at home with Cary Grant and Eva Marie Saint, or Gregory Peck and Audrey Hepburn, wasn't a cure for her troubles, but it was a Band-Aid that fit just fine.

"Who knows?" Roseann said. "If you joined one of those Alzheimer's groups, you might meet a nice, single man."

"Oh, yeah, right." Karen took one last gulp of the bad coffee, then poured the rest down the sink and rinsed out the cup. "Like I'd want to hook up with some guy whose life is just as screwed up as mine is, thanks to Alzheimer's. Talk about serious relationship baggage. No, thanks. Besides, I'd probably end up running the stupid meetings. You know I would."

"Probably," Roseann muttered, nodding. "But you'd do a damn good job of it. You're not so terrific at helping yourself, Karen. But you really know how to help other people."

Karen managed to chuckle. "Well, thanks a bunch. I—"

Her cell phone vibrated once more, and she checked the caller ID. Amelia again. Karen sighed. "I'm sorry, Roseann. I need to take this." She clicked on the phone. "Hello? Amelia?"

"Oh, thank God!" the girl began. "I'm sorry to bother you, Karen. But something awful has happened—"

"Where are you?"

"I'm sitting in Shane's car—in your driveway. I don't know anybody else I can talk to about this. You're the only one. I've had another blackout, and I think I did something—"

"It's going to be all right," Karen said calmly. She glanced at her wristwatch. "My housekeeper, Jessie, ought to be there very soon. Get her to let you in, and wait for me. If you want, help yourself to a Diet Coke in the fridge. I'll see you in about a half hour. Does that sound okay, Amelia?"

"Yes, thank you, Karen. Thank you so much."

"See you in a bit." Clicking off the line, Karen shoved the phone back in her pocket, and gave Roseann a pale smile. "Sorry, Ro. About that talk regarding my dad, can it wait until later in the week? I have an emergency with one of my clients."

Roseann nodded. "No sweat. Go help somebody. Like I say, it's what you're good at."

Karen patted Roseann's shoulder as she headed out of the employee lounge.

Before taking off, she stopped to peek in on her father. The orderly had cleaned him up, and now he looked so peaceful in his slumber. She wondered if in his dreams he was his old self again, if he wasn't frightened and confused. She took a long look at him, and remembered back in high school when it had been just her and her dad in their big, four-bedroom white stucco house near Seattle's Volunteer Park. Cancer had killed her mother when Karen was fourteen. Her brother, Frank, was married and living in Atlanta. Her sister, Sheila, was away at college. So Karen and her father looked after each other. They had a housekeeper, but Karen did most of the shopping and cooking. It was a lot of work, and took a bite out of her social life. Some afternoons, after school, all she wanted to do was nap. Her dad always let her sleep. He often snuck into her room while she was napping, and covered her with his plaid flannel robe. Then he'd wait a while and fix their dinner—either hamburgers or bacon and eggs. Those were the only things he knew how to cook. She remembered how she'd wake up to the smell of his cooking—and the feel of his soft flannel robe covering her. Sheila had brought him another robe years ago, a blue terry-cloth which he'd taken to the rest home with him. But the old plaid flannel robe still hung in his closet, and Karen sometimes still used it to cover herself when she took a late-afternoon nap.

She gazed at her father in his hospital-style bed and

began to cry. She'd been miserable throughout most of her high school years. But now she missed that time—and she missed her father. Wiping her eyes, Karen bent over and kissed his forehead. "See you tomorrow, Poppy," she whispered, though she knew he couldn't hear her.

Stepping out of the room, she wiped her eyes again and peered down the hallway. She spotted Amelia—at least she thought it was Amelia. The young, pretty brunette at the end of the corridor locked eyes with her for only a second. Then she turned and disappeared around the corner.

As he dialed the number for Helene Sumner in Wenatchee, George felt like a fool. He was overreacting. He'd let Amelia's weird premonition get to him. So Ina had promised to call this morning, and didn't. Big deal. She'd broken promises before. This wasn't the first time. Mark, Jenna, and Ina had probably decided to drive someplace else for breakfast. Or maybe they'd eaten at the house, then went hiking and lost track of the time.

Yet here he was, about to ask this old lady to schlep a quarter mile down the lake and check on his wife and in-laws. He listened to the first ring tone. Through the living room window's sheer drapes, he could see the kids still playing with Jody's friend.

"Yes, hello?" the woman answered on the other end of the line. She sounded frazzled.

"Hello. Is this Helene?"

"Yes. Is this the police? I thought someone would be here by now."

"No, this isn't the police," George replied, bewildered. "I'm calling from Seattle. Your neighbors down the lake, Mark and Jenna Faraday, they're my in-laws. My name's—"

"They're dead," the woman cried, cutting him off. "He shot the two women, and then himself. . . ."

George felt as if someone had just punched him in the stomach. For a moment, he couldn't breathe. Swallowing hard, he caught another glance of his children playing on the front lawn. Stephanie let out a loud scream and then laughed about something.

"I called the police twenty minutes ago," the woman said in a shaky voice. "They still aren't here yet. God, I still can't believe it. But I was in the house. I saw their bodies—and the blood. They're dead, they're all dead. . . ."

Chapter Five

Salem, Oregon—1996

Twenty-six-year-old Lauren Tully felt like the walking dead. The pretty, slightly plump brunette worked as a paralegal, and she'd just helped her boss finish up the Bensinger complaint. They'd toiled over the case all week, right up until 9:15 tonight. Her boss would file it in the morning, and said she could take the day off, thank God.

Now that she was outside, Lauren realized what a gorgeous day she'd missed, buried in her cubicle. It was one of those warm, balmy late-June nights. She hadn't had dinner yet, so she'd swung by Guji's Deli Stop on her way home. The four-aisle store was in a minimall, along with a hair salon, a Radio Shack, some teriyaki joint, and a real estate office, all of which were closed at this hour. Guji's was the only lit storefront. They closed at ten. There weren't many customers, and the parking lot was practically empty. Lauren picked up a frozen pizza, some wine, and—what the hell, she deserved it—a pint of Ben & Jerry's. She was coming out of the store when she noticed something a bit strange.

"Damn it!" the man yelled. "I'm sorry, honey. Daddy didn't mean to swear."

His minivan was parked over by the Dumpsters, near the bushes bordering one side of the lot. A big tree blocked out the streetlight, so Lauren hadn't noticed him and a child moving in and out of the shadows until now. The minivan's inside light was on, and the back door was open.

"No, no, no," the man was saying. "Don't try to lift that, honey. It's too heavy. Maybe someone in the store can help us."

Lauren opened her passenger door, and set the grocery bag on the seat. She glanced toward the minivan again. She could see the man now. He was on crutches. He and his little girl were trying to load groceries into the vehicle. One of the bags was tipped over, and two more stood upright. The man turned in her direction. "Excuse me!" he called softly. "Do you have a minute? I hate to bother you . . ."

Lauren didn't move for a moment. Something wasn't right, but she couldn't quite put her finger on it. Still, her heart broke as she watched the little girl struggling with one of the bags. She was about ten years old, and very pretty.

Lauren stepped toward them. "Do you folks need some help?"

"Oh, yes, thank you," the man said. "You're very kind."

"It's okay!" the little girl said—loudly. "I got it!" She loaded one bag into the backseat, and then quickly grabbed another. "It's not heavy at all! Thank you anyway!"

This close, she could see the man on crutches shoot a look at the young girl. He had such a hateful, murderous stare, it made Lauren stop in her tracks. Nothing in his malignant glare matched that soft, gentle voice coming out of the shadows just moments before.

But the child ignored him and loaded up the second grocery bag. She glanced at Lauren. "Thank you anyway!" she repeated. "You can go back to your car! Good-bye!"

The man turned to Lauren and tried to laugh, but she

could tell it almost hurt him to smile. "Well, thanks for stopping," he said with an awkward wave. "It looks like my daughter has the situation under control. Good night."

Lauren just nodded, then retreated toward her car.

On the way home, she wondered why they'd parked on the other side of the lot from Guji's Deli when there were plenty of spaces right in front of the store. Why walk all that way when he didn't have to? And the man was on crutches, too, though she didn't remember seeing a cast on his leg.

If Lauren Tully had turned her car around and driven back to Guji's Deli ten minutes later, she would have found that man on crutches and his little girl in the exact same spot. She would have seen the three grocery bags once again waiting to be loaded into the minivan.

If she had turned her car around, Lauren might have been able to warn 21-year-old Wendy Keefe that it was all a ploy.

The blond liberal arts major at Willamette University had ridden her bicycle to Guji's for a pack of cigarettes. Never mind that her boyfriend made fun of her for being both a smoker and a bicycle enthusiast. She was emerging from the store with her bike helmet under her arm when she spotted the minivan, along with the man on crutches and his daughter. The little girl was crying. Wendy hadn't been there ten minutes earlier, when the man had slapped the child across her face. And he'd slapped her hard. It was too dark for Wendy to see the red welt on the young girl's cheek.

"Excuse me!" the man called. He had a very gentle tone in his voice. "We're in kind of a bind here. I'm afraid we over-shopped. These bags are too heavy for my daughter. . . ."

Tucking the Salems in the pocket of her windbreaker, Wendy approached the minivan. The little girl had been struggling with one of three bags. But now she stopped to stare at Wendy. The child kept shaking her head over and over. Tears slid down her cheeks. She seemed to be mouthing something to her.

"Yes, it looks like you could use an extra hand," Wendy said.

Propped up on his crutches, the father smiled. "I really appreciate this. If you could just slide those bags into the backseat, we can take it from there."

"No problem." Wendy hoisted one of the bags into the back. The young girl stood by the open door. She whispered something, and Wendy turned to her. "What did you say, honey?"

"Run," the child whispered.

Bewildered, Wendy stopped to stare at her.

The father cleared his throat. "If you could get in there and slide the bag to the driver's side. Just climb right in there."

Wendy hesitated.

"Run," the young girl repeated under her breath.

For a second, Wendy was paralyzed. She squinted at the child, who began to back away from her. Wendy wasn't looking at the man.

She didn't see him coming toward her with one of his crutches in the air.

"Run!" the child screamed at her. "No!"

It was the last thing Wendy heard before the crutch cracked against her skull.

The nine-year-old sat alone in the front passenger seat of the minivan. Her face was swollen and throbbing. He'd parked the vehicle on an old dirt road by some railroad tracks. In all the times she'd sat alone in this minivan, parked in this spot, she'd never seen a train go by. And she'd spent many hours here.

Clouds swept across the dark horizon on this warm June night. She could only see the outlines of the tops of the trees ahead of her. The rest was just blackness. She couldn't tell where he'd taken the bicycle lady. The screams seemed far away, maybe somewhere beyond the trees.

She'd had to endure his wrath all the way there, while the woman lay unconscious and bleeding in the back. Usually, he knocked them out with one quick, bloodless blow while they were inside the minivan. But she'd screwed everything up with that nice chubby lady, and he'd heard her trying to warn the bike woman. He kept saying it was *her* fault he had to hit the woman with his crutch. She'd bled on him while he'd loaded her into the back.

He repeatedly reached over from the driver's side and swatted her on the back of the head. "Think you're really smart trying to trip me up," he growled. "That slap earlier was nothing. I haven't even started with you, yet. Would you look at the blood back there? Shit, I think she's hemorrhaging. I wouldn't be surprised if she dies before we even get to the woods. If you'd done what you were supposed to, I might have had time to load her bike in the car. You might have gotten a new bicycle tonight. But, no, too bad for you."

The young woman was still alive. He'd revived her while dragging her toward the darkened woods. Her screams had started out strong, but now they seemed to be weakening.

It wouldn't be much longer.

The nine-year-old dreaded going home. She wished she were older, and knew how this minivan worked. Then she'd just start up the engine, drive away, and never come back. But she had to stay—and endure his punishment later.

She stared out at the blackness beyond the windshield and listened to the screams fading. She thought about how it didn't pay trying to help some people.

That stupid woman had gotten her into a lot of trouble.

Seattle—eleven years later

She pulled over to the side of the tree-lined street and watched Karen Carlisle's Jetta turn into the driveway. Karen may have spotted her in the hallway at the convalescent center, but obviously didn't realize she'd been followed home.

In fact, Frank Carlisle's shrink daughter seemed to have no idea that for almost three weeks now, her comings and goings had been carefully monitored.

She knew Karen's routines: when she ate and slept and walked the dog, and what she wore to bed. She'd figured out the housekeeper's schedule, too. She knew when Karen was usually alone and when she was at her most vulnerable. She even knew where they hid the spare house key for emergencies (under a decorative stone in a garden by the back door).

Of course, Karen would wonder about seeing her in the hallway at the rest home today. She might even ask about it. Karen would get the usual wide-eyed, innocent denial, and a very sincere, "I was never there. I don't know what you're talking about."

Actually, today was her fifth visit to that nursing home, observing Karen at work with the patients—and with her dad. The last time, a few days ago, she'd ducked into a room across the hall and spied on Karen saying good-bye to her senile father as he lay in bed. Only moments after Karen had left, she'd snuck into the old man's room. She couldn't resist. He was clueless, totally out of it. His mouth open, he stared at her and blinked.

Just for fun, she'd bent over and kissed his wrinkly forehead—the same way Karen always did. "I'm going to kill your daughter," she'd whispered to him.

Switching off the ignition, she leaned back in the driver's seat. She watched Karen climb out of her car and head toward the house. Despite some neglect, the white stucco held its own among the stately old mansions on the block. As Karen walked up the stairs to the front porch, there was some barking from inside the house. Jessie, the housekeeper, opened the door and let the dog out. His tail wagging, the black cocker spaniel raced up to Karen and poked her leg with his snout. She patted him on the head and scratched him behind the ears. Then he scurried down the steps to take a leak at the trunk of a big elm tree in the front yard.

Jessie stepped outside and said something to Karen. She was a stout, sturdy, grandmotherly woman in her late sixties with cat's-eye glasses and bright red hair that was probably a wig. Jessie didn't usually work on Saturdays. She must have been making up for the fact that she'd only put in a half day on Wednesday.

Watching from inside the car, she rolled down her window.

Jessie was shaking her head at Karen. "Nope, nobody here but us chickens," she heard Jessie say. "I haven't seen hide nor hair of Amelia, and I've been here about twenty minutes."

Karen paused at the front door, muttered something, and then turned to glance over her shoulder. "C'mon, Rufus, let's get in the house." The dog obediently trotted to her.

"How's your dad doing?" Jessie asked.

"Not so hot," Karen said, leading the cocker spaniel inside the house. Then it sounded like she said, "Today wasn't a good day."

Sitting behind the wheel and staring beyond the dirty windshield, she smiled. "Poor thing," she whispered. "Think today was a bad day? Just wait, Karen. Just wait."

In the foyer, Karen took off her coat while Jessie and Rufus headed past the front stairs to the kitchen. The house's first floor still had the original wainscoting woodwork. A few well-scattered, old, worn Oriental rugs covered most of the hardwood floor.

Karen draped her coat and purse over the banister post at the bottom of the stairs, and then followed them into the kitchen. She opened a cookie jar on the counter, and tossed a dog biscuit at Rufus, who caught it in the air with his mouth. Over by the sink, Jessie was polishing a pair of silver candelabras that had belonged to Karen's parents.

Karen sat down at the breakfast table, which had a glass top and a yellow-painted wrought-iron frame and legs. It really belonged on a patio, but had been in the kitchen for decades. The matching wrought-iron chairs had always been uncomfortable, even with seat cushions. Her dad had bought all new white appliances about six years ago, and it brightened up the kitchen. But the ugly old table with the chairs-from-hell remained.

Rufus came over and put his head in her lap. He was nine years old, and had been her dad's main companion most of that time. They'd taken care of each other. At least once a week, she loaded Rufus into the car and drove him to the rest home to see his old buddy. Then she'd walk or wheel her dad outside, and Rufus would go nuts, pawing and poking at her father's leg, licking his hand. The visits with Rufus always cheered up her dad.

She thought about how much freedom her father would lose if they changed his routine and his medication. She replayed in her mind kissing him good-bye about twenty-five minutes ago. It was strange, seeing that young woman who looked so much like Amelia in the hallway, outside her father's door.

"I can't believe Amelia isn't here," Karen muttered. "She was so anxious to see me. I told her to wait."

"Did she say what it was about?" Jessie asked, toiling away on the candelabra.

"Something horrible happened. That's all I know. And that's all I can say without breaking patient-therapist confidentiality."

"Oh, yeah, like I have a direct line to Tom Brokaw. Who am I going to tell?" Jessie grinned at her. "You worry about her more than all your other patients. That Amelia is a sweet girl. The way she counts on you—and looks up to you. Three guesses who she reminds me of."

Karen just nodded. Amelia and Haley were alike in so many other ways, too: the drinking problems, the low self-esteem, and a penchant for blaming themselves for just about everything.

She remembered a discussion she'd once had with Haley, in which the fifteen-year-old blamed herself for her parents' breakup. "Hey, honey," Karen had told her, with a nudge. "If anyone's getting blamed for your parents' breakup, it's me."

That wasn't quite true. When Karen had first met Haley's father four years ago, he'd already separated from his wife. Karen had come to loathe her go-nowhere counseling job at Group Health. Her dad had just started to show early warning signs of something wrong with little episodes of depression and forgetfulness. Karen had recently fired his housekeeper, who had been robbing him blind for months. She'd moved back home temporarily to look after him and take him to his barrage of doctor appointments. As for Karen's love life, it was nonexistent.

It seemed like the only time she had for herself was the hour between returning home from work and cooking dinner for her dad. He was always glued to the TV and *Law and Order,* so she'd change into her sweats, jog to Volunteer Park, then run laps around the reservoir. That section of the park had a sweeping view of downtown Seattle, the Space Needle, and the Olympic Mountains. At sunset, it was gorgeous, and she could almost convince herself that she wasn't so bad off. There were always a few handsome men doing laps, too. Most of them were probably gay, but she still got an occasional, flirtatious smile from a fellow jogger. Hell, something like that could make her night.

And sometimes it could make her stumble and skin her knee. The jogger whose smile had caught her eye and tangled her feet on that warm September evening was about forty years old. He had brown hair that was receding badly, but the rest of him was awfully nice: dark eyes, a swarthy complexion, sexy smile, and a toned, sinewy body.

As soon as she hit the asphalt, Karen felt the searing pain in her knee. She also felt utterly humiliated. The handsome jogger swiveled around and ran to her aid. He kept saying he was sorry he'd distracted her. It was all his fault.

"Oh, no, it's okay," Karen babbled. "I'm fine. I—it really doesn't hurt."

The hell it didn't. But something left over from her tomboy period was putting up a brave, tearless front.

"Jesus, that's gotta smart," he said. "Look, you've got pebbles embedded in there—"

"Really, it's nothing." But then she took a look at all the blood, and suddenly felt a little woozy.

"I have a first-aid kit in my car," she heard him say. "Stay put. I'll be right back."

When he returned, he helped her to a park bench, sat her down, and went to work on her knee. The blood had trickled down to her ankle. He squatted in front of her and meticulously cleaned it up. He also recommended she put some ice on her knee once she got home. Karen tried not to wince while he picked out a few pebbles and applied the Neosporin.

"So, are you a doctor?" she asked, once she got past the pain. "You're really good at this."

"No, I'm an attorney. But I have a thirteen-year-old daughter who thinks she can outrun, out-throw, and out-dare any boy in her class. So I've tended to a lot of scrapes and cuts."

Karen looked for a wedding ring on his hand. There wasn't one.

"Her mother and I have been separated for seven months," he said, apparently reading her mind. But he seemed focused on her knee as he put a large Band-Aid over the wound. "You know, I should take another look at this knee in a couple of nights and see how it's healing. Are you free Saturday night?"

Karen hesitated. His slick yet corny approach took her totally by surprise.

He looked up at her and grinned.

Yes, she thought, *a very sexy smile.*

His name was Kurt Lombard. They had a great first date: dinner at the Pink Door, and a heavy make-out session afterward. Then he didn't call. After eight days, she finally phoned him. She was so relieved and grateful when he asked her out again that she ignored all the signs. Looking back on it, she could see Kurt had immediately established a pattern in their relationship. She'd fallen hard for a ruggedly handsome commitment-phobic charmer. Every time he showed he cared about her, it was intermittent reinforcement. He was like a bad slot machine that paid off just often enough to keep her hooked.

Karen had dated him off and on for three months before working up the nerve to ask how he felt about her. And was he ever planning to divorce his wife? Kurt couldn't even commit to *un*-commit.

When she had patients in unbalanced relationships like this, Karen always advised them to stand up for themselves or get the hell out. But she stuck with Kurt. Eventually, he did divorce his wife, and Karen was relieved he didn't take his new freedom to the limit by dumping her, too. More positive intermittent reinforcement came when he wanted her to meet his daughter, Haley. By then she was fourteen, and out of her tomboy phase. She'd already been arrested once, and rushed to the hospital twice for alcohol poisoning. On their first meeting—dinner at the 5-Spot Café—Kurt had dropped them off in front of the restaurant, and then went to park the car. Standing on the curb in front of the café, Karen found herself alone for the first time with Haley. The oversized

army fatigue jacket limply hung on the girl's slouched, ema-
ciated frame. She had a blue streak in her stringy brown hair.
And she might have been pretty if not for her perpetual
sneer. "So—you're the girlfriend," Haley said.

Playing along, Karen grinned. "And you're the daughter."

"Y'know, my mother's a lot prettier than you," Haley
said.

"Yeah? Well, my mother can beat up your mother." Karen
shot back.

Staring at her for a moment, Haley twirled a strand of hair
around her finger. Finally, she burst out laughing.

Karen realized she had no problem standing up to the
daughter—just the dad. She and Haley weren't exactly bosom
buddies, but they got along all right. By the time Haley
was fifteen, Karen and Kurt were living together in a two-
bedroom house in Seattle's Queen Anne district.

Karen's dad was doing better, thanks partly to his new
medication, but even more to his new housekeeper, Jessie.
She doted on him, but kept him in line, too.

Kurt was a hit with Karen's dad—and with her siblings,
Frank and Sheila, when they came to Seattle on vacation with
their families. Her friends liked him, too. But when Karen
asked Jessie what she thought of Kurt, the housekeeper just
smiled cryptically and said, "He's very charming."

"That's it?" Karen asked.

"He's very charming," Jessie repeated. "But he should
pay more attention to the women in his life, namely you and
his daughter, the poor thing."

Three weeks after Jessie had made that comment, a terrified Haley confided in Karen that she thought she had syphilis
or gonorrhea. Karen made an appointment for her at Group
Health, and went with her to the doctor's office. It turned out
Haley had a mild yeast infection.

"I won't say anything to your folks about this," Karen told

her as they left the office together. "And I'm not going to tell you how stupid it is for someone your age to be having sex—"

"Oops, I think you just did," Haley interjected.

Karen nodded. "Yeah, well, at least be smart enough to take some precautions, okay?"

"Thanks, Karen."

The following weekend, Haley bought her a coffee mug. It had a cartoon of a Garfield-like smiling cat with sunglasses, and said "KAREN is a Cool Cat!" She and Haley had a good laugh over how tacky it was. At first, Karen only used the mug for her morning coffee as a joke when Haley was staying with them. But then she began using it every morning.

Karen became Haley's confidante and surrogate big sister. Haley started to shape up, too, joining a support group to help kick her drinking problem. She was growing into a lovely young woman. But some things she confided in Karen weren't easy to hear: "My mother feels really threatened by you."

"Well, let her know as far as you're concerned she can't be replaced. And if that doesn't work, remind her that she's a lot prettier than I am."

Haley chuckled. "You'll never let me forget about that, will you?"

"Never."

Other things Haley revealed were damn difficult to take. "I was talking to Dad this morning," she told her while trying on dresses in the changing area at a downtown boutique. Karen was helping her pick out a formal for the junior prom. "I asked him if he was *ever* going to marry you, and he got all pissy with me. He said I should mind my own business. So, I told him, if you end up being my stepmother that certainly would be my business, and I'm all for it. But he just got madder and madder." Haley sighed, and nervously wrapped a strand of her hair around her finger. Karen had long ago noticed whenever Haley got perplexed she started playing with her hair like that. "God, he's my father and I love him," she went on. "But he's such an asshole sometimes. Still, you want to marry him, don't you Karen? I mean, you've discussed it with him, right?"

"You know," Karen managed to say after a moment. "I don't think you should wear a long formal to this thing. You'll just look like everyone else. What about a pair of black slacks and a fancy top? I have this sleeveless copper-sequined top at home—and these very sexy black heels. We'll fix your hair so it's up."

"Omigod, that sounds fantastic!" Haley gushed. "I'll look like I'm going to the friggin' Grammys!"

That was exactly how she looked—sleek, sexy, and sophisticated. Kurt couldn't believe it was his little girl going out the door with that awestruck teenage boy in an ill-fitting tuxedo. "It just floors me how she's grown up so fast," Kurt remarked. "In a little over a year, she'll be going off to college."

"And I don't even have a child of my own yet," Karen heard herself say.

But, obviously, he pretended not to hear it.

Lately she'd been watching families and women with babies, and most of those women were younger than her. Not only was her biological clock ticking, there was a race against time with her dad, too. He'd been slipping again; the Alzheimer's was advancing. Maybe it was selfish of her, but she wanted to have a child he could know and hold while he was still somewhat coherent.

"I want to get married, Kurt," she told him. "Is that ever going to happen? Do you see that in our future at all?"

His back to her, he stood at the living room window, watching the limo back out of the driveway. Haley, her date, and a bunch of their friends had hired the car and a chauffeur for the night.

"No," Kurt finally replied. "I don't see it happening."

Karen felt as if someone had just sucker punched her in the stomach. She'd expected him to waffle a bit, and leave her some room for hope. She sank down in a hardback chair, and gripped the armrests. "It's not even a possibility?" she asked.

Still staring out the window, he let out a long sigh. He wouldn't face her. Karen strained to catch his reflection in the darkened glass. "I've been married once and it didn't work out," he explained. "That was enough for me. I don't want to get married again, Karen."

"Well, *this* isn't enough for *me*," she murmured.

He turned and frowned at her. "Jesus, what's gotten into you all of a sudden?"

It wasn't so sudden. Karen knew she should have had this discussion with him three years ago. She was an idiot to wait this long. He'd never really misled her. She'd been lying to herself all this time.

Karen said nothing. She stood up, wandered into their bedroom, and started packing her overnight bag.

She slept at her father's house that night. Within a month, she'd moved out of the Queen Anne house she shared with Kurt. It was almost insulting the way he didn't put up much of a fight. But Haley was devastated. Karen assured her they'd still be friends. Hell, she *needed* friends. After the breakup, Karen had suffered several Kurt Casualties among her acquaintances—mostly other couples who suddenly seemed uncomfortable around her.

She stayed true to her word, and kept in touch with Haley. She felt good about herself with Haley. She'd helped a troubled little teen punkette develop into a sweet and lovely young woman. Karen wanted to rise above the manner of a vindictive ex. So she often had to remind the 17-year-old that talking about her father was verboten.

"You'll have to hear this whether you like it or not," Haley told her, five months after the breakup. They were jogging around the Volunteer Park reservoir together, where Karen had first met Kurt. "Dad's getting married," she said.

Karen stopped abruptly. "What?" she asked, even though she'd heard what Haley had said. A moment passed, and neither of them uttered a word. Karen got her breath back. Small wonder she hadn't tripped and fallen on her face upon hearing the news. To her amazement, she was still standing.

Kurt's fiancée was a 28-year-old Macy's saleswoman named Jennifer. Big surprise, a younger woman.

Haley expressed utter disgust with her father, and claimed his fiancée was a major dipshit. Karen told her they weren't going to talk about it. "When you're near me, you're in a no-Kurt-bashing zone. We don't need to do that here. Our friendship is based on better things."

It was tough sticking to that noble resolve after she'd received one particular e-mail from Kurt. They'd kept their distance since the breakup, and the only contact they'd had with each other had been infrequent e-mails. This one the son of a bitch copied to someone in his office—obviously to show he meant business:

Karen:

Since you've moved out, I've allowed Haley to continue seeing you, because I know your friendship means a lot to her. I think I've been very tolerant about this. Haley told me that she informed you of my marriage plans. So, I'm sure you will understand that I no longer feel your friendship with my daughter is appropriate. This is a somewhat confusing time for Haley, and she has had a few recent setbacks with the drinking. She has also had other problems at

school that I won't go into. Suffice it to say, I believe
her association with you is creating some inner
conflict. Please respect my wishes and give Haley a
chance to adapt to the positive changes in her home
life with me. Please stop seeing her.

Sincerely,
Kurt

Karen immediately fired off a two-page, single-spaced
tirade that began: "Dear Asshole," and went on to tell Kurt
what a lousy father he was. She cited several examples.

But at the end of the day, Karen didn't send the e-mail.
She didn't have it in her to fight with Kurt at that point.
Things were getting worse with her dad. He'd become quite
paranoid, and a few times the previous week, he'd been so
disoriented he hadn't even recognized her or Jessie. He'd
slapped poor Rufus on the snout for barking on two occasions, and that was totally unlike him. Karen's brother and
sister kept calling long distance for updates on his condition.
They wanted her to start looking for nursing homes, and she
almost came to blows with them on the subject.

"I know you don't want to give up on him," her brother
argued. "But you're being selfish keeping him at home,
Karen. He's better off in a full-care facility. It sounds horrible, but for his sake, you'll have to let go."

Karen knew he was right, but she wasn't ready to let go,
yet.

And she wasn't ready to abandon Haley either; though she
wondered if maybe—just maybe—Kurt was right, too. Even
with all her efforts not to badmouth Kurt, her friendship
with Haley still threatened the father-daughter relationship.
How couldn't it? Perhaps she was being selfish there, too.

Haley phoned her on the sly a few times over the next two

weeks. In each call, she cried hysterically and cursed her father. "How could he do this? He has no right! I can't believe you're going along with him on this."

Karen tried to explain that until she was eighteen, her father, indeed, had every right to slap a moratorium on their friendship. But it was only temporary and, in the meantime, why didn't she give this Jennifer a chance and cut her some slack? And what was this about her drinking again, and some trouble in school?

"C'mon, honey, you shape up, okay?" Karen told her, with a pang in her gut. "And you really need to stop calling me. You'll get us *both* in trouble."

Haley promised to stop calling if they could meet one more time. Karen reluctantly agreed to a dinner together at the Deluxe Bar and Grill, a cozy, trendy burger joint with an old-fashioned bar and a modern gas fireplace. She and Haley sat in a booth. After all those semi-hysterical phone calls, Haley was surprisingly calm and collected—almost at peace with the situation. She explained she wasn't going to plead or argue with her over her dad's decision. And she wasn't going to Kurt-bash either. No, this was about having a nice last dinner together.

"Now, don't make it sound so *final*," Karen said. "We'll be back in touch after you're eighteen, which is in—what—less than a year? By then you'll be in college and making a whole new batch of friends. You'll be fine, Haley. So don't cry in your Cobb salad about it."

Haley just nodded, and gave her a strange, sad smile.

Karen was mostly concerned about her recent setbacks with the drinking, and her problems at school. "I know you're not happy about this, but I understand why your dad thinks it's for the best. Do me a favor, and don't screw up your own life just because you're mad at him. You were doing so well for a while there, honey. Don't mess it up. If you're pissed at your father and want to get even with him, do it some other way. Short sheet his bed, bust up that awful country-and-western CD collection of his, poop in his favorite shoes, I don't care."

Haley rolled her eyes and laughed.

"Just don't ruin your own life to hurt him," Karen whispered. "Promise me you won't."

"I promise." Haley fiddled with a strand of her hair.

"And stop tugging at your hair."

Obediently, she smiled and glanced down at her plate. She played with her fork instead. "Karen, you're not going to forget me, are you?"

Karen reached across the table and took hold of her hand. "How could I? Every morning I have my coffee out of that tacky 'Karen is a Cool Cat' mug you gave me. I couldn't start my day without it."

They hugged good-bye alongside Haley's father's Toyota. Haley offered her a ride, but Karen decided to walk home. It was only a few blocks. She'd been keeping up a brave, everything-will-be-swell front with Haley, and needed time alone to have herself a good cry.

When she got home, she found her dad asleep in front of the TV. Jessie had fixed him fried chicken. Karen washed his dinner dishes, then woke him and got him into his bed. She was about to take a shower when the phone rang. She snatched up the receiver on the second ring, hoping her dad hadn't awoken. "Hello?"

"This is the Seattle Police calling for Karen Carlisle," said the man on the other end of the line.

"Yes, this is Karen." Her grip tightened on the receiver.

"Your name and phone number are listed in Haley Lombard's wallet as her emergency contact."

Karen had no idea. For a moment, she almost couldn't breathe.

"I'm afraid there's been an accident," he said.

"Where? Is Haley hurt?"

"She went off the freeway overpass at Lakeview and Bel-mont."

Karen knew that overpass. It curved above Interstate 5, and had a low guardrail along the edge. At one point, the drop was several stories down to the freeway.

"Is she—is she going to be all right?"

"They're taking her body to Harborview Medical Cen-ter," he answered grimly. "I'm sorry. Were you her parent or legal guardian?"

Karen closed her eyes. "No," she heard herself answer. "No, I was her friend."

The rest of the night was a blur. She couldn't get hold of Kurt, and there was no answer at Haley's mother's house, not even a machine. Karen didn't want to leave her dad alone; he'd woken up in the middle of the night before, and not known where he was. But she had no choice. All she could do was quietly hurry out the door, and pray he'd sleep until morning.

In the car, she was so frazzled she passed Twelfth Avenue, probably the quickest way to the hospital. The next possible route, Broadway, was gridlocked. Flustered, she headed down-hill to Belmont and the overpass where Haley had had her accident. That overpass eventually led to the highway on-ramp, and once on the interstate she could be at the hospital within two minutes.

But her thinking was muddled. Of course, they were rerouting traffic at the accident site. Cars lined up bumper to bumper as she approached the overpass. A detour sign had been placed at the last turn before the overpass, and a cop waved at her to make a left, where traffic seemed to move at a crawl. Ahead, Karen could see cones lined up, emergency flares sizzling on the concrete, and swirling red strobes from police cars parked at the start of the overpass. She saw something else, too: Kurt's Toyota.

"My God, they made a mistake," she whispered to herself. The cop had told her on the phone that Haley had gone off the overpass, yet there was Kurt's car, all in one piece. The front door was open, and someone shined a flashlight around inside the car. All she could think was *Maybe Haley's okay after all, maybe they got it wrong. . . .*

"Keep moving!" yelled the cop in front of the detour sign. He waved at her impatiently.

Karen rolled down her window. "The police called me fifteen minutes ago," she said. "They told me to go to Harborview. I'm a friend of Haley Lombard. But I think they made a mistake—"

"Okay, you can go ahead," he grumbled, motioning her forward.

Karen slowly continued down the hill, where the police kept onlookers at bay. She caught another look at Kurt's Toyota. The man inside with the flashlight was inspecting the glove compartment.

"You need to turn your car back around!" another cop screamed at her.

She shook her head and called out the window to him, repeating what she'd told the first patrolman. "I think there was some kind of mistake about the victim's identity." She nodded toward the Toyota. "That's Haley Lombard's father's car over there."

The cop had her pull over to a small lot by a chain-link fence overlooking the freeway. "Lemme get someone to clear this up with you," he grunted.

Karen parked her car and climbed out. For a moment, her legs were unsteady. She kept looking for a mangled section of the overpass's guardrail, some indication that another vehicle had plowed through it and careened down to the freeway. But she didn't see any damage at all. She wandered toward the railing edge and peered over it. About five stories below, on the interstate, a line of emergency flares cordoned off two lanes, and traffic was at a near standstill. Several squad cars, their flashers going, surrounded a smashed-up SUV. A tow truck was backing up toward it. From the skid marks on the pavement, it looked as if the SUV had swerved to avoid hitting something, and then crashed into the concrete divider. The tire markings on the pavement veered in front of a pool of blood. It almost looked black in the night.

Confused, Karen glanced to her right and tapped a young policewoman on the shoulder. "Excuse me. I'm a friend of Haley Lombard's, and they called me. They said she went off the overpass. But her father's car is right there, and I don't see where anyone could have driven off—"

"Haley Lombard, yes," the policewoman said, nodding. She seemed distracted by a voice crackling over the walkie-talkie on her belt. "Hell of a mess down there. An SUV almost hit the body. Thank God no one in the vehicle was seriously injured. Your friend didn't *drive* off the overpass. She *jumped*. It looks like she was drinking. They found a bottle of bourbon in her car. She was DOA at Harborview ten minutes ago. You need to talk to somebody there." She turned away and started barking a bunch of police code numbers on her radio.

Karen couldn't hear what she was saying. She just stood there by the overpass's guardrail, with the wind whipping at her. She was thinking that it all made sense now. She should have seen the signs. Some people about to commit suicide can appear very calm. After a period of torment, they can suddenly seem at peace, because they have come up with a solution for their problems. That had been Haley only two hours ago. She'd taken control of her situation and made up her mind about what to do.

"Karen, you're not going to forget me, are you?"

A loud *beep, beep, beep* from below made her turn toward the guardrail again and gaze down at the freeway. A cleanup truck had backed up toward the dark puddle. Its hoses went on and started to wash the blood away. Pink swirls formed in the water that rippled across the pavement to the high-way's shoulder.

Kurt and his ex-wife both blamed Karen. Haley had lied to them about where she'd been going that night. Kurt pointed out that he'd asked Karen to stop seeing Haley, but she'd met with her anyway, and just look what had happened. She must have said something to Haley during their secret dinner that helped push their girl over the edge.

Karen didn't have it in her to fight with Haley's grieving parents. She didn't go to the funeral. She knew she wasn't welcome.

Just three weeks after the burial, Karen had her first meeting with Amelia Faraday. For a while, Amelia reminded her so much of Haley, it hurt. But since then, she'd gotten to know Amelia, and really couldn't compare her to anyone.

The telephone rang, and Karen jumped up from the breakfast table. She figured it was Amelia again, and grabbed the phone before Jessie even had a chance to wipe off her hands. "Hello?" she said into the phone.

"Is Karen Carlisle there, please?" The man sounded as if he had asthma or something. His breathing wasn't right.

"This is Karen," she said.

"Um, my name's George McMillan. My niece is one of your patients, Amelia Faraday. . . ."

"Is Amelia all right?"

"She isn't with you?" he asked. "I just spoke with her five minutes ago, and she said she was at your house."

"Well, I'm sorry, Mr. McMillan, but she isn't," she replied. "Amelia called me, too. She indicated there was some kind of emergency. Is everything okay?"

"No, it's not." He cleared his throat, but it still sounded like something was wrong with his breathing. "She—she had this *premonition*. She phoned saying she thought her parents and my wife—that's her aunt—"

"Yes, Amelia has mentioned her."

"Well, see, they went away for the weekend at the family cabin on Lake Wenatchee, and Amelia was convinced they'd all been killed last night." His voice cracked, and Karen realized he was crying. That was why his breathing sounded so strange. "And she—she was right. I talked to someone who lives near the Lake Wenatchee house, and this neighbor, she found the bodies."

"Oh, my God," Karen whispered. She sank down in one of the chairs at the breakfast table. "I'm so sorry. . . ."

Karen heard him trying to stifle the sobs. He explained how he'd spoken to this neighbor—and then the police in Wenatchee. It appeared as if Amelia's father had shot his wife and sister-in-law with a hunting rifle, and then he'd turned the gun on himself.

"My God, Mr. McMillan—George—I'm so sorry," she repeated. "Poor Amelia. You—you said she had a *premonition* about this?"

"Yes, but she doesn't know yet that it's true. I called and tried to persuade her to come over here. But she said she needed to see you. I—I couldn't tell her over the phone what happened . . ."

Karen's front doorbell rang. Rufus started barking and scurried toward the front of the house.

"I think that's her at my door right now," she said into the phone. She turned to the housekeeper. "Jessie? Could you? If that's Amelia, could you please have her wait in my office?"

Jessie nodded, wiped off her hands and started out of the kitchen. "Rufus, knock it off!"

"Mr. McMillan, are you still there?" Karen said into the phone.

"Yes. Would you—would you mind driving Amelia over here? We live in West Seattle. I don't want her to be alone. And it might help my kids if their cousin was here." His voice cracked again. "They're playing outside. They still don't know. My son's eleven, and my daughter—she's only five years old. God, how am I going to tell them their mother's dead?"

Karen's heart ached for him. "I can drive Amelia over," she said finally. "It's no problem, Mr. McMillan. But if I insist on taking her to your house, she's bound to figure out something's wrong. Would you like me to tell her what happened?"

She could hear him sigh on the other end of the line. "Yes. Thank you, Karen. Thank you very much."

When she clicked off the phone, Karen could hear Jessie talking to Amelia: "You sit tight, hon. She'll be with you in a jiff. Rufus, get down!"

Pulling the dog by his collar, Jessie lumbered back into the kitchen and gave her a wary look. "Whew," she whispered. "That poor girl has the fidgets something fierce. She's practically bouncing off the walls in there. I think she's been crying, too."

Karen took hold of her arm. "Jess, do we still have some of Dad's sedatives?"

"You mean those light blue pills that made him a little dopey?"

Karen nodded. "Yes, the diazepam, for anxiety." It was times like this Karen wished she were a psychiatrist rather than just a therapist. Then she could have the proper medications on hand, instead of making do with some secondhand sedatives that were probably beyond their expiration date. "Amelia's going to need something to calm her down. Do we still have those pills?"

Jessie nodded. "On the crap shelf in the linen closet. I've been bugging you to let me clean that out. Good thing you never listen to a word I say. I'll get them." Jessie headed up the back stairs.

Karen went to the refrigerator and grabbed a bottle of water for Amelia. She gave Rufus a stern look. "Stay," she said. Then she took a deep breath and started toward her office at the front of the house.

The room used to be her father's study, and had always been one of Karen's favorite spots in the house. It was very comfy, with a fireplace and built-in bookshelves. But Amelia didn't appear at all comfortable. Dressed in jeans, a black top, and a bulky cardigan, she nervously paced in front of the sofa. Her wavy black hair was a windblown mess. Jessie was right. It looked as if she'd been crying.

She rushed to Karen and threw her arms around her. Karen wasn't in the habit of hugging her patients. But she held onto Amelia and gently patted her on the back.

"Where were you?" Karen asked, finally pulling away a little. "I thought you were going to wait for me here."

Tugging at a strand of hair, Amelia looked down at the floor and shrugged. "Well, I waited for Jessie, like you said to. But after about ten minutes, I got kind of anxious. So I just drove around for a while."

Karen bit her lip. "You, um, you didn't by any chance track me down at the Sandpoint View Convalescent Home? I thought I saw you there about twenty-five minutes ago."

"I have no idea where that even is," Amelia replied, wide-eyed. "What are you talking about?"

Karen shook her head. "Never mind. It's my mistake. Here, I got you some water. Sit down, try to relax."

"I can't sit down," Amelia said, pacing again. "I have a feeling something's happened to my parents."

"I understand," Karen said. "I just got off the phone with your uncle. He called. He was worried about you. He told me that . . ." She hesitated.

Amelia stopped pacing, and turned to stare at her.

Jessie came to the door with the diazepam and handed the bottle to Karen.

"Thanks, Jessie," Karen said. "Could you close the door, please?"

Jessie slid shut the big, bulky pocket door that came out of the wall. Karen shook two pills into her hand. "Amelia, I want you to take these. They're like Valium. They'll chill you out a little."

But Amelia didn't move. She just kept staring at Karen. Tears welled in her eyes. "You want me to take a sedative? What did Uncle George tell you?"

"Take the pills, Amelia."

"Oh, my God," she said, wincing. A shaky hand went over her mouth. She sank down on the sofa. "Then it's true. Aunt Ina . . . my Mom and Dad . . . they're all dead, aren't they?"

Karen swallowed hard and nodded. "I'm so sorry. . . ."

Chapter Six

No one said anything in the car while Karen drove across the West Seattle Bridge toward Amelia's uncle's house. Amelia sat on the passenger side, pensively gazing out her window. Jessie was in back with a grocery bag full of food from Karen's fridge. She'd insisted on fixing dinner for Amelia's uncle and his family.

A bit taken aback by the idea, Karen had wondered out loud if they'd be intruding on the family's grief.

"Nonsense, they gotta eat, don't they?" Jessie had replied while loading up the grocery bag. "You have all the fixings here for chicken tetrazzini—chicken, noodles, Parmesan cheese, sour cream. I'll whip up the casserole, stick it in the oven, and then you and I can beat a path out of there if it looks like we're wearing out our welcome."

Amelia had been inconsolable, sobbing hysterically for twenty minutes until the diazepam had kicked in. She finally slumped back on Karen's sofa. "I should go see Uncle George," she murmured, wiping her eyes. "Poor Jody and Steph . . ."

Sitting beside her on the couch, Karen handed her another Kleenex. "Your uncle asked me to drive you over. I said I'd be glad to."

Amelia nodded. "Thanks."

Biting her lip, Karen studied her for a moment. "You—you still haven't asked how it happened."

Silent, Amelia stared down at the wadded-up Kleenex in her hand.

"Your Uncle George said you had some kind of premonition."

Amelia shrugged helplessly. "It was just a feeling—an awful, awful feeling that something was wrong."

Karen's heart was breaking for her. "Honey, there's no easy way to tell you this. They haven't confirmed it. But it's possible your dad shot your mom and your aunt, and then he killed himself. They don't know for sure yet."

Amelia said nothing. She merely gave out an exhausted sigh, and closed her eyes.

Karen stroked her arm. "I'm so sorry," she whispered.

While they'd gotten ready to leave, Amelia had just sat quietly on the sofa. Her voice hadn't even cracked when she'd left Shane a phone message, explaining she was spending the night at her uncle's house. She'd told him he could pick up his car at Karen's. She'd said nothing about her parents' deaths. "I'll call you later tonight," she'd finished up listlessly.

Once they'd climbed inside Karen's Jetta, Amelia had suggested they take Highway 99 to the West Seattle Bridge. But after that, she hadn't said anything else.

Karen took her eyes off the road for a moment to look at her now. She was still staring out at the Seattle waterfront and skyline. There was a tiny, sad smile on her face.

"How are you doing, Amelia?" she asked.

She kept gazing out the window at the view from the bridge. "I was thinking about all the trips we took here to Aunt Ina and Uncle George's house—the Christmases, Thanksgivings, and birthdays. It's a long drive down from Bellingham, almost two hours." She traced a horizontal line on the window with her finger. "This bridge was always the landmark, the sign we were almost there. I remember when we were kids, Collin and I used to get so excited crossing this bridge. We loved going to Ina and George's." She let out a little laugh. "Last Thanksgiving on our way here, I noticed Collin had way too much product in his hair. He had his window open, but his hair didn't budge an inch. I could have broken off a piece of it. I remember teasing him, and Mom and Dad were laughing. Collin's face got red and he started cracking up too. He had the funniest laugh. You should have heard it. . . ."

Still staring out the window, she said nothing for a moment. Then the smile ran away from her face. "That was the last time I drove here with my family. I can't believe they're all gone now. I can't believe I actually could have . . ." She trailed off and shook her head.

From the backseat, Jessie leaned forward and patted Amelia on the shoulder.

Karen glanced at her on the passenger side. Amelia had her head down. She absently twirled a strand of her hair around her finger—the same nervous tic Haley had had.

Karen remembered Amelia doing that during their very first session.

Someone from Student Health Services at the University of Washington had referred the 19-year-old to Karen. Karen didn't have much information on her potential new client, except that her track record with therapists hadn't been too marvelous. She'd been having problems with alcohol and joined this campus group, Booze Busters. That had worked for a while, but she'd fallen off the wagon when her kid brother had drowned three weeks before.

When Karen answered her door for their first session that warm Friday afternoon, she was surprised at how beautiful Amelia was. The soft-spoken, polite girl had wavy black hair and blue eyes. She wore a pink oxford-cloth shirt, khaki shorts, and sandals. She said, "Yes, thank you," to a bottle of water, and sat at one end of the sofa in Karen's study. "So— what do you know about me?" she asked.

Karen settled in her easy chair with a notebook and pen. "Not very much, just what they told me at the U's Student Health Services. Do you know anything about *me*?"

"Not very much," Amelia echoed her, a tiny smile flickering on her face. "But I Googled you. Under 'Karen Carlisle, Counselor, Seattle,' there were a few links. I found out that you're thirty-six years old. You graduated with honors from UCLA. You have a master's in Social Work from the U, and you were a counselor at Group Health for five years before you started counseling on your own. Your name kept coming up in articles about that girl who got killed last month, Haley Something. Was she a client of yours?"

"She was a friend," Karen answered carefully. "But we're not here to talk about her."

"I guess you're right. This is my hour." Amelia sipped her water. "Well, I suppose you know I've been through a lot of therapists. I'm like a one-session wonder with them."

Karen shifted a bit in her chair. "Why is that?"

Amelia shrugged. "They were all dorks."

"Dorks," Karen repeated.

Amelia nodded. "For example, my Aunt Ina recommended this Dr. Racine, absolutely raved about her. And she turned out to be awful. The whole time I was talking to her, she sat there and stroked this ugly cat in her lap. I don't think she was even listening. Every once in a while, she just said something like, 'You own that,' or 'That's valid.' I mean, spare me."

"Okay, so that's one crummy therapist," Karen said. "What about the others?"

Amelia rolled her eyes. "Well, there was this hippie, who seemed very promising until the end of our first session, when he gave me a homework assignment. He wanted me to go home, get some magazines, and clip out pictures and words that made me feel happy—and pictures and words that made me sad. And then I was supposed to make two posters: a happy collage and a sad collage. So I went home, got some magazines, and found this picture of a little girl waving at someone from a car window. I think it was an auto insurance ad or something. I clipped that out, and cut out the word Good-bye. Then I made a little poster of that and mailed it to him."

Karen nodded. She was trying to figure out this young woman, who had come across as so vulnerable and sweet when they'd met just ten minutes ago. But she had a smart-ass streak, too. Karen wondered just how much of what Amelia said was true.

"Then there was this Arab guy—not that it makes any difference. I just couldn't understand him half the time because his English was terrible. He tried to hypnotize me, and kept screaming at me in his thick accent that I was *reseesting*. And I wasn't, I swear. Honest to God, I was trying to be a good subject."

"Why was he hypnotizing you?"

Amelia sipped her water. She brushed a piece of lint off the sofa arm. Her focus seemed intent on that. "He was trying to get me to remember stuff about my childhood, before the Faradays adopted me. Didn't Student Health Services tell you that I was adopted when I was four?"

Karen shook her head. She made a quick note: *Adopted @ 4 yrs old.* "Do you know what happened to your biological parents?" she asked.

"Nope. One of my first therapists was all hot on finding out about them. So my dad tried to get in touch with the adoption agency in Spokane. Turned out the place burned down after the Faradays adopted me. All their records went up in smoke. My folks thought about hiring a private detective to look into it further. I'm sure it couldn't be too tough tracking down state or county records. I mean, the information's there, somewhere. Am I right?"

"I suppose," Karen allowed. "So did they hire a private detective?"

"Nope. They dropped the idea when I dropped the therapist." She cocked her head to one side and squinted at Karen. "I have a feeling my folks would rather I not know about my biological parents."

"If that's true, it's certainly understandable," Karen said. "How do you feel? Do you want to know more about your birth parents?"

Amelia started to fiddle with her hair, and wrapped a strand around her finger. "I guess I'm curious."

Karen stared at her, and remembered Haley. She felt a little pang in her heart. "Well, that's normal enough," she said, smiling. "So, Amelia, what do you hope to get out of these sessions with me?"

"Well, I'd like to have more control in my life. I'm tired of being so screwed up."

"In what way do you feel screwed up?"

"I drink. I have blackouts. I don't remember doing certain things."

"What kind of things?" Karen asked.

"For example, I started seeing this really sweet guy, Shane, about two months ago. Well, one afternoon last week, he saw me at a stoplight in the University District in a beat-up Cadillac with some goony-looking urban-grunge type. He said I was all over this guy." Amelia shook her head. "I swear to God, I didn't remember any of it. But after Shane described the guy and his car to me, I had this vague impression that it really happened. I can't help thinking I might have had sex with this other guy. I went and got tested just to make sure I didn't pick up any STDs from this—this *stranger*."

"So how did the tests turn out?" Karen asked with concern.

"Negative—all around. I begged Shane to forgive me, and he did, thank God. He knows I didn't do it *consciously*." She gave a pitiful shrug. "Anyway, see what I mean about being screwed-up and not having any control?"

With a sigh, Karen leaned back in her chair. "Well, you know, Amelia, I don't mean to preach at you. But blackouts, memory loss, and erratic behavior generally come with the territory when people drink excessively."

"I wasn't drinking that afternoon. I was napping all day at a friend's house—at least I *thought* I was napping."

"Were you sick?"

"No. Hungover," she murmured. Her eyes wrestled with Karen's for a moment. "Listen, I was having blackouts when I was in Booze Busters and totally off the sauce. So it's not just connected to the drinking. I've always had this problem with—with *lost time,* ever since I was a kid. I was pretty screwed up back then, too, having nightmares all the time, along with these pains. My mom used to call them phantom pains. But they were real to me, they hurt like hell. I remember one in particular when I was six. I was playing in the backyard, by our dock, and out of nowhere, I suddenly got this terrible burning sensation on the back of my wrist. I let out such a shriek. I swear to God, it felt like someone was putting out a lit cigar on me. Mom thought a wasp might have stung me or something. But there was no sign of anything wrong. Still, it hurt like hell for days afterward.

"That's why I started drinking on the sly in early high school. It numbed these weird pains. And after a few drinks, I'd drag myself to bed and pass out. And I didn't have to lie there for an eternity with my usual tossing, turning, and worrying about the nightmares. Hell, for a long time, drinking was my *salvation*."

"So—do you think you're better off with an alcohol dependency?" Karen asked.

Amelia shook her head. "I'm not defending my drinking. I'm just saying that I was having these problems a long time before I tipped back my first shot of Jack Daniel's."

"Do you still get these pains?" Karen asked.

"No, thank God. They stopped around the time I was sixteen." Amelia sighed. "Anyway, that's why some of the other therapists wanted to explore my early childhood. I mean, something must have happened to me early on to make me this screwed up, right?"

Karen smiled. "Do us both a favor and stop referring to yourself as screwed up, okay?"

Amelia smiled back at her. "Okay."

"Can you remember anything from that time before the Faradays adopted you?"

She started to peel at the label on the water bottle. "Just fragments. I remember one night, sitting alone in a car, in the front seat. I was cold—and tired. The car was parked by this forest. It was dark all around me, and I could hear screams. I remember thinking, 'When the screaming stops, then we can go home.' "

Karen stared at her. She didn't write anything down. "Do you know who was screaming? By any chance, did you recognize the voice?"

Amelia shrugged. "Some woman, I don't know."

"Were you frightened?"

"No, I just remember wanting to go home. That's it. There's nothing else to it. Like I said, it's just fragments of memory."

"Do you recall who took you home?" Karen asked.

Amelia shook her head.

"I'm just trying to piece this together, Amelia," Karen explained. "Earlier you said, 'When the screaming stops, then we can go home.' Who's 'we'?"

"I told you, I don't remember," she replied, a bit edgy.

"Okay," Karen nodded, reading her discomfort. "Let's move on. Is there anything else from your early childhood you'd like to tell me about? Did you have any friends or playmates?"

Amelia took a moment to answer, and Karen quickly jotted in her notes: "Young A in car alone @ nite—screams outside—go home when screaming stops."

"I remember there was a little playhouse in a neighbor's yard. I think it was a toolshed, but he'd fixed it up like a playhouse with a small, red, plastic table and chair inside. I have this vague recollection of eating cookies at that little table."

"Tell me about this neighbor. He sounds nice."

She nodded. "He was Native American. I liked him, but I don't think I was supposed to be around him. He had beautiful, long black hair almost down to his shoulders. I couldn't tell you how old he was. Everyone over twelve at that time seemed like an adult to me. He wore a denim jacket. I wish I could remember his name, but I can't." She sighed. "When that one therapist tried to hypnotize me, that's what I was hoping for most of all—to remember the name of that nice neighbor man."

"Have *any* names from that time stuck with you?" Karen asked.

Amelia frowned. "Unca-dween. I'm not sure if it was a person or a place. It could have been a nickname. I know it wasn't my Native American friend, because when I think about Unca-dween, it doesn't make me happy."

Karen scribbled down the name, not quite sure of the spelling. "Any other fragments you might remember?"

Amelia took a swig from the water bottle. "Well, I have a feeling I might have been attacked or molested somewhere along the line. The other therapists all said I was repressing something. But I have this memory of being in my underpants and standing by a tub—I think it was in the bathroom at home. My mother was shaking me and asking me over and over again, 'Did he touch you down there?' I sort of knew what she meant. But she seemed so angry and upset that I pretended *not* to know. I just cried and said I was sorry. I don't know why I was apologizing. I guess I was just scared."

"But the incident she was questioning you about—"

"I don't remember it at all," Amelia said, shaking her head. "And I have only this vague impression of what my biological mother looked like. She had long, wavy black hair. I remember this one blouse of hers—white with a pattern of gold pocket watches and chains. I thought it was just gorgeous."

"Do you have any memories of your father?" Karen asked.

"None," Amelia answered quickly.

"You mentioned your mother talking to you in the bathroom. Do you remember any other room in the house?"

"I think there was a bomb shelter in the basement." Amelia fiddled with her hair for a moment. "It could have been someone else's house, maybe when I was older. But I remember standing in the basement just outside this big, thick door. I was talking to someone inside the little room. It could have been part of a dream for all I know. But the memory's there.

"The only other thing that stands out about that time was I used to talk to myself in the mirror a lot. I don't think I had many playmates my age, because all I remember is being alone and talking in the mirror." She let out a little laugh. "So what do you make of that? Early signs of a split personality?"

Karen laughed. "Boy, you *have* been to a lot of therapists, haven't you? But let me do the analysis, okay?"

Amelia had started them down memory lane, so Karen let her continue. She asked if she recalled spending time in any foster homes before the Faradays adopted her. In so many cases with adopted children, there were horror stories involving foster parents. But Amelia had no such memories. "I think they were all pretty nice. I didn't stay with anyone for very long. I have a feeling I was on the market for only a short while before the Faradays picked me up. My poor parents, they probably thought they were getting this great deal, because I was a pretty little girl. What a letdown it must have been to find out I was damaged goods."

"Why do you feel that way, Amelia?" Karen asked.

Amelia shrugged.

"Have your folks ever said or done anything to make you feel that way?"

Amelia smiled and shook her head. "No, from the very start, they made me feel loved. . . ." She described going for a walk with her potential new mother on her first day with the Faradays; her first impressions of a playground and a Baskin-Robbins 31 Flavors ice cream parlor not far from their house. She remembered some time later, after the adoption was official, when she learned she would soon have a baby brother or sister to play with. She had her first sleepover—at her Aunt Ina's apartment—the night Collin was born.

"Is this—the brother who died recently?" Karen asked hesitantly.

Amelia nodded.

"Do you have any other brothers or sisters?"

"No," she muttered. Then she cleared her throat. "It was just Collin and me."

"I'm sorry," Karen said. "Were you . . . very close to him?"

She nodded again. Amelia had tears brimming in her eyes, yet she was stone-faced. There was a box of Kleenex right beside her on the end table, but she didn't reach for one.

"I was told he died in a drowning accident. Is that right?"

"No, that's not right," she whispered, staring at Karen.

She was almost expressionless, yet a single tear slid down her cheek. "My brother's death wasn't an accident. I know it wasn't."

"How can you be so sure?"

Amelia quickly wiped away that one tear. "Because I killed him."

Karen remembered the silence in her study after Amelia had made that statement. It had lasted only a few seconds, but seemed longer, like the silence in the car now, as they reached the West Seattle side of the bridge.

"Stay on this road for a while," Amelia said tonelessly. "The turnoff for my uncle's house is after we pass California Avenue. I'll tell you when it's coming up."

Karen took her eyes off the road for a moment, and looked at her.

Her head tipped against the window, Amelia stared straight ahead with the same stone-faced expression she'd had after telling Karen that she'd killed her brother. And once again, there were tears locked in her eyes.

Chapter Seven

Amelia's Uncle George answered the door with his 5-year-old daughter in his arms.

Karen hadn't expected him to be so handsome. He wore jeans and a long-sleeved white T-shirt that showed off his lean, athletic physique. He had a strong jaw with a slight five o'clock shadow, and wavy black hair that was ceding to gray. Though his green eyes were still red from crying, there was a certain quiet strength to him.

Karen watched him set down the little girl so he could hug Amelia. The child then wrapped herself around his leg, and pressed her face against his hip. George held on to Amelia for a few moments, whispering in her ear.

"Thanks, Uncle George," she said, sniffling. She turned and nodded toward Karen and Jessie. "This is my therapist—and she's also my friend—"

"Hi, I'm Karen," she said, stepping in from the doorway to shake his hand. "I'm so sorry for your loss." She introduced him to Jessie, who was carrying the bag full of food.

"Jessie figured you and the children could use a home-cooked dinner tonight—"

"Just point us to the kitchen," Jessie announced. "Oh, never mind, I see it—straight ahead." And she started off in that direction.

Karen took off her coat, but held on to it. "If we're at all in the way, please, just let us know," she told George.

"No, you're not," he said. "You're a lifesaver, Karen."

Amelia bent down and pried Stephanie off George's leg. The child clung to her now. Amelia looked so forlorn as she rocked Stephanie. "I'm sorry," she whispered tearfully. "I'm so sorry, Steffie. . . ."

"Why are you sorry?" the child asked. "You didn't do anything wrong."

Amelia winced, and then she seemed to hug her young cousin even tighter.

Watching them, Karen felt so horrible for Amelia and everyone in this house.

George collected his daughter from her. "Amelia, sweetie, do you think you could talk to Jody?" he asked. "He won't come out of his room. I'm really worried about him. Maybe he'll talk to you."

Wiping her eyes, Amelia nodded, and then started through the living room toward a back hallway.

"Jody's my son," George whispered to Karen. He stroked his daughter's hair. They trailed after Amelia. "Five minutes after I told him the news about his mom, Jody ducked into his room and shut the door."

In the hallway, they stayed back and watched Amelia knock on the bedroom door.

"He did the exact same thing a few months ago when his cousin died," George explained. "Jody just worshiped Collin. He was holed up in his room for two whole days. I thought he'd miss the funeral. My wife had to leave his meals outside the door and even then, he hardly ate a thing. He only came out to go to the bathroom." George's voice cracked a little. "God, I don't know what to do. It's such an awful helpless feeling to know your child's hurting. . . ."

Karen felt the same way watching Amelia. She wished there was something she could do to make the pain go away.

Amelia knocked on Jody's door again and called to her cousin, but he didn't answer. "Jody? Please let me in," she called. "I know how you feel, believe me. . . ."

"I'm sorry!" he replied in a strained, raspy voice. "I gotta be alone right now, Amelia. Could you go away, please?"

Her head down, Amelia slinked away from his door. She looked at her uncle, and shrugged hopelessly. "Sorry, Uncle George," she murmured. "Guess I'm just useless. I—I'm so tired. Would it be okay if I went to lie down for a while?"

He nodded, and kissed her forehead. "Sure, sweetie, your bed's all made down there."

Amelia gently patted Stephanie on the back, then wandered through the living room and foyer to a set of stairs leading to a lower level. Looking over her shoulder, she glanced at Karen, and then started down the steps.

"Do you think maybe you could talk to him?"

Karen turned at George and blinked. "You want *me* to talk to your son?"

He shrugged. "Well, you're a therapist. Maybe you'd have a better idea about the right thing to say. . . ."

"You know, I think we should just respect Jody's need to be alone," she whispered, touching his arm, "For a while, at least. If this is how he grieved for his cousin, then it's what he knows. That's how he got through it last time. Why don't we give him until dinner's ready, and try again? Okay?"

He stared at her for a moment, then nodded. "I think you're a very smart lady," he said. "Thanks, Karen."

She smiled at him. "Well, um, I'll go down and check on Amelia."

"Take a right at the bottom of the stairs. The guest room's the first door on your left."

Downstairs, Karen paused in the large recreation room. It had a linoleum floor and high windows that didn't let in much sunlight. There was a big-screen TV, a sectional sofa, and someone's treadmill. Stashed in one corner were a bunch of toys, including a dollhouse. Karen draped her coat over a chair. She gazed at the collection of framed family photos on the wall. She figured the stylish, attractive redhead in the pictures was George's murdered wife. There were also a few photos of Amelia with her family. Karen had been hearing about the Faradays for months, but this was her first actual look at them. She could see a resemblance between the sisters, Jenna and Ina. Studying the pictures of Mark Faraday, she wondered how that pleasant-looking, slightly dumpy man could have shot those two women and then himself. It was hard to comprehend that they were all dead now. In one night, Amelia had lost nearly all of her family—and in such a violent, heinous way.

There were photos of Collin Faraday, too. From the way Amelia talked about her dead brother, Karen had expected him to have been this stunningly handsome, golden-haired teenager. Instead, he just seemed like a normal, nice-looking kid with a goofy smile.

"My brother's death wasn't an accident. I know it wasn't," Amelia had told her during their first session. "Because I killed him."

Karen remembered staring at her, and wondering exactly what she'd meant.

"I promised myself I wouldn't mention anything about it," Amelia had said, squirming on Karen's sofa. "It's too soon to drop a bombshell like that on you. And now the session's almost over. Jesus. Please, tell me you'll see me again,

Karen. I trust you, and I can't keep this to myself any longer. Please, don't send me away—"

"It's okay, I'm listening," Karen had said calmly. "We've got time." She wasn't one of those clock-watching therapists. If a patient was in the middle of something important, she never cut them off because of time. In this instance, she luckily hadn't scheduled any other sessions that afternoon, so Karen could go on for another hour or so if it meant understanding Amelia Faraday better. Already, she wanted to help and protect this girl.

"What do you mean, *you killed him*?" Karen asked as gently as possible. "Can you talk about it?"

Amelia nodded. "I was at a Booze Busters retreat in Port Townsend," she replied, sniffling. "Six of us took an RV there for the weekend and camped out. But I had this *premonition* about Collin the whole weekend, all these feelings of hatred for him that I can't explain. I kept thinking about how I would kill him, and it was crazy. I didn't want that to happen. I couldn't have meant it. I didn't even want to think about it. I loved my brother. He was the sweetest guy. . . ." She started sobbing again. "I'm sorry."

"Take your time."

Amelia wiped her eyes and took a deep breath. "I must have blacked out, because all I have are fragments of what happened."

Fragments again, Karen thought. She scribbled the word down in her notes.

"I was standing on the dock in our backyard with Collin," Amelia explained. "Our house is up in Bellingham—on Lake Whatcom. I hit him with a board or something—a piece of plank, I think. He just—just looked at me, stunned, and—and an awful gash started to open up on his forehead. He let out this garbled, frail cry. . . ." Wincing, she shook her head. "God, it was this weird, warble-type of sound, almost inhuman. And then he toppled off the dock into the water.

"I don't remember anything else. It's like I lost nearly everything from that afternoon, because the next thing I knew, I was waking up from a nap in the RV in Port Townsend—and it was dinnertime. But I had those images in my head. It's how come I knew about Collin before anyone else. I tried to call my folks and tell them something had happened, but they were spending the weekend at their cabin, and the cell phone service is lousy out there—"

"There was no one else staying with Collin?" Karen asked.

Amelia shook her head. "He was alone in the house for the weekend. Before my folks left, I teased him about how he'd be raiding the booze cabinet, watching porn, and having a big party while they were gone. He had a friend coming over that afternoon. He's the one who found him. When Collin didn't answer the door, his buddy went around to the back and saw him floating by the dock. His sleeve had gotten caught on something. They figured he'd had too much to drink, then fallen off the dock, and hit his head on some pilings. Turned out he had alcohol in his system. And maybe that's true, but he didn't die the way they think."

Karen squinted at her. "Have you talked to anyone about this?"

Amelia sighed. "Just my Aunt Ina. She said I was crazy with grief, and that I shouldn't repeat it to anyone. It would just upset people even more."

"You said you were with people from Booze Busters that weekend," Karen pointed out. "How did you manage to break away from the camp, then drive to Bellingham and back without them noticing? It's at least a hundred miles and a ferry ride each way. You'd have been gone the entire afternoon."

Amelia seemed to shrink into the corner of Karen's sofa. She rubbed her forehead. "I don't know how I got there. But I remember what happened. And a neighbor saw me there, too. The police determined Collin must have died around two or three o'clock that Saturday afternoon. Our neighbor, Mrs. Ormsby, said she saw me hosing down our dock around that time. But because I was supposed to be gone the whole weekend, no one really believed her. She's an old woman. They figured she was senile or just wanted some attention. Mrs. Ormsby later said she might have been mistaken. But I don't think she was."

Karen leaned forward in her seat. "But she must have been wrong, Amelia. Don't you see? Your friends would have noticed if you'd left the campsite—"

"I know, I know," she cried. Her whole body was shaking. "But I have these—these *pieces of memory* that tell me I killed him. When I'm alone in bed at night, I can still hear him making that strange, horrible sound after I hit him with the plank. I still hear Collin dying."

Karen let her cry it out. "There are a lot of explanations for what you were feeling—for these sensory *fragments*," she said finally. "It doesn't mean you killed your brother, Amelia. Your sudden rage toward him, that's not entirely uncommon. I've heard many stories from people who suddenly, for no good reason, became irritable or distant with a loved one— only to lose them within a few days of this inexplicable anger. Even when the death is unexpected, our extrasensory perception can sometimes kick in and start to protect us from the impending loss."

Curled up in the corner of the sofa, Amelia gave her a slightly skeptical look. But at least she'd stopped crying.

"You said that you and Collin were close," Karen went on. "Often with family members and loved ones, we can sense when something is wrong—even if that loved one is over a hundred miles away. We can still pick up a frequency that there's trouble. Maybe you just tapped into Collin's frequency. Maybe you have a bit of ESP."

"Do you really believe that?" Amelia murmured, still eyeing her dubiously.

"Well, it makes a lot more sense than the notion that you traveled over two hundred miles without ever really leaving your campsite in Port Townsend. Doesn't it?"

Amelia sighed and then reached for her bottle of water.

"I've just met you, Amelia," she continued. "But you don't seem like a murderer to me. And what would your motive be, anyway? You loved your brother. As for that neighbor woman who saw you, why do you still believe her even after she recanted what she said? No one else believed her, but *you* did. Why do you want to take the blame?"

Karen remembered going on like that for a few more minutes, until Amelia had started to calm down. She'd made her promise to go back to Booze Busters, and they'd agreed to meet twice a week.

That had been four months ago. Karen didn't need to hear bits of a flashback in which Amelia's biological mother asked if someone had touched her "down there" to presume she'd been abused in some way as a young child. All the classic attributions of child abuse were there in the 19-year-old: her low self-esteem, nightmares, flashbacks, lost time, and her assuming guilt for just about everything.

A perfect example of this was Amelia's episode with her boyfriend, Shane, and how quickly Amelia had assumed she'd done something wrong when he said he'd seen her in that car with another man. Amelia had gone and gotten herself tested, because she'd automatically figured herself guilty of infidelity. It never seemed to have occurred to her that Shane might have been mistaken.

There were a lot of problems they worked on over the next four months. And in that time, Karen felt a special bond forming with this young woman who depended on her so much. She was more like Amelia's big sister than her therapist.

Amelia had kept her promise and went back to Booze

Busters. And though things still got a little rocky with Shane from time to time, they continued to see each other. Her grades were improving at school. Mark and Jenna Faraday had both e-mailed Karen to tell her what a wonderful job she'd been doing with Amelia. *Her whole outlook has improved 100 percent since she started seeing you,* Jenna Faraday had written.

Karen e-mailed back and thanked them. She'd been tempted to ask the Faradays to reconsider hiring a private detective to look into what had happened to Amelia's biological parents. But she'd left that up to Amelia instead. Amelia was nineteen, and old enough to discuss it with her parents herself. Unfortunately, for the last two months, Amelia had been procrastinating. She admitted she was afraid. "It's not so much I'm worried about having been abused or anything like that," she'd said. "I'm just scared that I might have done something really, really horrible."

"Well, you were only four, Amelia," Karen had replied. "You couldn't have done anything *that* awful. Except for Damien in *The Omen*, how many totally evil four-year-olds do you know? We need to explore this time period in your life."

Amelia's problems couldn't be completely treated until they knew what had happened to her as a child.

Now Karen stared at a framed photo of Jenna and Mark Faraday. They stood on a dock in sporty summer clothes with their arms around each other. The beautiful lake glistened in the background. Karen wondered if it was the same spot where their son had been killed. If so, the photo certainly must have been taken before that tragedy, at a happier time. How could they have known what would occur there? And just a few months later, they would be dead, too.

With a long sigh, Karen started toward the first door on the left. According to George's directions, it was the guest room. The door was closed. Karen was about to knock, but hesitated. She heard Amelia murmuring something. Karen couldn't tell if she was awake—or talking in her sleep.

"No," Amelia said in a hushed tone. "You really don't want that to happen. You don't mean it. You mustn't even think that."

"Yes, well, thank you," George said into the cordless phone. He sat at the breakfast table with Stephanie in his lap. "I'll be here—waiting. Good-bye."

Dazed, he clicked off the phone. "That was the police," he said to Jessie.

Hovering over the stove with a fork in her hand, she gave him an expectant look.

"They're coming over to ask me some questions. Could I ask you or Karen to stick around and keep an eye on the kids until the cops leave? They'll probably want to talk to Amelia, too. I figure my study's the best place." He glanced down at Stephanie and resituated her in his lap.

Jessie nodded. "No sweat. I can stay here as long as you need me."

He reached back for his wallet. "I'd like to pay you something for all your—"

"Your money's no good here tonight, no sir," Jessie said. "If you need someone to cook, clean, and babysit after today, I'll gladly take your dough. But tonight, you put that wallet away."

Following her instructions, George worked up a smile. "I don't know you very well, Jessie. But I have a feeling you're a gem."

She grinned at him, and then her gaze shifted to Stephanie. "Hey, sweetheart, could you help me fix dinner?"

Warily staring back at her, Stephanie shifted in his lap.

"Oh, c'mon, what do you say? Help me out. Stir the sauce for me, okay?"

" 'Kay," Stephanie murmured, scooting off her father's lap.

Jessie pulled out one of the chairs from the breakfast table and put a bowl full of the sauce mixture on it. She gave Stephanie a plastic spoon. George watched his daughter, with a determined look on her face, stirring the concoction.

He felt a tightness in his throat. George told himself he wasn't going to break down in front of her, not when she'd just stopped crying herself.

He thought about the police, now on their way. They'd have all sorts of questions about the Faradays' personal problems, their deep, dirty secrets. They'd want to know what had driven Mark Faraday to snap and do such violent, horrific things.

George would have to tell them how Mark and Jenna's marriage had suffered in the wake of Collin's death. Still, he'd never imagined his brother-in-law as the type of man who could harm anyone intentionally. Then again, not too long ago, he'd never imagined Mark as the type of man who would sleep with his wife's sister, either.

Should he admit that to the police? God, he didn't want to go into that with them. Still, he wondered if Ina and Mark's indiscretion had anything to do with what had happened last night. George couldn't begin to guess what had been going through Mark's head when he'd picked up that gun and started shooting.

The three of them were dead. Couldn't people just leave them alone?

No. The media coverage would be crazy. What a scoop: the *love triangle* behind the bloody murders. The scandal might blow over by the time Stephanie was old enough to understand what people were gossiping about. But poor

Jody—all his friends would know his mother had screwed his uncle just two months before the guy shot her, his wife, and then himself.

Part of him was so mad at Ina right now for doing this to her family and herself. The irony was she'd always been so concerned with keeping up appearances and impressing people. How would Ina have felt if she knew her sad little affair would become public knowledge?

Maybe he could strike a deal with the police to leave the more delicate matters out of the newspapers. It was worth a try. He really didn't have much of a choice.

He thought about Amelia, napping downstairs. Telling the police about Ina and Mark meant telling Amelia, too. And God only knew how that already fragile girl would take it.

"Am I doing good, Daddy?" Stephanie asked, looking up from her work.

"Oh, you're doing great, sweetie," he said.

She went back to stirring the cream of chicken soup and sour cream concoction. With tears in his eyes, George leaned over and kissed the top of her head.

"Amelia, are you awake?" Karen whispered. Opening the door, she peeked into the dimly lit guest room.

Amelia was lying on one of the twin beds. The pale-green paisley quilts matched the material for the drapes, which were closed. The place looked like something out of a Pottery Barn catalogue. The décor—with all the carefully chosen accents—had that pleasant, slightly generic ambiance. There were two framed Robert Capra posters on the walls—black-and-white Paris scenes.

Stirring, Amelia sat up and squinted at Karen. "Oh, hi."

"Were you on your cell just now?" she asked. "I heard you whispering to someone."

"I—um, must have been talking in my sleep," she said, shrugging.

Karen closed the door behind her, then sat down on the bed across from Amelia. She reached for the lamp on the nightstand between them.

"No, don't, please," Amelia said.

So they sat in the darkness for a few moments. Karen heard muffled sobbing, and looked up toward a vent in the ceiling.

"That's coming from Jody's room," Amelia explained.

Karen listened for another moment, and then sighed. "You're not feeling in any way responsible for what happened at the cabin last night, are you?"

She quickly shook her head. "God, no."

"Honey, it'll help you to talk about it."

Amelia glanced up toward the vent. Jody's muted sobbing seemed to devastate her. She wiped a tear from her cheek.

"You're not responsible for that," Karen whispered.

"Yes, I am," she murmured. Grabbing her pillow, she reclined on the bed and curled up on her side. "It's just how it happened when Collin was killed. All day yesterday, I had these awful feelings that Mom, Dad, and Aunt Ina deserved to die."

"Why did you feel that way?"

"I don't know. It was something evil inside me. I thought about going to the Lake Wenatchee house and shooting them all. It's horrid, I know. It doesn't make any sense. I was so confused. I tried calling you, but you weren't home. I couldn't talk about it with Shane. We went to a party last night, and I just wanted to get drunk. I only had a couple of beers. But it was enough to make me a little crazy. I stole a half-full bottle of tequila, borrowed Shane's car, and just started driving. That's all I remember. I blacked out."

"Oh, Lord," Karen whispered, shaking her head.

"Next thing I knew, I woke up this morning in this empty parking lot in Easton. Do you know where Easton is?" Amelia sat up and stared at her. "It's off I-90, halfway between here and Wenatchee. I must have stopped there to rest on my way back. At first I thought I'd had a nightmare. I kept praying it wasn't real. But I knew it was. I didn't need you to tell me they were dead. I knew how it happened, too, because I'm the one who killed them."

"But you said you had a blackout," Karen argued. "You can't know for sure—"

"It wasn't a dream, Karen. I remember my dad in the rocking chair by the fireplace." Amelia started weeping inconsolably. "I—I shot him in the head. My mom, she must have woken up. God, I can still see her running out of their bedroom. I shot her too—I shot her in the face. . . ." She curled up again, and sobbed into the pillow. "Aunt Ina . . .with her it seemed like later, but I'm not sure. I just remember her standing there in the living room, staring at my dad, and then at me. She said, 'My God, honey, what have you done?' And I didn't say anything. I just shot her in the chest. . . ."

Horrified, Karen gaped at her. "Amelia, you couldn't have. You're just not capable of that kind of coldhearted—"

"Then how come I know what happened?" she cut her off. "Nobody in this house knows yet except me. I must have been there, don't you see? I'm the one who killed them all."

"It's not true, Amelia," she said, rubbing her shoulder. "It didn't happen like that. Listen to me. Are you listening? If you really did this, what kind of gun did you use?"

Amelia shrugged. "I'm not sure. My dad's hunting rifle, I think. I remember it felt like someone hitting me in the shoulder with a baseball bat every time I fired it."

"Was that the first time you've ever used it—last night?"

"I guess so."

"And you knew how to operate it right away? You knew how to load it and work the safety?" Karen didn't wait for

Amelia to answer. She switched on the nightstand lamp. "Are those the same clothes you had on last night? To hear you tell it, you shot them all at close range. Where's the blood on your clothes, Amelia?"

"I must have washed it off," she muttered, glancing down at herself.

"Where? When? During your blackout? Blood doesn't wash off that easily."

Amelia just shrugged and shook her head.

"Honey, you weren't there," Karen said. "I mean, just consider this. How much money did you have on you last night?"

"I don't know, about twelve dollars. Why?"

"It's—what—a hundred and fifty miles to Lake Wenatchee? That's at least three hundred miles round-trip, even longer if you took I-90. You'd have had to stop for gas. Do you remember going to a gas station?"

Biting her lip, Amelia shook her head again.

"Of course not," Karen said. She felt like she was starting to get through to her. "You didn't have enough money for gas, and you couldn't have used your credit card, because you told me during your session on Thursday that you maxed out your Visa. You were talking about how you had to control your spending. Check your purse. I'll bet that twelve bucks is still there." Karen reached for Amelia's purse on the floor between them. "Can I look through this?

Amelia nodded. "Go ahead."

Karen rummaged through the purse. She found a loose dollar bill, some change, and then in Amelia's wallet, two fives and a single. "I have exactly twelve dollars and sixty-two cents here, Amelia. You didn't buy any gas."

"Maybe not," Amelia said. "But—well, I've driven to Wenatchee and back on one tank of gas before."

"Then call Shane. Find out when he last filled up the car. Have him look at the fuel gauge now. That'll give us an idea how far you drove. You may have headed off to Wenatchee last night, but I'll bet you never got there." She tucked the money back in Amelia's wallet, and dropped it in her purse. Then she fished out Amelia's cell phone. "It's bad enough this horrible thing even happened. Please, Amelia, don't make it worse by blaming yourself for it. You couldn't have done it. So here—call Shane. Ask him about the gas."

Amelia hesitated, and then took the cell phone from her.

Karen heard something outside. She got up, parted the curtain and peeked out the window. A white sedan and a police car both pulled in to the McMillans' driveway—one after the other. "It's the police," she murmured almost to herself.

"Oh, my God." Amelia switched off the cell phone. A look of panic swept across her face. "They'll want to talk to me. Karen, please help me. What am I going to say to them?"

Karen turned toward her. "You won't have to say anything." She grabbed her own purse on the bed and found the bottle of diazepam. "You're in no condition. I want you to take another one of these pills. I'll tell the police you're sleeping and can't be disturbed. And you will be asleep, honey, if you just lie back and relax and let the pill take effect. Go ahead and call Shane, just be quiet about it. I'll get you some water."

Karen slipped out of the guest room and found the bathroom next door. She could hear someone in the foyer upstairs. She quickly rinsed out the tumbler, then filled it with cold water. She paused in front of the mirror, then pulled it open to inspect the medicine chest. There it was: a bottle of aspirin in cylindrical tablets, like the diazepam. They weren't light blue, but in the dark bedroom, Amelia probably wouldn't notice. Karen didn't really want her taking another diazepam; she just needed Amelia to think she should be relaxed and sleepy.

As Karen stepped out of the bathroom, she heard them talking upstairs.

"I think she's asleep right now," George was saying. "Her therapist is looking after her downstairs in the guest room. Could you let her rest for a while longer, and question me first?"

Someone—whoever he was talking to—muttered a response.

"Thanks," George said. "We can talk in here. . . ."

Karen ducked back into the bedroom, then quietly closed the door.

"I've really got to go," Amelia was whispering into her cell phone. "I'll explain everything later, I promise. Love you, too. Bye." She clicked off the line and gazed up at Karen, a tiny look of hope in her eyes. "He just picked up the car at your place. The gas is just under a quarter of a tank. He said it was about three-quarters full when we went to the party last night."

Switching off the light, Karen sat down next to her. She handed her the aspirin and the tumbler of water. "That's about right, isn't it? Approximately a hundred and sixty miles to and from Easton, that's around half a tank. You couldn't have made it to Wenatchee and back without refueling."

Amelia nodded. She swallowed the aspirin with some water, then handed the tumbler back to her. Tears welled in her eyes, and she winced. "It still doesn't make sense. If I didn't do it, how come I have these images in my head?"

"I don't know yet, but we'll find out. I promise." Karen stroked her arm. "Just because you have certain images in your head, it doesn't mean they're true. We don't even know how it happened yet, Amelia."

Pulling away, Amelia laid back and wrapped her arms around her pillow. "Why don't you talk to the police, Karen? Then we'll know whether or not I'm wrong."

Chapter Eight

Karen sat in the dark while Amelia tossed and turned in the bed across from her. The muffled sobs emitting through the vent from Jody's room upstairs had ceased. Karen guessed the police had been grilling George McMillan for about an hour now, and they were probably getting warmed up for Amelia.

She heard someone coming down the stairs. Karen climbed off the bed just as a knock came on the door.

Amelia sat up, suddenly awake.

Karen opened the door to find Jessie, her face in the shadows. "They sent me down here to fetch Amelia," she whispered. "They'd like a statement, which means they'll be asking her all sorts of rude, tactless, personal questions for the next two hours."

"Well, that's just too much for her right now," Karen said under her breath.

"It's the treatment they've been giving her uncle."

Karen glanced over her shoulder at Amelia, who stared back at them, visibly trembling. Karen couldn't let the police

interrogate her, not when Amelia was so distraught and disoriented. "Go back to sleep, honey," she whispered to her.
"And if you can't nod off, just lie there quietly until they go."

She stepped out of the guest room and gently closed the
door.

"They want her uncle to go to Wenatchee tonight to identify the bodies," Jessie whispered. "He might not be back
until very late. I promised him we'd stick around and hold
down the fort."

"Yes, of course," Karen said.

"I told you we wouldn't be in the way, but you never listen to me." Jessie tapped her shoulder. "And if we hadn't
come here, you wouldn't have met George. Talk about a
sweetheart. Oh, and the way he is with his little girl. He's
just the kind of man I've always wanted to see you with."

Karen frowned at her. "For God's sake, Jessie, his wife
was just murdered last night."

"Well, I know that," she whispered. "Doesn't mean you
can't call him in a couple of months and find out how he's
doing." Jessie sighed. "I put the little one down for a nap.
The poor lamb cried herself to sleep."

They headed up the stairs. Karen could hear George talking as she approached the study.

She knocked, and then opened the door. A handsome,
mustached, gray-haired man in his fifties was pacing in front
of George, who sat in an easy chair. The man wore a blue
suit that looked slept in, and he stopped to glance at her.

George got to his feet as Karen stepped inside the room.
He was wearing glasses, the Clark Kent type, which made
him look even more handsome—and gentle.

A young, beefy, uniformed cop was also in the room. He
sat in a swivel chair by the computer desk. He also stood up
long enough to lean over and switch off a small recording
device on the coffee table. The three men seemed slightly
cramped in the close quarters. There was a small window

above the desk, and two walls of shelves packed with books and framed photos of the McMillan clan.

"Detective Goodwin," George said. "This is Amelia's therapist, Karen Carlisle."

"Hello." She shook the detective's hand. "I understand you wanted to meet with Amelia. But I'm afraid I kind of threw a wrench in that. You won't be able to get a statement from her this afternoon—or even tonight. She's heavily sedated right now."

The detective frowned. "But we need to talk to her."

Karen shrugged. "Well, I'm sorry. She's asleep. It's my fault. She was hysterical earlier, and I had to give her some tranquilizers to calm her down—the maximum dosage."

"The poor thing, it would have broken your heart to see her," Jessie chimed in from the doorway. "All the crying and carrying on, she was just beside herself. Thank God Dr. Carlisle was here."

Karen shot her a look over her shoulder. She knew Jessie was trying to help. But did she have to pour it on so thick—especially with the *doctor* bit? Jessie quietly retreated toward the kitchen.

Turning, Karen locked eyes with George. He hadn't witnessed Amelia in hysterics. He hadn't seen his niece *crying and carrying on* to a level that required her to be sedated. Yet he seemed to know she was protecting Amelia right now. Karen could see he understood.

His gaze shifted to the detective. "Haven't you gotten enough for the time being? Do you really need to question Amelia *now*?"

The gray-haired detective rubbed his chin and stared at Karen. "How long have you been treating Amelia?"

"Since the beginning of the summer," she replied.

"In any of her therapy sessions, do you recall her mentioning anything about her father that would shed more light on what happened at the Lake Wenatchee house last night?"

She shook her head. "I can't think of anything significant—at least, nothing that would help your investigation."

"Sure you're not holding out on me?" he pressed. "This isn't one of those doctor-patient confidentiality things you're pulling on me, is it?"

"No, sir. If you were infringing on that, I'd tell you."

Frowning, he let out a little huff. "I still want to talk to her."

Karen shrugged helplessly. "Well, I'm sorry."

"Listen," George interjected. "If you're after more information about her dad's state of mind, you won't get much. Amelia has been away at school these last two months. I don't think she knows about her dad and Ina." He turned to Karen. "My wife and Amelia's dad, they had an affair in August. It was very short-lived. Has Amelia mentioned anything to you?"

Karen bit her lip. "No. This is the first I've heard about it."

He turned to the detective. "See what I mean? You won't get much from Amelia. So leave the poor girl alone—at least for tonight."

"Fine," Goodwin grumbled. Then he glanced at Karen. "But I'd like her in my office at the West Seattle precinct tomorrow morning at nine o'clock—sharp."

Karen nodded. "I'll drive her myself. I'm sorry I couldn't be more help. If that's all, can I go now?"

He sighed. "Fine."

But Karen couldn't leave it at that. She was thinking about Amelia's fantastic *confession* to last night's shootings. She hesitated in the doorway. "May I ask you a question, detective?"

"Go ahead," he muttered.

"I had to tell Amelia about what happened last night—based on an early report from Mr. McMillan. I really didn't have a very clear idea." She stole a glance at George, hoping this wouldn't bother him too much. "I told Amelia it appeared her father had shot her mother and aunt—and then himself. Amelia asked me what kind of gun he'd used—and where the police had found the bodies. She—um, she wanted details I couldn't give."

The detective stared back at her, unyielding.

"Mark had a hunting rifle, he used that," George answered—almost bitterly, as if he were just so sick and depleted from discussing it. Still, there was a tremor in his voice as he spoke. "My sister-in-law, she was shot in the face. They found her in the upstairs hallway. Ina—my wife—she—um, she was shot in the chest. She was in the living room with Mark. And Mark, he sat down in his rocking chair by the fireplace and shot himself in the head." Over the rims of his glasses, George looked at the older cop. "Did I get everything right, Detective?"

The plainclothesman said nothing.

Neither did Karen. She was thinking about Amelia's version of how it had happened last night. Amelia's story wasn't part of a nightmare or some delusion. The details she'd recalled were horribly real.

In the darkened guest room, Amelia lay in bed staring up at the ceiling. She listened to the voices upstairs in Uncle George's study, distant undecipherable murmuring. But she recognized Karen's voice. Maybe Karen could keep the police from talking to her for a while. But eventually they'd figure out who had killed her parents and her aunt. Karen couldn't keep that from happening.

In fact, Karen couldn't do much to help her at all.

Amelia wondered if she was even that good a therapist. Probably not.

"Stop it," she whispered to herself. "Don't even think it."

Amelia clung to her pillow and curled up into a fetal position. She suddenly felt sick, because along with her doubts, another thought raced through her head—an ugly thought that Karen Carlisle deserved to die.

Around five o'clock, after George and the two policemen had left, Karen went down to the guest room to check on Amelia again. But she wasn't there. Karen felt a little wave of panic in her gut. She glanced toward the bathroom, and saw the door was closed. But she still felt wary, thanks to memories of Haley. While checking the medicine chest earlier, she hadn't been looking for razor blades or sleeping pills.

She gently tapped on the bathroom door. "Amelia?"

"Karen?" she replied in a lazy voice. "If it's just you, come on in."

A warm waft of steam engulfed her as she stepped into the bathroom. The shower curtain had a pattern of fish and seahorses. It was halfway open to reveal Amelia sitting in the tub. Her hair was pinned up, but some wet black strands cascaded over her pale shoulders. Her head was tipped back, and her eyes half closed. "Did the police leave?" she asked.

"Yes, they're gone," Karen replied. She was glad no one had heard the water running down here. They would have known Amelia was awake after all. She wondered if Amelia, on some subconscious level, was trying to give herself away.

"Sit down," Amelia said, with a nod toward the toilet.

Karen lowered the lid and sat down. The tub faucet dripped steadily, and the sound echoed off the blue and white tiles. Amelia didn't seem a bit shy. She had a beautiful body, and Karen was reminded of high school, and her own teenage envy toward bigger-breasted girls. She felt a resurgence of that now.

"So you talked to them," Amelia said. She took a deep breath. "Was I right about how it happened?"

Karen nodded. "You might be close," she allowed.

She didn't know what else to say. How could Amelia have known—without being told—exactly where the bodies were found and how each one had been slain?

The only possible explanation was that perhaps Amelia had some kind of extrasensory perception or clairvoyance. But that was a stretch, and it still didn't account for why Amelia had assumed she'd committed the murders.

With a vague, forlorn look in the direction of the faucet, Amelia soaped up her arms. She wouldn't even glance at Karen. "Do the police still think my dad did it?" she asked.

"Yes," Karen replied. "There's no reason to doubt them, Amelia. It's a terrible thing to comprehend. But your father did this—not you. We'll never know why he did it. But there are things about your dad that will come out now, because of what happened, some things you might not be aware of."

Amelia slowly shook her head. "He would never do anything to hurt my mom—or Aunt Ina. I knew him. He was a good man."

"Well, he was human, too. But you're right. He wouldn't *intentionally* hurt anybody. Amelia, you'll have to brace yourself for certain . . . revelations about him."

"Like what? If you know something, tell me."

Karen hesitated.

"Is it something the cops are going to tell me?" Amelia asked. "I'd rather hear it from you, Karen. Tell me."

Karen wondered: Did she really need to know? At the same time, for Amelia to start believing her own innocence in the shootings, she needed to start accepting the fact that her father was guilty. "Okay," she said, finally. "Your uncle just told this to the police. I'm not sure if you know. But it sounds like your dad and your Aunt Ina had a—an affair. I guess it was very brief and happened about two months ago."

Amelia said nothing. She absently rinsed the soap suds from her arms and shoulders. "I thought Ina was acting a little weird back in August," she mumbled, closing her eyes. "I should have guessed it was something like that."

"I'm sorry," Karen muttered.

"I'm glad to hear it from you instead of the police—or Uncle George."

Karen didn't say anything for a minute. Finally, she sighed. "The police want to see you tomorrow morning," she said. "I think they're mostly interested in what you can tell them about your parents—especially your dad. But if they ask what you were doing last night, you need to be very careful how you answer them. I don't want you wrongly incriminating yourself, because you've had these disturbing . . . visions."

"Don't worry, Karen. I won't say anything to the police. Amelia slid further below the surface, and water sluiced around in the tub. It was up to her chin now. "I was a closet drinker for three years, and no one knew. I became pretty good at covering up and lying. I'll be okay tomorrow."

"Well, I don't want you *lying* to the police. Just—just don't incriminate yourself."

All she could think about was what would happen if Amelia *confessed* to the shootings. Guilty or innocent, they'd book her immediately. And if Amelia didn't end up in jail, she'd end up in an institution. She'd be destroyed.

"Listen," Karen said, "why don't you call Shane back? Invite him to dinner. I'm sure there's plenty. Knowing Jessie, she's made enough to feed an army."

Amelia nodded. "Yeah, I think I'd feel better if Shane was here. But you're not leaving, are you?"

"Not unless you want me to," she said.

"No, I'd really like it if you stuck around, Karen."

She smiled and got to her feet. "Okay, then. I'll go tell Jessie to expect one more for dinner."

*   *   *

Forty-five minutes later, Karen met Shane as he was parking his car in front of the McMillans' house. She knew him from all the times he'd picked up Amelia after her sessions. With his messy, light brown hair, scruffy beard, and perfect white teeth, he looked like a surfer dude, and talked like one half the time. But he had a good heart and was totally devoted to Amelia.

As Shane climbed out of his VW Golf, Karen saw he'd forgone his usual semi-grunge attire and was dressed up in a blue oxford-cloth shirt and khakis. The unruly hair was slicked back with some product. And she saw something else very out of character for Shane: he was crying.

He gave her a forceful hug, and dropped his head on her shoulder. "Shit, I can't believe they're dead," he cried. "How is she? How's Amelia doing?"

"She's okay. She just had a bath." Karen patted his back, then gently pulled away. "Listen, Amelia can't remember exactly where she took the car last night. She talked to you earlier about the gas."

He wiped his nose with the back of his hand and nodded. "Yeah, looks like she used up about half a tank, but I don't care. Screw the car. I just feel so bad—"

"How many miles can you get on half a tank in that car?" she asked.

He glanced back at the VW and shrugged. "About a hundred and fifty. What's the big deal with the car?"

She didn't go to Wenatchee, Karen assured herself. That was at least 150 miles *one way.* "Listen, have you cleaned or swept out your car at all since picking it up at my place?"

Mystified, Shane shook his head.

"Amelia thinks she might have left something in it. Do you mind if I take a look?"

He shrugged. "Knock yourself out."

Karen checked the seat and floor on the driver's side.

There wasn't a drop of blood or a bloody rag anywhere; there was nothing unusual except an empty tequila bottle. Karen checked the glove compartment, then popped the trunk and checked in there. Nothing.

"Busted," Shane said, nodding at the tequila bottle. "Did she tell you she fell off the wagon last night?"

"Yes, but we'll worry about that later." Karen tossed the empty bottle in a recycling bin at the end of the McMillans' driveway. Then she gave Shane a nudge. "C'mon, I'm counting on you to make sure Amelia puts away some dinner. She hasn't eaten a thing all day."

Amelia ate, thank God. Shane sat next to her at the kitchen table. Jessie had set all six places in hopes that Jody might come out of his bedroom and join them. She'd used her charms, along with a root beer and a plateful of chicken tetrazzini and garlic bread, to gain temporary access to his room.

To Karen's amazement, fifteen minutes into their dinner, Jody shuffled in with a near-empty plate in his hand. He was a good-looking kid, lean with brown eyes and wavy brown hair. "Is there any more of this stuff?" he asked quietly.

Jessie sprung up from the table and grabbed his plate. She got him a second helping—and got him to sit with them at the table. Shane asked Jody if he could crash in his room for the night. Whichever bunk was free, he didn't care. He just didn't want to be far from Amelia. If Jody still needed to be alone, he didn't show it. In fact, he seemed honored to have his cousin's boyfriend, a college guy, asking to bunk with him for the night.

Karen sat at the head of the crowded table in Ina McMillan's breakfast nook. She remembered how she'd eaten dinner alone in front of the TV the night after Haley had died, and she'd done the same thing the night she'd put her father in Sandpoint View Convalescent Home. She wasn't feeling sorry for herself; she just wished she had family.

She looked at Amelia on the other side of the table. Shane

had his arm around her. But Amelia stared back at her with a sad little smile. She nodded, and silently mouthed the words, *Thank you, Karen*.

Karen smiled and nodded back. And she felt as if she had family after all.

When George trudged through the front door at 12:40 A.M., Jessie began heating up his dinner. He made the rounds, checking in on his kids, kissing them goodnight, and then briefly chatting with Amelia and Shane, who were down in the basement, watching TV.

When he came back up upstairs, Karen asked to talk to him alone. He looked so tired and depleted, but said, "Of course." They stopped by the kitchen, where he poured them each a glass of wine—and another for Jessie. Then Karen followed him into the study. He closed the door after her, then nodded toward the easy chair. "Please, have a seat."

Karen sat down. "Thanks. And thank you for getting the police off Amelia's case today. She was very confused and distraught this afternoon, understandably so. But—well, it wouldn't have been good for her to talk to anyone, especially the police."

"Did she tell you about her premonition?" he asked.

Karen nodded. "Yes, sort of."

George sipped his wine. "Does Amelia think she's responsible for what happened? Is that why you wanted to talk to me?"

Dumbfounded, Karen just stared up him. "How did you know?"

"She had a *premonition* about Collin's death too. At one point, she even told Ina she thought she'd murdered him. Didn't make any sense. She was a hundred miles away when he drowned." George sighed, and ran a hand through his salt-and-pepper-colored hair. "When Amelia called me today with her premonition about trouble at the lake house, I could tell she felt somehow responsible for it. And then her premonition turned out to be true. Anyway, this afternoon, when you wouldn't let the cops talk to her, that cinched it. I figured you were covering for her."

He had another hit of wine, and frowned. "It's crazy. Thank God she didn't say anything about it in front of the kids. You're her therapist. Why would she blame herself for this? I mean, is it some guilt thing left over from her childhood or what?"

"I'm really not sure what it is in Amelia's case," Karen admitted. "But you're right, a childhood trauma could explain a lot. Amelia doesn't have much recollection from the time before the Faradays adopted her. I understand they had problems trying to track down information about the biological parents."

He nodded. "There was a fire at the adoption agency."

"Do you know the name of the place?"

"No, but it was in Spokane. I'm sure the adoption papers are somewhere at Mark and Jenna's house. Amelia and I need to drive up there this week to go over whatever legal documents need going over. I'll keep an eye open for those adoption papers, if you think they might help."

Karen nodded. "Yes, thank you. They might end up helping Amelia—a lot."

He plopped down in the desk chair. "God, I don't want her knowing about this. . . . *thing* that happened between her dad and her aunt." He slowly shook his head. "I'm pretty sure it was just one time, one little episode. Still, for a while there, I didn't think I could ever forgive Ina. Then I saw her tonight, lying on that gurney. Suddenly, her stupid little sin didn't matter anymore." His tired eyes filled with tears. He sat up, and cleared his throat. "Sorry, I hardly know you. I didn't mean to—"

"Oh, no, it's okay," Karen said, waving away the apology.

"I'm a therapist. People get emotional around me all the time. It's a hazard of my occupation. I'm used to it."

He just rubbed his forehead.

Karen winced a little at what she'd just said. It sounded stupid. She shifted around in her chair. "Listen, George, if it's any help, I already talked to Amelia about what happened between your wife and . . . and Mark."

He took his hand away from his forehead and stared at her. "You told her . . . about my wife's indiscretions?"

"Yes, I—I needed to convince Amelia that her father was responsible for last night—and not her. She didn't have any idea about how difficult things were at home for her parents."

"But she didn't have to know," he argued. "I discussed it with the cops. They weren't going to put it in the official report. Don't you see? Amelia didn't need to know."

"Oh, God, I'm sorry," Karen said, wincing. "I was worried the police were going to tell her. I didn't want her to hear it from them. If it—if it's any consolation, Amelia seemed to take the news in her stride. And she even thanked me for telling her."

"Well, please don't expect me to thank you," he muttered.

"I think I should probably go," Karen said. "After everything you've been through today, the last thing I wanted to do was upset you. I'm sorry."

"No, don't go. Forget it. I'm just very, very tired," he grumbled. Then he swilled down the rest of his wine.

Karen didn't say anything. She felt awful. At the same time, she tried not to take his abrupt sullenness too personally. The poor man was exhausted, and emotionally devastated.

George pulled himself up from the chair. "Then we're done?"

Karen stood up, too. "Actually, I wanted to ask if you recall Amelia ever having any other premonitions, before the one she had about Collin's death. When she was growing up, did she show signs of being clairvoyant?"

"You mean like ESP?" He shook his head. "No. I didn't hear about any special gifts along those lines. I heard a lot about the nightmares when she was a kid. She had these weird phantom pains, too."

Karen nodded. "Yes, I heard about those. That's why in junior high school she started sneaking into her parents' liquor cabinet. She was scared to go to sleep, because of the nightmares. The alcohol made her not worry so much, and she'd pass out. It helped numb the pain, too."

He brandished his empty wine glass. "Well, right now, that sounds like an excellent idea."

Karen kept a distance as she followed him from the study back to the kitchen. He refilled his glass with wine, then topped off Karen's and Jessie's glasses. He thanked Jessie profusely as she served him a plateful of chicken tetrazzini. Then he sat down at the head of the breakfast table. He took two bites, and said, "Wow, this is good." But he suddenly seemed to have difficulty swallowing.

Karen stood back near the stove, but she could see tears in his eyes.

George McMillan started to sob over his dinner. "I'm sorry, I can't eat," he cried. "I'm sorry—after you went to all that trouble. . . ."

Jessie patted his shoulder. She pulled a chair over, and then plopped down beside George. Her chubby arms went around him while he wept on her shoulder. "It's okay, honey," she whispered. "Don't you worry about it."

Karen remained by the stove, watching them. She knew, from eating alone so often and on certain nights, that it was hard to swallow while crying.

Chapter Nine

Springfield, Oregon—October 2001

Tracy Atkinson felt silly for having reservations about shopping at Gateway Mall that beautiful October night. But there were all sorts of alerts on the news about the spread of anthrax and another possible terrorist attack. Big shopping malls were supposed to be a prime target. She'd been avoiding crowded places for over a month now. The 26-year-old blond dental technician wished she were more like her fiancé, Zach, who kept telling her: "Hey, when your number's up, it's up, and there's nothing you can do about it."

He'd had no qualms about getting on a plane yesterday and flying to Boston for a sales conference. She had to admire him for it.

After a half hour inside the shopping mall, with visits to Target and Kohl's, she started to relax. On her way into Fantastic Footwear, she noticed a backpack left unattended beside a bench. It made her nervous, and she didn't linger in the shoe store for long before coming out and checking if the backpack was still there. Tracy let out a grateful sigh as she watched a teenage boy grab the backpack and strap it on. Sipping from Taco Time containers, he and his buddies wandered toward the cinemas at the other end of the mall.

"Excuse me, do you own a green SUV with an American flag decal on the rear passenger window?"

Tracy swiveled around and blinked at the middle-aged man. He held a teenage girl by the arm. She was pretty, with gorgeous blue eyes, but her black hair was unwashed. She wore the usual punk attire: black jeans and a black sweatshirt, also unwashed. She sneered at Tracy, and then tried to jerk her arm away from the man. But he didn't let go, not even when he pulled a wallet from his windbreaker pocket and flashed his badge at Tracy. "I'm Officer Simms," he said with a polite smile.

He was balding and slightly paunchy, but his eyes had a certain intensity that made him oddly attractive. His smile was nice, too. "I'm sorry to bother you, but I think this young lady keyed the driver's side of your SUV."

"It's just a little scratch," the girl grumbled, rolling her eyes. "Shit . . ."

"It's destruction of private property and vandalism," the man said.

Tracy gaped at them both. She and Zach had bought the green SUV only two months ago. They planned to start having kids right after they got married, and the SUV, though a bit premature, was part of that plan. Zach called it their *babymobile*. He'd put the U.S. flag in the window a few days after 9/11. Tracy couldn't believe this little urchin had keyed their brand-new babymobile. Zach would have a cow.

"Why would you do that?" she asked the girl. Tracy guessed she was about thirteen. "What did I ever do to you? I don't even know you, for God's sake."

The bratty girl merely rolled her eyes again.

"Pointless, just pointless," the man said, frowning. "Listen, ma'am. Why don't you walk out to the parking lot with us? You can review the damage to your vehicle, and decide whether or not you want to press charges."

"Of course," Tracy muttered, still bewildered. "I'm parked outside the furniture store."

But then, he was already aware of that, Tracy reminded herself. In order to know who she was, the man must have seen her parking the SUV in front of the furniture store. Obviously, the kid had keyed the babymobile just moments later, the little bitch.

The funny thing was, Tracy hadn't seen anyone else in the area when she'd left the car forty-five minutes ago. That section of the mall was usually the least crowded. She'd figured the new SUV would be safe there.

She imagined the cop looking for her, and dragging this punk girl around the mall for the last forty-five minutes. Why hadn't he just asked them to make an announcement over the mall's PA system? *Would the owner of a green SUV, license plate number COL216, report to the information desk?* That certainly would have been easier.

"Are you with mall security?" Tracy asked the man. They were walking through the furniture store, the dining room section. He still had the girl by her arm. She seemed to be resisting a little as they neared the exit.

"No, I'm a cop, off duty right now," he replied. "At least, I *was* off duty. If you'd like to press charges—and I think you should—I can radio it in to the station and they'll start filling out the paperwork right away. I'll drive you to the station. I promise it won't take that long."

He held the door open for Tracy, and they stepped outside. It had grown dark out, and chilly. But the lot was illuminated by halogen lights, which gave the area a stark, eerie, bluish glow. There weren't many cars left in this section. Tracy could see the SUV ahead, and on the driver's side, one long uninterrupted scratch. It started above the front tire and continued across the driver's door, then along the back door to the rear bumper. "Oh, damn it," Tracy muttered.

"That's my minivan over there," the man said, nodding at a blue Dodge Caravan parked nearby. "Come with me, and I'll radio this in."

Tracy stared at the girl, who didn't seem to have an ounce of remorse in her. She just looked annoyed, as if they were bothering her. "What the hell is wrong with you?" Tracy asked.

"Don't even try," the man said, dragging the girl toward his minivan. "C'mon . . ."

The girl didn't put up much of a fight as the man slid open the back door, put a hand on top of her head and guided her into the backseat. "Buckle up!" he barked.

He shut the door, then opened the front passenger door for Tracy. "I promise this won't take long."

Tracy climbed into the front. She watched him walk around the front of the vehicle toward the driver's side. The minivan was a bit stuffy, and smelled like a dirty ashtray. Tracy immediately rolled down her window a little. She glanced at the girl in the rearview mirror. The teenager was very sullen and quiet. But she stared back at Tracy in the mirror and shook her head. "Stupid," she grumbled.

"What?" Tracy asked. "What did you just say to me?"

The man opened the driver's door and climbed behind the wheel. "You should buckle up, too," he said. "This shouldn't take long. The station isn't far from here."

Tracy automatically started to reach back for her seat belt, but then she glanced out the window at her and Zach's SUV. It didn't make sense to leave the SUV behind. Wouldn't they want to take pictures of the damage? And doing it this way, he'd have to drive her back to the mall later. Following him to the station in the SUV would be easier. She let the seat belt slide back to its original position.

"Say, you know . . ." Tracy trailed off as she gazed at the dashboard.

He'd said he would radio in a report to the police station. But there was no radio in the car. Then it dawned on her: He's not a cop.

"Stupid," the girl repeated.

"Oh, no," Tracy murmured. "God, no! Wait—"

In one quick motion, the man had her by the throat.

All at once, she couldn't breathe. Tracy tried to fight him off, pounding away at him and, at the same time, frantically groping at the door. But she couldn't find the handle. And she couldn't stop him. He was too strong.

With one hand taut around her neck, he practically lifted her off the seat. He was crushing her windpipe. Tracy thought he'd snap her head off. He held a blackjack in his other hand.

For a second, everything froze, and Tracy caught a glimpse in the rearview mirror.

Nibbling at a fingernail, the girl stared at her. There was something in her eyes, something Tracy hadn't seen earlier. It was remorse.

Then everything went out of focus. Tracy desperately clawed at the hand around her throat. She felt something hard hit her on the side of her head.

She didn't feel anything after that.

In the kitchen, it sounded as if the faint, distant moaning might be something in the water pipes, maybe a plumbing problem. The girl had to listen very carefully to hear it. The drip in the kitchen sink, where she'd just washed the dinner dishes, made a more pronounced sound.

She scooped up Neely, the tabby who had been rubbing against the side of her leg for the last few moments. Cradling the cat in her arms, she opened the basement door. She could hear it better: a murmuring that might have been mistaken

for one of the other cats meowing. As she started down the
cellar stairs, the creaking steps temporarily drowned out that
other faint sound.

The 13-year-old stopped at the bottom of the stairs. She
stroked Neely's head. She could hear the woman's voice
from here, muffled and undecipherable, but sounding human
now, a woman crying out.

The girl flicked on the light switch as she stepped into the
laundry room. The basement was unfinished, with a concrete
floor and muddy-looking walls. Above the washer and dryer,
there was a small window and a shelf full of houseplants her
mother had collected and nurtured in old coffee cans and
cheesy planters. One was a pink ceramic pot with WORLD'S
GREATEST MOM in faded swirling gold script on it. That held
the philodendron with the vines that draped down across the
top of the washing machine operation panel.

Exposed pipes and support beams ran across the ceiling
throughout the basement. It was from the far right support
beam here in the laundry room where her mother had hanged
herself nine years before. The girl had found her there at the
end of a rope, dressed in a black skirt and her favorite blouse—
white with pictures of gold pocket watches and chains on it.
One of her slippers had come off, probably when she'd
kicked the stool out from under her. It would have been a
horrific discovery for almost any child. But by that time, the
four-year-old girl had become quite accustomed to death
and suffering.

The girl still watered her mother's plants when she did the
laundry twice a week, like some people tended to flowers on
a grave.

She continued on to the furnace room, where the muffled
cries didn't seem so far away anymore. She could make out
parts of what Tracy was screaming: "Please, please . . . can
somebody hear me? Help me! My parents have money!
They'll pay you . . . please! God, somebody . . ."

She knew the woman's name, because she'd looked at her driver's license: Tracy Eileen Atkinson. Born: 2-20-1975; Ht: 5-06; Wt: 119; Eyes: Brn.

She reached up and pulled the string attached to the furnace room light that dangled from the ceiling. She stared at the big, heavy metal door to the bomb shelter. He'd lodged a crowbar in the door handle, so no matter how hard Tracy pulled and tugged at the door, it wouldn't budge.

"Can anyone hear me? Please! Help me!"

If Tracy was like the others before her, she'd grow tired and stop screaming for help in a day or two. And a day or two after that, he'd grow tired of Tracy and slit her throat.

But until then, Tracy would learn that if she cooperated with him, he would give her some food scraps, maybe even an orange or an apple. If she put up a fight, she wouldn't get anything, except maybe cat food.

Neely meowed, and the girl continued to pet her head as she approached the bomb shelter door. "There now, Neely," she said.

"Is someone out there? Hello?"

She leaned close to the thick metal door. "I can hear you," she called softly. "Can you hear me?"

"Yes, yes. Oh, thank God! You have to help me . . ."

"Listen," she said. "I just want you to know. I didn't touch your car. He's the one who scratched it up."

"What? I don't care . . . you've got to let me out of here. . . . Are you still there?"

Tracy started screaming and pounding on the metal door. But the sound was so muffled outside the bomb shelter, it was quite easy to ignore.

Stroking Neely and pressing her cheek against the tabby's fur, she turned away from the door. She pulled the string to the single overhead light, and the furnace room went dark once again. She switched off the light in the laundry room, then ascended the basement stairs.

She could hardly hear Tracy anymore—unless she tried. And even then, it was just a faint, distant moaning.

Seattle—six years later

"Your father always loved my fried chicken."

Jessie seemed so flattered by the way Frank gorged on her chicken, Karen didn't have the heart to tell her that he'd attacked his serving of shepherd's pie with the same relish last week—and that was the most revolting dish the rest home cafeteria served. "Well, Dad obviously misses your cooking," she said.

Frank sat in a hardback chair with Jessie's home-cooked dinner on a hospital table in front of him. He was dressed in a plaid shirt, yellow pants, a white belt, and slippers. He had a towel in his lap in lieu of a napkin. He'd turned into a very messy eater in the last few years.

Sitting with Jessie on the foot of his hospital bed, Karen was dressed in a black skirt and a dark blue tailored shirt. Sometimes, watching her father gnaw away at a meal—especially finger foods—was pure torture for her. Corn on the cob and spareribs were the worst, but fried chicken ranked high up there, too. Forcing a smile, she could only glance at her father momentarily before turning away.

Karen looked out his window, and the smile vanished from her face.

There it was again—the old black Cadillac with the bent antenna. She'd seen the car several times the last few days. She'd started noticing it after that Saturday Amelia had come to her about the deaths of her parents and aunt. Twice the banged-up Cadillac was parked on her block; another time it cruised along the drive at Volunteer Park while she'd been running laps around the reservoir. She'd spotted the same vehicle in her rearview mirror on her way to pick up Jessie this afternoon. And now it was in the parking lot at the convalescent home.

Karen got to her feet and moved to the window. From this distance, she couldn't tell if anyone was in the car.

"Frank, slow down," Jessie was saying. "The chicken's all yours. It's not going anywhere. Take your sweet time."

"Jessie, come here and look at this," Karen said, gazing out the window. Jessie waddled up beside her. "See that Cadillac out there, the one with the broken antenna? Does it look familiar? I think someone in that car has been following me."

Rubbing her chin, Jessie squinted out the window. "You know, I'm not sure. These old peepers aren't what they used to be. I—"

Karen heard the chair legs scrape against the tiled floor. She swiveled around to see her father with his mouth open and eyes bulging. He pounded at his chest. "Oh, my God, he's choking!" she cried.

"I got him!" Jessie pushed her aside and rushed behind the chair where Karen's father sat, writhing. Within a moment, the big woman scooped him up out of the chair and locked her chubby arms around his stomach. Jessie jerked her forearms under his ribs—lifting him off his feet with every squeeze. Once, twice, three times, four times. Then a piece of food shot out of his mouth.

Karen's father let out a cry, and then he gasped for air. He seemed to sag in Jessie's arms. She lowered him back into the chair, and patted his shoulder. Karen hovered over him. "Just sit there and get your breath back, Poppy," she said. He seemed okay, just a bit shaken.

But Jessie wasn't so well off. Karen gazed at her. She staggered toward the bed and plopped down on the edge. Wincing, she put a hand over her heart. The color had drained from her face, and she started wheezing.

Karen hurried to her side. "Jessie, are you okay?

She didn't respond. She just sat there, struggling for her breath.

Karen snatched up the phone and called for the doctor on staff. "There's a woman here with breathing problems. Could you come to room 204, quickly please?"

As she hung up the phone, she heard Jessie say, "Aren't you—aren't you supposed to say 'stat'?"

Karen sat down on the bed, and gently patted her back. "I'd feel like an idiot saying 'stat;' that's for the nurses and doctors. How are you?"

Jessie nodded. "I just overdid it a bit. I'll be peachy in another minute or two." She glanced over at Karen's father and started to chuckle. "Well, I'm glad he didn't let my having a coronary slow him down."

Frank was sitting up and gorging on his fried chicken once again.

Karen managed to laugh, but she noticed Jessie wincing again. She stayed at her side until the doctor arrived with a nurse. Dr. Chang felt Jessie's throat, then put a stethoscope to her chest. He asked if she could walk with him to his office down the hall. Jessie nodded. But she seemed a bit unsteady on her feet as Dr. Chang and the nurse led her out of the room.

Karen hated to see her looking so feeble. Jessie was her rock. She couldn't have managed without her these last four years.

Now that she'd moved her dad into Sandpoint View, Karen was getting pressured by her older brother and sister to sell the house. But she didn't want to sell it yet. She kept Jessie on three days a week. They often took these trips to the convalescent home together.

Her father's face and hands were a greasy mess. Karen got him cleaned up. Then she washed off the plate and utensils in his bathroom sink, along with Jessie's Tupperware containers. All the while, she thought about Jessie, down the hall, being examined by Dr. Chang. The reality of it was,

Jessie wasn't much younger than Dr. Chang's regular patients here.

One good thing, at least she hadn't heard an ambulance yet. Whenever there was a severe medical emergency, they sent for an ambulance and rushed the patient to University Hospital. Many of the ones from this place died on the way.

Karen finished drying off Jessie's Tupperware, and then checked on her father again. He'd moved into the cushioned easy chair, and was dozing peacefully. She decided to give Dr. Chang another five minutes with Jessie before going to his office and finding out how she was doing.

She glanced outside her father's window, and once again focused on that beat-up, old black Cadillac. Was someone really following her? Maybe one of her patients? Most of her clients weren't a threat to anyone, except maybe themselves. Every once in a while she got a truly disturbed new patient. But Karen sent those to a more qualified specialist.

Some of them didn't like being sent away.

Karen looked at her dad again. He was snoring now. He wouldn't be going anywhere for a while.

Grabbing her purse, she retreated down the hallway to the side door, and then out to the parking lot. The cold wind hit her, and Karen shivered as she headed toward the old, black Cadillac. She wanted to get the license plate number. She still had a few connections with the police department from when she'd worked at Group Health Hospital, counseling the occasional crime victim or criminal. She could pull a few strings and maybe get a trace on the plates through the Department of Motor Vehicles.

Approaching the car, she didn't see anyone inside. She wasn't close enough to read the license plate, but started to reach into her purse for a pen and paper. Then she heard a faint, distant wail, and Karen stopped in her tracks. The siren's high-pitched cry grew louder and louder.

The ambulance sped up the street, its red flashers swirl-ing on the roof. It turned into Sandpoint View's parking lot. "Oh, my God, Jessie," she murmured to herself.

Running back to the side door, she ducked inside and raced down the hallway toward B wing, where Dr. Chang had his office. But as she turned the corner, Karen came upon about a dozen elderly residents hovering outside the TV room. Roseann was trying to get them to disperse. "C'mon now, clear the door, folks," she was saying. "The paramedics need to get to Peggy, and you're blocking the way."

Karen approached her. "What happened?"

"Peggy Henderson fell and hit her head," Roseann whis-pered. "There's blood everywhere. I think she might have had a minor stroke, too, poor thing. Dr. Pollard is in there with her now. Help me get these people out of here."

Karen glanced in the TV room, and saw the frail old woman lying on the sofa, with the other doctor on staff and a nurse hovering over her. Two bloodstained hand towels were wadded up in a ball by their feet. Pollard was checking her vital signs. Karen didn't have much time for more than a glance. Two paramedics were barreling down the hallway with a collapsible gurney.

Karen turned to Dwight, a tall, spry 85-year-old who was a bit of a know-it-all. Except for his slippers, he dressed as if ready for a round of golf, in a green cardigan sweater and plaid pants. Among those gawking at poor Peggy, he was the least likely to budge. "Dwight, we need you," she said ur-gently. "Could you help me get these people to clear the way?"

The old man relished being an authority figure. "All right, let's give them some room here!" He kept clapping his hands and poking at his fellow residents' shoulders and backs until they shuffled aside. Of the dozen or so spectators, two had walkers and one was in a wheelchair. Karen helped corral them down the hallway while the paramedics rushed into the TV room.

In the middle of all the commotion, she saw a young brunette in a windbreaker emerging from a nurse's station alcove down the corridor. Karen froze. "Amelia?" she called.

The young woman glanced at her for a second, then hurried farther down the hallway. Karen started after her. "Amelia? Wait a minute!" She wondered why she was running away. Up ahead, the young woman ducked into a stairwell. The door was on a hydraulic spring, and still hadn't closed all the way by the time Karen swung it open again. She heard footsteps echoing in the dim gray stairwell. The walls were cinder block, and the unpainted concrete steps went down to a lower level and then to the basement. Karen paused at the top of the stairs and peered over the banister. She could see a shadow moving on the steps below. "Amelia? Is that you?" she called.

Karen rushed down the stairs, pausing only for a moment when she heard a door squeak open on the basement level. A mechanical, grinding noise suddenly resounded through the stairwell, probably from the boiler. She continued down the steps to the landing and pushed open the door. Karen found herself in a long, dim corridor. Two tall metal oxygen cylinders stood against the wall, along with a broken-down metal tray table on wheels. Someone had left an old rusty crowbar on top of it. Straight ahead, Karen saw the open door to the boiler room. She poked her head in. The room was huge, with a grated floor, a big old-fashioned boiler, a furnace, and a labyrinth of pipes and ducts. She didn't see anyone. Most of the maintenance people went home at 2:00 P.M. on Saturdays.

"Amelia?" she called, over the din from the boiler.

Turning, she glanced back at the corridor. A set of double doors farther down the hall was gently swinging in and out.

She would have noticed if they'd been moving before. Had someone just ducked into that room?

Karen hadn't been down here since Roseann had given her an employee tour of the place months ago. If memory served her right, there was a storage room beyond those swinging doors. Approaching them, she cautiously glanced over her shoulder at the passageway to another part of the basement. She didn't see anyone, just two large bins full of dirty laundry.

Karen pushed open the swinging doors, and stepped into the dark, cavernous room. The spotlights overhead seemed spaced too far apart, leaving several large, shadowy pockets amid the clutter. To Karen's right was a graveyard of broken gurneys, metal tray tables and other hospital equipment. There were also about a dozen more tall oxygen cylinders.

"Is someone in here?" she called. "Amelia? Can you hear me? It's Karen."

She studied the rows of boxes to her left, some neatly stacked as high as five feet. But others had been torn open, revealing their contents: toilet paper rolls, lightbulbs, paper towels, soap bars, and cleaning supplies. One huge, open carton held bedpans that gleamed in the dim light. Still more boxes were opened and emptied, lying discarded on the floor.

As Karen ventured deeper into the room, she wondered what the hell Amelia would be doing down here. And if it had indeed been Amelia she'd seen upstairs, why had she run away?

Something crunched under her shoe. Karen stopped and gazed down at the thin shards of glass on the floor. Then she looked up toward the ceiling. The hanging spotlight above her was broken. She studied the line of spotlights; most of them had been shattered. No wonder there were so many dark areas in this cellar room. Someone had made it that way.

"Who's down here?" she called.

Karen didn't move for a moment. Her eyes scanned the rows upon rows of boxes, some sections engulfed in the shadows. About twenty feet away, she detected some movement amid the maze of cartons. Suddenly, a dark figure darted between the stacks.

Karen gasped. It looked like a man in black clothes, with a stocking cap on his head. She hadn't seen his face; he'd moved too quickly.

Her heart was racing, and she started to back up toward the double doors. She thought she heard something—a faint murmuring.

"Do it now!" a woman whispered urgently. "Get her!"

Karen turned around and ran for the exit as fast as she could. Flinging open the double doors, she retreated down the basement hallway. As she reached the metal table by the stairwell, she paused and glanced over her shoulder. The storage room doors were still swinging in and out. But no one had come out after her.

She noticed once again the rusty crowbar on top of the table and snatched it up. She took a minute to catch her breath. With her gaze riveted on the swinging doors, Karen reached into her purse for her cell phone.

She had Roseann's number on speed dial. Her friend answered after two rings: "Sandpoint View, this is Roseann."

"Ro, it's Karen," she said, still trying to get her breath.

"Where did you disappear to? One minute, you're with me working crowd control, and the next—"

"I'm in the basement," Karen cut in. "I followed someone down here. I can't explain right now. But could you send Lamar down?" Lamar was an orderly around thirty years old, one of the sweetest guys Karen knew. But he also had a linebacker's build, a shaved head, and an ugly scar on his handsome face. With his formidable looks, Lamar would have made a good bodyguard. And that was what Karen needed right now, because she'd made up her mind to go back into that storage room.

"Tell Lamar I'm by the door to stairwell C, right across from the boiler room. And could you tell him to hurry, please?"

Karen clicked off the line, and stashed the phone back in her purse. She kept her eyes on the double doors, now motionless. She clutched the crowbar tightly in her fist, and waited.

"Are you going to call the police?" Lamar asked.

He'd given Karen his white orderly jacket to keep her warm, and she felt so small wrapped in it. They stood by a set of concrete steps leading down to a fire door to the convalescent home's basement. The old door, with chicken wire crisscrossed in the fogged window, had had a fire alarm attached to the inside lever. But someone had managed to dislodge the mechanism. Karen and Lamar had found the door half open during their search of the storage room. Five overhead lights had been broken—and recently, too. Using Karen's cell, Lamar had phoned Marco, the head of maintenance. Marco had been in the storage area shortly before going home at 2:00 P.M. According to him, all the lights down there had been working fine three hours ago.

The outside stairwell to the basement was nearly hidden behind a row of bushes on the side of the long, two-story, beige brick building. But from where Karen stood, she had a clear view of the parking lot. The black Cadillac wasn't there anymore.

Lamar nudged her. "So, are you going to call the police, Karen?" He spoke with a very crisp Jamaican accent.

Frowning, she shook her head. Even with her old connections on the force, she'd sound pretty stupid trying to explain what had happened. She'd followed someone down to the basement, to the storage room. She'd seen a man, but couldn't really describe him. She'd heard a woman whispering to him. It had sounded like they'd planned to attack her or kill her—she couldn't be sure. And oh, yes, one more thing: the young woman she'd followed down to the basement was a client, and a friend of hers.

"So, do you think you might have a stalker?" Lamar asked.

"I—I'm not sure," she said, shrugging. She was thinking about last Saturday, when she'd spotted someone who looked like Amelia in the corridor outside her dad's room.

"It's almost dinnertime," Lamar said, gently taking her arm. He led the way through a break in the bushes to the parking lot. "They'll need me back inside. Will you be okay?"

She gave him his jacket back. "Yes. Thank you, Lamar. I'm sorry to drag you down to the basement for nothing."

He shook his head. "It wasn't for nothing, Karen, not after what they did to the lights and the door. I think you were being set up. You watch out for yourself, okay? I don't want anything bad to happen to you. You're one of the nicest people here."

"Well, thank you, Lamar," she said. "Thanks very much."

Biting her lip, Karen watched him lumber away toward the side door. She thought she'd been set up, too. But why?

It was getting dark out, and colder. Shivering, Karen glanced at her watch: 5:05. Poor Jessie had been waiting for her for fifteen minutes. While in the basement with Lamar, Karen had phoned Dr. Chang's office. Apparently, Jessie was all right.

She pulled out her cell phone again, and dialed Amelia's cell number. After two rings, she got a recording.

"Amelia, this is Karen," she said, after the beep. "It's a little after five, and I'm wondering where you are right now. Can you call me as soon as you get this? We need to talk. Thanks."

She clicked off the line, and then shoved the phone back

inside her purse. She wondered if she'd called that number twenty-five minutes ago while down in that gloomy basement storage room alone, would she have heard a cell phone ringing?

She remembered something Amelia had told her during their first session. She'd said, as a child, she used to talk to herself in the mirror a lot. She'd tried to make a joke of it. "So what do you make of that? Early signs of a split personality?"

Karen wondered if Amelia would claim to have had one of her *blackouts* this afternoon. Would she only remember *fragments* of this incident, too?

She thought she knew Amelia. She'd believed her incapable of killing anyone. She'd been certain about that.

But now Karen wasn't sure of anything.

"I was sitting there with my blouse off in your Dr. Chang's examining room for twenty-five minutes and for absolutely no reason, except maybe because I'm the *youngest* female patient he's had since he started working there. If that isn't pathetic, I don't know what is."

Karen kept checking the rearview mirror while Jessie, in the passenger seat, explained how her emergency checkup had been a total waste of time. Karen needed convincing that Jessie was all right. She also needed to make sure an old black Cadillac with a bent antenna wasn't following them. But she couldn't make out much in the rearview mirror beyond a string of glaring headlights behind her on Twenty-fourth Avenue.

She'd decided not to tell Jessie about the incident in the basement. No need to put any more stress or strain on her. At the same time, she hated to think she might be leading a pair of potential killers to Jessie's home in the Beacon Hill district.

"You know, I don't like leaving you alone," Karen said, eyes on the road. "I mean, what if you have another spell in the middle of the night?"

"I highly doubt I'll be wrapping my arms around another 170-pound man and repeatedly lifting him off his feet tonight. But if I end up doing that, the fella and I would like a little privacy, please." She chuckled and waved away Karen's concern. "Quit worrying. There's nothing wrong with me except I'm old as the hills and big as a house."

"Sure you haven't been overworking yourself at the McMillans'?" Karen asked. Jessie had babysat, cooked, and cleaned at George's house three days during the past week.

"Oh, it's been a breeze. Those kids are so sweet. And Amelia's been there practically every day, and she helps out a lot. By the way, I've been putting in a good word for you now and then with Gorgeous George. Just planting the seed for when he's ready to start dating again."

"You're wasting your time, Jess. George doesn't like me much. He thinks I'm a busybody."

"Oh, phooey, where did you get that idea?"

Karen said nothing. She briefly checked the rearview mirror again.

She hadn't seen George since the funeral three days ago, where she'd given him a brief, polite hello. Before that, he'd distractedly nodded and waved at her—while on the phone— when she'd stopped by his house on Sunday morning to drive Amelia to the West Seattle Precinct. Amelia's much-dreaded interview with the police had turned out to be rather benign.

They'd talked with her for only forty-five minutes. They hadn't asked about her premonition, and hadn't seemed very interested in where she was at the time of the shootings. The questioning had focused mostly on her family, especially her father, and his behavior during the last few months.

Since then, Amelia had phoned Karen every day, sometimes even twice a day. Karen always took the calls, and tried to reassure her that she'd survive this. Amelia never mentioned whether or not she still felt responsible for the deaths of her parents and her aunt. But Karen knew it was an issue. They would work on it during their next scheduled session on Monday.

In the meantime, Karen reviewed her notes from several of Amelia's past sessions. She wondered about the origins of her nightmares and those memory fragments, some of which were eerily real. Amelia herself had joked she might have a split personality. But genuine cases of multiple personality disorder were very rare, and all the textbooks pointed out the dangers of misdiagnosing a patient as having MPD. Just the suggestion of it could make certain susceptible patients splinter off into several versions of themselves, worsening their problems, and delaying any kind of real treatment.

Still, multiple personality disorder could have caused Amelia's blackouts, her *lost time*. Maybe it could also explain why Amelia had been at the rest home today, luring her down to that basement storage room. Lamar had said she was being set up, but for what? Her murder? Was Amelia the host to another personality that was killing everyone close to her?

It started to drizzle, and Karen switched on the windshield wipers. "Jessie, I need your opinion," she said, eyes on the road. "I have a client who says she's seeing and feeling things that are happening miles and miles away to people in her family—"

"Are you talking about Amelia?"

"A client," Karen said, knowing she wasn't fooling Jessie for a second. "Anyway, what do you think of that? Do you believe in ESP or telepathy?"

She was waiting for Jessie to respond with one of those alternative words for *bullshit* only people over sixty used nowadays: *hogwash, balderdash,* or *bunk.*

"I believe in it," Jessie said, after a moment. "If we're talking about picking up signals and pain from other people, then I say, yes, definitely, especially if you're close to that other person. I'm a believer now. When my Andy was so sick, I felt every pain he had. Sometimes I'd even wake up in the middle of the night with the pain. And I knew it was Andy, suffering."

Karen glanced over at Jessie. The headlights, raindrops, and windshield wipers cast shadows across her careworn face. Andy was her son, who had died at age twenty-nine back in 1993.

"He was in Chicago and I was in Seattle. Yet, I felt what he was feeling. If I was sick to my stomach one evening, sure enough, I'd hear the next day that he'd been throwing up half the night. If I had a headache or a dizzy spell, that's what he was having. I've never felt so physically sick and horrible as I did his last week, when he was in the hospice. I was there with him, and for a while, I thought I was going to die there, too."

Jessie let out a sad, little laugh. "You're going to think I'm crazy, but did I ever tell you that Andy still visits me every Christmas? It was his favorite time of year, you know. When he was younger, he used to go crazy decorating the house for Christmas. If it were up to him, he would have put a Christmas tree in every room. That Christmas after he died, my daughter, Megan, and my granddaughter, Josie, were staying with me. Josie was five at the time. I was about to go to bed when I heard her talking to someone. So I stepped into Andy's bedroom, where she was sleeping and almost walked into . . . something that fluttered away, like a bird. It was the weirdest thing. I can't describe it; it was like a ball of air that whirled around and disappeared. For a minute there, I thought I was going nuts. I asked Josie what was happening. And she said, 'I was just dreaming about Uncle Andy, Grandma.'

"Something like that has happened every Christmas since," Jessie continued. "It can be a weird little coincidence, or just this overwhelming feeling, and I know Andy's there. It's funny. Even though I know he's going to show up somehow, he still manages to sneak up on me when I'm not expecting him. So, anyway, I'm no expert on telepathy and ESP and that sort of stuff. But I do know for a fact there are forces out there that keep us connected to the people we love, even after we've lost them."

Karen nodded pensively. She could see Jessie's block up ahead.

"So tell Amelia if she's feeling a connection to someone who has died recently, and she's seeing things, well, she's not really all that crazy, at least, no crazier than yours truly."

"I didn't say it was Amelia, remember?" Karen felt obliged to say.

"Oh, yes, that's right," Jessie replied, deadpan.

She turned down Jessie's block, and checked the rearview mirror again. No one seemed to be following them. Despite Jessie's protests that she was double-parked and getting wet in the rain, Karen walked her to her front door. She made Jessie promise to call if she felt dizzy or short of breath. Jessie assured her that she'd be fine.

But Karen was worried about leaving Jessie alone, and it wasn't just because of her little spell earlier, scary as that had been. No, it was because of the other scare Karen had experienced, in the rest home's basement. Whoever had come after her might decide to go after Jessie.

"Listen," she said. "I don't want to worry you, but I read in the *Post-Intelligencer* there have been some robberies in this neighborhood. So lock your doors tonight, and set the alarm." It was a fib about the robberies, but she wanted Jessie to take precautions.

"Well, there isn't a thing in here worth stealing," Jessie replied, unlocking her door. "I hardly ever set the alarm."

"Well, set it tonight, for me, okay? Humor me."

"Okay, okay, I'll batten down the hatches. Worrywart."

Karen hugged Jessie in the doorway, then scurried back into her car. She started up the engine, but sat in the idle car for a moment. The windshield wipers squeaked back and forth, and raindrops pattered on the roof.

She thought about how Jessie had felt her son's pain, though two thousand miles away from him. Had Amelia made the same kind of connection with her family members when they were killed? Were her nightmarelike visions of their murders a form of telepathy?

Until this afternoon, Karen would have never considered it a possibility. But perhaps Amelia hadn't really felt a telepathic connection with her loved ones at the time of their deaths.

Maybe she was connected to the person who had killed all of them.

In the shadows of a tall evergreen at the edge of the lot next to Jessie's house, she stood in the rain. The hood to her windbreaker was up, covering the top of her head. The old Cadillac was parked around the corner. She already knew where Karen's housekeeper lived; it hadn't been necessary to follow Jessie down the block. But she'd wanted to hear what Karen and Jessie were saying to each other. So she'd climbed out of the Cadillac and skulked into the neighbor's yard. She'd only caught snippets of the conversation through the sounds of the wind and rain. It was sweet how Karen had been so worried about Jessie, and even kind of funny, because they'd both be dead before the week was through.

Karen probably had only a slight inkling of how close she'd come to having her throat slit in the basement at the rest home an hour before. Now there was no mistaking it; Karen had seen her. It wasn't the same as last week's brush with her in the corridor outside the old man's room. This time, Karen wouldn't just *ask* if she'd been at the rest home. She'd *accuse*. And this time, the innocent routine or the blackout excuse wouldn't work. Karen would keep pounding away at her for an explanation.

So she'd have to move fast and kill her, before the bitch started talking about her to other shrinks or maybe even to the police. Karen slept every night alone in the big relic of a house. The dog was a slight obstacle. But she'd killed plenty of animals in her time. This one wouldn't be a problem. And there were plenty of ways to break into that old house, plenty of opportunities.

She watched Karen duck back inside her car, then she just sat idle in the driver's seat for a few minutes. What was Karen Carlisle thinking about right now?

She had a thought of her own, and it made her smile. She was wondering what they'd tell that senile old man at the rest home next week when he asked why the visits from his daughter had suddenly stopped.

Chapter Ten

"Hi, this is Amelia. Sorry I can't take your call. Leave a message, and I'll get back to you as soon as I can. Bye."

Beep.

"Amelia, it's Karen again at about 6:15," she said into her cell. She'd just pulled into her driveway and switched off the ignition. The rain had subsided to a light drizzle. "Listen, I'm home now. So call me, either at home or on my cell. It's important. Talk to you soon, I hope." She clicked off the line, shoved her cell phone in her purse, and reached for the car door handle. But she noticed something in her rearview mirror, and suddenly froze. She saw the silhouette of a man as he came up her driveway, toward the car. He was tall and slender with short hair so blond it was almost white. The streetlight was at his back, so she still couldn't see his face. He wore gray slacks and a dark suit jacket with the lapels turned up to protect him from the drizzle. As he reached the back of the car, Karen quickly locked her door.

He knocked on her window. "Karen?" he called. "Karen Carlisle?"

She stared at him through the rain-beaded glass. He was very handsome, with chiseled cheekbones and pale-blue eyes. She guessed he was in his early thirties. "Yes? What do you want?" she called back.

He grinned, and made a little whirling motion with his hand like he wanted her to roll down the window.

Karen started up the car engine again. She pressed the control switch, and with a hum, the window lowered only an inch before she stopped it. "I said, '*What do you want?*'" she repeated loudly.

As he reached into his suit jacket, Karen tensed up, until she realized he was pulling out his wallet. He opened it, and showed her a Seattle Police Department identification card. *Det. Russell Koehler* it said, under a very macho-somber photo of him. "I'd like to ask you a few questions about Amelia Faraday," he said, almost too loudly, as if he wanted to get across to her that he was becoming annoyed by the window between them. "You're her therapist, aren't you?"

Karen flicked the switch, lowering the window some more. "Yes, I'm her therapist," she said. "What's this about?"

"I'm investigating the deaths of her parents and her aunt."

"I thought the police had already determined that Mr. Faraday shot his wife and sister-in-law and then himself," Karen replied warily. "Besides, the shootings happened in Wenatchee. Isn't that out of your jurisdiction?"

"Let's just say I have a special interest in the case."

Despite what had happened in the rest home basement and all her new uncertainty about Amelia, Karen still felt very protective of her. She shrugged. "Well, I can't tell you much, at least nothing Amelia has shared with me during our sessions. That's strictly confidential; I'm sure you understand."

He chuckled. "I wouldn't dream of treading on your doctor-patient confidentiality. But the fact of the matter is, Karen, I've read the police reports. Amelia came to your house on

Saturday afternoon, saying she had a premonition about something bad happening at the family getaway at Lake Wenatchee. That doesn't quite count as a doctor-patient session, does it?"

She stared back at him. "I treat any client emergency as a professional session."

"Really? So are you going to charge her for Saturday?" he asked pointedly.

"That's none of your business," Karen replied.

He smirked—that same cocky grin again. "You know, Karen, it looks like I've started off on the wrong foot with you. The thing is, I don't believe Mark Faraday shot anyone. I think someone else killed Mark, along with his wife and sister-in-law. Maybe you'd be more willing to cooperate if we sat down together over a cup of coffee and you let me explain where I'm coming from." He glanced over her shoulder at the house as if it were her cue to invite him in, and then he smirked at her. "'Where I'm coming from,' that's one of those therapy terms, isn't it?"

Karen eyed him warily. She wasn't about to invite this guy into her home. She still wasn't a hundred percent sure he was really a cop. "There's a coffee place on Fifteenth called Victrola. It's about a five-minute walk from here. I'll meet you there in ten. I just need to make a call."

"Who are you calling? Amelia? Or your lawyer?"

Karen flicked the switch and started to raise the window up on him. "Neither."

He grabbed the top of the window to delay its ascent. "You aren't *hiding* Amelia, are you?"

She released the switch for a moment. "No. Why do you ask that?"

"Because I've been trying to get in touch with her since one o'clock this afternoon, and she's MIA. No one knows where she is—not her uncle, her roommate, or her boyfriend." He glanced back at the house again. "Are you sure

Amelia's not in there? That's an awfully big place for just one person. Do you live there alone?"

"It's my father's house. He's in a rest home with Alzheimer's. So, yes, I'm living here alone. And yes, I'm sure Amelia's not in there."

"And you don't have any idea where she might be?"

Karen shook her head. "No, I don't." She flicked the switch, raising the window again. "I'll see you at Victrola in ten minutes," she said over the humming noise. She watched him in the rearview mirror as he turned and strutted down the driveway toward the street. Then she looked at her house, and couldn't help wondering, *Are you sure Amelia's not in there?*

Climbing out of the car, Karen kept her eyes riveted on the house, watching for any movement within the dark windows. She should have turned on a light before running out the front door this afternoon. At least she'd remembered to set the alarm. She glanced at her wristwatch: 6:25. It was strange to feel so nervous about walking into a dark house by herself at this early hour. But then, it had been a very strange day.

Karen approached the front stoop, then tested the doorknob. Still locked; that was a good sign. She unlocked the door and opened it. Flicking on the light, she headed for the alarm box and quickly punched in the code.

She paused for a moment, and felt a pang of dread in the pit of her stomach. Something was wrong. Why wasn't Rufus barking? She anxiously glanced around, then ventured down the hallway to the kitchen. Switching on the light, she hurried to the backdoor. Still locked. Good. She noticed the basement door was ajar. She turned on the light at the top of the stairs and peered down at the steps. "Rufus?" she said. "Here, boy!"

Nothing. Karen shut and locked the basement door in

practically one swift motion. She headed toward the front of the house again. "Rufus?" she called out. "Where are you?"

Poking her head in the living room, she stopped dead. The dog was trying to sneak down from the lounge chair her father had had re-covered to the tune of $850 only ten months ago. Naturally, it had become Rufus's favorite spot to nap, when no one was around. "You stinker!" she yelled. "No wonder you didn't bark when I came in. You know you're not supposed to be on that chair. Some watchdog. I could have been strangled, and you wouldn't care, as long as it didn't interrupt your nap."

His head down, the dog slinked toward the kitchen.

"Don't even *think* you're getting a cookie," Karen growled, retreating into her office. She checked her address book. Her contact with the Seattle Police from her days at Group Health was Cal Hinshaw, a smart, dependable, good old boy. She found his number, then grabbed the phone, and dialed. She kept glancing over her shoulder to make sure no one was sneaking up behind her. She could hear Rufus's paws clicking on the kitchen floor, but nothing else.

"Lieutenant Hinshaw," he answered after three rings.

"Cal? It's Karen Carlisle calling, you know, from Group—"

"Karen? How the hell are you? It's been an age. Listen, I'm running late for something and just about to head out. Can I call you back?"

"Actually, I just wanted to hit you up for some quick information."

"Lay it on me. What can I do you for?"

"I'm wondering if you know anything about a Detective Russell Koehler. He just came by asking a lot of questions about one of my clients, and I'm stalling him. Is he on the level?"

"Koehler? Yeah, I know the guy. He thinks his shit is cake. He's been on *paternity leave* the last two weeks. He found something in the employee regs that allowed him to take a month off with pay while his wife pops out a kid, not that I'd think for one minute he'd be any help to her. He's kind of a sleaze. But I hear he knows somebody in the mayor's office, and gets away with a lot of crap at work. You say he's flashing his police credentials and asking questions?"

"Yes, about those shootings in Wenatchee last week, the Faraday murder-suicide case. My client is their daughter. I'm wondering why this cop—on leave—is investigating a practically closed case out of his jurisdiction."

"You got me, Karen. He's always working some angle."

She shot a cautious glance toward the front hallway. "Maybe this man isn't really Koehler. Is he in his midthirties with pale blond hair and blue eyes? Good looking?"

"Not half as good looking as he thinks he is. That's Koehler, all right. Watch your back with him, Karen." Cal let out a sigh. "Listen, I need to scram. Let's get together for coffee sometime and catch up. And keep me posted if you find out why Koehler's sniffing around this Wenatchee case. You've got me curious now."

"Will do. Thanks, Cal," Karen replied, and then she hung up the phone.

Grabbing her umbrella, she set the alarm again, and ran out of the house.

"Do you know how much Ina and Jenna were worth?" Russell Koehler asked in a hushed voice. "The Basner sisters had a little over three mil between them."

Karen leaned over the small table, so she could hear him better in the crowded coffeehouse. They sat by the window. An eclectic art collection hung on the walls with price tags next to each work. About two thirds of the customers sat with their laptops in front of them. Chet Baker's horn and velvet vocals purred over the sound system.

"Guess who now stands to inherit those millions?" Koehler continued. "Nineteen-year-old Amelia Faraday and her favorite uncle, George McMillan."

Karen leaned back and shrugged. "So?"

"According to the Faradays' neighbors up in Bellingham, Amelia was a real hell-raiser. And from *Uncle George's* own testimony, we know his wife was banging his brother-in-law. A close friend of Ina McMillan's confirmed it. So you've got a rebel daughter pissed off at her parents, and this cuckolded history professor, both due to inherit a shitload of money. You do the math. One, or both, of them could have done the job on Ina, Mark, and Jenna last Friday night—or they hired someone to do it."

Karen frowned over her latte. "Well, you're wrong. Without breaching any therapist-client confidentiality, I can tell you this. Amelia never once complained to me about her parents. If anything, it was the other way around. Amelia said she'd caused her folks some heartache over the years, and wanted to make it up to them."

"She *told* you that. She probably figured you'd be repeating it to some cop, like you are right now. How do you know Amelia wasn't just setting you up?"

"Amelia genuinely loved her parents, Lieutenant. Also, I was with George McMillan hours after he learned of his wife's death, and he was devastated. It wasn't an act. If you're trying to pin the Wenatchee shootings on either one of them simply because they're in line for some money, then you don't have a leg to stand on. Besides, three million split between two people isn't a huge fortune nowadays."

"Maybe not to you," Koehler replied, drumming his fingers on the tabletop. "Not everybody lives in a *castle*, like you do. The police based their conclusion that Mark Faraday was unstable mostly on the testimony of Amelia and her Uncle George, the beneficiaries of this little windfall. I mean, isn't that pretty damn convenient? Maybe three mil isn't such a gold mine nowadays, but it's still a damn fine nest egg. Two people could live very comfortably on that. Not everyone is as lucky as you, inheriting a mansion. Some people have to make their own luck."

Amelia glared at him. "I don't think it's lucky that my father lost his mind. And I'm sure Amelia Faraday and George McMillan don't feel lucky about what happened to their loved ones."

"All right, all right, take it easy," he said, rolling his eyes. "You'd be thinking along the same lines as me if you'd seen the house by Lake Wenatchee. I walked through it the day after. I didn't go in there suspecting your client and her uncle. But that's how I felt when I walked out of the place. For starters, there are footprints all around the outside of the house. But there were other partial footprints in the mud they weren't so sure about. The cops figured that most of the prints belonged to Mark, after examining his slippers. And I'm wondering, what the hell was Mark doing out there in his slippers? He must have gone to check on something, maybe a noise, or maybe one of the women saw someone lurking outside the house."

Karen shrugged. "He could have been chasing away a raccoon for all we know." She shook her head. "You're jumping to conclusions—"

"I saw the bloodstains, Karen. I saw them in the upstairs hallway where Jenna got shot in the face. There was a big stain on the living room floor, where Ina got it . . ."

Karen remembered Amelia's description of the scene. It was so dead on.

"But the bloodstain on the living room wall, behind the rocking chair where they found Mark Faraday with his hunting rifle still in his hands, that's what really stopped me. The bullet entered above his left eye and shot out the back of his head about two inches above the hairline on the back of his neck. The stain on the wall was almost parallel to the top of the rocking chair. He couldn't have held a hunting rifle to his face that way, not parallel. He'd need arms like an orangutan to manage that. If Mark Faraday really killed himself with that rifle, the barrel would have been at a diagonal slant, blowing off the top-back of his head. The only way the exit wound and the bloodstain on the wall could be like that was if someone else held the rifle parallel to his face."

Karen automatically shook her head. "But he was in a rocking chair. It might have tipped back—"

"Yeah, yeah, one of the Wenatchee cops gave me the same song and dance about the rocking chair. That might account for Faraday's blood and brains being where they were on the wall. But there's still the exit wound. You can't explain that away. And I'll tell you something else there's no explanation for: the whereabouts of both Amelia and her Uncle George on the night of the shootings. Their alibis aren't worth shit. Uncle George says he was home with the kiddies at the time of the murders. But he could have easily driven to Lake Wenatchee, pulled off the killings, and driven back while the kids were in bed. It's about 150 miles from Seattle to Lake Wenatchee and, driving at night, he could have cinched the round-trip in less than five hours. The guy had the motive and the opportunity.

"As for your client, she ditched her boyfriend at a party around eleven, and then went for a 'drive.' No one saw her or talked to her for the next twelve hours. The coroner estimates her parents expired sometime between two and three in the morning. The aunt died a little later, closer to dawn. They think she must have lingered for a while, after being shot. Either way, that's three or four hours after Amelia left the party, plenty of time for her to get to Lake Wenatchee. She told the police she'd driven as far as Snoqualmie Falls, then fell asleep in a parking lot. Hell, you'd think she'd try to be a little more creative with her alibi."

"She couldn't have driven to Lake Wenatchee," Karen argued. "There wasn't enough gas in her boyfriend's car to get her there and back. And Amelia didn't have the money or credit cards to buy gas."

"So, she could have siphoned some gas. Or maybe she just drove to some designated spot and met her uncle. Then he could have driven the rest of the way so they could pull off the job together."

"That's crazy," Karen whispered. "I saw Amelia on Saturday afternoon, and I got a good look at the clothes she had on, the same clothes she'd worn to the party the night before. Everyone was shot at close range. There would have been bloodstains."

"Yeah, so? She could have easily changed into something else before she started shooting, and then discarded the bloody clothes later. Or maybe she let *Uncle George* do the shooting."

Karen just shook her head at him.

"Obviously, you've considered the possibility that Amelia killed them," he pointed out. "Otherwise, you wouldn't be so fast with your counterarguments about her clothes and the gas in her boyfriend's car. You must have discussed this with her. What did she say to convince you she was innocent? I'd like to hear it, Karen. You convince *me*."

"I didn't need convincing," Karen replied. "I *know* Amelia. I know she couldn't kill anyone."

He cracked a tiny smile. "I'm pretty good at reading people, Karen. And I could tell just now you really weren't sure you believed what you were saying. I'm certainly not buying it."

It was all she could do to keep from squirming in her chair. "You grossly overestimate your powers of perception, Lieutenant," Karen managed to say. "And it's got you jumping to a lot of wrong conclusions. You've already made up your mind about Amelia and her uncle, haven't you? Anything I tell you that doesn't fit into your preconceived scenario, you simply disregard. Why bother even talking to me? Have you talked to Amelia yet, or her uncle?"

Koehler nodded. "The uncle, yes. But he clammed up pretty tight after a few questions. As for your client, she keeps giving me the slip."

"Then your investigation isn't official police business, is it?" Karen said.

Grinning, he shrugged, "Well, I . . ."

"Before coming here, I called a friend of mine on the police force," she went on. "He said you're on paternity leave right now. What's your angle, lieutenant? Why is this so important to you that you'd take time away from your wife and newborn baby to investigate a case that isn't even in your jurisdiction?"

"Because I care about the truth," he said, with a straight face.

"I'm pretty good at reading people, too, Lieutenant. And you're full of shit." Karen got to her feet. "I've talked to you all I want to right now. If you come around my place again asking me a lot of questions, you better bring your checkbook, because I'm charging you for my time."

She started for the exit, and he called to her, his voice rising above the noise inside the café. "I'll just have to chase down your client and talk to her," he said ominously.

Karen headed out the door, and pretended not to hear him.

"You have—no—messages," said the prerecorded voice on her answering machine.

"Damn," Karen muttered, hanging up the cordless phone in the study.

Amelia still hadn't called her back. Karen felt so torn. She'd just returned from the coffeehouse, where she'd argued Amelia's innocence to that cocky cop. Yet, while walking home in the light drizzle, she'd repeatedly looked over her shoulder for that broken-down black Cadillac.

How could Amelia be so innocent, and at the same time be a potential threat to her? Could she really have multiple personality disorder?

This *other* Amelia had never emerged during any of their sessions. Sandpoint View was the only place Karen had seen her. Why there of all places?

Biting her lip, Karen picked up the cordless phone again and dialed the rest home. One of the night nurses answered: "Good evening, Sandpoint View Convalescent Home."

Karen recognized her voice. "Hi, this is Karen Carlisle. Is this Rita?"

"Sure is. What's going on, Karen? I heard someone was stalking you this afternoon down in the laundry room or something. What's up with that?"

"Beats the hell out of me, Rita. But it's got me a little nervous about my dad. Would you mind checking on him for me?"

"Don't have to. I just saw him five minutes ago in the lounge, watching TV with a bunch of them. Frank's just fine."

"Could you check on something else for me, Rita? Could you take a look out at the parking lot and tell me if you see a . . . an old black Cadillac with a broken antenna?"

"Sure, no sweat. I'll just go look out the side door. Hold on a minute."

With the cordless phone to her ear, Karen wandered to the front hallway. She glanced up the stairs to the darkened second floor. She hadn't been up there since leaving the house early this afternoon. She kept staring up at the second floor hallway. Suddenly a shadow swept across the wall.

She gasped and started backing away from the stairs. Then she saw the shadow race across the wall again and realized it was just a car passing outside, the headlights shining through the upstairs windows. She let out a sigh. "You idiot, Karen," she muttered to herself.

"Karen, are you still there?" Rita asked, getting back on the line.

"Yes, Rita?"

"I didn't see a Cadillac in the lot, or parked on the street, either. Does this have anything to do with the whacko who was stalking you?"

"It might. Listen, how late are you working tonight?"

"Until midnight, lucky me."

"Could you give my dad an extra check now and then for me, Rita?"

"Of course I will, Karen. Don't you worry about Frank. I'll make sure he's okay. You look after yourself, girl. Do you have pepper spray? I don't leave home without mine. If you don't have pepper spray or mace, you should keep a knitting needle in your purse."

"Well, I've had a minicanister of mace in the bottom of my purse for years, but I've never had a reason to use it."

"Better make sure it still works. Test it, girl."

"I will. Thanks, Rita. Thanks a million. And if you happen to notice a black Cadillac in the parking lot, would you call me?"

"No sweat. Your cell number's right here at the nurse's station."

After she hung up, Karen was still worried about her father, so feeble and helpless. Visitors wandered in and out of that rest home all day. And there were plenty of temps on the nursing staff. Amelia could have easily passed as one of them.

If there was a photo of Amelia by the nurses' station, the staff could keep a lookout for her, and Karen would feel a lot better. But she didn't have a picture of Amelia. They'd done a pretty good job of keeping her photo out of the newspapers last week.

George McMillan certainly had a picture of his niece among the family snapshots. Karen needed to call him anyway. Even if he didn't like her, she had a good reason to phone him right now. Maybe he had an idea where Amelia was.

Jessie had left the McMillans' number by the phone in the kitchen. Karen went in there, and called him.

George picked up on the second ring. "Hi, Jessie."

Karen balked. "Um, this isn't Jessie. It's Karen Carlisle."

"Oh, I'm sorry. Your name came up on the caller ID, but I just figured it was Jessie."

"No, it's—it's me, Karen," she said, feeling awkward. "I hope I'm not interrupting your dinner."

"No, we just finished. It was spaghetti, the only thing I know how to cook that my kids like. What can I do for you, Karen?"

"I'm wondering if you know where Amelia is. I've been trying to get ahold of her."

"She's incommunicado right now," George replied. "Shane phoned earlier today, all worried about her. He just called back an hour ago. Amelia's roommate said she mentioned something this morning about needing to get away. It looks like she just took off someplace for the weekend. She used to pull this on her parents every once in a while, and it drove them crazy. I hope she's not drinking again. She was doing so well this week, considering everything she's been through."

"Listen, would you mind if I came by tonight? I need to talk with you, and I don't want to discuss this over the phone."

"No problem, Karen," he said. "When can I expect you?"

"I'm leaving the house right now."

"I had a bellyful of Koehler myself," George said. He stood at the kitchen sink, scrubbing a saucepan. Karen stood beside him with a dishtowel in her hand. Despite George's protests, she'd insisted on helping him clean up. His daughter,

Stephanie, was in bed, playing with her stuffed animals. Jody and a neighbor friend were watching TV downstairs.

"When he came by yesterday, I thought it was official police business," George continued. "So I let him in, and talked to him for a while. But then Koehler started in about Amelia, saying she could have killed her parents and my wife. He even insinuated that Amelia and I could have been having an affair. He pointed out that, after all, she isn't a blood relative, and niece or no niece, a hot-looking 19-year-old is hard to pass up. That's when I threw him out on his ass."

He handed Karen the saucepan. "Then I called Dennis," he said. "Dennis Goodwin, he was that detective who was here last Saturday. We drove to Wenatchee together. He turned out to be a pretty nice guy. I could tell he liked me, or at least felt sorry for me. He told me Koehler's on leave—"

"*Paternity* leave," Karen interjected. "His wife just had a baby."

"Mazel tov," George grunted. "Anyway, apparently Koehler thinks he'll make a big name for himself if he cracks this case wide open. He was talking to another cop about the potential for a book deal and movie rights. Anyway, he's not afraid of treading on anyone's toes on the force, because he's very well connected with the powers that be. I guess I didn't do myself any good by pissing him off, but I really don't care."

"Do you mean that?" Karen asked, studying him.

He let out a little laugh. "Well, actually I am a bit worried about what he might do. I'm thinking about Amelia, mostly."

Karen nodded. "So am I. Remember what we talked about last week? It took a lot of persuading on my part to assure Amelia she didn't kill her parents, and your wife. I'm not sure exactly how much I succeeded in convincing her. She's probably still pretty confused. If Koehler goes to work on her, God knows what she'll end up telling him."

"Then he'll go to the media, and make Amelia out to be a deranged killer." George reached over and turned off the water. "God, I don't want my kids to read that."

Karen said nothing for a moment. Gnawing away at her was the idea that it could be true about Amelia. She dried off her hands, then folded up the dishtowel. "Listen, something happened to me when I went to visit my father in the rest home today. It involves Amelia . . ."

They sat down at the kitchen table, and she told George about her bizarre, scary experience in the basement storage room. She explained her reluctance to diagnose Amelia as having a split personality, and asked if he'd ever noticed any abrupt behavioral changes in his niece. "Not just mood swings," Karen clarified. "But a total shift in her persona, when she might have sounded or even looked different to you."

He shrugged. "I don't remember ever seeing Amelia act like anybody except Amelia. Ina never said anything to me about personality shifts, and she and Amelia were pretty close this last year. Mark and Jenna never mentioned anything either. I . . ." He hesitated. "Wait a sec. You know, Collin said something to me about a month before he died. He and some friends were eating lunch on the bleachers at his school in Bellingham, when he spotted Amelia watching them from across the street. He called to her, and she started to walk away. It struck him as weird, because Amelia was supposed to be in Seattle, and he usually knew when she was coming home to visit. Anyway, when he caught up with her, Amelia acted like a total stranger, he said."

"You mean she didn't recognize him?" Karen asked.

"No, she knew who he was, all right. They talked for a minute or two, then Amelia said she had to go and asked Collin not to tell their parents that she'd been there. I remember Collin saying to me, 'I felt like Amelia was a different person.' He said she didn't seem drunk or anything. She just didn't seem like his sister. Collin was spending the weekend here when he told me this story." George let out a sad sigh. "Huh. You know, that weekend was the last time I saw him."

Karen was about to reach over and put her hand over his, but she hesitated. She cleared her throat. "Um, I don't know much about multiple personality disorder. We'd have to get Amelia to a specialist. We also have to prepare ourselves for the awful possibility that Koehler is right about Amelia."

George frowned. "Do you really think she could have killed her own parents—and my wife? I know my niece, and she could never—"

"Yes, I agree with you," Karen cut in. "The Amelia *we know* isn't capable of murder. I'm saying there could be another person inside Amelia we don't know. Maybe this *other* Amelia was in the rest home earlier today. Maybe she's the one Collin spotted outside his high school that time. Collin said she was like a stranger. We don't know this other Amelia either. We don't know what she's capable of."

George slowly shook his head. "I can't believe it. I mean, Jesus, I've had her here alone with the kids this week. Are you sure?"

"I'm just saying it's a possibility we have to consider. In fact, one reason I wanted to stop by tonight was to borrow a photo of Amelia, any recent photo of her that you might have. I want to post it at the nurses' station in my dad's rest home so they'll keep a lookout for her. You probably think I'm overreacting."

"No, not at all," he said. "We have plenty of family pictures. I'll make sure you get a current one of Amelia before you leave tonight."

"Thank you, George," she said, sitting back in the kitchen chair. "About Amelia, I'd like to get her to someone more qualified in multiple personality disorder. I've never had a true MPD case. There are theories it can be caused by an early childhood trauma. But that's just a theory. And Amelia's early childhood is still a mystery to us. I really—"

"God, I forgot to call and tell you," he interrupted. "I was up at Mark and Jenna's house in Bellingham the day before yesterday with Amelia, and I found the adoption papers." He got to his feet. "They're in my study. I'm not sure how much help they'll be."

Karen eagerly followed him into the study. She remembered some of those fragmented memories Amelia had shared with her about her early childhood: a woman screaming in the woods while young Amelia sat alone in a car; the Native American neighbor she liked; a person or place called Unca-dween; and her mother standing over her in the bathroom, asking, "Did he touch you down there?"

If they could track down more information about Amelia's biological parents, they might discover what those fragments meant. Maybe they'd find the key to Amelia's problems.

George put on his glasses and sifted through a stack of papers on his computer desk. "Here's the file," he said, handing her a folder. "I'm afraid there isn't a lot of information here—no mention of the biological parents or even where Amelia was born, just her first name and the birthday, May 21, 1988."

Karen glanced at the records: sixteen pages of legal documents, most of it boilerplate stuff. But the adoption date was there: April 5, 1993; and so was the name of the agency: Jamison Group Adoption Services, Spokane, Washington.

Karen nodded at his computer screen. "Could I get online for a minute?"

"Sure, I'll start it up for you." Sitting down, he switched on the monitor, then worked the keyboards for a minute until he connected to the Internet. He quickly vacated the chair for her. "What are you looking up?"

"This adoption agency. I want to read about the fire. Maybe they'll say something about where all their records went, besides up in smoke." She sat down, and did a Google search for Jamison Group Adoption Services, Spokane, WA.

The first four listings were for other adoption agencies in Spokane, and three more, picking up the key words, were for *Jamison* Auto *Services* in *Spokane*. And there was a Jim *Jamison* offering *group* rates for his limousine *services* in *Spokane*.

Frowning, Karen went to the next page, and then she found something halfway down the list:

FOUR DIE IN SHOOTING . . . Gunman Sets Adoption Agency on Fire . . .
Duane Lee Savitt, 33, walked into the **Jamison Group Adoption Agency** on East Sprague Street at 1:35 P.M. Within minutes, he had shot and killed office manager Donna . . .
www.spokesmanreview.com/news/shooting/042993 – 14k.

"My God," George murmured, peering over her shoulder. "All this time, I thought the fire was accidental."

Karen clicked on the link, and pulled up an article in the *Spokesman Review* archives, dated April 28, 1993:

FOUR DIE IN SHOOTING RAMPAGE

*Gunman Sets Adoption Agency on
Fire After Shooting Spree*

SPOKANE: Police investigators are still trying to determine the motive for a Pasco man's shooting spree at an adoption agency, which left three employees dead on Monday afternoon. Before it was over, the gunman set ablaze the small, two-story Tudor

house which served as the adoption
agency's office. He was shot and killed
as he opened fire on police and fire-
fighters arriving at the scene.

Armed with two handguns, several clips of ammunition, and an in-
cendiary device, Duane Lee Savitt,
33, walked into the Jamison Group
Adoption Agency on East Sprague
Street at 1:35 P.M. Within minutes,
he had shot and killed office manager
Donna Houston, 51, and Scott Larabee, 40, an attorney for the agency.
Anita Jamison, 44, vice president and
part owner, was also shot.

"I heard screams, and several loud
pops next door," said Margarita Brady,
a receptionist at a neighboring archi-
tecture firm, D. Renner & Company.
Brady immediately called 911. "There
were still screams coming from inside the house when I saw the smoke
start to pour out the windows . . ."

Karen glanced at the adoption documents again. Both
Scott Larabee and Anita Jamison had signed the contracts.

According to the article, Anita Jamison was still alive when
the police finally gunned down Duane Lee Savitt. But she'd
been badly burned in the fire and died in the ambulance on
the way to Sacred Heart Medical Center.

The article also mentioned that the fire had destroyed vol-
umes of records on file at the agency.

"It probably doesn't have anything to do with my niece,"
George said, still standing behind her. "But we should
Google this Duane Savitt."

"Duane," Karen repeated, staring at the killer's name in the news article. She could almost hear a four-year-old girl trying to pronounce it. "Dween."

"What?" George asked. "What is it?"

"My God," Karen whispered, her eyes still riveted to that name on the screen. "I think we might have just found Amelia's other uncle."

Chapter Eleven

"None of the women I met last week through that Internet service were worth a second date. Four women, and not one could hold a candle to you."

Karen managed a patient, placid smile for the man seated across from her on the sofa in her study. He was a skinny 42-year-old divorcé with receding strawberry-blond hair, fishlike eyes, and a huge Adam's apple.

"Now, Laird, we've been over this before," she said. "It's called transference, and it's perfectly normal to get a little crush on your therapist. But you need to move on from that. Now, tell me about these women, and why they didn't measure up to your standards."

"Well, for starters, none of them liked *Star Trek*."

"That's not a good reason. Your ex-wife was a huge *Star Trek* fan, and the two of you fought like cats. You'll have to do better than that."

Laird started listing the faults of date number one. She just wasn't pretty enough for him—this from a guy who looked like a blond Don Knotts. Of course, she was in no position to criticize people for their fickle romantic notions, not when she had feelings for a man whose wife had just been murdered a week ago.

She and George McMillan had spent over an hour last night in front of his computer screen, checking search engine listings for Duane Lee Savitt. George had pulled up a chair and sat beside her. They hadn't found much about the man who might have been Amelia's Unca Dween. Apparently, the police never determined a motive behind his killing spree. There were no records of him ever working at Jamison Group, and as far as anyone could tell, he hadn't known any of his victims. One article suggested Savitt might have been the birth father to a child adopted through the agency. But it was difficult to determine that, since he'd destroyed all their files. A thorough search of county and state records yielded nothing for investigators.

Karen was getting frustrated by what looked more and more like a dead end. But she had George at her side, occasionally touching her arm or shoulder as they found each new potential lead, even if it didn't pan out. She wasn't alone in her concern about Amelia; she had an ally.

She understood why he was a history professor. He seemed obsessed over getting every single fact about this tragedy from nearly fifteen years ago. He was doing it for Amelia, of course. But Karen liked to think he was doing it partly for her, too.

Before she left his house, he gave her a photo of Amelia, so she could post it at the nurses' station at the convalescent home. He walked her to her car, and assured her that he'd keep digging for more information about Duane Lee Savitt.

Karen hesitated before climbing into the car. She couldn't leave there without resolving something, though a sixth sense told her to leave it the hell alone. "Listen, I still feel bad about upsetting you last week. If I was out of line, I'm sorry—"

"What are you talking about?" George asked.

"When I told Amelia about her father and—and your wife," Karen explained. "I meant well. But you're right, it wasn't my place to—"

"Karen, please," he said, shaking his head. "It was a misunderstanding. You don't have to apologize for anything. If I got curt with you, I'm sorry. I was half out of my mind that night. If it weren't for you and Jessie, I don't think I could have gotten through it."

She shrugged. "Well, I didn't do much."

"Are you kidding? You broke the news to Amelia for me that her parents and Ina were dead. That was the last thing in the world I wanted to do. You drove her over here, and made sure she didn't get herself in trouble with the police. Even after what happened to you today—at your dad's rest home, and with Koehler—you're still in Amelia's corner. My niece is very lucky to have you for a friend. You're selling yourself short, Karen. I think you're terrific."

"Well, thank you, George," she said. She felt herself blushing. "I'll talk to you tomorrow, okay?"

George shook her hand, then lingered as she backed out of the driveway. He threw her a little wave. Karen blinked her headlights, and then started down the street.

She thought about him while driving to Sandpoint View and, for a few minutes, she actually wasn't scared. It didn't even occur to her to check the rearview mirror for the old black Cadillac.

All it took to jolt Karen back to scary reality was a long walk down that cold, dark, stale-smelling corridor at the rest home. She posted the snapshot of Amelia on the bulletin board at the nurses' station, along with a note: "If you see this young woman anywhere in or around here, please call me immediately. Many thanks, Karen Carlisle." She wrote her home and cell phone numbers at the bottom of the note.

She checked in on her dad, who was asleep. "G'night, Poppy," she whispered, kissing him on the forehead.

She chatted briefly with Rita, thanking her again for helping her earlier in the evening. Then she walked back out toward her car. The lot wasn't very well lit, and her eyes scanned the bushes bordering the rest home for anyone who might be lurking there. She had her key out, and picked up her pace the last few steps to the car. She made sure to check the backseat before climbing behind the wheel. Then she quickly shut the door and locked it.

All the way home, she kept glancing in the rearview mirror. No one seemed to be following her. Once she stepped inside the house, Karen switched on several lights. She took Rufus on a room-to-room check. While in Sheila's old room (now the guest room) she went into the closet. Her dad used to keep a gun under his bed, but when he'd started showing signs of depression and early Alzheimer's, Jessie and Karen had decided to hide the gun and bullets in another part of the house. They were inside a shoebox on the guest room closet shelf. If her dad had noticed the gun was missing, he hadn't said anything about it.

Karen dug the gun out of its hiding place. As far as she knew, her father had never fired the thing. The same clip had probably been inside the gun since 1987. She didn't know much about guns, but after so many years without use or maintenance, this one probably didn't work. Still, Karen felt better having it, especially when she crept down the basement stairs for the last round of her house check. She kept the gun pointed away from her toward the floor. The main part of the cellar had once been a recreation room for Karen's older brother and sister, but now it was just a storage area. The cheaply paneled walls used to be covered with posters that had come down decades ago. It was impossible to see the top of the Ping-Pong table, now loaded down with her old dollhouse, her brother's ancient 8-track tape player, and boxes of junk. Jessie kept the laundry room neat. But the latch was broken on the window above the big sink, and everyone at one time or another had used it to climb inside the house when they'd forgotten their keys. The furnace room was like something out of a horror movie. Even with a strong light, there were still dark areas behind the furnace, and a maze of pipes that cast shadows on the paint-chipped walls. Spiderwebs stretched across those old pipes. Jessie admitted she never cleaned that room. "You have to be a contortionist to make your way around that furnace. God knows what's back there; I don't even want to think about it. That's the creepiest room in this house." Karen agreed with her. And once she'd checked it, she hurried back up the stairs, shut the basement door, and locked it.

She let Rufus do his business in the backyard, while she stood, shivering at the back door. Then Karen heated up a Healthy Choice pizza for her late-night dinner in front of the TV and a mediocre *Saturday Night Live*. Of course, it was hard to laugh when she felt the need to keep a handgun tucked under the sofa cushion—*just in case*.

She'd fallen asleep on that sofa, with her dad's old robe over her and the gun beneath her. Rufus was curled up on the floor beside her. The TV and several lights remained on. The last thing she'd thought about was the gun. Did she really expect to use it, and on whom? Amelia?

Karen spent most of the morning on the phone with old contacts from Group Health, trying to track down psychiatrists who had experience with multiple personality disorder cases. *You can't be serious* was the most frequent response, and several people just laughed. But Karen did come up with a few names, and left some messages. She figured if Amelia was indeed suffering from MPD, then someone more qualified than herself had to be brought in—and soon. Karen felt out of her league here.

She had two client sessions scheduled that Sunday afternoon, and the second one was with Laird, who always complained about his love life.

"She ordered a Cosmopolitan with some fancy-schmancy-brand vodka, and all I had was a lousy Bud Light," Laird was saying of his most recent Internet date. "And afterward, she tells me we should split the tab fifty-fifty, and I'm like, the hell with that. She wasn't even pretty—"

The doorbell rang, and Rufus started barking. Karen got to her feet. "I'm sorry, Laird. I'll be right back. In the meantime, think about why this woman's prettiness, or lack of it, comes up as an issue here."

She stepped out to the foyer and shut the study door behind her. "Quiet, Rufus!" she called. She always kept him locked up in the kitchen when she had clients over. She wasn't expecting anyone. Amelia still hadn't called back. But it wouldn't have been like her to come over unannounced, anyway. Even with her emergency last week, Amelia had tried to call first.

Karen checked the peephole. "Damn it," she muttered, and then she opened the door.

Detective Russ Koehler stood on her front stoop, wearing a leather aviator jacket, khakis, and a smug expression. He had a tall beverage cup from Starbucks in his hand. "You told me to bring my checkbook next time I came by," he announced. "But I decided to bring a peace offering instead—a tall latte."

He tried to hand it to her, but Karen didn't move a muscle. She just stared at him.

"Listen, I admire the way you stuck up for your client yesterday. But if you really want to help Amelia, you'll cooperate with me. And you know something? I think you'll feel better once we've talked. We're going to connect, Karen. I'm feeling lucky about it. In fact, I have my lucky shirt on today."

Eyes narrowed, Karen glanced down at his shirt for a second: a white button-down oxford with wide stripes of blue that matched his eyes. She might have been attracted to him, if only he weren't such a snake. He held out the Starbucks cup again.

"C'mon, aren't you at least going to take my peace offering?"

"I'm in the middle of a session with a client right now," she said finally. "And you're interrupting."

"I can wait," he said with a crooked grin.

Karen started to shake her head. "Well, I'm afraid you . . ."

She fell silent at the sight of someone coming up the driveway toward them. She wore jeans, a red blouse, and a black cardigan, and nervously clutched a big leather purse to her side. Her hair was swept back and up from her neck with a barrette. "Amelia?" Karen whispered. She could see she was wearing makeup, a rarity for her. The crimson lipstick and dark mascara looked startling against her creamy complexion.

Koehler turned and glanced at the 19-year-old. Obviously he liked what he saw. Karen noticed the shift in his posture, and even with only a quarter of his face in view she saw a smirk on his face that was almost predatory. "Well, well, Amelia Faraday, at last we meet," he said.

Stopping a few steps from him, she seemed bewildered.

"This is Detective Russ Koehler, with the Seattle Police," Karen piped up.

Wide-eyed, she politely nodded at him.

He grabbed her hand and shook it. "Sorry for your loss. Listen, I'd really like to chat with you—"

"Amelia, I need to see you inside for a minute," Karen said loudly, cutting him off.

"Oh, okay," she murmured, still looking baffled. She turned away from Koehler and started toward the doorway.

But he took hold of her arm. "Now, wait a minute—"

From the doorway, Karen shot him a look. "What do you think you're doing?"

He froze for a moment, then let go of the 19-year-old. "Okay, fine," he grumbled. "Everything's cool."

"Wait here, please." Karen shut the door on Koehler, and ushered her into the house. "Come on, Amelia." Passing the study, she called out, "Laird? I'll be with you in a minute!"

They hurried into the kitchen. Rufus backed away, and barked at them. He even growled a little. "Stop that," Karen hissed. "You know Amelia, for God's sake."

"What's wrong with him?"

"I don't know," Karen said, reaching into the cookie jar. "Too much excitement around here, I guess." She fished out a dog biscuit, opened the basement door, and tossed it down the stairs. Rufus let out a final bark, then eagerly chased after the treat. Karen shut the basement door after him.

"Amelia, where have you been?" she whispered, taking hold of her arm. "I left you four messages yesterday."

"Oh, Karen, I'm so sorry," she said. "I needed to get away. So I rented a car and just started driving. I didn't check my messages. Please, don't be mad—"

"I'm not mad. I'm just confused, and worried about you." Karen patted her shoulder. "Listen, I need you to be honest with me about something. It's important. What were you doing yesterday around five o'clock?"

She shrugged. "I'm really not sure. I've been driving all over. I think I was up near Deception Pass, but that might have been earlier in the day. Why are you asking?"

"You didn't stop by the Sandpoint View Convalescent Home yesterday?"

She shook her head. "I don't even know where that is, Karen."

"Do you recall running down a gray stairwell to a basement area with a boiler room, and another room that was a storage area?"

She shook her head again. "No—"

"Think hard, Amelia. You don't remember a storage area

full of boxes and hospital equipment? There were broken lights on the ceiling, and it was dark. There was a fire door—"

"I don't know what you're talking about." She backed into the hallway.

"You don't have any memory of it at all? Not even fragments?"

"Goddamn it, no!" she cried angrily. "Why are you asking me all these fucking questions? Why are you picking on me?"

Dumbstruck, Karen stared at her. Amelia had never snapped at her like that before. And for a moment, Karen wondered if she was talking to the *other* Amelia right now. Between the makeup and her manner, she almost seemed like a different person. Then again, maybe Karen was looking too hard for a *different* Amelia right now.

She took a deep breath, and tried to smile. "I thought I saw you yesterday at the rest home where my father's staying," she said calmly. She took a small step toward her. "I— I must have been mistaken. I didn't mean to jump on your case."

"Well, you're scaring me, Karen," she said with a shaky voice. "I don't understand why you're acting like this. What happened?" She glanced toward the front door. "What's that police detective doing here?"

"If I seem on edge, he's one reason why," Karen explained. "He's *unofficially* investigating the deaths of your parents and aunt. By *unofficially*, I mean he's snooping around on his own without any backing from the police department. At least, he doesn't have any backing, yet. He's got a bunch of crazy theories and notions about what might have happened last weekend. This guy's bad news, Amelia. You shouldn't talk to him. And you don't have to—"

The doorbell rang. Rufus started barking and scratching on the other side of the basement door. The doorbell rang again and again until the chiming was continuous. The study door slid open, and Laird stuck his head out. "Is anyone going to answer that?" he asked, over the incessant ringing and the dog's yelping.

Karen moved down the hallway, and gave her client a gentle push back into the study. "Laird, I'll be with you in just one more minute. Sorry about the interruption." She shut the door to the study. "Rufus, can it!" she yelled. Then she swiveled around and yanked open the front door to find Russ Koehler, with his finger on the bell. "Do you mind?" she growled.

"As a matter of fact, I do mind," he replied, finally taking his finger off the doorbell. "I'm going to talk with your client whether you like it or not. And the more trouble you give me, the more trouble I'll make for you—and believe me, I can deliver on that."

Not backing down, Karen shook her head at him. "Amelia doesn't have to talk to you—"

"Oh, Karen, never mind, really, please," she interrupted. She touched Karen's shoulder as she edged past her toward Koehler. "I don't want you getting in trouble on my account. I'll talk to him. It'll be okay. Don't worry."

"No, Amelia, wait—"

But she hurried out the door.

Koehler took hold of her arm, and he grinned back at Karen. "You heard what Amelia said. *Don't worry.*" Then he led her toward the driveway. "My car's parked just down the block. We can go for a drive." He handed her the Starbucks container. "Could you use a tall latte? I bought it for Karen, but she didn't want it."

She took the drink, then glanced over her shoulder at Karen. "I'll call you later, okay?"

From her front door, Karen watched them start down the sidewalk together. "Damn it," she muttered.

They disappeared behind some tall hedges bordering the neighbor's yard. But she could still hear Russ Koehler talking. "You know, Amelia, I had no idea you were such a lovely girl. . . ."

Then his voice faded in the distance, and Karen couldn't hear him anymore.

"I swear, I don't remember much about that night at all," she said, quietly sobbing in the passenger seat.

She'd finished the latte he'd given her about ten minutes ago when they'd taken the Issaquah exit off Interstate 90, about a half hour east of Seattle. The empty container was in the cup holder between them. Russ had been a little worried about potential spilling on the plush interior of his new Audi TT Coupe (one of the benefits of marrying into money). He reminded her a few times to be careful with the coffee. Now he could relax a little, and he focused on getting a confession out of this tasty-looking young thing. He figured her Uncle George probably couldn't keep his hands off her. He couldn't really blame the guy, either. He was convinced the uncle had manipulated her into helping him kill his wife and her parents.

He'd asked that she show him where she'd gone on the night her parents and aunt had died. According to police reports, she'd driven to Snoqualmie Falls. But this Issaquah route was sure a screwy way of getting there. Following her instructions, he'd almost gotten lost on all these winding forest roads around Cougar Mountain Wildland Park. He'd finally pulled into a little alcove at the start of a hiking trail, and shut off the engine to his Audi. By the hiking path, there was a little sign with a cartoon of Dennis the Menace wearing a backpack, and the caption "Don't Be a Litterbug!" Only somebody had crossed out the *Don't*. No one else was parked in the area. The sun was just starting to set behind the tall evergreens to the west.

"Listen, Amelia, I'm going to make sure you get a break

for talking candidly with me," he said, letting his hand slide down from the gear shift to her seat. His pinky brushed against her thigh. "I'm very well connected. So you can tell me the truth, and we'll work something out. I don't really blame you. It was your uncle's idea, wasn't it?"

Her head down, she kept crying. She held her purse in her lap. "I haven't been able to talk to anyone about it, not even Karen."

"Is he screwing you?" Koehler asked.

Wincing, she nodded. "I'm so ashamed. My boyfriend, Shane, he's so sweet. I can't believe I've been doing this behind his back. But it's been going on for—for years now."

Koehler couldn't believe his luck. Incest and pedophilia now factored into the story. "How old were you when your uncle started in on you?"

She wept quietly, and set her purse down between the seat and her door. She wouldn't look him in the eye. She leaned forward, and didn't seem to realize it made her blouse open in front. Koehler could see one white, round breast, and the rose-colored nipple grazing at the fabric of her blouse.

He moved his hand to her thigh and stroked it. He was starting to get hard. "It's okay, Amelia. Take your time answering. I'm here for you."

Koehler couldn't stop staring at her breasts. He wanted so much to undo the rest of those buttons on her blouse. His head was swimming.

He didn't notice that she was reaching inside her purse.

All at once, she swung her arm out and hit him in the forehead with something hard. A searing pain shot through his head, and for a moment, all he could see was white. "Fuck!" he howled.

He touched his forehead and felt blood. It was trickling down into his left eye. Blinking, he tried to focus on her.

Then he noticed the gun in her hand.

* * *

"They left here together over two hours ago," Karen said into the phone. She was at her desk, behind stacks of work files. She'd been meaning to straighten them out for months. It was just the busywork she needed while waiting around for Amelia to call. So far, she'd reorganized the *A* through *D* patient records, had two cups of coffee, and given herself a paper cut.

"I tried calling Amelia an hour ago, and nothing," she continued. "I even called Koehler's cell phone, and there was no answer there either."

"I can't believe she went off with him," George muttered on the other end of the line.

"And voluntarily," Karen added. "I tried to stop her. Now all I can think about is Amelia making some sort of confession to that creep. I wasn't going to call you until I heard back from her. I didn't want to worry you for nothing. But now I . . ." She sighed. "Well, I thought you should know. Maybe you want to contact a lawyer or something."

"I appreciate it, Karen," he replied. She could hear the TV on and Stephanie laughing in the distant background. "Let's just wait it out for now. You're the only one Amelia has confessed to, for lack of a better word. She's a very smart young woman. She kept her mouth shut with the police and everyone else about her *visions*. Let's just hope she does the same thing with Koehler."

"You're right. I probably shouldn't have called you this soon."

"Nonsense, I'm glad you told me, Karen," he said. "Why should you be the only one who's worried? Besides, Amelia's my niece. Jody, Steph, and I are her only living relatives. Or maybe I should qualify that—only *known* living relatives. Listen, I've checked the Spokane and Pasco newspaper archives and still haven't come up with very much on Duane

Lee Savitt. All I know is that he was an auto mechanic and, according to the people who worked with him at this garage in Pasco, he pretty much kept to himself. No one seemed to really know him. He had a sister, Joy, who died a few weeks before his rampage at the adoption agency. I kept hoping to find the name of another surviving family member in one of the articles, but no dice. But there was something in his obituary in the Pasco *Tri-City Herald*. They mentioned he was buried at Arbor Heights Memorial Park in Salem, Oregon."

"Uh-huh," Karen said. "And—that's a lead?"

"Someone had to pay for the burial, and his headstone, if there is one. It's a pretty safe bet that person knew Duane, too. But so far, that party is nameless. I checked the office hours for Arbor Heights Memorial Park, and they're closed right now. But I'll get in touch with them tomorrow morning. Keep your fingers crossed they still have billing records from 1993."

"I will," Karen replied tentatively. "That—that's great, George."

She didn't want to remind him it was a long shot that Duane Lee Savitt had been Amelia's uncle. If he had been, and they discovered something in Amelia's childhood to explain her condition today, then George might be gathering evidence to exonerate his niece for murdering her parents, and his wife.

She wondered if George was aware of that. Or was he still so convinced of Amelia's innocence that such a notion hadn't even occurred to him?

Until yesterday, Karen had felt exactly the same way. It helped that George knew about Amelia going off with Koehler. And it helped that he was doing extensive research into what had happened at the adoption agency.

But Karen still felt as if she were the only one worried about Amelia—and what that young woman was capable of.

* * *

Russ Koehler was shivering. He wore a T-shirt, and nothing else. She'd made him strip off his shoes, socks, trousers, and underpants after they'd veered off the main hiking trial. Then she'd told him to remove his shirt and start tearing it into small, thin strips. Every forty or fifty feet that they stomped through those woods, branches from shrubs scraping at his naked legs, rocks and sticks chewing away at his cold, bare feet, she made him tie a strip from his shirt to a branch. He'd been marking a trail for her return trip.

"Once I feel we've walked far enough, I'm going to leave you here—alone," she explained coolly. "I'll take down these trail markings, so it's not going to be easy for you to find your way out. Even then, you won't have any money. You won't have your clothes or your precious car. And I'll be far, far away, where you won't ever find me."

Russ was ordinarily quite proud of his body, but now he clutched what was left of his shirt over his genitals. They were shrunken up from the cold. He felt so vulnerable with her walking behind him, staring at his naked ass. She didn't tease him, giggle, or make any lewd comments as they continued through the forest. She seemed so passionless, almost detached from everything. And that scared the shit out of him.

"Listen, Amelia," he said, glancing over his shoulder for a second. "Your plan isn't going to work. If you're on the run, you won't be able to collect your inheritance. Your uncle will get it all. Everyone will think you did it alone."

"Then do you think I might be better off if I just killed you here?" she asked, without a hint of irony or sarcasm in her voice.

"Jesus, no," he gasped. "No, no. I'm saying we can make a deal, and pin the brunt of it on your uncle. He manipulated you, didn't he? And I told you, I know people who have a lot of clout. . . ."

"Tie another strip to that evergreen branch, will you?" she said.

His hands shook violently as he tried to make a knot around the branch with the shirt strip. Russ glanced up at the darkening sky. Within a few minutes, the forest would be swallowed up in blackness, and he'd be lucky to see his hand in front of his face.

He turned to her, and clutched the torn shirt in front of his crotch. "I—I'm never getting out of here, am I?" he asked.

"Well, you have a lot of challenges," she said, the gun pointed at him. "You'll have bears, coyotes, and maybe even a cougar or two to contend with. Most of the real interesting creatures in these woods come out at night. Did you ever hear that story about the woman who went camping in the woods while she was having her period, and she got mauled to death by a bear? Apparently, the bear smelled the blood, and he tracked her down. So, I'd watch that cut on your forehead, Russ. It could be your death sentence out here. Now, turn around and keep walking. Just a little farther, we're almost there."

He stared at her for a moment. She was screwing around with him. He could tell. She planned to kill him in these woods. Turning, he continued to stagger through the brush. His feet were cold and bleeding. "Listen, Amelia," he said, starting to cry. "My wife just had a baby, for God's sake. You can't kill me . . . please. My son's only a week old."

"If your baby son's so important, why weren't you with him today? Why didn't you buy a station wagon instead of your flashy sports car?"

"Please . . ." he repeated. Just a few feet ahead, there was a small clearing in the forest. He noticed a large, oblong rock on the ground. It was about the size of his fist. He imagined bashing her brains in with that rock, once he had her down.

He weaved forward and continued to make sobbing noises for her benefit. He was banking on the element of surprise. She wouldn't expect a weeping, sniveling man to suddenly attack her. The rock was just in front of him now. He stumbled, then hurled himself to the ground. He even let out a defeated cry. Then he grabbed the rock.

A loud shot rang out.

The rock flew from his gasp. A spray of blood hit him in the face. It felt as if his hand had exploded. He howled in pain. Grabbing his wrist, he brought his hand up to his face so he could focus on it.

To his horror, Russ Koehler saw a bloody, bone-exposed stub where his index finger used to be.

"You fucking bitch!" he yelled, real tears streaming down his face. Curled up on the ground, he held onto his mangled hand, and glared at her.

Expressionless, she stood over him with the gun.

"Goddamn you!" he hissed. "You've been jerking me around for the last hour, and I've known it. You have no intention of leaving me alive in these woods."

She nodded. "You're right about that."

"You're stupid," he said, gasping for air. "Everyone on the police force knows I'm checking on you. When I disappear, they'll figure out it was you. And when they find my body—"

"Oh, they won't find you, not right away," she cut in. "What I was telling you earlier about all the wild animals in these woods, that wasn't bullshit. They'll take care of you, the hungry ones. They're always hungry. Some of them will even bury your bones. I learned that from *him*. He didn't bury every one of them, you know. Sometimes, he just let nature take its course. If there's enough exposed flesh and enough blood—and enough carnivorous creatures around to smell it—then, it isn't always that necessary to bury a dead body."

"Jesus, you're insane," he murmured, still curled up on the ground. "Did you hear what I said, Amelia? You're in-fucking-sane, you stupid—"

"I'm not Amelia," she said. "I'm Annabelle. And you're the one who's stupid—for not seeing that earlier."

Wide eyed, he stared at her as she aimed the gun at him again. "NO! NO, WAIT! GOD, PLEASE. . . ." He screamed and screamed. But there was no one around to hear him.

And no one heard the gun go off . . . three times.

"Hello?"

Karen heard a baby crying in the background on the other end of the line. "Yes, hello," she said. "Is Russ Koehler there, please?"

"Who is this?" Mrs. Koehler asked, sounding haggard.

"My name is Karen Carlisle." She glanced at her wristwatch: 10:35. "Um, I'm sorry to call so late, but I've been trying to get ahold of your husband, and he's not answering his cell phone."

"I know, I've been trying to reach him too," she replied. "What's this about? How do you know Russ?"

"He came by my office today regarding an investigation," Karen explained. She figured the less she said about it, the better. She decided not to mention Amelia, who still hadn't gotten in touch with her. "Um, Detective Koehler was supposed to call me back, and never did. I was just checking in."

"Well, he isn't here," Mrs. Koehler said abruptly. "If you happen to hear from him, Miss—"

"Carlisle," Karen finished for her.

"Yes. Well, tell him his wife and son are waiting up for him."

Karen heard a click on the other end of the line, and then—nothing.

Chapter Twelve

"Your homework assignment this week is to be good to yourself," Karen said, walking out of her office with her last patient of the day. Cecilia was a divorced forty-something woman with curly gray-brown hair and low self-esteem. Karen opened the front door for her. "List ten things you consider life's little pleasures and do three of them for yourself this week. Treat yourself, okay?"

Nodding, Cecilia smiled at her. "Okay, Karen. Thanks. See you next Monday."

Ordinarily, Karen would have gone back into her study and jotted down some notes about the session, but she still hadn't heard back from Amelia. Twenty-four hours, and still no word. No one had heard from her—not George, Shane, or Amelia's roommate.

Karen always switched off her cellular and set the home phone answering machine for immediate pickup during client sessions. Between each of her three sessions today, she'd anxiously checked her messages.

With Cecilia out the door, Karen made a beeline to her

purse, which was on the chair in the front hallway. She dug out her cell phone and clicked on the messages display. There was one. She recognized Amelia's cell phone number. She knew it by heart, now. Karen pressed the playback code. "Hi, Karen. You're not answering at home, either. You must be with a client. Um, looks like you called me a bunch of times. Sorry, but I've been out of town, and I switched off my phone. I just had to get away from everything and everyone. Shane and my Uncle George left a ton of messages too. I didn't mean to worry you guys. Anyway, I'm back. Call me, and I'll answer this time, I promise! Bye."

Baffled, Karen played the message again. It didn't make sense. Amelia was acting as if yesterday with Koehler had never even happened.

She hit the last caller return, and Amelia answered after two rings. "Karen, is that you?"

"Hi, Amelia. I just got your message."

"And I just got all of yours. Sorry if I gave you a scare. I should have told you—"

"You were out of town?" Karen asked, cutting her off.

"Yes. I rented a car and drove up and down the coast. Now that my credit card's working again, I—"

"And you just got back *today*?"

"Yes, about an hour ago. I blew off a morning class. Why? What's going on, Karen?"

"Did you happen to have a blackout over the weekend? Any lost time?"

"Why do you ask that?" Amelia replied, a sudden edge in her voice.

"Well, I . . ." Karen trailed off at the sound of someone on the front stoop. Rufus started barking in the kitchen. Then the doorbell rang. "Amelia, just a minute," she said, moving to the door. She glanced through the peephole to see a petite, very pretty black woman and a stocky, Caucasian man in his late forties with a bad comb-over. From their somber expressions, office clothes, and the odd pairing, Karen figured they were police detectives.

She backed away from the door. "Listen, Amelia," she whispered into the phone. Rufus's barking competed with her. "I have to call you back."

"Karen, for God's sake, you can't just ask me if I've had a blackout, then say you'll call me back. What's going on? Did something happen over the weekend that I should know about?"

"I can't talk right now," Karen whispered urgently. "There are people at my front door. I'll call you back as soon as I can." She clicked off the line. "Rufus, calm down!" she yelled. Then she opened the door, and put on her best cordial smile for the two of them. "Can I help you?" She still clutched the cell phone in her hand.

The woman flashed her police badge. "Karen Carlisle?"

She nodded. "Yes?"

"Good afternoon, I'm Jacqueline Peyton and this is Warren Rooney." Behind her, the man gave a little nod. Neither one of them cracked a smile. "We're with the Seattle Police," she continued. "We're hoping you might help us locate a missing person. I understand Detective Russ Koehler was here yesterday afternoon."

Karen stared at them and blinked. "He's *missing*?"

"Was he here yesterday afternoon?" the woman pressed.

Karen nodded more times than necessary. "Um, yes, he showed up around this time yesterday—two o'clock. He was here for about ten minutes."

"Mrs. Koehler said you telephoned her last night."

"Yes, I thought I'd be hearing back from him, and never did." Karen opened the door wider. "I'm sorry. Would you like to come in?"

The two detectives stepped inside the foyer. Karen closed the door after them. The cell phone went off in her hand, and she glanced at the caller ID: Amelia again.

She switched off the phone and stashed it in her purse. "I always thought a certain amount of time had to go by—like forty-eight or seventy-two hours—before the police considered anyone officially missing."

The man shook his head. "In Washington State, there's no waiting period. He's been missing since yesterday afternoon. And at three o'clock this morning, we picked up a DUI driving Koehler's car, a brand-new Audi. He claims he found it—abandoned, unlocked with the keys inside—on Aurora Boulevard."

"What was the nature of Detective Koehler's visit here?" the woman asked.

Karen hesitated. She remembered Koehler walking off with Amelia yesterday. "My car's parked just down the block," he'd told her. "We can go for a drive."

"Ms. Carlisle?" the policewoman said.

Karen folded her arms in front of her. "Um, I'm a therapist, and Detective Koehler was asking about one of my clients, Amelia Faraday. I believe he was conducting some sort of follow-up investigation into the deaths of her parents and aunt in Wenatchee last week." She figured this wasn't any news to them. George had already told her that other cops on the force knew about Koehler's interest in the case. But they didn't know Koehler had driven off yesterday afternoon with Amelia.

She needed to talk to Amelia before the police did.

"I'm afraid I wasn't much help," Karen added. "I told Detective Koehler it would be unethical to repeat anything a patient shared with me during a session. Not that there's anything to conceal. I've read the newspaper reports, and I don't think Amelia held back on anything when she spoke to the police."

The policewoman cocked her head to one side. Her eyes narrowed at her. "When Detective Koehler left here yesterday, did he indicate where he was going?"

Karen shrugged. "I have no idea where he was headed." All the while, she thought, *God, I'm lying to the police now.*

"But he said he'd call you," the man interjected. "What about?"

Karen shrugged again. "I'm not sure, actually. He didn't specify the reason."

"And when you didn't hear from him, you tried calling him."

She nodded. "That's right."

"You told Mrs. Koehler you'd been trying his cell before phoning his home." The cop finally cracked a tiny smile. "Sounds like you felt his calling back was pretty darn important."

Karen swallowed hard. "I just didn't like the idea of having unfinished police business hanging over my head at the end of the day," she answered carefully.

Neither one of the detectives seemed to be buying her story. The woman cleared her throat. "Ms. Carlisle—Karen, you don't have to answer this. But it would be a big help to us. Do you have a—a *personal* relationship with Russ Koehler?"

"With Detective Koehler?" She let out a little laugh. "God, no, I only just met him the day before yesterday. What, did his wife think that I—"

"Do you suppose Koehler went to see Amelia Faraday after leaving here?" the man asked, cutting her off.

"Um, I really can't say," Karen replied, shrugging.

"Do you have a contact address and phone number for Ms. Faraday?" he asked.

"Yes, I have that on file. I'll write it down for you." She retreated into her office, took a deep breath, then looked up Amelia's campus address and phone number. She scribbled down the information, then returned to the foyer and gave the piece of paper to the policewoman. "That's her room number in Terry Hall, along with the phone there."

The woman took it. "You don't happen to have her cell phone number, do you?"

Karen hesitated. "Um, I . . ."

"Never mind," she said. "This is good enough. Thank you for your time, Ms. Carlisle."

As soon as Karen ushered them out the door, she ducked back inside, and dug her cell phone out of her purse again. Amelia answered on the first ring. Karen asked her if she was in her room at the dorm.

"Yeah," Amelia replied. "Why did you ask me if I had a blackout? What's going on?"

"Listen," Karen said. "Do me a favor. Finish up whatever you're doing there and get out. Some people might be on their way to see you, and it's best you don't talk to them until I meet with you. Don't answer the phone either. I'll meet you in twenty minutes at the U Library, the Graduate Reading Room. Don't tell anyone else where you're going, okay?"

"Well, okay, I guess. But I wish I knew what the hell was going on."

"I'll explain everything when I see you. Take care."

Karen clicked off the line. Then she headed to the closet and grabbed her coat.

"So, the way I understand it, your niece was adopted through the agency when she was four and, within a month, this Duane Lee Savitt character walked into the adoption place, shot three employees, and set their offices on fire. Is that about right?"

George nodded. He stood by Professor Lori Kim's desk and watched her load her briefcase with books and papers. Her Family and Juvenile Law class had just let out, and the classroom was empty except for the two of them. Lori Kim was a stout Asian woman in her late thirties. She had a few gray streaks in her close-cropped hair and wore designer glasses with her dark-blue power suit. Lori's brisk, no-nonsense manner was occasionally punctuated by a sweet, disarming smile. George had called a few friends at the university, and had heard Professor Kim had a background in law enforcement as well as child psychology.

"I'm wondering if there's a connection between this girl and the shootings at the adoption agency," George explained. "I heard you know something about adoption laws. Do you think Savitt might have gone to the agency, trying to track down the child? At the same time, he torched the place, so I'm wondering if he wanted to destroy records that might link him with one particular child."

"That one particular child being your niece?" Lori Kim asked.

"It's a stretch, yes. But she does have vague memories of an Uncle Duane. "

Professor Kim zipped up her briefcase. "Do you mind if we walk and talk? I have a dental appointment at two-fifteen, and my car's parked on the other side of the campus."

"Not at all," George replied. "In fact, I'll even carry your briefcase for you. I was hoping to get some information on my niece's biological parents, but—"

"Oh, that won't be easy," she cut in. She unloaded the briefcase on him, and it was damn heavy. "Those records are closed in Washington State."

George had already found that out the hard way. He'd been on the phone for two hours this morning with several government agencies, talking to a lot of apathetic, curt, and often rude clerks who had told him the same thing: the information he wanted was "confidential . . . unavailable . . . restricted." Finally, he'd given up and started phoning people, asking if there was a professor who knew a lot about adoption procedures. He hoped against hope that Lori Kim might know a way for him to get past all the legal stumbling blocks.

Lugging the briefcase, he walked down the corridor with

her on the law school's second floor. She moved at a brisk clip. "If your niece remembers an Uncle Duane before she was adopted by your in-laws, it means she had to be at least three or four years old before she lost her parents—or they gave her up. It's unusual that she'd end up adopted through an agency. She should have gone through the foster care system."

"She did spend time in some foster homes before my in-laws took her," George said. They ducked into the stairwell and started down the steps. "I was still dating Amelia's aunt when Amelia's parents were going through the adoption process. They lived in Spokane at the time. But I know they had a lot of visits back and forth, and a trial period."

"That's how they do it in foster care. Maybe the adoption agency was involved for some other reason." Professor Kim stopped at the bottom of the steps. "You said your niece spent time in other foster homes. Did the child have any problems or disorders?"

He nodded. "She had frequent nightmares, and she got these phantom pains and illnesses. She practically drove her parents nuts. But that didn't start up until after the adoption went through. By then my in-laws had moved to Bellingham and had a baby boy of their own. We figured Amelia was just vying for their attention."

Lori Kim frowned. "Then again, maybe those nightmares and phantom pains were what got the child bounced out of one foster home and into the next. Might even be why her real parents gave up on her. Children learn very quickly. Your niece might have been on her best behavior with your in-laws during that trial period. When she saw her baby brother cried without getting the boot, she might have figured it was safe to let her pain and fear be heard."

They stepped outside into the sun and a cool autumn breeze. This section of the campus was graced with stately old buildings and magnificent trees with their leaves changing. The grounds were bathed in a riot of fall colors. Classes were in session, so there wasn't the usual mob scene. Only a few students and teachers lingered about.

"Of course, I'm just speculating," Professor Kim continued, as they walked along a paved pathway across the leaf-scattered lawn. "Once in a while, if the foster system has problems placing a child, they may turn to an adoption agency for assistance. It's possible that's what happened with your niece."

"I always assumed Amelia's biological parents were dead," George remarked. "But you mentioned they might have just given her up. Do you think they could still be alive?"

"Anything's possible," Lori Kim replied. "If you want me to come up with a potential reason for why this Duane Lee Savitt did what he did, I can give you about a dozen different scenarios."

"Give me your best one."

"Well, since there weren't any state, city, or county records connecting Savitt with the adoption agency, I'd say he wasn't the child's legal father. But there's a chance he was the birth father. The mother could have lied about it on the birth certificate and transfer papers. Savitt may have also been your niece's natural uncle, just as she remembers. But once again, they didn't come across his name in any records, which means he was most likely a family friend or possibly a blood uncle on the mother's side, and she was married. The maiden names aren't always flagged on those records."

George nodded. "Savitt had a sister named Joy who died just a few weeks before he went berserk at the adoption agency."

Lori Kim stopped abruptly. "It's strange that Savitt waited until the mother died before he tried to track down the child."

"Well, maybe he tried to get custody after his sister died—"

"There would be a record of that," she argued. "You said

Savitt shot up the adoption place less than a month after your niece was officially adopted. But under the foster care system, it's a gradual process toward the final adoption. And you said your niece had some false starts in other foster homes. So she had to be in foster care for at least three months, which means the mother was still alive, and therefore gave up the child. Maybe she was too sick to take care of her at the time. One thing for sure, she didn't want her brother to have the girl or she would have given him custody. So, obviously, Savitt waited until his sister was dead before he went searching for his niece. And when he came to the agency, looking for her—"

"They couldn't tell him where she'd gone, because those adoption records are closed," George finished for her. "So, Uncle Duane went crazy."

"Well, I don't quite agree with you on that," she said, resuming her quick gait along the path. "I doubt he'd armed himself for his first trip to that agency. He probably went there once to make inquiries, became frustrated, and then returned with his arsenal."

George got winded carrying the heavy briefcase and trying to keep up with her. "You know, it's weird the police couldn't figure this out."

"Well, they couldn't connect him to anyone at that agency. But you have—if you're right about him being this girl's uncle. And so far, we're just hypothesizing."

"Why do you think he burned the place down?"

"Did any of those articles you read say if he used hollow-point bullets to shoot those people?"

"Yeah. How did you know—"

"Hollow-points are the bullets of choice for most mass murderers. Only God knows what other function they serve. Hunters don't use them. Hollow-points inflict the most damage. And that's probably why Duane Savitt set fire to the place, to inflict the most damage."

"You don't think he was trying to destroy some records?"

"It's possible. But if he was really related to your niece, those same records would be in the foster care system, and he should have known that. Then again, you're trying to figure out the logic of some asshole who took it upon himself to shoot three people who never did a single thing to hurt him. I hope I never comprehend the way someone like that thinks."

"If those records exist in the foster care system, how can I get to them?" George pressed. "You must know some way."

"Get your lawyer, get your niece, and file a petition."

"There's no alternate route?"

"Try to track down someone who knew Uncle Duane."

"I'm giving that a shot right now," George replied. "One of the articles I read mentioned he was buried in a cemetery in Salem, Oregon. I'm trying to track down whoever paid for the plot and the tombstone, if there is one. I figure this person must know Duane pretty well."

"That's good thinking," she said. They headed toward a small parking lot.

"I called the cemetery office this morning," George explained. "The guy there said they *might* be able to help me if I come down tomorrow and talk to him in person."

"Sounds like someone wants his palm greased. Bring money." Professor Kim took her key out of her purse and unlocked the driver door to her blue Geo. "Did you think I'd have some connection, a shortcut way of getting the lowdown on your niece's biological parents?"

George gave her the briefcase. "I'd be lying if I said I wasn't hoping for that."

"Sorry, George," Professor Kim said. She tossed her briefcase onto the passenger seat, and then climbed behind the wheel.

"You were still a lot of help. Thanks."

"Have a nice trip to Salem. And if you end up meeting that friend of Duane's, would you find out something for me?"

"What's that?" he asked.

"Find out why Duane waited until his sister was dead to go looking for the girl. Or maybe I should say to go *hunting* for the little girl. I have a feeling that's closer to what he had in mind. Good luck, George." She shut the door, started up the car and backed out of the parking spot.

George watched her drive away until the car disappeared around a curve in the winding road.

"Karen, I swear, I didn't get back to town until this morning," Amelia whispered.

They sat at the end of a beautiful long wood table. There were twenty matching tables in the Graduate Reading Room of UW's Suzzallo Library arranged like pews in a church, ten on each side. The tall stained-glass windows, ornate hanging light fixtures, and cathedral ceiling inspired quiet meditation. Bookcases were pressed against the stone walls. There were at least sixty other students in the library, and only the slightest murmuring could be heard among them.

Amelia looked pretty in a lavender sweater and khakis. She wasn't wearing much makeup today, and she had her hair pulled back in a ponytail. "I was driving around Olympic National Park yesterday afternoon," she told Karen in a hushed voice. "That's as close to Seattle as I got. I ended up spending last night at a B & B in Port Angeles. I can show you the receipt if you don't believe me. It's in my other purse."

"So, you don't remember coming by my place yesterday?" Karen asked.

Amelia adamantly shook her head.

"We talked in the kitchen," Karen said, trying to jog her memory. "Rufus was acting strange, growling at us."

Amelia glanced down at the library table and frowned. "I'm sorry."

"And you never met a Detective Koehler? The name isn't even familiar?"

"No."

"He gave you coffee, and took you for a drive. . . ."

Amelia brought a hand up to her mouth, and stared back at Karen. "He gave me coffee?" she repeated.

Karen nodded. "Koehler's tall and good-looking with pale-blond hair. He's got a very cocky smile. . . ."

"Are his eyes blue?" she asked.

"Yes," Karen whispered, leaning forward.

"His eyes match the blue stripes in his shirt," Amelia murmured, staring down at the tabletop.

"Yes, that's right."

"I make him take it off and tear it into strips," Amelia continued, almost in a trance. "He ties the pieces of his shirt onto branches in the forest. They're markers. I—I'll need to find my way back to the main trail after I kill him."

Karen swallowed hard. She waited a moment before saying anything. "What forest, Amelia?"

She gazed at Karen. Her lip quivered. "This really happened, didn't it? Oh, Jesus!"

A student one desk down loudly cleared his throat and scowled over his textbook at them.

"I need you to remember, Amelia," Karen whispered. She stroked her arm. "It'll be okay. We're going to work this out. Do you remember where you where? What forest?"

"God, Karen, you must be right," Amelia said, under her breath. "I don't remember being at your house at all, but I was with him. We were driving for long time. He was worried about me spilling coffee in his new car. I remember keeping my purse shut and in my lap most of the time. I—I didn't want him to see that I had a gun in there." She shook her head. "It doesn't make sense. Karen, I don't own a gun. . . ."

"You mentioned Olympic National Park," Karen pressed. "Was this forest anywhere around there?"

Tears brimmed in her eyes. "No. Oh, God, Karen, this is so screwed up. How could I think I was in one place and be in another? I didn't have anything to drink at all yesterday, I swear. . . ."

"We'll straighten all that out. Just try to remember where you went with Koehler."

"Cougar Mountain Park, over in Issaquah," she replied numbly. "It's nowhere near where I thought I was. But I remember the signs for the park. We walked at least a mile before we veered off the trail."

"They have a lot of hiking trails there. Do you recall which one it was? Did it have a name?"

Amelia shook her head. "I'm sorry."

"Do you remember where you parked, or the name of the road you took there? Anything?"

Amelia closed her eyes for a moment. "It was, um, Newcastle-Coal Creek Road," Amelia whispered. "I remember the turnoff. We went to the fourth or fifth little parking area off that road. At the start of the trail, there's a small sign with a cartoon of Dennis the Menace on it. I don't remember what the sign said, but someone wrote on it. We—we were parked there for a while. He started touching me, and I—I hit him!" Her voice cracked. "God, I hit him with that gun."

Several people shushed her. Karen quickly helped Amelia to her feet. "C'mon, let's get out of here."

"And then later, in the forest, I shot him." Amelia cried, clutching Karen's arm. "He was begging for his life and I shot him in the head. . . ."

People were staring as Karen hurried Amelia down the aisle between the rows of tables. By the time they stepped outside together, Amelia was sobbing and recounting—in fragments—what had happened in that forest. She'd left Koehler's seminaked corpse where she'd shot him four times. She'd found her way back to the main trail, but didn't remember removing any of the homemade markers from the branches and shrubs along the way. She'd taken Koehler's car, and by then it had grown dark. She didn't remember anything until she was back in Seattle, catching a bus in a sketchy neighborhood along Aurora Boulevard.

"I don't understand it," Amelia said, shaking her head over and over. They sat down on a park bench outside the library. "I woke up this morning at a B & B all the way over in Port Angeles. I could have sworn I spent all of yesterday there. Karen, if you saw me with this man yesterday, and I remember all these horrible things, then they must have really happened. Do you see what that means? I killed this guy. And I probably killed my parents and Aunt Ina and my brother—"

"We don't know that yet," Karen said, rubbing her back. "You could be wrong about what happened to Koehler. You can't hold yourself accountable, not until I've looked into this further. Are you listening to me? You're not responsible for killing anyone, Amelia. We'll work this out together, but you'll have to trust me."

Amelia's cell phone went off—a low hum. Wiping her eyes, she reached inside her purse and checked the caller ID. "It's that policewoman again, the one you told me about," she said, her voice raspy. "Same number as last time."

"Don't answer it. I don't want you talking to her or anyone else until we figure out what really happened. Let her leave another message." She patted Amelia's arm. "Listen, I think it's best you lay low and stay at my place tonight. But I need to check out your story first."

"What, are you driving to Port Angeles?"

"No, Cougar Mountain Park." She glanced up at the sky. "And I'd like to get there before dark."

"You can't go alone," Amelia said. "I should go with you."

"No, you shouldn't. If something really did happen in that forest yesterday, you're in no condition to relive it. I'll be back by six if traffic isn't too nuts." Karen got to her feet, and so did Amelia. "You'll probably need some overnight things. Let's swing by the dorm. We'll call Shane and see if he can take you someplace for the next two or three hours. Maybe you guys can take in a movie."

Amelia nodded. She pressed the keypad on her cell phone, and then listened to her voice mail. "Oh, no," she murmured. "That policewoman, she and her partner are at the dorm now, waiting for me."

"What?" Karen asked.

"She said she's calling from the lobby downstairs at Terry Hall, and they want to ask me some questions."

"Damn," she whispered, rubbing her forehead. "Okay, call Shane. Tell him we need him to do something for us right away."

Twenty-five minutes later, Shane emerged from the crowd in Red Square, the campus's redbrick-paved central plaza and hub. He ambled toward them with a backpack slung over his shoulder. His blond hair was covered up with a stocking cap, and he wore a T-shirt over a long-sleeved T, and baggy jeans.

Jumping up from the park bench, Amelia ran to Shane and embraced him. They kissed feverishly. Amelia broke away, nodded toward Karen, and whispered something to him. Then holding hands, they approached her together.

Karen stood up. "Thanks, Shane. Did you have any problems?"

"Pulled it off without a hitch," he said with a crooked grin. "You were right though, Karen. The two of them were sitting in the lobby—a nice-looking black chick, and this older white guy with Donald Trump hair. They looked like total narcs. But they hardly paid any attention to my coming and going."

"Did you remember my robe?" Amelia asked with her arm linked around his. "And my copy of *Washington Square*? I need it for English Lit."

He kissed her forehead and pointed to his backpack. "It's all in there, along with your black jeans, the pink T-shirt you sleep in, and everything else you wanted. I called the Neptune Theater while I was in your room. They're showing a new print of *The 400 Blows* at 4:15. We're all set."

Karen glanced up at the sky, and guessed she only had about an hour of sunlight left. She didn't want to start hiking down that forest trail after dusk. "Um, Shane, can I talk to you for a moment?" she asked.

"Sure, Karen, what's up?" he said, uncoupling with Amelia for a moment, and stepping toward her.

"I need you to be very, very careful," she whispered. "This may sound strange, but—"

"Are you telling him that I'm *dangerous*?" Amelia asked in a loud voice.

Karen looked at her and sighed. "Amelia—"

"You should. He won't believe it if I tell him." Her voice cracked. "So warn him, Karen. Tell him to watch out for me. I don't want to hurt him, okay?"

Karen patted Shane's shoulder. "Amelia's right," she said in a low voice. "You need to keep an eye on her. If you notice a sudden change or a severe mood swing, call me."

He chuckled. "Are you shitting me, Karen?"

"I'm serious, Shane," she whispered. "You have my number, don't you?

He nodded. The lopsided smile ran away from his face.

"Stay in public places with her," Karen warned. "Make sure there are always other people around. Don't let her out of your sight for a minute. I'll see you in two or three hours."

"Okay, Karen, sure thing," he murmured. He looked like a hurt, confused little boy as he backed away from her. He slung his arm around Amelia again, and gave her another kiss on the forehead.

"Whatever she told you," Amelia said, "it's true. Okay?"

"Sure, it's cool," he muttered. But he wouldn't look at Karen. "C'mon, sweetheart, let's get out of here. We'll be late for the movie."

They started walking away. Amelia glanced over her shoulder. "Karen, be safe, okay?"

She nodded, and then watched them merge into the crowd of people mingling around Red Square. Karen glanced up at the sky again, and saw clouds moving across the slate-colored horizon. She didn't have much time.

All too soon, it would be dark.

Chapter Thirteen

The other cars on Newcastle-Coal Creek Road had their headlights on. Karen reluctantly switched her lights on, too. It was like admitting defeat. She'd hoped to reach the hiking trail in Cougar Mountain Park before nightfall. But traffic on I-90 had been miserable, and the thirty-mile trip had taken nearly two hours.

Now it grew darker by the minute. Driving along the snaky, wooded road, she'd passed three parking areas for hikers and other visitors entering the wildlife area. Only a few cars occupied those lots, a bad sign, not many hikers left. As much as she didn't need an audience for this gruesome expedition, Karen loathed the thought of being completely alone in those woods. It would have been nice to know someone was at least within screaming distance.

Karen slowed down as she drove past the fourth parking area: only one car, and no signs posted by the trail. Amelia had said they'd pulled into the fourth or fifth bay.

Biting her lip, Karen watched for the next parking area. She almost missed it, and had to slam on the brakes to turn in to the small, unlit alcove. There were only six spaces, and no other cars. She couldn't even see the beginning of a trail. But then it was awfully dark.

She reached into the glove compartment for the flashlight, and then climbed out of the car. She glanced over at the trees and bushes bordering the alcove, and finally noticed a gap in the foliage. She saw a sign with a cartoon of Dennis the Menace, carrying a backpack. From the distance, Karen couldn't read it in the dark. She shined the flashlight on it: "Don't Be a Litterbug!" Someone had crossed out the *Don't*. It was just as Amelia had said.

Karen couldn't help wondering if everything else Amelia had told her would turn out to be true.

She kept the flashlight on, took a deep breath, and started down the trail. She could hear some people talking not very far away, and that made her feel a bit safer, but only for a few minutes. Soon, she saw them heading toward her, a middle-aged couple wearing hiking gear. They gave her a puzzled look, and Karen realized how odd she must have appeared, on a hiking trail, dressed in her black blazer and slacks, and a blue tuxedo blouse. "You aren't just getting started, are you?" the man asked with concern.

"I'm only going for a mile or so," Karen said. "There are still other hikers around, aren't there?"

"I think you have the place to yourself," the man replied. "We're finishing up."

"Be careful," the woman said ominously. "There are bears in these woods at night, and cougars. It's not called Cougar Mountain Park for nothing."

"Thanks," Karen said with a pale smile. "Good night."

They continued on, and Karen could hear the woman clicking her tongue against her teeth. "Stupid girl . . . at this hour . . . Just wait, we'll hear it on the news tomorrow that she's missing or dead."

Karen trudged on through the gloomy woods. She kept the flashlight directed on the path in front of her. She guessed it would be at least another five minutes before she should start looking for the trail markers Amelia had told her about.

She didn't hear anyone else in the forest, just leaves and bushes rustling in the night wind. Karen felt dread in the pit of her stomach. She tried to brace herself for what she might find. Having volunteered at the rest home for the last few months, she'd seen her share of dead bodies, and had cleaned up blood after several messy accidents. She told herself that she could get through this. She simply had to be dispassionate about it. And, if she found Koehler's corpse, she would turn around, go back to her car, and call George. The two of them would figure out what to do from there.

She started shining the light on the bushes and trees that hovered over both sides of the crude, snakelike path. She didn't see any trail markers, just a few squirrels and raccoons. Their eyes looked iridescent in the flashlight's glow as they gazed at her, and then scurried away. Karen checked her wristwatch. Only 6:20, but it felt like midnight. If she didn't find one of Amelia's markers by 6:35, she'd quit and turn back.

She almost tripped on a tangle of tree roots across her path. And then she heard something that made her stop. Twigs snapped underfoot. "Is anyone there?" Karen called. The noise was unmistakably someone—or *something*—prowling through the bushes. They didn't stop, and they didn't answer her, either. "Hello?" Karen called nervously.

She directed the flashlight in the general area where the noise was coming from. But she didn't see anyone. The sound was fading. The trees and bushes seemed to move as the beam of light swept across them. Then Karen saw it—only a few feet away. A piece of white fabric with a blue stripe was tied to the low-hanging branch of a small, bare brittle-looking tree. She made her way through the brush to get a closer look. She remembered the fabric pattern from yesterday. Koehler had said it was his lucky shirt.

Standing very still, she listened for a moment. Whatever she'd heard earlier, it was gone now. Karen shined the light in the trees, searching for the second piece of Koehler's lucky shirt. She found it through the thick overgrowth, about thirty feet away. She seemed headed in the right direction, but there was no real path. It was nearly impossible to navigate her way in the dark. At one point, she walked right into a branch, and just missed scratching her eye. Touching her cheek, she glanced at her fingertip and saw blood. "Good one, Karen," she muttered, pressing on.

Part of her wanted to turn back. Amelia had been right about everything so far. Karen knew she was close to finding Koehler's corpse. Did she really need to see it? Once she set eyes on it, she'd have to call the police. And then how would she be any help to Amelia?

Still, she forged ahead, following one trail marker after another. She'd counted seventeen of them, and guessed by now she was about a quarter of a mile off the trail she'd started on. Karen found another rough trail, and then came upon a clearing, a little bald spot in the woods, no more than ten or twelve square feet. With her flashlight, she scanned the tree branches for the next marking, but there wasn't one. She had no idea which direction to go from there.

Something darted across the ground in front of her. Karen gasped and tried to catch a look at it with her flashlight. But the thing scampered by so quickly all she saw was a shadow before it was gone. "Relax," she said to herself. "Probably just a rabbit."

She still had the flashlight directed on the forest floor when she noticed something else amid the leaves, twigs, and dirt. One part of the ground was darker, as if stained. The leaves were a different color. Karen took a step closer. Something smelled horrible—like death. She knew that putrid odor from the nursing home. It filled the room when a patient had died.

With the light shining on that dark patch, she could see some of the leaves were the burgundy color of dried blood. Part of the ground was covered with a slimy substance that had attracted bugs. Was this where Amelia had left Koehler's corpse? No doubt, some person or thing had been there for a while. It had started to decay before being moved. Karen wondered if a bear, or maybe even a cougar, had dragged off the carcass.

The fetid smell was too much for her, and she backed away. Shaking, she felt sick to her stomach.

Karen took a few deep breaths, then scanned the forest floor with the flashlight's beam. She was looking for a mound of dirt that might indicate a grave, or maybe even a piece of clothing. But there was nothing.

Still, she knew Amelia must have killed Koehler on this spot. It was where the lucky-shirt markers ended.

She heard something—a rustling sound, and twigs snapping again. She made a wide arc around the slimy patch of ground and directed the flashlight into the woods on the other side. The sound seemed to be coming from that direction. Karen could see only the first row of illuminated bushes and trees. Beyond that, it was just blackness. She thought she saw a bush move. Or was it just the shadows playing a trick on her. "Who's there?" she called.

The rustling noise abruptly stopped. Karen realized no forest creature would freeze up like that. This was a person.

She was paralyzed for a moment, waiting for the next sound.

All at once, there was a shuffling noise, footsteps.

Karen turned and ran, but suddenly the ground seemed to slip out from under her. She fell backward into that oily patch of leaves and dirt. She let out a sharp cry. The flashlight had rolled out of her hands, and she desperately scurried along the ground to retrieve it. Then she struggled to her feet. Leaves stuck to her clothes. As she frantically brushed them away, she felt that slimy, jelly-like substance that had come from Russ Koehler's decaying corpse.

Karen could hear the footsteps coming closer. She spotted the last marker, tied to the bough of a bush by the crude pathway. She ran toward it, and anxiously searched for the next marker. All the while, she could hear that rustling behind her, pursuing her. The trail suddenly disappeared, and so did the markers. Panic stricken, Karen waved the flashlight around, hoping to find a piece of Koehler's shirt on a nearby tree or shrub. Without them, she couldn't hope to find her way back to the main trail.

Had she taken a wrong turn? She noticed a short path amid the foliage, and hurried along until her flashlight illuminated something on the ground in front of her. Karen froze. "Oh, God, no," she murmured. For a moment she couldn't breathe.

At least a dozen strips of Koehler's shirt littered the pathway.

All this time, someone had been behind her, removing Amelia's markers. That someone didn't want her finding her way back to the main trail.

She heard the footsteps again, coming closer. Karen blindly ran through the brush, zigzagging around trees and shrubs, staggering over rocks on the ground. She didn't know where she was headed. She could have been totally turned around and forging even deeper into the woods. Branches lashed at her face, arms, and legs. At every turn, she expected a hand to grab out at her. She prayed for some sign ahead, a light through the trees, some signal that she was near the edge of the forest. She didn't want to die in these woods, as Koehler so obviously had.

All the while, she heard the footsteps thumping behind her, the bushes rustling.

But she could hear something else, too. It sounded like a car approaching. Up ahead in the distance, she saw the beam from a pair of headlights sweep across the bushes and trees. After a few moments, another car sailed by. Karen raced toward the road, and civilization. Her lungs burning, she pressed on. She could actually see the edge of the forest now, and cars whooshing past. By the time she emerged from the woods and felt the pavement beneath her, Karen was almost delirious. She didn't know if she had stumbled back onto Newcastle-Coal Creek Road, or if it was another street. She didn't have any idea how to get to her car from this spot.

She tried to wave down an SUV, but it passed her by, its horn blaring. Karen swiveled around and shined her flashlight into the woods.

She saw him for only a second—a tall figure ducking behind a tree. He had a small shovel in his hand. He couldn't have been more than a hundred feet away.

Karen swiveled around. "Help! Help me, please!" she screamed, waving at another approaching car, a beat-up Taurus.

The car pulled over to the side of the road.

Karen caught her breath. "Thank you, God," she whispered.

"This teenager in the Taurus was so sweet. The poor kid, I had him driving one way and then the other before we finally found where I'd left my car."

The cell phone to her ear, Karen stood outside a RiteAid in a Bellevue strip mall. Under the glaring halogen lights, she could see her reflection in the storefront window. With her brown hair a mess, dirt on her clothes, and scratch marks on her face, she looked as if she'd been beaten up.

"Are you sure you're all right?" George asked for the second time.

"Somewhat traumatized, but okay," Karen replied with a shaky laugh.

"And you don't want to call the police?"

"Well, at this point, we don't have a body," she said. "And I'm sure all of those trail markings will be gone by the time anyone goes back into those woods, searching for one. I don't think calling the police would do any good right now. Besides, I'd like to get Amelia some help before the cops and the press start going to town on her. And you'll think I'm crazy, but there's still a part of me that believes she's innocent."

"I feel the same way, Karen," he said. "Still, she could be dangerous, you said so yourself. There's every indication that she killed Koehler."

"I know," Karen sighed. "But that man chasing me through the woods tonight, I think he's the same one who was in the basement at my father's rest home yesterday. I'm more worried about him than I am about Amelia. Shane spotted her being very intimate with some strange man in a car a few months ago. It could be this same guy. Maybe he has some kind of weird power over Amelia. Maybe he's hypnotizing her or something, I don't know."

"I was planning to go to Salem tomorrow," George said. "Jessie's supposed to look after the kids. It was just a day trip, but maybe now, I ought to stay put. You shouldn't have to take care of Amelia all by yourself. She's my responsibility—"

"You're going to Salem?"

"Yeah, I want to find out who paid for Duane Lee Savitt's cemetery plot. They wouldn't tell me over the phone and suggested I come down there."

"You should go," Karen urged him. "If we can find out more about her early childhood, it could end up helping Amelia

quite a lot. Go. I'll watch over Amelia. We'll be fine. I don't
think the police will be looking for her at my place tonight.
They've already been by today. In the morning, I'll get her to
a specialist. I have some names."

"Well, your faith in Amelia's innocence is a lot stronger
than mine," he said. "She's my niece, and I love her. But I
wouldn't trust her around my kids right now. And I don't
think I'd sleep very well under the same roof as her."

Karen peered through the RiteAid window. She noticed
an aisle marker that said Sleep Aids. "I know what you mean,"
she said. "I probably won't sleep too well, myself. But I'll
make sure Amelia does. Will you call me from Salem tomorrow
as soon as you find out anything?"

"Of course, Karen," he replied. "And phone me tonight if
anything happens. Even if it's just that you're scared and
can't sleep. I want you to call me, okay?"

She smiled. "Okay, George. Thank you."

Karen stirred the ingredients from four sleeping capsules
into the chocolate sauce as she heated it over the stove. The
diazepam she'd given Amelia last week had calmed her a bit,
but hadn't made her sleep. And Karen needed to make sure
Amelia was conked out tonight.

Rufus sat at her feet, watching her every move. He always
did that while she was cooking in case she accidentally
dropped a piece of food.

Amelia was upstairs, changing into her pajamas. She and
Shane had watched *The 400 Blows* and then eaten dinner at
My Brother's Pizza. Before calling them, Karen had left a
message with Dr. Danielle Richards, the most qualified psy-
chologist on her contact list. Dr. Richards had called back,
and agreed to meet with Amelia in the morning.

Shane had dropped Amelia off at 9:20. By then, Karen
had already showered, changed the sheets in the guest room,

and taken Rufus for a quick walk. After what had happened in Cougar Mountain Park, she'd decided to tuck her father's gun in her coat pocket for the short trip down the block and back. She wished she'd had it with her during that hike in the forest.

Amelia let out a gasp when she saw the scratch marks on Karen's face and hands. Karen reassured her that she was all right. She told her what had happened in the woods, focusing on the fact that there was no actual corpse, and no reason to go to the police just yet.

At the same time, she wondered out loud about the man who had chased her through the forest. Did Amelia know someone who could have done that? It couldn't have been Shane. Did she have any other male friends, maybe someone Shane didn't know about?

Amelia couldn't think of anyone. She became more upset the more Karen pressed the issue, and finally Karen just dropped it. She suggested Amelia change into her pajamas, and they could watch a movie on TV.

That had been about fifteen minutes ago.

She could hear Amelia coming down the stairs now. The crystals from the sleeping pill capsules still showed up in the chocolate sauce. Karen turned up the burner, and rapidly stirred the concoction. Then she went to the refrigerator freezer for the ice cream.

Amelia stepped into the kitchen. Her hair was pinned up; and she wore an oversized pink T-shirt, flannel pajama bottoms, and thick gray socks. She sat down at the kitchen table. Rufus strolled over to her and put his head in her lap.

"I'm making sundaes," Karen announced.

Scratching Rufus behind the ears, Amelia sighed. "Oh, I think I'll pass. I've had a nervous stomach ever since this afternoon. Thanks, anyway."

Standing by the stove, Karen turned to gaze at her. "But I heated up the chocolate sauce just for you," she said. She tested the sauce with a little dab from her spoon. It didn't have any detectable foreign taste. "Hmm, it's good stuff too. And I know you like chocolate. C'mon, one scoop won't kill you." She prepared Amelia's dish, dousing the ice cream with chocolate sauce. Then she set it on the table in front of Amelia.

Perking up, Rufus showed more interest in the dessert than Amelia did. Karen dished out a scoop of ice cream for herself, and brought it over to the table. She sat down. "Go ahead, dig in," she urged her.

Amelia gazed at Karen's bowl and frowned. "Why aren't you having any chocolate on yours?"

"Because chocolate goes right from my lips to my hips. It's bad enough I'm having this ice cream." With her spoon, she pointed to the bowl in front of Amelia. "C'mon, don't let me be the only one pigging out here. Have some."

Amelia sighed. "I'm sorry, Karen. I don't want it."

"Well, can I—can I fix you something else?" She put down her spoon. "I have the sauce right there. How about some hot chocolate?"

"No, thanks." Amelia stared down at Rufus, and patted his head. "God, I'm so screwed up. You know, for a while, you had me convinced I couldn't have hurt my parents and Ina. And for the last few months, I actually thought I didn't have anything to do with Collin's death. But now, with this Koehler business, it brings everything back again. And the weirdest part about it is, I still don't really *remember* him. It's more like I *dreamt* about him or something. And I still feel like I was in Port Angeles yesterday. Talk about fouled up."

"Remember our first session?" Karen asked. "You told me about your blackouts and that time Shane saw you in a car with some other man. Shane confronted you pretty much the same way I asked you about Koehler. I started to describe him, and then you remembered."

Amelia nodded.

"Do you recall who Shane saw you with? Can you describe him to me now?"

She grimaced. "God, I've been trying to forget him. I don't like thinking about that time."

"Please, it's important," Karen said.

"His name's Blade," Amelia muttered, absently gazing down at the glass tabletop. "At least that's what he calls himself. He's twenty-five. His hair's cut short with little bangs and he's dyed it jet-black. He wears sunglasses a lot, even at night, sometimes."

"Then you still know him?" Karen asked.

Amelia looked up at her. "Still know who?"

"Blade." Karen let out an exasperated little laugh. "The man Shane saw you with in the car that time. You were talking like you still know him."

"Well, I don't—"

"Is he a friend of a friend's?"

Biting her lip, Amelia nodded. "I think so. He must be. I guess that's how I know about him."

Karen reached over and patted her arm. "Amelia, do you remember running down a gray stairwell to a basement? This happened recently. There's a boiler, and it's making all sorts of racket. Down the hall is a large storage room full of boxes and old hospital equipment. Blade is waiting there for you. The lights on the ceiling are broken, and the place is dark. You're down there with Blade . . ."

Amelia yanked her arm away. "Karen, please . . ."

Startled, Karen recoiled a bit. Even Rufus backed away from her.

"I'm sorry," Amelia murmured, her voice cracking. "Could you just—*chill* for a few minutes? I'm so worn out and frazzled and tired. I really don't want to talk about this now. I'm sorry. Please don't be mad."

"No, it's—it's fine," Karen said. She nodded at the bowl

in front of Amelia. Most of the ice cream had melted. "You sure you don't want any of that?"

Amelia just shook her head.

Getting to her feet, Karen collected both bowls and took them to the sink. She rinsed them out, and watched the chocolate sauce swirl down the drain.

"I just want to go to sleep and not think about anything for a while," Amelia said. "This is one of those nights when I used to drink until I'd passed out so I didn't have to worry or think about anything. Karen, you don't have any sleeping pills, do you?"

Karen switched off the water. She turned, and gave Amelia a patient, understanding smile. "You know, I think I might."

Ina McMillan was the name on the address label on the old *Vanity Fair* he'd fished out of the recycling bin in front of the house. That was the aunt, the one she'd shot in the chest. Aunt Ina.

He'd been to the house in Bellingham twice, and to their weekend retreat on Lake Wenatchee several times. But Blade hadn't been to this place in West Seattle until tonight. It was a Craftsman-style house at the end of a cul-de-sac. He'd parked the Cadillac a little further up the block. Through the open curtains in the living room, he could see all the way back to the kitchen. Now that he knew whose place it was, he could attach a name to the tall guy he'd seen going in and out of the kitchen. That was Uncle George. And the two brats were her cousins.

She hadn't told him whose place it was. She'd just given him the address, and told him to go check it out. He was supposed to give the place the once-over, because he had to do a job for her there tomorrow. Blade figured it would be a robbery, but he never knew with her.

She hadn't told him exactly what kind of job yet. She

would call him on his cell at eleven o'clock, and then let him know. She was kind of a tease that way. She made a game of everything. He liked that about her, but it could also drive him nuts at times. Sex with her was always a game, and it was fantastic. Blade always felt the crazier a woman was, the better the sex. And this one was *crazy*.

He'd checked the windows around the McMillan house. They were about seven feet above ground level, but he could use one of the trash cans or recycling bins to boost himself up and break in. Besides the front door, there was another door off the kitchen in back. In the bushes by the front stoop, there was a little sign for some home security service—no surprise. But he knew how to dismantle those stupid security alarms.

He glanced at his wristwatch: 10:50. Even though the cul-de-sac wasn't well lit, Blade put his sunglasses back on. She said they made him look cool. She also liked the shiny black suit he wore practically everywhere. He sometimes enjoyed posing in front of the mirror wearing his sunglasses and his trademark black suit, brandishing his guns. She took a bunch of pictures of him posing like that.

Tucking the *Vanity Fair* under his arm, Blade strolled back to his car. He sat in the front seat. He could still see the McMillan house from here, but his eyes grew tired and he closed them for a spell.

Funny about that corpse in the woods. He was supposed to have buried the guy last night. She'd even left trail markers for him. But after driving to the park, he just didn't fucking feel like doing all that work. Plus those woods were full of wild animals.

So this morning, she was all over his ass for slacking off. And so he drove back to the park late this afternoon. He'd brought along a small shovel she'd gotten at some army-navy surplus store. He hadn't exactly been looking forward to burying a decayed stiff. But the notion of possibly encountering—and shooting—some forest creatures suddenly intrigued him.

Well, he didn't find any forest creatures, but the stiff sure did. What was left of the guy was covered with crows when he'd found him. Blade puked twice as he dragged the stinking, picked-over corpse to a ditch off the marked trail. He didn't have to dig much to make the shallow oblong hole. With the shovel, he quickly covered him with a layer of dirt, then scattered some leaves and branches over that.

He was headed back to the car when he's spotted Amelia's shrink making her way along the trail. There was no mistaking it. She was looking for the dead guy.

It had been kind of fun, chasing her, and scaring the crap out of her. Of course, killing her would have been even more fun, and so easy. He'd had his heart set on killing *something* in that forest.

But he'd had his instructions not to touch her. She wasn't supposed to die in those woods. No, that was happening later.

His cell phone rang, startling him. Blade reached inside his suit-jacket pocket, pulled out the cell and switched it on. "Yeah?"

"It's me," she whispered. "Are you at the address I gave you?"

"Yeah, and I'm sitting in the car, parked down the street. But I can see the place from here. I even figured out who lives there. Uncle George, right?"

"Very good, baby."

"What kind of job do you want me to pull here tomorrow? Can you at least give me a hint?"

"Not over the phone. But I've written it down for you somewhere."

"You and your fucking games," he muttered.

"You love it," she whispered. "I'm at Karen's house. Why don't you come over?"

"Now?"

"Yeah. I'll be watching for you. You said you're in the car?"

"Uh-huh." He put the keys in the ignition. "I'll be right over."

"First, reach under the driver's seat."

Blade bent forward and felt around until his fingers brushed against something.

"I left a note for you," she said. "Take another long look at the house, then read my note. Okay? I'll see you soon."

She clicked off.

Grinning, Blade switched off his phone. He pulled an envelope from under the car seat. Following her advice, he took off his sunglasses and stared at the McMillan house for a few moments. Then he tore open the envelope and read her note:

"Tomorrow, after 4 P.M.: Kill everyone in the house, and take whatever you want."

Chapter Fourteen

"Karen!" she screamed. "Karen, where are you?"

At her desk with a glass of chardonnay, Karen was studying notes from earlier sessions with Amelia. She sprang to her feet and hurried for the stairs. Rufus followed her.

She'd talked Amelia into taking three sleeping pills, just to ensure they did the trick. Amelia had gone to bed in the guest room about fifteen minutes ago. There hadn't been a peep out of her, and now this screaming.

Karen raced up the second floor hallway and flung open the guest room door. Between the two quilt-covered twin beds, the table lamp was on. Trembling, Amelia sat up in the bed that was farther from the door, her hands covering her face.

"What is it? What's going on?" Karen asked. Rufus followed her into the bedroom.

"I'm sorry," Amelia cried, still covering her face. "I'm so sorry. I didn't mean to scream out like that. I feel like such a baby." She lowered her hands, then slumped back against her pillow. "It's just—I'm used to the dorm and all the noise. It's so damn quiet here, I was going crazy. I started hearing things, and got scared."

Karen sat on the other bed. "Why don't you come downstairs and watch TV for a while?"

She shook her head. "No, I just want to sleep. More than anything, I wish I could have a couple of shots of Jack Daniel's right now, just to relax."

"Not after those sleeping pills," Karen said. "You've been so good lately. I wouldn't let you slide back now anyway. I can bring a radio in here. Or what about a sound machine? My sister gave one to my dad a few years ago. I think it has ocean waves or something."

Amelia let out a weak laugh. "Sure, might be worth a shot. Anything but this awful silence. I'm sorry to be so much trouble."

Karen got up and started out of the room. "No sweat. I think it's just down the hall in the closet. Be right back."

She retrieved the sound machine from the closet's bottom shelf. Karen prayed it would do the trick.

She returned to the bedroom with the sound machine, set it on the nightstand, and plugged it in. The sound came on: waves rolling onto the shore, and the occasional, distant cry of a seagull. "Tranquil enough for you?" Karen asked, with a tiny smile.

Amelia sighed. "As long as I don't have to listen to the sounds inside my head. Do you know what I was hearing when I finally screamed for you?"

"What were you hearing?" Karen asked.

"It was that weird, frail warble Collin made after I hit him in the head with the plank." Tears came to her eyes, and she covered her face again. "I kept hearing my brother dying. . . ."

"You didn't do it," Karen whispered, stroking Amelia's hair. "You're not responsible for it, Amelia. Now, lie down and listen to the waves. Don't think about anything else. Rufus and I can stick around until you fall asleep. Would that help?"

"Thanks, I'm sorry to be so—"

"Oh, hush, it's no bother," Karen said, tucking her in. Then she switched off the nightstand lamp, and made her way to the rocking chair by the window. She settled back in it, and Rufus curled up near her feet.

"You're sweet, Karen," Amelia murmured, over the sound of the fake distant waves. "I often wonder why you don't have a boyfriend. Doesn't make sense, you're so nice, and pretty." Karen heard her yawn. "I—I sometimes think about how lonely you must be."

"Oh, I'm doing all right," Karen answered almost automatically.

"Always helping people, taking care of people, and no one to take care of you, it's not right. Karen, you . . . you deserve to be happy."

Karen said nothing. She felt a horrible ache in the pit of her stomach, and tears welled up in her eyes. But she remained silent. She just kept rocking in the chair, and listened to Amelia surrender to sleep.

Amelia felt herself drifting off as she spoke to Karen. The sleeping pills must have worked after all. In the darkness, she could see Karen sitting over in the corner of the room, by the window. Amelia heard herself slurring her words, and Karen's silhouette seemed to blur.

For a second, just as she started to fall asleep, Amelia no longer saw Karen Carlisle across the bedroom. Instead, she had a fleeting image of her father in that rocking chair, the moment before she shot him through the head.

Bellingham, Washington—six months before

A notice came up on the 36-inch flat-screen TV in the Faradays' den: ALL MODELS ARE EIGHTEEN YEARS OR OVER.

Collin had been looking forward to this moment. His parents had left for Lake Wenatchee that Saturday morning. This was the 16-year-old's first weekend home alone ever, and to get the debauchery rolling, he'd borrowed three DVDs from his friend, Matt Leonard, whose brother had smuggled them home from college: *Whore of the Worlds*, *Booty Call 9-1-1,* and *Missionary Impossible*.

He was having some of the guys over for poker tonight; at least, that was the plan, if one of them could get his hands on a case of beer and some cigars. Matt would be coming over in about two hours, which gave Collin plenty of time to watch one of the movies and whack off. He'd drawn all the shades and peeled down to his underpants. His hand was already inching past the elastic waistband of his briefs as he watched the opening photo credits for *Whore of the Worlds*. A pretty brunette with perky breasts was shown from the waist up, gyrating on something that seemed to have the kick of a me-chanical bull. The credits ran: Amber Anniston as Tami Cruz. Next, a long-haired blonde with a huge rack stared seduc-tively at the camera with her finger in her mouth: Sheridan Madrid as Sheri Savoy.

And then the front doorbell rang.

"Damn it!" Collin hissed, switching off the DVD player. Springing up from the sofa, he frantically dressed and hid the DVD covers behind a sofa pillow. The doorbell rang again and again. "Matt, if that's you, I'm gonna kill you," Collin muttered. He hurried to the front door, and checked the peep-hole. "What the hell?" he whispered. Then he unlocked the door and opened it. "Amelia, what are you doing here?"

"Oh, nice way to greet your sister," she said with an abrupt laugh. She brushed past him and sauntered into the house. "Mom and Dad are in Lake Wenatchee, and little brother is home alone, which means I caught you in the middle of get-ting drunk or bopping the bologna. Which is it?"

Collin ignored the question. "Aren't you supposed to be at some Booze Busters retreat in Port Townsend?"

She headed into the kitchen and started hunting through the cupboards. "Don't remind me. They just dropped me off. I told them I needed to get my allergy medication."

"Allergy medication?" Collin repeated.

"Yeah. Good one, huh? Anyway, they're coming back to pick me up in a half hour." She started checking the lower cabinets. "Where the fuck are they hiding the booze nowadays?"

"To the left of the sink, where they've always kept it," Collin replied, squinting at her. "Why are you acting so weird?"

She pulled a bottle of bourbon out of the cabinet. "Well, I'm not drunk, if that's what you mean, little brother." She took two highball glasses from the upper cupboard. "At least, I'm not drunk, *yet*."

Collin stared at her as she filled both glasses about halfway. He didn't think his sister was drunk. She just wasn't acting much like herself. Since when did she ever refer to him as little brother? He'd never seen Amelia wearing so much makeup in the middle of the day. She was acting like she did that time a few weeks back when she'd unexpectedly shown up at his school. He wondered if it was being away at college that had changed her. "What's going on?" he asked. "What's with the hotshot act?"

She handed him a glass. "You're the hotshot, all alone for the weekend. If you plan to get shitfaced, I want to see it." She clinked her glass against his. "C'mon, chug it."

"Are you nuts? I'm not getting drunk with you."

"Oh, c'mon, don't be such a pussy. Have some fun."

Collin shook his head and put down the half-full glass. "I'm not sure this is such a great idea, Amelia. You know you shouldn't . . ."

She frowned at him. "You know, you can be a real asshole sometimes."

He looked at her, incredulous. *"What?"*

"You heard me," she muttered, plopping down at the breakfast table. "When's the last time we saw each other?"

"Three weeks ago, when you came home for the weekend," he replied, folding his arms. "And before that it was the time you dropped by my school in the middle of the day. Of course, later, you didn't remember that, so maybe it doesn't count."

Apparently, it had been one of her episodes with *lost time*. He wondered if later she'd have any memory of this afternoon. She sure was acting bizarre.

"Three weeks we haven't seen each other," she said. "I come by to say hello, and what do I get?" She made a face and dropped her voice an octave to sound like a surly Neanderthal. " 'What are you doing here?' Real sweet, Collin. Thanks a lot. How do you think that makes me feel?"

Collin sighed. "I didn't mean it that way."

"It's bad enough everyone considers me the family fuckup, and you—you pee perfume. Of course, I'm not even really part of this family, being adopted and all."

"Oh, c'mon, Amelia," he said, sitting down at the table with her. "That's bullshit. Why do you even say stuff like that?"

"You're always so disgustingly good," she sneered. "With Mom and Dad gone for the weekend, I figured you'd finally let loose a little, maybe get drunk or high or something. And I just wanted to be here to see it. Plus to be perfectly honest, I could really use a drink. Sorry if that offends you. But you're making me feel like shit. Are you too fucking good to have a couple of shots with me?"

"All right, okay, fine. I'll have a drink. Jeesh!" He got up from the table and retrieved the highball glass. He quickly tipped it back and took a swallow. It burned. Unlike most of his friends, he really wasn't much of a drinker. Since his sister had a problem with alcohol, he'd purposely avoided it.

She broke into applause. "Way to go! Finish it!"

His throat was still on fire, but Collin forced down the rest of the glass. He gasped for air. The strong, medicine-like taste was still in his mouth. "Okay?" he asked. "God, Amelia, I don't know how you can stand to drink this stuff."

"I'm so proud of you," she said, laughing. "You're gonna feel fantastic in a few minutes."

Collin numbly stared at her. When she laughed, she didn't sound like herself. Or maybe he was drunk already? It couldn't happen that fast, could it?

"I'll make a deal with you." With a sly grin, she nodded at her glass. "I won't have this if you drink it for me."

"No way!" he protested. "Give me a break."

"Why not? C'mon, it'll be fun. You can be the drunken screwup for a change, and I'll be the perfect child and stay on the wagon. It's role reversal. You're not driving anyplace. Go for it. You'll be doing us both some good."

Collin was shaking his head.

"What can happen? At the very worst, you'll get hammered. You were gonna do that later tonight, anyway. Right?"

"Okay, okay," he said, feeling a little funny as he walked to the breakfast table. Collin picked up her glass, and guzzled down the bourbon in two gulps. He coughed and his eyes watered up.

She applauded again. "That's just like you—rescuing me from myself. You took a bullet for me, little brother."

He sank down on the chair beside her and caught his breath. There she went again with that *little brother* bit. Maybe it was something she'd picked up at school. Why was it so important that she see him get drunk?

He started to laugh. "You're acting so completely weird today," he said, grinning wildly. "I swear to God, it's like I don't even know you, *big sister*. I mean, you've *always* been weird, and I've always loved you for it, Amelia. But this—today—

is a whole different type of weird. Ha! Or maybe it's me. Am I shitfaced already?" He snickered again, and realized he must indeed be drunk, because he couldn't stop babbling.

Collin reminisced out loud about the times Amelia had raised hell growing up, all the trouble she'd gotten into. He talked about how she'd driven their parents crazy, and he imitated their dad when he went ballistic over something she'd done: " 'Ye Gods, what's wrong with her?' Ha! When Dad starts in with the Ye Gods, then watch out, we're all in trouble!" Collin couldn't stop laughing.

But then he took a moment to look at her, and Collin realized she hadn't laughed once. She just sat there with a cryptic smile on her face.

"I'm sorry, Amelia," he muttered. "You—you know I love you. I do. It's just that, *Ye Gods*, I think I'm drunk!" He chuckled again.

"We need to get you some fresh air." She stood, and then helped him to his feet. "This might not have been such a terrific idea. I don't want you sick. C'mon, little brother. . . ."

Collin felt a bit woozy, but he could certainly walk on his own. He didn't need her helping him. As they moved into the den, he stole a look at the sofa, where, for the moment, the throw pillow covered up those porn DVDs.

She went to the sliding glass door, and opened the curtain. She struggled to move the door until she finally seemed to notice the stubby, thick beam of wood braced on the floor, tracking for extra insurance against break-ins. Funny, she seemed to have completely forgotten it was there. She moved the beam aside, then slid open the door. "There now," she said. "Why don't we sit down on the couch, watch some TV—"

"No, no, no," he protested, shaking his head. All Collin could think about was his sister switching on the TV and discovering *Whore of the Worlds* there. "Let's go outside, down to the dock. You're right, I need some air. C'mon . . ."

Leading the way, Collin staggered down the slight slope

in their backyard toward the dock, and he realized he was truly drunk.

It was a cool, crisp May afternoon. The sun glistened off Lake Whatcom, and across the calm water he could see the mountains in the distance. The wooden dock was slightly neglected, because they didn't have a boat. But it was still sturdy, with an upper deck that had a railing, and a lower platform that had nothing between it and the water directly below. Ever since they were kids, he and Amelia and their friends often used the dock to sun themselves, and Lake Whatcom was quite swimmable.

Collin glanced over his shoulder. She was following him with the stubby wood beam in her hand. One moment, she had it slung over her shoulder like a baseball bat, the next, she used it like a walking stick as she made her way down the grassy slope. Her black hair fluttered in the wind, and she grinned at him. She seemed to enjoy seeing him inebriated.

Though he might have felt more secure up on the dock's upper platform—with the railing—Collin ventured down three steps to the lower, open tier. The water lapped up almost to the edge of its wooden planks. He could hear her stepping down behind him. "Boy, the lake is beautiful today," he murmured, squinting out at its glimmering surface.

"You're slurring your words," she said. "You got drunk a lot faster than I expected you would."

He wasn't sure exactly what she meant. She'd been *expecting* him to get drunk? But Collin nodded anyway, and kept gazing at the lake and mountains. "Yeah, I am pretty hammered. Do me a favor, okay?"

"What's that?" she asked.

"Please make sure I don't do anything stupid. I hear all these stories about dumb-ass teenagers getting drunk and they somehow end up getting themselves killed. I don't want that to happen to me."

"Oh, I'm afraid it's too late," she replied.

Collin froze. That wasn't his sister's voice.

"You're not Amelia," he murmured.

He swiveled around to see her raising the wooden beam over her head. Collin didn't even have time to react, or ward off the blow. All of a sudden, that thing came crashing down on him, and Collin Faraday heard his own skull crack.

While hosing the blood off the dock, she thought about the funny, garbled cry Collin had made before falling into the lake. He'd sounded like a feeble old woman. And that strange, gurgling noise, it must have been the blood in his throat when he'd tried to scream out. Whatever it had been, she snickered as she remembered it now.

Her brother's foot had caught on some of the pilings under the dock, and he was floating facedown in the water just below her.

He was their favorite, the child they'd been hoping and trying for until deciding to adopt, and she'd been a mere compromise.

They would mourn him. But they wouldn't have to grieve for very long. Soon enough, they would be dead, too. Soon enough, she would have no family—or friends. She would be the only one left.

And that was exactly the way she wanted it.

Seattle—six months later

Karen woke up, and suddenly she knew someone else was in her bedroom.

Lying in bed with the covers up to her neck, she'd been lightly dozing for the last three hours. She hadn't heard a peep from Amelia down the hall, just that machine churning out the sounds of waves and seagulls. Rufus had fallen asleep at the foot of Karen's bed, but now she heard him sitting up. His dog tags jingled. He started to growl.

She heard a floorboard creak. For a moment, she couldn't move.

Finally, and very slowly, Karen reached under the extra pillow beside her and found her father's revolver.

She could almost feel someone hovering over her.

She quickly sat up in bed. "I've got a gun!" she said.

Rufus started barking furiously.

"God, Karen, no, wait!"

Blindly reaching for the nightstand lamp, she fanned at the air for a moment before she found the light and switched it on. "Amelia," she murmured, catching her breath. "Rufus, hush! That's enough."

"Oh, Karen, I'm so sorry," she whispered, a hand clutching at the lapels of her robe. "I got turned around. I thought this was the bathroom. . . ."

Rufus kept growling at her, punctuating it with an occasional bark.

"Rufus, cease and desist," Karen said. Her heart was still racing. She tried to smile at her. "It's the next door down, Amelia."

"Thanks. Sorry I woke you." She hesitated in the doorway, and frowned at her. "Do you always sleep with a gun? Or do you think I'm dangerous?"

Karen shook her head. "No, I don't usually sleep with a gun. And no, I don't think you're dangerous. This is about something else, Amelia." She was thinking of the young man who called himself Blade. That was why she had the gun at her side tonight; and why Rufus was sleeping in her bedroom instead of his own little bed in the corner of the kitchen. But part of her still couldn't trust Amelia—not if she was sick.

"Think you'll be able to get back to sleep?" Karen asked.

Yawning, she nodded and turned toward the hall. "G'night, Karen. Sorry I scared you." She gently closed the door behind her.

Rufus let out one last growl, and then settled back down at the foot of her bed. Karen listened for a few moments until she heard the toilet flushing. It was strange. Earlier tonight, Amelia had come down to the kitchen in her T-shirt and pajama bottoms. But she'd put on a robe in the middle of the night, just to go to the bathroom?

Karen checked the digital clock on her nightstand: 4:11 A.M. She switched off the light, slipped the gun back under the pillow beside her, and lay there for several minutes. She thought she heard murmuring. She peeled back the covers, quietly crept out of bed, and then listened at the door. "She's got a gun, for chrissake . . . I can't . . . goddamn mutt . . ."

It was a woman's voice, but it didn't sound like Amelia.

Karen crept back to the bed and retrieved her father's revolver again. Rufus scurried to his feet and looked at her. "Stay!" Karen whispered to him. Then she opened the door and gazed down the darkened hallway. She held the gun tightly. The guest room door was open, but the light was off. Past the waves and seagulls from the sound machine, she could hear the woman whispering again: "We'll just have to take care of it tomorrow . . ."

Karen tiptoed down the corridor, but the floorboards creaked and she froze. Rufus poked his head past her bedroom doorway and let out an abrupt bark. The murmuring down the hallway suddenly stopped. Karen heard a rustling sound. "Amelia?" she said. She had the gun poised.

She skulked toward the guest room. She could hear whispering again, only this time, it sounded more like Amelia: "I want two baskets of flowers. Yes, you can . . . But I'm taking my dog . . ."

Karen peeked into the doorway. In the darkness, she saw the silhouette of someone in the far twin bed, nestled beneath the covers. "But I have a ticket . . ." she said in a sleepy voice—Amelia's voice. "That train doesn't leave for a while . . ."

With a sigh, Karen retreated back to her own room, and crawled back into bed once again. She shouldn't have been surprised Amelia talked in her sleep, in addition to everything else. Karen tried to go to sleep, but merely tossed and turned. She told herself everything was okay. She'd be taking Amelia to a specialist in just a few hours.

She kept checking the clock on her nightstand. The last time she looked it was 5:17. She could hear birds chirping. An unsettling thought occurred to her: *What if that wasn't Amelia under the covers? What if it was someone else?*

But Karen told herself she was being silly. And she finally drifted off to sleep.

The clock on Shane's nightstand read: 6:02 A.M. Barely lifting his head from his pillow, he squinted at it. He wondered what the hell that tapping noise was. He and four other guys shared a dilapidated house on Forty-third Street, just a few blocks from the campus. His bedroom was on the first floor, right off the kitchen. It took him a moment to realize the tapping was on his window. Against the faint light of dawn, he could see the silhouette of someone on the other side of the old venetian blinds.

"What the . . ." he muttered, crawling out of bed. He staggered across the cluttered room in his underpants. The tapping continued.

Some of the venetian blind slats were bent and broken and, through the gaps, he could see who was out there. He immediately raised the blinds, and then tugged the window open. He had to crouch so that he could talk to her face-to-face. "Amelia, sweetheart, what's going on?" he asked, in a groggy voice.

She wore a rain slicker and stood on her tiptoes. "Sorry to wake you," she whispered. "I just had to see you, baby."

He started to straighten up. "Well, go around to the kitchen door, and I'll let you in."

"No, no, I can't stay. Karen's practically holding me prisoner at her place. She doesn't know I'm gone. I need to get back there and sneak in before she wakes up."

He crouched down again and hovered by the open window. "Shit, you shouldn't have to stay there if you don't want to. . . ."

She smiled. "It's okay. But I need to meet you later, someplace where we can be alone, with no one else around. You know that boat place by Husky Stadium?"

"You mean where they rent canoes?"

She nodded. "I want you to rent one and take it out on Lake Washington to Foster Island, near the Arboretum. It's over past the Museum of History and Industry—"

"I remember where it is," he interrupted. "We've been there before." Foster Island was a secluded little patch of land accessible by a long, winding, nature path that included a few footbridges. They'd had a picnic there during the summer.

"Good. I'll meet you out there at eleven-thirty."

"Oh, shit," he murmured. "I'm sorry, sweetheart, but I've got my psychology class at eleven."

She frowned. "Can't you skip it for *me*? This is important."

He hesitated. "Sure, I guess."

"I knew I could count on you. Don't tell anyone you're meeting me or mention where you're going. And that includes Karen. I don't trust her anymore."

"What?" He let out a dazed laugh. "But you *love* Karen. You were just bending my ear last night over pizza about how goddamn wonderful she is."

She shook her head. "Not anymore. If Karen calls you, don't even pick up."

"Well, why go back there if you don't trust her? Why all the secrecy? I don't get this, Amelia. . . ."

"I'll explain everything to you on Foster Island at eleven-thirty, and take a canoe out there. It's very important. Will you just do it for me, please?"

"Of course," he murmured. He didn't understand any of this. Most of all, he couldn't understand her. She wasn't acting like herself. "Of course, I'll be there," he reiterated.

"Thanks, baby," she said. Reaching up, she ran her fingers through his messy, light brown hair, then pulled his head down to her. She gave him a long kiss, and slipped her tongue into his mouth. He wanted more, but she pulled away.

"Sorry, I've got morning breath," he whispered with a little laugh.

"It's okay," she grinned and licked her lips. "Do you have morning wood, too?"

Indeed he did. He'd woken up—as usual—with a morning hard-on, which had been revived by that arousing kiss. Shane blushed.

She giggled. "Stand up straight, so I can see it."

He was obedient. "Little Shane's standing up straight, too, babe."

She reached inside the window, and fondled his erection through his underpants. She made this moaning sound he'd never heard her make before. He was embarrassed, but very turned on at the same time.

"I want more of that later," she purred, giving him one final, gentle tug.

Then she suddenly turned around and hurried toward the alley off the backyard. In a stupor, Shane watched her duck inside a black Jetta. It looked like her therapist's car. The engine started up, and the car drove away.

Shane's erection quickly subsided as he stood there in the window. He remembered something Karen had told him the previous afternoon. "You need to keep an eye on her. If you notice a sudden change in her or a severe mood swing, call me."

For a few moments, Shane thought about calling Karen, maybe waking her up, and telling her what had just happened.

But he went back to sleep, instead.

Chapter Fifteen

The phone woke her up.

Blurry eyed, Karen glanced at the clock on her night-stand: 8:32 A.M. She hadn't meant to sleep this late. But after almost shooting her own houseguest in the predawn hours, she'd been so shaken up, she'd just tossed and turned. She must have nodded off at some point, because Rufus had awoken her with some sudden and inexplicable barking at around 5:45. Then, just as suddenly, he'd gone back to sleep. But Karen hadn't been quite as lucky. The last time she'd looked at the clock, it was 6:41.

At least she'd gotten nearly two uninterrupted hours. Still, she'd overslept—and the damn phone was ringing.

Propping herself up on one elbow, Karen reached for the cell phone on her nightstand. She didn't recognize the caller number. She cleared her throat, then switched it on. "Hello?"

"Karen Carlisle?"

"Yes. Who's calling?"

"This is Jacqueline Peyton with the Seattle Police. I spoke with you yesterday."

Karen quickly sat up. She felt a pang of dread in her gut. They must have found Koehler's body. Despite everything that had happened in those woods last night, Karen still clung to some hope that Koehler was still alive. As of 7:00 last night, there had been no body, and only speculation. She wondered if that was all about to change.

"Ms. Carlisle?" the policewoman asked.

"Yes, I'm here," she said, rubbing her forehead. "How can I help you?"

"We've been trying to locate Amelia Faraday ever since we spoke with you yesterday afternoon. She hasn't been to her dorm. She isn't answering her phone. We've talked with her roommate, her boyfriend, and her uncle, and none of them have any idea where she is. I was wondering if you might have heard from her."

Karen hesitated. "Um, is this about Detective Koehler? Is he still missing?"

"I'm afraid so, yes. We think Amelia Faraday might have been one of the last people to see him, after you, that is."

"I see," was all Karen could think to say.

"Has Amelia contacted you? Do you have any idea where we might be able to reach her?

"Um, you know, I—I might be able to help you," Karen stammered. "But I just woke up, and I'm a little out of it right now. I was up late last night. Could I get back to you in about twenty minutes, Jacqueline? I have your number here on my cell. Could I phone you back?"

"That would be fine. I'll be waiting to hear from you," she replied.

"Talk to you soon," Karen said, and then she clicked off. "God help me."

She threw back the covers and jumped out of bed. Rufus barked once and got to his feet. He scurried after Karen, down the hallway toward the guest room. All the while,

Karen thought about how much she hated lying to the police. And yet here she was, doing just that. If she could hold them off for just two hours, she'd get Amelia to Dr. Richards. She'd have an expert opinion on Amelia's condition. It could help their case. Despite everything, Karen still believed Amelia was innocent on some level.

"Amelia?" she called. "Amelia, are you up?"

No response. The bathroom door was open. No one was in there. She didn't hear anyone downstairs.

Karen got to the guest room doorway and stopped dead. The bed was unmade and empty. Amelia's clothes and her knapsack were gone.

But the sleep machine was still churning out the sounds of ocean waves and seagulls in flight.

"Let me double-check on that," said the thin young man in a swivel chair. Seated across the desk from him, George guessed he was about twenty-four and gay, or metrosexual. He probably hated wearing that cheap-looking blue suit. His blond hair looked painstakingly mussed, and was loaded with product. The young man smiled at George, then turned toward his computer keyboard, and started typing.

He was the only person on duty in the small, modern ranch-style office across the street from Arbor Heights Memorial Park. The hedges bordering the cemetery were neatly trimmed, and the tall wrought-iron gates stood open.

But across the street, George had had to ring the doorbell before being buzzed in by the young man, who introduced himself as Todd. The office had a large picture window, which offered a view of the cemetery. There were three potted palms and two desks, both with computers. One wall was all file drawers, while another had a huge map of the cemetery with color-coded decals over certain areas.

George sat on the edge of his chair while Todd frowned at the computer screen. "No, I'm sorry," he said at last. "We don't have any billing records for Savitt, Duane Lee. I show he passed away in 1993, and he's in plot E-22 on the east hill. But there's nothing else here."

"Are you sure?" George asked. "I called yesterday, and someone here told me they might be able to help me if I came by in person."

Todd sighed. "Well, we don't have any billing information in the computers for burials prior to 1996. There's no paperwork, either. Everything over ten years old gets shredded. Who did you talk to?"

George started fuming. He shook his head. "I don't know. But he told me to come by today. I live in Seattle. I flew down to Portland, rented a car, and drove an hour here to Salem because this guy told me he could help me." George decided not to mention that he'd also paid for a cab to schlep Jessie over to his house at 5:30 in the morning, and then take him to the airport. She'd phoned an hour ago. She'd gotten Jody off to school and Steffie to the daycare center.

"You must have talked to Murray," Todd surmised. "He has the day off. He's been here since the late eighties. But I don't know how he could possibly remember a transaction from 1993—"

"Could you call him?" George asked.

Reaching for the phone, Todd winced a bit. "Um, he said he was going hunting today. But I can try."

George said nothing. He knew why Murray remembered that transaction from 1993. It was because the man buried in plot E-22 had murdered three people.

"Hi, Murray, this is Todd," the young man was saying into his phone. "If you get this message, call me at work. You talked to a man in Seattle yesterday, and told him if he came here, you could give him some billing information on the burial of a—" he glanced at his computer—"Savitt, Duane Lee, from 1993. Well, the gentleman is here, and waiting. So call me as soon as you get this." He hung up, then rolled his eyes at George. "I don't know if he'll call back. Like I said, I think he's out shooting Bambi's mother."

The remark was probably meant to elicit a chuckle, but George just glared at him. "Could you give me directions to this plot E-22?" he growled. "As long as I came all this way, I might as well take a look at the grave."

Todd nodded, then reached for a preprinted diagram of the cemetery. He circled a tiny square near the lower corner of the map. "Um, just go along the main drive, veer to your right. You'll see a big oak tree and, down the hill from there, a statue of a soldier from World War I. At least, I think it's the First World War. He's wearing one of those weird pith helmets, almost like a hubcap."

George just nodded.

"Anyway, after the soldier, take a left, and E-22 is there." He handed George the diagram.

"Thank you," he muttered. "Listen, I'm sorry to be short with you, because it's not your fault. But I'm just very frustrated and furious right now."

"I understand," Todd whispered meekly.

George stomped out of the office, then crossed the street, almost hoping some driver would honk at him at the pedestrian crosswalk so he'd have an excuse to scream at someone. But there were no cars around. He passed through the cemetery gates, and checked the diagram as he followed the main, two-lane road. It was a cool, overcast morning. The sky was the same light gray color as some of the tombstones. George noticed a few of the markers had photographs of the deceased on them. Printed on laminated oval metal discs, they looked like large, faded campaign buttons. He found the oak tree, then spotted a weathered old statue of the WWI infantryman, which stood out among the other headstones. Walking on the grass, he tried to avoid tramping over the graves. His shoes became wet with the morning dew. He finally found the headstone, a simple, squat slab of dark gray marble: Duane Lee Savitt, 1960–1993.

Beside it was the exact same type of headstone. But this one had a crucifix engraved above the inscription: Joy Savitt Schlessinger, 1963–1993, Beloved Wife & Mother.

"Yes, there are other Schlessingers buried here," Todd told him, ten minutes later. His fingers poised over the keyboard, he studied his computer screen. "Two more, Lon Rudyard and Annabelle Faye Schlessinger." He grabbed another diagram of the cemetery and circled two tiny squares right beside each other. "They're in the same general neighborhood, only you take a right when you get to the soldier statue," he explained.

"Thank you very much," George said.

George retraced his steps from before. He didn't know exactly what he expected to find—perhaps the graves of Joy Savitt's in-laws, or maybe her husband and a second wife. These Schlessingers might not have been at all related to Duane's sister. He turned right at the statue of the infantryman, then started checking the headstones lined up in front of a long, neatly manicured shrub.

George found them, two rose-colored headstones.

LON RUDYARD SCHLESSINGER
Husband and Father
22 October 1958 – 13 July 2004

And beside him:

ANNABELLE FAYE SCHLESSINGER
Beloved Daughter, Rest with the Angels
21 May 1988 – 13 July 2004

"They died the same day," George murmured to himself. He wondered if they'd been killed together in an accident. The girl was only sixteen years old. Were Lon and Annabelle Schlessinger the husband and child of Joy Savitt?

Biting his lip, George took another look at Annabelle's date of birth. She was born on the exact same day as Amelia.

"My God," George whispered. "Amelia and Annabelle, they were twins."

"She took the car. I had about sixty dollars in my purse. She took that, too."

With the cell phone to her ear, Karen held Rufus on a leash in the backyard. He hadn't been out yet this morning and needed to go. She kept the kitchen door open so she could hear the home phone if it rang.

"My dog started barking at around a quarter to six this morning," Karen explained. "I'm guessing that's when Amelia snuck out of the house. I called Jessie at your place, and she hasn't seen her. But she'll keep a lookout for my car. Amelia's roommate, Rachel, hasn't seen or heard from Amelia this morning either. Neither has Shane. I also called the rest home where my dad is, and they didn't see Amelia over there, either. I'm grateful for that. I didn't want to bother you, George. I know you're in Salem. But has Amelia called you?"

"No, she hasn't." He let out a long sigh. "This isn't like Amelia at all. I mean, she's disappeared for a day or two before, like she did this weekend. But she's never stolen a car, or money. This is nuts."

"Do you think she might have driven up to the house in Bellingham?" Karen asked.

"Well, I have the phone number for Mark and Jenna's neighbors up there," George said. "Nice couple, Jim and Barb Church. I'll give them a call, and find out if there's any activity next door. You drive a black Jetta, right?"

"That's right." She heard a beep on the line. *God, please, let it be Amelia*, she thought.

"I'll ask the Churches to keep their eyes peeled for your car," he was saying.

"Just a second, George. I have another call." She checked the caller ID, and then quickly got back on the line with George. "Oh, God, it's this policewoman phoning, the third time. I've been dodging her all morning. They've been looking for Amelia since yesterday."

"Listen, I think you better come clean and tell them what's happening, Karen. You don't want to get yourself into any more hot water with the police. Plus, at this stage, you aren't doing Amelia any favors by not reporting this. I hate to even think it, but she could hurt somebody else."

"I suppose you're right," she said, feeling a pang in her already knotted-up stomach. Rufus tugged at the leash, and Karen let him drag her toward the edge of the garden. She wondered who would walk her dog if she ended up in jail for aiding and abetting a fugitive.

"I may try Shane one more time," she said into the phone. "I had to call him three times before he finally picked up. And when I talked to him, I had a feeling he might have been holding back on something. Once you hear back from Amelia's neighbors up in Bellingham, will you give me a call?"

"Will do," he said. "By the way, I've been to the cemetery, and now I'm parked down the block from the public library in Salem. I need to look up some information. Has Amelia ever mentioned someone named Annabelle to you?"

"*Annabelle?* No, I don't think so. Why?"

"Because I'm pretty sure that's her twin sister."

"Amelia has a twin?" Karen murmured.

"*Had,*" he said, correcting her. "Annabelle died three years ago, the same day as her father. That's why I'm here at the library. Maybe there's something in the local newspaper archives about it."

"She never mentioned a twin," Karen muttered, almost to herself. Amelia had recalled sometimes talking to herself in the mirror as a child. Was that as close as she could come to remembering her twin sister?

While George explained about Joy Savitt and the Schlessinger graves, it suddenly seemed to make sense why Amelia had all these issues—the guilt, the low self-esteem, and the nightmares. At age four, her parents had discarded her, and kept her twin. But why?

"Listen, George, call me as soon as you find out anything," she said, pulling Rufus on his leash as she headed toward the house. "I'll see what I can dig up on the Internet. What was that date the father and daughter died again?"

> July 13, 2004 . . .
> Lon Schlessinger . . .
> Annabelle Schlessinger . . .
> Joy Savitt Schlessinger

None of those keywords yielded a result on the search engines Karen had tried. There wasn't anything in the *Oregonian* either. And nothing came up in the *Salem Statesman Journal* archives index. She hoped George might have better luck following a paper trail at the Salem library.

Karen glanced at her wristwatch: 11:20. She tried phoning Shane once more. He didn't answer his cell. She left another message: "Hi, Shane, it's Karen again. I still haven't heard from Amelia, and I'm very worried. I've just talked with her uncle, and we both agree it's time to call the police and tell them what's happened. If you have any idea where Amelia is, please, please, call me back."

Shane stopped rowing for a minute so he could listen to Karen's message.

It was cool and overcast, with a breeze that made the lake slightly choppy, not exactly a great day to be out on the water. Nevertheless Shane had forked over his driver's license and five bucks for the canoe rental. And now his was the only boat in this area of Lake Washington. He'd already crept by the Montlake Bridge, and was edging along the shore near the nature path. He saw two people fishing off one of the footbridges, but no one else.

He couldn't believe Karen was ready to call the cops just because Amelia had borrowed her car. But it was more than that, he knew. Last night, Amelia had been singing Karen's praises and, this morning, she'd told him not to trust her. It didn't make sense.

Shane slipped the cell phone back in his jacket pocket, and recommenced rowing. He saw a little piece of land with grass and trees jutting out from the wild overgrowth along the shore. He started looking for Amelia. She'd told him she would be there, and she would explain what all this was about. But he didn't see any sign of her, yet.

The water became a bit rough, and his canoe rocked back and forth as he rowed closer to Foster Island. The spot looked deserted. Shane pulled past some reeds and around a bend, where he found a clear spot to maneuver the boat into the shore. He felt the tip of the canoe hit the muddy bottom, then reluctantly he stepped into the water and tied up the boat to a tree trunk.

"Shit," he muttered.

Even though he'd moved quickly from the muddy bank to the grass, his feet had been totally immersed in the frigid lake. His shoes were soaked, along with his socks and his jeans, from the knees down. "Damn it to hell," he growled.

He heard her laughing in the distance.

Then he saw her, emerging from behind a tree. She was wearing the same lavender sweater she'd had on yesterday, and the black jeans he'd packed for her. She had her knapsack slung over her shoulder. She looked very pretty, laughing, with her wavy black hair loose and windblown around her shoulders.

He snarled at her, but couldn't help chuckling, too. "Well, Amelia, my feet are wet, my fucking toes are frozen, and I hope you're happy."

In response, she hoisted up her sweater to flash him her bare breasts. "Does that warm you up a little, baby?"

"Jesus," he murmured with a startled grin. "What the hell has gotten into you today?"

She kissed him. "Right now, I think we both should be getting into this canoe before it floats away." She grabbed him by the hand and started to lead him to the shore.

But Shane balked. "Hold on. Don't you think you ought to tell me what's happening? I mean, this is pretty bizarre. Karen's called me four times this morning. She's freaking out because you took her car, along with some money from her purse."

"Karen's a fucking liar." She scowled at him. "Did you talk to her?"

He sighed. "Yeah, I took one of the calls. She's really worried. The cops have been calling her about you. And she's not a liar. You did take her car. I saw you drive away in it this morning from my place."

"Well, I brought it right back to her house. And if she says I still have it, she's lying. I can't believe you talked to her after I asked you not to. You can't trust her. I told you that."

"Well, what the hell happened? Last night, you were all gaga for Karen, and today, she's a lying skanky bitch. What did she do to you?"

"Can't you guess?" she asked. "Isn't it obvious? She couldn't keep her goddamn hands off me all last night. And then she got really angry with me, because I didn't want to have sex with her. To think, I trusted her and bared my soul to her and, all the while, she just wanted to get into my pants."

"My God, you're kidding," he muttered.

"I'll tell you all about it in the boat," she said, stroking his cheek. "You're the only one I can talk to about this. C'mon, baby, I just need to be with *you* right now, nobody else. Could you pick me up and carry me into the canoe? I promise to warm your feet for you later."

"Sure, sweetheart," he said, obediently hoisting her in his arms. He kissed her forehead and carried her down the grassy slope toward the canoe.

Once he'd pushed the boat away from the shore and hopped inside, she untied his wet shoes and pried them off. Then she rolled down his soggy white socks and wrung them out over the lake. She rubbed his feet, and took turns tucking each one between her legs. Pressing her pelvis against his cold, wiggly toes, she gyrated and purred. Shane grinned at her. She could see the erection growing inside his jeans. She giggled at how much more feverishly he rowed in response to her foot-warming tactics.

"Thanks for rescuing me from her, baby," she said. "You can slow down now. We're not in any hurry. I brought along something else to keep us both warm." She unzipped her knapsack and pulled out a pint of Wild Turkey.

Shane stopped rowing, and gave her a disapproving look. "Oh, I'm not sure if that's such a great idea, Amelia. You know you shouldn't."

She just smiled at him. She thought it was funny, because her brother had said the exact same thing shortly before she'd bashed his skull in.

She saw the caller ID and quickly answered the cell phone. "George?"

"Yeah, hi," he said. "I just talked to Barb Church up in

Bellingham. There's nothing going on next door at Mark and Jenna's house. No sign of your car, either."

Karen was still seated in front of her computer trying to get information on the Schlessingers, but to no avail. She rubbed her forehead. "Well, Shane didn't answer when I called. I left another message."

"I know you don't want to, Karen, but it's time to let the police in on this. Amelia took your car and stole some money. That's not like her. She's not herself. I don't want anyone else hurt because we procrastinated on this. I'm being selfish here, too. Amelia knows where I live. And my kids will be home from school in a few hours."

"I understand," Karen said. "I'll call them." But she hated the idea. All she could think about was how scared, confused, and desperate Amelia must have been to run away like that. She imagined the police hunting her down, maybe even a high-speed chase that would end with Amelia dying in a car crash.

Maybe Karen didn't know that *other* Amelia. But the young woman she knew wouldn't hurt anyone. In fact, Amelia would have wanted to get as far away as possible from her family and friends if she believed herself a danger to them. But where would she go?

"The Lake Wenatchee house," she murmured. No one else was at the lake house, except ghosts.

"What?" George asked.

"Do you think she could have driven to the Lake Wenatchee house?"

"It's possible."

"Didn't you tell me last week you'd phoned a neighbor, some woman who lived down the lake from them? Do you still have her number?"

"It might be in my study someplace. But I don't have it on me."

"Do you remember her name?"

"Helene Something . . . Summers . . . no, Sumner. Helene Sumner."

"Helene Sumner in the Lake Wenatchee area," Karen said, scribbling it down. "I'll call information. Maybe this Helene has noticed some activity over there today."

"And if she *has* seen something over at the house, then what?" George asked.

"Then I'll warn her to stay away. And I'll need you to give me directions to the cabin."

"What, are you nuts? If Amelia's in that house, I'm not letting you go there. That's insane. Besides, you don't even have a car."

"I could rent one."

"Karen—"

"Listen, George, let's not argue about it just yet. For all we know, Amelia might not even be at Lake Wenatchee." Karen sighed. "Have you come up with anything about the Schlessingers at the Salem Library? I'm not having any luck on the Internet."

"I had the same problem on the computers here. But I went to the periodicals desk, and they're digging up some newspaper microfiche files for me right now. I just stepped outside to take the call from Barb in Bellingham. I'm heading back in there now." He paused. "So—you'll talk to this policewoman, right? Report your car stolen, and Amelia missing. . . ."

"Yes, George, I will," she replied. But she knew it wouldn't be easy. The police would have a lot of questions for her, and maybe a few charges, starting with obstruction of justice.

"Okay. Talk to you soon," he said.

"Bye, George."

She quickly clicked off the line, and then dialed directory assistance for Wenatchee, Washington.

*   *   *

At the periodicals desk, George gave the librarian his driver's license as a deposit for a microfiche file for the *Salem Statesman Journal* for the week of July 11– 18, 2004. The two microfiche-viewing machines were at a desk near a bookcase full of reference books and in front of a window looking into the lobby and the Friends of the Library Bookstore.

He switched on the machine, and it made a soft, hairdryer-like humming noise. George quickly scanned the file until he came to the front page for July 14, 2004, the day after Lon and Annabelle Schlessinger had died. He wasn't sure what he hoped to find—perhaps a story about a car crash or a local boating accident. Maybe the story wasn't even in the local paper. Like Uncle Duane, they may not have even died in Salem.

He didn't see anything on page one, but noticed the newspaper's index in the bottom left corner said the obituaries were on page A 19. George fast-forwarded to it, but didn't see any Schlessingers among the dead. He went back to the first page. These were *A.M.* Editions. If Lon and Annabelle had died late in the evening on July 13, it might not have made the morning paper.

He scanned forward to July 15, and searched the front page. His eyes were drawn to a headline near the bottom right of the page, taking up three columns. He anxiously read the article:

LOCAL RANCHER AND DAUGHTER PERISH IN BLAZE

Widower & Teen were Salem
Residents for 11 years

MARION COUNTY: The two-story house of a secluded ranch outside

> Salem became the site of a fiery in-
> ferno Wednesday night, claiming the
> lives of widower, Lon Schlessinger,
> 45, and his daughter, Annabelle Faye
> Schlessinger, 16. Marion County in-
> vestigators believe the fire started in
> the upstairs master bedroom . . .

"Another fire," George murmured to himself. He was thinking about Duane Lee Savitt burning down the adoption agency.

The article didn't exactly say Lon Schlessinger had fallen
asleep while smoking in bed, but they sure hinted at it.
Annabelle's charred remains were discovered in the hallway
by her bedroom door. The Schlessingers had moved to the
area in 1993. Mrs. Schlessinger died that same year, "an apparent suicide," according to the article. There was no mention of her dead brother, and his murder rampage, at least,
not on page one.

George anxiously scanned down to page two, where there
were side-by-side photos of Lon and Annabelle Schlessinger.
He was a slightly paunchy, balding man who looked like an
ex-jock gone to seed. The high school portrait of Annabelle
was startling. George might as well have been staring at a
three-year-old photo of his niece.

Biting his lip, George went back to the article, which
talked about Lon's membership in two civic organizations,
and his love for hunting and fishing. George was more interested in what they reported about Amelia's twin:

> "Annabelle was an extremely
> bright student," said Caroline Cad-
> well, her sophomore homeroom
> teacher at East Marion High School.
> "She was very driven. With her intel-
> ligence, beauty, and determination,

we were all expecting great things in
her future. It's a tragic loss. . . ."

The article ended with a quote from Annabelle's friend
and classmate, Erin Gottlieb:

> "Annabelle was like a force of
> nature. She was so strong and deter-
> mined. She never let anyone get in
> her way when she made her mind up
> to go after something, and you have
> to admire that. I guess it took another
> force of nature, like fire, to stop
> her."

It struck George as a slightly cryptic epitaph, almost un-
flattering.

There was a coin slot at the side of the microfiche viewer
and, for two quarters, George made a copy of each page.
Then he returned the microfiche file to the reference desk,
and asked for a local phone book.

He hoped Caroline Cadwell and Erin Gottlieb still lived
in the area. Maybe Annabelle's teacher and her friend could
tell him something about Mrs. Schlessinger's apparent suicide and Uncle Duane's killing rampage. Maybe one of them
knew about Annabelle's twin sister.

She got Helene Sumner's machine.

Karen waited for the beep, then started in: "Hello, Ms.
Sumner. I'm Karen Carlisle, a friend of Amelia Faraday. I'm
sorry to bother you, but—"

There was a click on the other end of the line. "Yes,
hello," the woman said. "This isn't a reporter, is it?"

"No," Karen said, suddenly sitting erect in her desk chair.
"I'm a friend of Amelia Faraday. I'm calling from Seattle.

She drove off early this morning in my car, a black Volkswagen Jetta. I've been trying to locate her. I was wondering—"

"Well, I can tell you where she was as of nine o'clock today," Helene interrupted. "She was at their house, just down the lake from here. It's got the police tape on the front door, but that didn't stop her from going inside, though I suppose she has a right to go in there."

"Then you saw her?"

"I heard screams," Helene said. "That's what got my attention. The sound travels across the water. I've been keeping an eye on the place. The police told me to report any trespassers. Well, I almost phoned them this morning when I heard the screaming and laughing over there. But then I got out the binoculars, and saw it was Amelia."

"Just Amelia, and no one else?"

"I only saw her, though it sure sounded like someone else was there, maybe that boyfriend of hers."

"Boyfriend?" Karen said. "You mean Shane?"

"I don't know his name. I'm sorry. I know you're Amelia's friend, but . . ." Helene paused for a moment. "Are you in college with Amelia?"

"I'm Amelia's therapist, Ms. Sumner," Karen admitted.

"Well, then you must know, for someone so sweet and pretty, she has terrible taste in boyfriends."

"Does he have black hair and wear sunglasses?" Karen asked.

"Yeah, that's him. I'm sorry, I hate to say the word, but he looks like a *pimp*, what with his cheap suit and those sunglasses. But I didn't see him today, just Amelia."

"You said she was at the house around nine o'clock. Have you seen or heard anything over there since then?"

"No. She may have left. She may have gone back inside the house. I'm not sure."

"Is there a black Jetta or an old Cadillac in the driveway?"

"They don't have a driveway. There's a short trail through

the woods to the top of a hill, where the road is. The Faradays always parked their car in this inlet up there. Do you want me to go over to the house, and check if she's—"

"No," Karen cut her off. "No, please, don't do that. It could be dangerous, especially if her boyfriend is there. I agree with you, Ms. Sumner. He's a bad influence on Amelia. I don't want you going over there. If you see him or Amelia anywhere on your property, you should call the police. I don't mean to frighten you—"

"I'm sixty-seven years old, miss," Helene said. "Not many things scare me anymore. I've lived alone in this house by the lake for the last nine years. I have a good watchdog and a loaded rifle. I'll be all right."

"I'm glad to hear it," Karen replied.

This was the only lead she had. And from what Amelia had told her, there was no way to get in touch with anyone at the lake house, except through Helene's landline next door. Karen would have to drive three hours to Lake Wenatchee and hope Amelia was still there. She wondered if Blade was indeed with her this morning. Or was Amelia's multiple personality disorder so severe that she was *screaming and laughing over there* by herself?

"Miss? Are you still there?"

"Um, yes, Ms. Sumner," she said. "Can I ask you for one more favor? Could you give me directions to the Faradays' house?"

"Have another hit," she said, handing him the Wild Turkey bottle.

His hands on the oars, Shane grinned at her. "I think I've had enough. They say booze and boating is a bad mix."

"This is a stupid little canoe," she said, still offering him the half-drained pint bottle. "I don't think it counts. C'mon, have another blast. It'll warm you up."

Shane shook his head. He already had a little buzz, and unlike Amelia, he knew his limits. Though so far, she'd downed surprisingly little for someone who had seemed bent on getting drunk less than an hour ago.

She was acting awfully strange, a total turnaround from last night. She'd been nervous and on edge throughout the movie and pizza, needy, but in a good way that made him feel like the most important person in the world. But then, since her bizarre visit with him this morning, she didn't seem stressed out at all. She wasn't making him feel needed, just manipulated and jerked around. That wasn't like Amelia at all. Her flirting—the foot rubs, flashing him, the kisses, and her dirty talk—had all been a turn-on, yeah, but it all seemed like an act.

Last night, she hadn't been able to tell him why the cops were waiting for her in her dorm lobby. She'd promised to explain later, and begged him to be patient with her. But when he'd pressed her about it again just a few minutes ago, she'd dismissed it, and said they were bugging her with more personal questions about her father. "I just didn't feel like discussing my dad's hang-ups with them again, that's all," she'd explained. "So screw them."

She didn't want to talk about Karen coming on to her last night either. At first she'd acted like Karen had attacked her or something. But now, in the boat, she didn't seem too traumatized about it. Shane began to wonder if anything really did happen with Karen.

He glanced up at the darkening sky, the clouds almost obscuring Mount Rainier in the distance. "Looks like rain. We should head back," he said, working the oars again.

"Party pooper," she muttered. She put the cap back on the Wild Turkey bottle, then slipped it into her knapsack. She kept the knapsack in her lap. "What's wrong with you today anyway?" she asked. "You're acting totally weird."

"*I'm* acting weird?" Shane shot back.

She nodded. "You know, I should be really sore at you. This morning, I specifically asked you not to talk to Karen, and you talked to her anyway. Did you tell her about meeting me here today?"

"No. I didn't tell her shit. I didn't tell anyone." He rowed more fervently. "I'm sorry, but this whole thing is totally schizoid. You show up at my window at dawn, dragging me out of bed. You've got me ditching psych class and renting a canoe, so we can schlep out here in the middle of the god-damn lake for this secret meeting. My favorite shoes are all wet, and we're about to get rained on. And you're telling me I'm acting weird, because I'm not exactly thrilled to be jumping through all these hoops for you. . . ."

Her head bowed, she hugged her knapsack in her lap and quietly cried.

Shane sighed. "Okay, okay, I'll shut up. I'm sorry. Let's just go back to my place and talk, okay? Nobody's there right now."

"Well, nobody's out here right now, either," she said, pouting. "That's why I wanted to come here—so we could be alone. But you're acting like you don't want to be alone with me."

"That's not true, sweetheart." He stopped rowing, and they drifted for a few moments.

"You're treating me like I'm a stranger," she said, wiping a tear from her cheek. "I've felt it ever since we met on the island. You've been pulling away from me. We're out here alone in this beautiful, romantic spot, and all you want to do is go home."

"I'm sorry, Amelia." He shrugged and shook his head. "I didn't mean to pull away. I just can't figure out what you're up to today. I—"

"What I'm *up to* today?" she repeated, giving him a wounded look. "What does that mean? You sound like you don't trust me."

"Of course, I trust you."

"Prove it," she said, reaching into the knapsack again.

"What?"

"I said, prove it. Prove to me that I have your trust." She pulled a revolver out of the knapsack.

Shane recoiled, and the boat rocked a bit. "What the hell? Amelia . . ."

Tears in her eyes, she pointed the gun at him.

"Sweetheart, what are you doing?" he whispered. If he'd had a little buzz from the Wild Turkey, he was very sober now. He stayed perfectly still.

"I want to see if you really trust me, if you love me," she said.

Gaping at the gun, he shook his head. "I—I didn't know you had that. Where did you even get that?"

He shrunk back as she got to her feet. The boat swayed back and forth, but she kept the gun trained on him. "Oh, Jesus, be careful," he murmured, wincing.

She sat down close to him. Their legs pressed against each other, knees bumping. Shane tried not to make any sudden moves.

She stared into his eyes. "A minute ago, you said you didn't mean to pull away from me. If I put this gun in your mouth, would you pull away?"

"Sweetheart, please stop. . . ."

"Then you don't trust me," she cried. "You don't love me. I might as well use this gun on myself. Don't you see? You're all I have left, Shane."

"Don't, please, Amelia. Just—just—just put that thing down."

She held the revolver a few inches from his face. He was so terrified, he could hardly breathe.

"Prove to me that you love me," she whispered. "Let me put this in your mouth. Can't you trust me that much? Just for a couple of seconds? If you won't let me, I swear to God, I'll shoot myself right here. I mean it."

He shook his head.

"Fine," she muttered, then she suddenly turned the gun on herself.

"No!" he screamed. The sound seemed to echo over the lake.

She froze. Her eyes wrestled with his.

"You can put it in my mouth," he said. "If it's that important to you, go ahead."

Shane told himself that she'd had the chance to shoot him ever since they'd gotten out on the lake, if that was what she wanted to do. In some totally screwed-up way, maybe she was right; he'd have to trust her, and this was one way of showing it.

But as she turned the gun toward him, he felt his stomach lurch. Shane thought he might be sick. His hands shook on the oars. "Why?" he whispered. "Amelia, why are you doing this?"

Her forehead was wrinkled in concentration, but there was a strange coolness about her, too, a determined gaze past the tears in her eyes.

She brushed the end of the gun against his lips.

Shane opened his mouth wider, and tasted the dirty metal on his tongue.

"I'm doing this to make certain you love Amelia," she said.

He sat there, trying not to shake, and counting the seconds while she kept the gun in his mouth. It struck him as bizarre, the way she'd said *Amelia* instead of *me*, as if Amelia were someone else entirely: "I'm doing this to make certain you love Amelia."

The notion that she might not be Amelia didn't occur to him at all. Shane didn't have a chance. Before the thought even entered his head a bullet already had.

* * *

She dipped her hand in the cold lake water to rinse it off. Blood had sprayed on her face and hair, too. She licked her lips and tasted it: salty and warm. Then she bent over the side of the canoe and washed off her face.

Shane had flopped back so violently that the boat had almost tipped over. Water had sluiced in, and one of the oars had gotten knocked into the lake. Now he lay there on the floor of the canoe in an awkward contortion. The small puddle of water lapping around him was almost completely red now.

She checked his wallet. There were only seventeen dollars in there. She kept ten. She'd noticed the ring on his right hand earlier. It was gold with a beautiful black onyx stone. She twisted it off his finger and dropped it into her purse. Wiping off the gun, she carefully placed it beside his lifeless hand. Then with the one oar they had left, she paddled toward the little island. The small patch of land was still unoccupied. She let the canoe hit the muddy bank. Climbing out of the canoe, she stepped knee-deep into the icy lake. She hoisted the knapsack over her shoulder. She had a change of clothes in there, among other things.

Giving the boat a shove, she watched it drift away from the shore.

Then she turned and headed for dry land.

Chapter Sixteen

"Sorry I didn't call back sooner," Karen said into her cell. She walked along Boylston Avenue at a brisk clip. She wore a trench coat over her black jeans and her dark green V-neck sweater.

She'd cancelled all her afternoon appointments before running out of the house. It was eleven blocks to her destination, and Karen was in a hurry. She might have taken a cab, but this wasn't a phone conversation she wanted to conduct in the back of a taxi. She'd turned down Boylston to avoid the crowds and the traffic noise along the main drag, Broadway. This street was more residential, with an eclectic mix of brand-new and very old apartment buildings. Trees lined the parkways, and their fallen leaves covered the sidewalk. Karen hadn't encountered too many other pedestrians taking this route.

"I wasn't ignoring you, Detective," she explained on the phone. "The last couple of hours, I've been busy making calls, hoping to find out where Amelia might have gone. You see, I probably should have told you this morning, but, well, Amelia stayed over at my place last night."

"Is that so?" Jacqueline Peyton said on the other end of the line. "You knew we wanted to get in touch with Amelia. And yet you deliberately kept her from talking to us. Why?"

Karen hesitated. She didn't want to say anything to incriminate Amelia or herself. Hell, she didn't even want to be talking to the police right now. But if there was *another* Amelia out there endangering people's lives, then the police had to be told. At the same time, the Amelia she knew was probably scared, confused, and hiding somewhere, like at the lake house in Wenatchee. And Karen didn't want to see her hurt.

Yet, she'd slipped her dad's revolver into her purse before leaving the house a few minutes ago. Exactly who she intended to use it on she didn't know.

"I'm sorry," she said at last. "But I'm Amelia's therapist, and my first duty is to my client. She's a very sweet, very confused young woman—"

"Did she meet with Koehler on Sunday?" Jacqueline Peyton pressed.

"I can't say," Karen replied, picking up her pace. "I can't tell you anything we discussed in confidence—"

"You know, Karen, that won't hold up in court."

"Maybe not, but I'm sticking to it. So, here's what I can tell you right now. Okay?"

"Go ahead. I'm listening."

"Amelia stayed at my house last night. After you called me this morning, I went to check on her, and she was gone. So was my car, and about sixty dollars from my purse. My car is a 1999 black Volkswagen Jetta, license plate number EMK903. Are you taking this down?"

"Yes, black VW Jetta, Washington plates EMK903."

"Amelia's uncle, her boyfriend, and her roommate don't have any idea where she is," Karen continued. "Her uncle and I checked, and she's not up at her parents' house in Bellingham. Amelia would never intentionally hurt anybody. But there's someone who could be with her, and I think he's trouble. His name's Blade and he's in his midtwenties. He has dyed black hair, and wears sunglasses a lot. I believe he drives an old black Cadillac with a bent antenna. I don't have any other information about him."

"All right," the policewoman said. "Where are you right now? Are you at home?"

"No, I'm not," Karen said. Just half a block ahead, she could see a green sandwich-board sign on the sidewalk. It had ENTERPRISE RENTAL CAR written on it.

"We'll need to talk to you in person, Karen. And you might want to have your lawyer present."

"Yes, I was afraid of that," she murmured into the phone. And then she clicked off.

While they got her compact economy car ready for her, Karen asked to use the restroom. It was a small, gray-tiled unisex bathroom off the garage. She stood by the dirty white sink, and pulled out her cell phone again. She counted three ring tones.

"Sandpoint View Convalescent Home," Roseann answered.

"Hi, Ro, it's Karen again, just checking in. How's my dad?"

"He's up and around, and having a good day. Still no sign of that girl you asked about."

"Well, good," Karen said, relieved. "You might not be able to get ahold of me later this afternoon. If you do see her, call this number right away. Do you have a pen?"

"Just a sec. Okay, shoot."

"555-9225, that's a Detective Jacqueline Peyton. Tell her you're a friend of mine, and you've found Amelia Faraday."

"555-9225," Roseann repeated. "I'm a friend of yours and I found Amelia Faraday. Got it."

"Detective Peyton will know what to do from there."

"Are you going to tell me what this is all about?"

"I can't right now. But later, Ro, I promise."

"Sounds like you're in a hurry to get someplace."

"Yes, I need to take off soon," Karen said.

"Well, you caught me in the lounge, and Frank's right here. Do you have time to talk with him? Like I said, he's having a good day."

"Oh, yes, thank you. Ro. Please, put him on." She waited, and heard some faint murmuring on the other end.

"Hello, Karen?" he said, at last.

"Hi, Poppy, how are you?"

"Fine. How's my girl doing?"

"I'm okay," she lied. Her voice even cracked a little, because this was one of those rare moments when she felt like she was talking to her father again. Part of her just wanted to say, *Poppy, I'm in trouble.* Instead, she cleared her throat. "Um, I hope to come by to visit you tomorrow."

"Well, I'll be here. Could you bring Rufus?"

"Sure, I will. You sound great, Poppy."

"We're having ham for dinner tonight," he said. "They serve a good ham here."

"Well, enjoy. And I'll see you tomorrow, okay?"

"Okay, sweetie. Take care of yourself."

Then she heard him talking to Roseann: "That was my daughter, Karen. How do you hang up this thing? Oh . . . I see . . ." There was a click on the line.

"Bye, Poppy," she said to no one.

"Why do you want to talk to Erin?" asked the woman on the telephone.

There were five Gottliebs in the Salem phone book, and this was the third one George had called. It was Erin's mother, M. Gottlieb.

"I'm trying to track down some information on Annabelle Schlessinger," George said. He was sitting inside his car, still parked down the street from the Salem Library. "I understand Erin and Annabelle were friends."

There was a silence on the other end of the line. "Mrs. Gottlieb?"

"Um, how did you know Annabelle?" she asked finally.

"I didn't," he admitted. "That's why I wanted to talk to Erin. You see, I'm doing some research on my family tree— a master's thesis on genealogy, actually. There's a chance I could be related to Annabelle. I was hoping Erin might be able to give me some information about the Schlessingers."

"I don't think she could tell you much. Erin and Annabelle really weren't friends for very long."

"Anything would be helpful, Mrs. Gottlieb."

"Well, I suppose you could phone her at work. You can reach her at the Pampered Pup."

It was a doggie daycare and grooming place located in a strip mall near Willamette University. George had decided he'd get more information out of Erin if they talked face-to-face.

Apparently Erin had been expecting him, one way or another. When he told the Pampered Pup receptionist he was looking for Erin, the heavyset, terminally bored-looking young woman came around the lobby desk, then escorted him to the back. She opened a door that must have been soundproof, because the sudden din of yelps and barking startled him. She led him to an alcove, where about two dozen small- and medium-sized dogs were in cages, stacked one on top of the other.

"Hey, Erin," the receptionist yelled over the racket. "You've got a visitor." Then she wandered back toward the front office.

Erin was thin with straight, dark-blond hair, glasses, and a pierced nostril. She stood at a long steel sink, washing a slightly hyper Jack Russell terrier. She wore a dark-blue work apron over her black sweater and jeans. She nodded instead of shaking his hand. She had on yellow rubber gloves, and worked a portable shower nozzle over the soapy dog.

"Hi, I'm George," he said. "Sorry to bother you here at work."

"It's okay. My mom called to tell me you might be calling or coming by." Erin gave him a wry grin. She had to talk loudly over the continuous barking. "All these alarms probably went off when you told her you were related to Annabelle Schlessinger. Mom always thought Annabelle was a terrible influence on me. So, what did you want to know?"

"Well, I read that story in the *Statesman Journal* about the fire, and what you said about Annabelle." George leaned against the dry end of the long sink. "It was an interesting quote, very poetic . . ."

"Oh, that *force of nature* speech," she said, chuckling. "I got so much shit from my other friends about that. But I honestly couldn't think of anything *nice* to say. Annabelle and I were officially avoiding each other weeks before the fire. But I guess I knew her better than anyone else, so I had to come up with something for that stupid reporter."

"Your mom indicated that you and Annabelle weren't friends for very long," George said.

Washing under the dog's tail, she nodded. "Yeah, she was just a little too clingy and possessive. Can I be totally honest with you? I mean, you didn't know her, right? You don't want me blowing smoke up your ass, right?"

"No, I'd appreciate your honesty. Really, it won't offend me at all."

"Well, it's funny. All the guys were hot for Annabelle, because she was pretty and had big boobs. But she just used them. It didn't take long for me to realize she was a manipulative bitch, and you can throw *crazy* into that soup, too."

"Crazy, how?"

"Well, I guess this goes with the clingy, possessive part of her character. But she wanted us to work out our own secret language, so we could write and talk to each other, and no one else would understand. She even wanted us to dress alike at school. I mean, how queer is that? Oh, and she claimed she could read my thoughts. That was another thing. Annabelle said she was telepathic. I remember laughing at her and saying she was tele-*pathetic,* and she got really pissed off at me. I think that was the beginning of the end for us."

She picked up the terrier and moved it farther down the steel sink. "Better back up," she said.

But George didn't hear her past all the barking and yelping. He was thinking about the matching clothes, a secret language, and some telepathic connection. Was Annabelle hoping Erin would take the place of the twin she'd lost?

"Hey," Erin said loudly. "Unless you want to get doused, better stand back. He's gonna shake it off."

George backed up toward the cages, and watched the dog shake off the excess water. Erin started working a towel over him.

"Did Annabelle ever mention to you that she had a twin sister?" he asked.

"Oh, yeah, *Andrea.*" Erin said, nodding. "She told me *Andrea* was abducted by some pervert neighbor when the kid was four, and he raped and killed her. I mean, talk about creepy and tragic, right? And then I talked to another girl in my class, Deborah Wothers. Annabelle tried to be Deborah's friend for a while, because Deborah's so nice and everybody loves her. But Deborah was smart enough to keep her distance. Anyway, she told Deborah that her twin sister, *Alicia,* slipped and fell in the tub and drowned or some bullshit like that. So, you're telling me she really did have a twin?"

George just nodded. He knew both stories were fabrications, of course. But he wondered if there was a sliver of truth to the abduction incident.

Erin had stopped drying the dog. She stared at George. "So, this twin, how did she really die?"

"She didn't. She's alive, and her name's Amelia," he explained. "The Schlessingers put her up for adoption when she was four. I'm trying to find out why. Amelia doesn't know anything about her birth family. I was hoping you could fill in a lot of blanks for me, Erin. Did Annabelle ever talk about her mother?"

With a dumbfounded look, Erin shook her head.

"Nothing?" he pressed.

"Well, I heard she offed herself when Annabelle was just a kid. She hanged herself in the basement or something. Annabelle was supposed to have found her. I never had the guts to ask her for details."

"What about the father?"

She shrugged. "I used to see him at church, that's it."

"Didn't you ever see him at Annabelle's house?"

"I never went there. I don't think anyone in the class did, either." Erin wrapped the dog in the towel, then carried him to a cage, and set him inside. With a sigh, she pulled off her gloves. "Anyway, I never set foot in the place," she said. "Annabelle always came over to my house. She pretty much hated living out there at that ranch in the middle of nowhere."

"Did Annabelle ever talk about her Uncle Duane?" George asked.

Erin pried a stick of Juicy Fruit out of her pants pocket, then unwrapped it and put it in her mouth. "Nope, sorry."

She put her work gloves back on, opened another cage, and pulled out a miniature schnauzer. "C'mon, bath time, you mangy son of a bitch," she muttered. She set the dog in the steel tub, then stopped and turned to George. "You know who you should talk to? Mrs. Cadwell, our homeroom teacher sophomore year. Caroline Cadwell, she was practically a friend of the family. I think she even knew Mrs. Schlessinger. She could tell you a lot."

"Caroline Cadwell," George repeated. Along with Erin, she'd been quoted in the newspaper account about the fire.

Stroking the dog's head, Erin paused to glance at George. "As far as the Schlessingers go, Mrs. Cadwell knows more than anybody else, and she's *seen* more than anybody else. She can tell you all about the fire, too."

"Really?" George asked.

"Oh, yeah," she replied, nodding. "Mrs. Cadwell's the one who identified the bodies."

Salem, Oregon—July 2004

It was 8:50 P.M., and still light out—still pretty hot, too. But she felt a soft, cool evening wind against her bare legs.

Eighteen-year-old Sandra Hartman cut across the deserted baseball field. Her shoulder-length black hair was freshly washed, and she wore a blue blouse, khaki shorts, and sandals. She warily eyed the empty bleachers. The place kind of gave her the creeps at night, even with the late sunset.

She was on her way to meet some friends at Lancaster Mall. They planned to see *Dodgeball*, of all things. The only reason for going was because a bunch of guys she knew were supposed to show up.

Sandra lived eight blocks from the mall. It wasn't very pedestrian-friendly right around there. Ordinarily, she would have driven over. But her parents had taken the car for some business dinner her dad had. When she'd mentioned she might go to the movies, he'd insisted she grab a ride from a friend or stay home.

Everyone was still in a panic over the disappearance of Gina Fernetti just ten days before. The story was on TV and in the newspapers. Regina Marie Fernetti was twenty, a journalism major at the University of Colorado, and home for summer break. She and two girlfriends had gone to the Walker Pool on a busy Saturday afternoon. Gina had driven. They'd just claimed a spot on the grass, and laid out their blankets when Gina announced she wanted to get a certain tape cassette out of the car for her Walkman. She left her purse and blanket behind, and went off toward the parking lot with her car keys. When she didn't return fifteen minutes later, her friends checked the lot. Gina's car was still there, still locked. They searched the pool area, and had her paged over the public address system. The lifeguards even made everyone get out of the pool for ten minutes just to make sure Gina hadn't missed the announcement. Gina's girlfriends finally called Mr. and Mrs. Fernetti who, in turn, called the police.

No one had seen Gina Fernetti since. She'd just vanished.

So Sandra's father was being a bit crazy-overprotective. To appease him, Sandra had tried to get one of her friends to pick her up at the last minute, but with no luck. They were carpooling over to the mall, and it was already crammed. Sandra figured she could get a ride home later from one of the guys, and her dad would be none the wiser about her walking to the mall alone.

She had about twenty minutes until the movie started, and figured she'd be at the mall in ten. Sandra noticed the streetlights go on as she made her way across the baseball field. She slipped through an opening in the fence, and started down a residential street. She didn't see anyone else around. It was a bit eerie and unsettling. On a warm night like this, more people should have been out. Was what had happened to Gina keeping people inside with their doors locked?

Sandra picked up her pace, but then suddenly balked when a shadow swept in front of her. She realized a car was pulling up behind her with its headlights on. She glanced over her shoulder: a silver SUV.

Strange, five minutes ago, she'd noticed a silver SUV coming up the road toward her before she'd cut through the baseball field. Was this the same one?

The vehicle slowed down and pulled over to the curb in front of her.

"Shit," Sandra murmured. A little alarm went off inside her. She quickly crossed the street, and watched the SUV slowly creep over toward her. She walked as fast as she could without breaking into a sprint. She told herself not to run. As long as she pretended not to notice them, they wouldn't know she was scared and they wouldn't start chasing her—not just yet. Somehow, maybe it would buy her time. She could be overreacting too. Would someone really try anything in a residential neighborhood, where people could hear her screaming? Plus, it was still kind of light out, for God's sake.

Then again, the light hadn't protected Gina Fernetti. She'd vanished in the middle of a sunny afternoon, and no one had heard her scream.

The silver SUV crawled down the street, keeping pace with her. Sandra's stomach was in knots. Could it be some friend of hers, playing a joke? Well, it wasn't funny, damn it. On her left, Sandra saw a two-story white stucco house with a car in the driveway and lights on in the front windows. She thought about running up the walkway and pounding on the door.

She casually glanced to her right at that silver SUV. The driver's window went down. "Hey, Sandra! Are you going to the mall? Do you need a ride?"

It took Sandra a few moments to recognize the driver, and when she did, she let out a weak chuckle. "Oh, my God, you scared the shit out of me."

"Sorry," said the girl behind the wheel, smiling. "I wasn't really sure if it was you or not. I'm headed to the mall. Do you need a lift?"

Sandra hesitated. If she accepted the ride, she'd feel obligated to invite her along to the movie. It was the polite thing to do. But she really didn't like this girl very much. In fact she hardly knew her. She was a sophomore, two years behind her. It was weird how the girl had called out to her from the car window like they were good friends. The only other time they'd ever talked was in the school cafeteria two months before. The sophomore had approached Sandra while she'd been eating lunch with her friends.

"You must be Sandra Hartman," she'd said. "You wouldn't believe how many times people mistake me for you."

"Oh, really?" Sandra had said, with a baffled smile.

"Yeah, I can totally see the resemblance now. We're almost like twins."

"Well, huh, maybe. Anyway, nice meeting you," Sandra had said. Then she'd turned away. Her friends at the table had started teasing her. "Who the hell was that?" Sandra had whispered. And then one of her friends had told her.

That had been the only other time she'd talked to Annabelle Schlessinger.

"Sandra? Are you headed to the mall?" Annabelle asked from the driver's seat of the SUV.

She worked up a smile and nodded. She figured her dad was probably right. In the wake of Gina Fernetti's disappearance, it wasn't smart to walk around alone at night. And it was starting to get dark. She'd be better off riding the rest of the way. So what if Annabelle ended up tagging along to the movie with her? There was no reason to be snobby toward her. In fact, Sandra realized as she stepped closer to the SUV and locked eyes with Annabelle that there was indeed a resemblance between them. "I'm meeting some friends to see *Dodgeball*. Do you want to join us?"

Her mouth open, Annabelle stared back at her and blinked. Stopping, Sandra saw tears well up in Annabelle's eyes. "What's wrong?" she asked.

"I—I really wish I could go to the movie with you guys, more than anything," Annabelle murmured. Then she cleared her throat, and straightened up behind the wheel. "Thanks anyway, but I can't," she said, more control in her tone. She gazed at the road in front of her. "I'm headed to the mall to run an errand for my father. Hurry up, get in."

Sandra walked around the front of the car, a bit puzzled by Annabelle's strange reaction to such a casual invitation. At the same time, everything was coming out all right for her. She had a ride to the mall with no strings attached. She didn't have to spend the rest of the night with Annabelle clinging to her.

"Oh, you've got the air-conditioning on in here," Sandra said, sliding into the front seat. "Feels like heaven."

Annabelle said nothing. She stared straight ahead.

Once Sandra shut the passenger door and buckled her seatbelt, the SUV started to inch forward. After a few moments, Sandra glanced at the speedometer: 10 mph. "What, are you afraid of getting a ticket?" she asked. "Why are you going so slowly?"

Annabelle didn't answer. The SUV crawled past the end of the block toward a turnaround area by some woods. The headlights and interior lights went off, and suddenly they were swallowed up in darkness. "What the hell's going on?" Sandra asked.

The car stopped. Hands on the wheel, Annabelle wouldn't look at her. Instead, she glanced up at the rearview mirror. "I'm sorry, Sandra," she muttered listlessly. "I guess you haven't met my father."

"What?" Sandra checked the rearview mirror, and saw a shadowy figure suddenly spring up from the floor. She gasped.

All at once, he grabbed her hair and yanked her head back. It happened so fast, she couldn't fight him off. He slapped a wet cloth over her mouth. It must have been soaked with some chemical, because it burned her face. Sandra's eyes watered up. She tried not to breathe in, and desperately clawed at his hand.

But he wouldn't let go. Almost unwillingly, she gasped for air, and then realized it was too late. Sandra had never experienced this sensation before. She wasn't passing out, or falling asleep, or even fainting. No, this was something different.

Sandra Hartman felt herself surrendering to something very close to death.

Seattle—three years later

"Nope, sorry, I still haven't seen hide nor hair of Amelia," Jessie said into the phone. In front of her on the McMillans' kitchen table, was a pile of laundry, still warm from the dryer. "No calls either, except from Karen, checking up on me about a half hour ago."

"Okay, Jessie, thanks," George said on the other end of the line. "Jody should be home from school in about an hour. Could you take him with you when you go to pick up Steffie at Rainbow Junction Daycare?"

"You asked me that this morning, and I will," Jessie said. "Now, can I tell you something? That cleaning woman of yours isn't worth the powder to blow her to hell. There are dust balls behind your sofa and under the cushions, I found three old French fries, a plastic barrette, some popcorn and forty-seven cents in change."

"Well, you can keep the barrette, but I want the forty-seven cents," George said. "You sure everything's okay there?"

"Peachy," Jessie assured him. "I'm folding laundry, and after this I'm taking out your recycling. Pretty exciting, huh?"

"Well, take a break, for God's sake," George replied. "I'll talk to you later, Jess."

She hung up the phone, and finished folding the clothes. Then Jessie got the recycling bin out of the pantry, and carried it out the kitchen door. She lumbered up to the edge of the driveway and let out a groan as she set the bin on the front curb.

Jessie paused to take a look down the block. She spotted a black car parked about four houses down on the other side of the street. But it wasn't Karen's Jetta, and that was the one she was supposed to be on the lookout for.

This car was just a beat-up old Cadillac.

With a sigh, Jessie turned and headed back for the house.

Chapter Seventeen

Karen took the turnoff at Coles Corner to Lake Wenatchee Highway. The scenery along Stevens Pass had been gorgeous: the mountains and rivers, the trees so vibrant with their fall colors, and even a few small waterfalls. But she'd barely noticed any of it. She couldn't stop thinking about what George had discovered, that Amelia had a twin sister.

No wonder Amelia had developed so many neuroses, having been torn apart from her twin at such a young age. With the sudden absence of her sister, Amelia might have taken on her twin's persona. Perhaps she assumed her sister felt abandoned, angry and bitter, even destructive. And maybe Amelia was adopting those traits during her blackouts while the twin sister part of her took over. That *lost time* Amelia experienced kept her from knowing about this sister-half and her activities.

"Or maybe they're just alcohol-related blackouts," Karen muttered to herself. "And you're making way too much of this twin thing."

She passed a sign for Lake Wenatchee State Park, and

knew she was on the right track, at least as far as her driving was concerned. According to Helene's directions, she would be at the Faradays' lake house in another fifteen minutes.

Amelia's separation from her twin certainly explained other things: the nightmares and those phantom pains and "faked" illnesses that had plagued her all the way through adolescence. Karen had read accounts of twin telepathy when she was in graduate school. Some were rather dull, dry studies. "Though separated, both twins picked the red ball for the first two experiments, and the green ball for the third, and the red ball again for the fourth. The choice patterns of the separated twins matched in 96 percent of the test cases."

Other accounts were a bit more like a *Twilight Zone* episode. Karen recalled one story about a 55-year-old businessman who woke up in the middle of the night in his Zurich hotel room with severe abdominal pains and a high fever. The doctors in the emergency room at the hospital couldn't find anything actually wrong with him, and his fever went away by the next morning. He got back to the hotel to find a message from his sister-in-law in Columbus, Ohio. His twin brother had been rushed to the hospital the night before with a ruptured appendix.

Karen remembered one of her professors dismissing such stories, though apparently dozens of similar cases were on record.

Had young Amelia, with her unexplained maladies, been feeling the pains and illnesses of her twin sister? Karen remembered some of Amelia's descriptions. *It felt like someone was kicking me. . . . Like my arm was being twisted off . . . It felt like someone was putting out a lit cigar on me. . . .*

She wondered about the awful things being done to Annabelle Schlessinger when her estranged twin sister—miles and miles away—had felt those horrible sensations. What kind of violence had that child endured? Amelia had said she'd stopped experiencing the phantom pains and ill-nesses about three years ago, when she was sixteen. And Annabelle Schlessinger had died at age sixteen.

Perhaps Amelia's violent nightmares while growing up had been the result of some kind of telepathy. Maybe she was picking up real incidents as they happened to her twin.

Karen could almost imagine her professor laughing at her for such far-fetched speculation. It might not hold up with an American Psychological Association review panel, but there were all sorts of phenomena that couldn't be easily ex-plained. And twin telepathy was one of them.

Karen kept a lookout for the street signs. Along the forest road, she could see the placid lake peeking through the trees. She finally spotted a sign, with a red and white checkered border:

DANNY'S DINER
Breakfast, Lunch, or Dinner
You'll Come Up a Winner!

1 MILE AHEAD ↑

That was the restaurant both Amelia and Helene had de-scribed to her—the one near the gravel road that led to the Faradays' lake house.

Karen still didn't know what she expected to find when she got to the cabin. She might have driven all this way for nothing. If Amelia was hiding out there, Karen would calm her down and talk to her. They certainly couldn't put off going to the police any longer. Hell, they were both probably *persons of interest* in Koehler's disappearance, and about a notch away from *fugitive* status, if not there already. But Karen was still determined to protect Amelia, and make sure she got the help she needed.

Up the road a piece, she saw Danny's Diner, a small

chalet-style restaurant with flower boxes in the windows and four picnic tables in front. The parking lot was big enough for a dozen cars, and at the moment, half full. As Karen drove by, she noticed the phone booth by the front door.

Eyes on the road, she reached over for her cell phone, and tried to dial her home number. A mechanical voice told her, "We're sorry. Your call cannot be completed. Please hang up and try again."

Helene was right, cell phones didn't work around here. That would make things extremely difficult if she ran into trouble at the cabin. She had to prepare herself for the possibility that Amelia was indeed at the cabin, but not at all herself right now. She might even have Blade with her.

Karen noticed the turn off to Holden Trail, a gravel road that sloped down and wound through the forest. The tiny stones made a hail-like racket under her rental car, and the occasional divot gave her a jolt. Karen had an awful foreboding feeling in the pit of her stomach, along with nerves and hunger, too. She hadn't eaten all day.

She spotted a turnaround on her left. Helene had told her to ignore that one. The inlet the Faradays used was up ahead. Karen slowed down. She could see a little plateau off the bay with enough room for two small cars. As she inched into the spot, Karen could see other tire marks in the gravel and dirt.

After the two-and-a-half-hour drive, Karen's legs cramped a bit as she climbed out of the rental. Grabbing her purse, she took another look at the gun inside. Along with the tire tracks, she noticed a cigarette butt and footprints, too. It looked like more than one person.

So Amelia hadn't come here alone this morning. She must have been with Blade.

Karen saw the footprints again as she made her way down the trail, which was mostly dirt, but some patches were covered in gravel. There were a few stone steps, too, and an old wooden railing at a few precarious spots. She caught a glimpse

of the lake between the trees. Finally, the terrain started to
flatten out. Karen could see a clearing and the Faradays'
house ahead.

A crude flagstone path led to the front stoop of the weathered, two-story Cape Cod home. Karen tried to peek inside
the windows as she passed. But it was dark in the house, and
she couldn't see anything beyond her own timid reflection.

Strips of yellow police tape with CRIME SCENE—DO NOT
CROSS written on them had been taped across the front door.
But someone had torn past them, and the loose tape strips now
fluttered in the wind. There was also a notice taped to the
front door—a green sheet of paper with a police shield logo
and CITY OF WENATCHEE POLICE DEPARTMENT along the top.
Karen glanced at it. There were two paragraphs of legal jar-
gon, but the last words were in bold print: NO TRESPASSING—
VIOLATORS WILL BE PROSECTUED.

Obviously, someone else had already ignored those warn-
ings. Karen was about to knock on the front door, but hesitated. If Blade and Amelia were in there, did she really want
to announce her arrival?

Biting her lip, Karen tried the doorknob. To her amazement, the door wasn't locked. Slowly, she opened it. Reaching into her purse, she took out her father's revolver, and
then stepped over the threshold. All the blinds were half
drawn, and the windows closed. It was dark and stuffy inside
the house. Nearly every stick of furniture had been dusted
for fingerprints. A dirt trail covered the carpet and floors,
obviously from all the police traipsing in and out of the
crime scene. By the fireplace, Karen noticed the rocking
chair where Amelia's father was found. Behind it, she saw
the large splotch on the wall, now a rust color. There were
bloodstains on the beige carpet, too, beneath the rocker, and
also a few feet away, where George's wife must have been
shot. Everything was just as Amelia—and Koehler—had described it.

Karen followed the investigators' trail toward the kitchen, but abruptly stopped at the sound of something creaking. It seemed to have come from upstairs, but she wasn't sure. With the gun in her trembling hand, Karen listened and waited for the next little noise. She counted to ten, and didn't hear anything. She told herself it was just the house settling. She crept into the kitchen. It had gingerbread trim on the shelves and a yellow, fifties-style dinette set. Through the window in the kitchen door, she noticed the yellow police tape again, only this time, it was intact and crisscrossed over the entry.

There was another door in the kitchen, open about two inches. Beyond that, all Karen could see was darkness. She moved the door, and it creaked on the hinges. She froze. Was that the same sound she'd heard earlier?

She gazed at the wood-plank stairs leading down to the pitch-black basement. Turning to look for a light switch by the door, she saw something dart past the kitchen window. Karen gasped. For a moment, she was paralyzed. She didn't know what to do. It had looked like a person, but she'd only caught a glimpse of her—or him. Whoever it was, they must have been outside, peeking in at her. And they'd moved away from that window so quickly, all Karen had seen was a human-shaped blur.

Clutching the revolver, Karen made her way toward the front door again. She kept checking the windows for whoever was outside the house, but didn't see anybody. "Amelia?" she called. Karen edged toward the door, which she'd left open. She still had the gun poised. "Amelia, is that you? It's Karen. Amelia?"

A dog started barking. "Who's in there?" someone called from outside.

Karen looked out, and saw an older woman with close-cropped gray hair, glasses, and a bulky gray sweater. She had a collie on a leash. "Hush, Abby," she whispered.

Karen quickly stashed the gun in her purse. "Are you Helene?"

Scowling at her, the old woman nodded. "Are you the one I talked to on the phone earlier?"

"Yes," she said, catching her breath. "I'm Karen Carlisle, Amelia's therapist."

"Well, Amelia must have skedaddled," Helene said. "No one's in there. I checked a little while ago."

Karen closed the door behind her. "You went in there after I warned you not to?"

Helene shrugged. "Why should I listen to you? I don't even know you. Anyway, the place is empty." She bent down and scratched her dog behind the ears. "I have no idea when she left. Like I told you on the phone, I saw only Amelia earlier, though it sure sounded like two people were here."

Karen nodded. She was thinking about the double footprints on the dirt trail that led to the house. "Ms. Sumner, before today, when was the last time you noticed Amelia here?"

"Well, she and that boyfriend of hers were carrying on out by the lake a week ago Monday," Helene answered, still hovering over her dog.

"The Monday before the shootings?" Karen asked. She was almost certain she'd had a therapy session with Amelia that Monday. "The fifteenth?"

Helene nodded.

"Are you sure?"

Helene nodded again emphatically. "Monday is my shopping day. When you get to be my age, and you live alone, different rituals become like your companion. . . ."

Karen nodded. She knew exactly what the old woman meant, and it scared her a little that she was already becoming so set in her ways.

"So Monday afternoon, before I headed out to the store, I took Abby for a walk, and I saw Amelia and that creepy young man by the lake. The way they were carrying on, I think they might have been doing drugs."

"What time was this?" Karen asked.

"Smack dab in the middle of the day, around one o'clock."

Karen shook her head. It didn't make sense. If she remembered correctly, her appointment with Amelia that Monday had been in the early afternoon. "Are you sure of the time?" she pressed. "Are you sure it was Amelia?"

Frowning, Helene stopped petting her dog and straightened up. "Miss, I may be old. But I'm not senile—not yet, at least."

"I'm sorry, but I'm almost positive I was with Amelia, in Seattle, around that exact same time."

Helene scowled at her. "Well, if you were with Amelia on that Monday afternoon, then who was that girl I saw by the lake?"

"Jessie, could you do me a huge favor?" Karen asked. She was in the phone booth by the entrance to Danny's Diner. "Could you drive over to my place and check something out for me?"

"Now?"

"I know my timing stinks with rush hour about to start, but this is important."

"Oh, I guess it's no problem," Jessie said. "Jody just got home from school. I'm supposed to pick up Steffie from daycare at four anyway. We'll just keep driving. The kids can meet Rufus. So what do you want me to do over there?"

"I need you to take a look at my appointment book on my desk, and find out if I had a session with Amelia on Monday afternoon, October fifteenth."

"That's all? I don't get to snoop through anything else of yours?"

"Sorry. I just need to confirm that I saw Amelia on that particular day."

"Monday, the fifteenth," Jessie repeated. "I'll check it out, and give you a ring on your cell in about a half hour."

"Um, cell phones don't work around here for some reason. I'm in a phone booth. I'll call you back."

"Try me at your place in about a half hour. We ought to be there by then."

"Okay. Thanks, Jessie. You're the best."

Karen hung up the phone for only a moment before picking up the receiver again. She punched in her American Express account, and then George's cell phone number.

She caught him waiting for Annabelle Schlessinger's high school teacher, who was busy coaching the cheerleading squad. Her name was Caroline Cadwell, and apparently she'd known the Schlessingers better than anyone else in Salem. "I was going to call you after I talked with her," George told Karen. "So, where are you?"

Through the phone booth's glass wall, Karen glanced at some patrons leaving the diner. "Oh, I'm out and about, running some errands."

"In Central Washington?" he asked pointedly. "Karen, the area code on my caller ID shows 509. Are you anywhere near Lake Wenatchee?"

"I'm in the phone booth at Danny's Diner," Karen admitted. "And before you start in, I've already been to the lake house. Helene Sumner spotted Amelia there this morning. But the place is empty now. The important thing is—"

"I can't believe you went there when you knew I didn't want you to," he interrupted. "Damn it, Karen. You could have gotten yourself killed."

"Well, I didn't," she murmured. The fact that he actually cared touched her. "Anyway, I'm sorry, George."

"Did you even call the police, like we discussed?" he asked. "And please, don't lie again, because I can check."

"Yes, I spoke to them. They still want to talk with Amelia about Koehler's disappearance. I avoided the subject, but told them about her taking my car and the money. I also gave them a description of the car, the plate number, the whole shebang. So, Amelia is officially a fugitive, which scares the hell out of me." She sighed. "Then again, I'm not doing so hot either. That's one more reason I decided to get the hell out of town and come here. The police want to talk to me and advised I have my lawyer present. Anyway, next time you see me, it may be through a Plexiglas window on visiting day."

"I'm not going to let that happen," George said soberly.

Karen let out a grateful little laugh. "You know something? I believe you. Thank you, George." She glanced down at the mud on her shoes from climbing up and down the trail to the lake house. "So, have you found out anything more about Annabelle Schlessinger? How she died?"

"Funny you should ask," George replied. He filled her in on what he'd learned from the newspaper account of the fire, and from Erin Gottlieb.

Karen listened intently. "So Annabelle supposedly died in a fire," she said, almost to herself.

"What do you mean *supposedly*?" George asked.

"I'm just wondering. If Annabelle isn't really dead, it would explain a lot."

"I still don't understand," he said.

"George, do me a favor. Find out as much as you can from Annabelle's teacher about this fire, and how they identified the bodies. Find out if there's any chance Annabelle could still be alive."

George figured he must have looked suspect, a 38-year-old man sitting all alone on the bleachers. His hands in the pockets of his sports jacket, he tried not to stare at the high school cheerleaders on the field. They worked on their routines while a boom box blasted music with an incessant drumbeat. George had noticed a few of the girls looking at him, whispering among themselves, and giggling. He'd also gotten a few strange glances from the guys on the football team as they'd hurtled past him, running their laps around the track.

He didn't feel vindicated until Caroline Cadwell backed away from the cheerleading squad and sat beside him on the bleachers. "Who's the hunk, Ms. C?" one of the girls called. "Your boyfriend?" Another cheerleader let out a wolf whistle.

"Okay, girls, you want to impress this guy?" she shot back. "Let's see a routine in sync for a change! Rachel Porter, you can kick higher than that!"

Caroline Cadwell was a skinny, forty-something woman with short tawny hair and big hazel eyes. Though pretty, she also had a certain gangly quality that reminded George of an ostrich.

When he'd approached Caroline after her last class had let out at 3:00, George had explained he was a relative of Joy Savitt Schlessinger. He'd used the same family tree thesis cover story he'd given Erin Gottlieb's mother. Caroline had seemed a bit dubious at first, but said she could talk with him later while she monitored cheerleading practice. After waiting on the bleachers for the last twenty minutes, George hoped this Schlessinger family friend would open up to him.

"So, George, you're studying your genealogy," Caroline said, smoothing back her hair from the wind. The pulsating music from the boom box droned on, and the girls went through their routine, but Caroline seemed oblivious to it all. "Tell me, how are you related to Joy? Are you a long-lost cousin, or what?"

The way she looked him in the eye and smiled, Caroline had the teacher stare down pat. Despite all his years in front of a class, George hadn't quite perfected that Don't-Give-Me-Any-Nonsense look.

"I'm not doing a thesis, Caroline," he admitted.

She nodded. "Yeah, the more I thought about that, the more I wasn't really buying it. What do you want, Mr. McMillan?"

"I'm trying to find out some information about my 19-year-old niece's birth parents. She was adopted when she was four. Her name is Amelia Faraday, but I believe it was Schlessinger before that."

Caroline's eyes wrestled with his for a moment. Then she sighed, shifted around on the bleacher bench, and glanced toward the cheerleaders again. "What kind of information are you after?" she asked.

"Anything that might help," George replied. "Amelia is a sweet, intelligent, pretty young woman. But she also has a lot of problems. She's had problems ever since she was a child. I'm hoping you could help us understand why that is."

"By *us,* do you mean Amelia's parents and yourself? Why aren't *they* here?"

"They were killed, along with my wife, a little over a week ago," George explained. "My two children and I are Amelia's only living relatives, at least, the only ones I'm aware of."

"I—I'm sorry for your loss," she murmured, visibly flustered. Then she covered her mouth and slowly shook her head. "My Lord, both families gone. It's as if that poor girl were cursed."

"I hear you were friends with Joy Schlessinger," George said.

She sighed. "Well, I probably knew her better than anyone else around here. I met her and Lon when they first moved to Salem in 1993. I was part of the Salem Cares Committee, and one of our functions was to roll out the welcome wagon to new residents. Depending how sociable people were, we could be a blessing or a major pain in the ass. Anyway, the Schlessingers seemed to appreciate our efforts. They were from Moses Lake, Washington."

"And that's where the twins were born, in Moses Lake?" George asked.

Nodding, she scrutinized the cheerleading squad again as they took a break between routines. "Not bad, ladies!" she called. "Let's see the next routine. Nancy Abbe, do me a favor and turn down the music a notch."

She turned to George again. "Anyway, I felt sorry for Joy. The poor thing was in a new city, and didn't know a soul. Plus she was stuck on this ranch on the outskirts of town. Lon was very, I don't know, remote, always off hunting and fishing. I got the feeling in the course of a normal day at that ranch he probably said a total of eleven words to her. He and Joy's brother, Duane, used to go camping and hunting together. Duane lived in Pasco. He's the one who introduced Lon to Joy. I only met Duane once, which was quite enough for me, thank you very much."

"You didn't care for him?" George asked.

"No, sir," she replied, frowning. "He was one of those short, wiry, overly macho types—very high strung, like a little pit bull."

"Sounds as if you had him pegged pretty quickly, and early, considering what he went on to achieve."

"Then you know about it," she said, rubbing her arms. "Yes, he struck me as a time bomb ready to go off. He wasn't very social. I don't think anyone in Salem ever met him. He just showed up to go hunting with Lon—that's it. No stops in town, no dinners out, nothing. The only reason I met him is because I used to drive out to the ranch to visit Joy, and he happened to be there that day. He and Joy were both odd ducks. She was a bit overzealous on the Bible thumping for me. I mean, I'm a Christian and very spiritual. It's why I stayed friends with Joy, even though I never really felt close to her. Being a friend in need seemed the Christian thing to do, y'know? I think, deep down, she had a good soul. But Joy was one of those fire-and-brimstone fundamentalists. She used religion the way some people use alcohol, as an escape from reality. I don't think she had a handle on what was going on around her." Caroline shrugged. "Then again, considering what life had to offer poor Joy, it's no wonder she needed some escape."

"What about her daughters?" George asked. "How was she with them?"

"There was only Annabelle when they moved here from Moses Lake," she explained.

George nodded. It made sense, because Amelia had been adopted through an agency in Spokane, Washington—about a ninety-minute drive from Moses Lake. Obviously, the Schlessingers had transplanted to Salem without her.

"Did Joy ever tell you what happened to Amelia?" he asked.

Caroline winced a bit, then sighed. "Amelia's the main reason they moved away. When the girl was four years old, she was abducted and molested by a neighbor man. Later, they found out this same man had raped and murdered a young woman who worked in a restaurant in Moses Lake."

George just stared at her. This was what Karen had been looking for, the *incident* in Amelia's early childhood.

"Lon shot the man dead," Caroline continued, "just as the police were closing in on him. They rescued Amelia, but the little girl wasn't the same after that. Joy and Lon had the worst time with her. They took her to several doctors, but I guess she was beyond help. She kept trying to run away. She even tried to kill herself—a four-year-old, for God's sake. Joy caught her with one of Lon's guns. They finally had to put her into foster care. It just broke Joy's heart, but they couldn't handle her anymore. Apparently, Lon didn't want to, but Joy totally relinquished custody. She had no idea where her child was. They told all their acquaintances in Moses Lake that Amelia had been sent to live with relatives up in Winnipeg.

"Anyway, not long after they moved here, Joy's mental

health started to deteriorate. I don't think she ever recovered from what happened to Annabelle's twin. They weren't here very long, just a few months when, one day, little Annabelle discovered her mother dead in the basement. She'd hanged herself. She left a note, apologizing to God and her family, and asking *me* to look after Annabelle."

"And a few weeks later," George interjected. "Duane Savitt went on a killing rampage at the adoption agency in Spokane. Do you know why? Do you have any idea what that was about?"

A pained look passed over Caroline's face for a moment. She turned to glance at the cheerleaders, and then stood up. "Okay, ladies! That looked great. You can wrap it up a little early today. Nancy, can you drop off the boom box in my office? Thanks!"

Hands in the pockets of her sweater, she stood on the bleachers and watched the cheerleaders disperse. She waited until the last girl left the field, and then she glanced down at George. "No one else in town knew about Amelia," she said quietly. "Joy had asked me to keep it a secret. I believe Annabelle got similar instructions. Growing up, she didn't talk about her twin—not until high school. Then I hear she told a few friends different stories about a twin who had died. But I believe Annabelle, her father, and I were the only ones who knew the truth."

She sat down beside George again. "When I read about Duane Savitt shooting those people and setting that adoption agency on fire, I knew what it was about, at least, remotely."

"But you didn't go to the police," George said.

Caroline sighed and shook her head. She stared out at the empty spot on the field, where the cheerleading squad had been practicing minutes before. "No. I heard they spoke to Lon. The story he gave them was that his brother-in-law had been estranged from the family for years. I was the only one in town who knew differently. I suppose Duane was as elusive with the good people of Moses Lake as he was with Salem folk. Because no one from Moses Lake stepped forward, claiming to know Duane. I know, because I read a lot of articles about that Spokane massacre."

"I read them too," George said. "You, um, you could have given the police some idea as to Duane's motive. They never did come up with one."

She nodded. "I know. But Lon asked me not to say anything—for Annabelle's sake. She'd been through a lot, and was still trying to get over her mother's suicide. This awful news about her Uncle Duane was devastating." Caroline slowly shook her head. "I felt a certain responsibility to Annabelle. After all, Joy had asked me to look after her. So, I didn't say anything. The police never approached me about it. I was never forced to lie, thank God. I just didn't say anything to anybody." She turned and gave George a sad smile. "You're the first one I've told."

"I understand," George murmured, nodding.

Caroline glanced out at the playing field again. "You know, years later, when Annabelle was fourteen, she asked me to explain what her uncle had done. I told her what I could. And then Annabelle said something very strange. She remembered her Uncle Duane asking her several times if she knew where Amelia was. Isn't that peculiar?"

Caroline pushed back her windblown hair and sighed. "How did he expect that little girl to know where her sister was living when her own father didn't even know?"

"Yep, I have the appointment book right in front of me," Jessie said on the other end of the line. "I'm in your office. It's here in the book: Amelia Faraday, Monday, October fifteenth, two P.M. And there's a red checkmark beside it."

That was Karen's way of indicating the client had shown up for the appointment and needed to be billed.

"Then her twin must be alive," Karen whispered. She slouched back against the phone booth's door.

"What are you talking about? Whose twin?"

"Um, I'll explain later, Jessie."

The lights went on outside Danny's Diner, and Karen realized it was getting dark. "Listen," she said into the phone. "Is everything okay there?"

"Terrific. The kids are playing with Rufus in the kitchen, and he's lapping up the attention. We'll take him out to the backyard so he can do his business. Is there anything else you need done here before we head back to George's?"

"No, thanks. You're great, Jessie. Remember everything I told you this morning? Well, it still stands. If you happen to see my car or if Amelia shows up at George's—"

"I know," Jessie cut in. "Be careful . . . she could be dangerous . . . call the police . . . do not pass Go, do not collect $200 . . ."

"I'm serious," Karen said, "doubly serious now."

"We'll be careful, hon. You drive safe. Talk to you soon."

"Thank you again, Jess."

She hung up, then immediately called George again. She was charging all these calls. Her American Express bill would be nuts, but right now she didn't care.

George answered on the second ring. "Karen?"

"Yes, hi—"

"Looks like you're still in that phone booth by the diner," he said. "I have the number on my cell. Let me call you back there in fifteen minutes, okay?"

She hesitated. "All right. But have you talked with Annabelle's teacher yet?"

"I'm doing that right now. Sorry to make you stick around there. Go inside the diner and grab a Coke or something. I'll call you in fifteen."

"Okay, but you should know—" Karen heard a click.

"Annabelle's alive," she said to no one.

* * *

"Can we take Rufus home with us?" Stephanie asked. She wouldn't stop petting him, even while the dog lifted a leg and peed on the hydrangea bushes near Karen's back door.

"Well, I don't think Karen would like coming home to an empty house tonight," Jessie said, standing on the back steps. The kitchen door was open behind her.

Jody held Rufus by his leash. He pulled his kid sister away from the dog. "Leave him alone for a minute so he can take a dump. Jeez!"

Stephanie resisted for a few moments, and finally turned toward Jessie. "Why don't Karen and Rufus come live with us?"

"I'm working on that one, honey," she replied. "Now, Jody's right, you have to leave Rufus be for just a minute or two. And you need to calm down, too."

Stephanie had asthma, and she'd left her inhaler at Rainbow Junction Daycare this afternoon. They'd be on pins and needles until they got back home, where she had two more inhalers. In the meantime, Steffie wasn't supposed to exert herself or get overexcited.

"Just take it easy, sweetheart," she called to her. "Why don't you . . ." Jessie trailed off as she heard a noise behind her in the kitchen.

She turned around, and gasped.

Standing by the breakfast table, she wore a rain slicker and clutched her purse to her side. She had a tiny, cryptic smile on her face.

"Oh, my God, you scared me," Jessie said, a hand on her heart. "What are you doing here, Amelia?"

Chapter Eighteen

"Sorry about the interruption," George said, tucking the cell phone in his sports coat pocket. He'd stepped down to the playing field to take Karen's call. Now he made his way back up the bleachers. "Where was I?"

"You asked me about the fire," Caroline Cadwell said.

Nodding, he sat down beside her. "So the police called you late one night in July. . . ."

"Yes, I had no idea Lon put me down on his insurance policy as his emergency contact. There was no next of kin, so they called me to identify the remains."

"Did you drive out to the ranch that night?"

"Oh, no. They didn't get the bodies out of there until about two in the morning. Because the ranch was so remote, it took a while for the fire trucks to arrive and even longer to get water in the hoses. In the meantime, the whole upstairs was burnt, along with most of the first floor. You can still see what's left of the place if you drive a couple of miles outside town. They haven't leveled it yet."

Shuddering, Caroline rubbed her arms. "Do you mind if we head inside? I'm starting to feel a chill."

"Not at all," George murmured.

"Can you imagine?" she said, heading down the bleacher steps with him. "All that destruction, a house left in cinders, because someone was smoking in bed. But that's how it happened, just like the old cliché. Lon had a Camel going, and he dozed off. What a stupid waste. Anyway, they asked me to come to the morgue the following morning at 9:30. I don't know why they put me through it. I mean, the fire was at the Schlessinger ranch. Lon was forty-six and Annabelle was sixteen. The two bodies were a male in his late forties and a female in her late teens. It wasn't too tough to figure out who they were."

George walked with her along the playing field toward a side door into the school. It was an ugly, three-story granite building from the Reagan era. Eyes downcast, Caroline kept rubbing her arms. "It was pretty awful," she muttered. "I had to go into this cold, little room that smelled rancid. I'm sorry, but the stench was horrible. That was one of the worst parts. The bodies were covered with white sheets, and they had them on metal slabs. First, I identified Lon. There was nothing left of his hair. His face was just blood, blisters, and burn marks, but I still recognized him. However, Annabelle—well, she was a skull with blackened skin stretched over it. Her mouth was wide open like she was screaming. . . ."

George noticed tears in Caroline's eyes. He gently rested his hand on her shoulder.

"I'd known her since she was a little girl," she said, her voice quivering. "I'd watched her grow up into a beautiful young lady. I had a hard time believing that—*thing* was Annabelle. The height and body type were Annabelle's, but I couldn't say for sure it was her. Then I remembered the bracelet."

"What bracelet?" George stopped with Caroline as she pulled out a handkerchief and blew her nose.

"Annabelle had a favorite bracelet, silver with these pretty roses engraved on it," Caroline explained. "She wore it all the time. It used to be her mother's. The bracelet was about two inches wide, and covered up an ugly scar. Annabelle had burned the back of her wrist rather badly when she was a child.

"Anyway, I asked the attendant in the morgue if I could see her left arm. He lifted the sheet and showed me. And there was the wide silver bracelet, almost melded to her burnt skin and bones. Then I knew it was her."

"That's how you identified Annabelle's body?" George asked. He wondered if the local police and coroner realized Ms. Cadwell had based her positive ID on a piece of jewelry around the wrist of a charred corpse.

"Well, what other proof do you want?" she shot back.

"Maybe dental records," he muttered. "Did they check their dental records?"

"I don't think so. Why should they?"

Because I know someone who thinks Annabelle could still be alive, George wanted to answer. But he didn't want to argue with Caroline Cadwell over something that had happened three years ago. She had no reason to be suspicious about the fire. And she'd been very forthright with him.

George held open the door for her, and Caroline strode into the school, murmuring a thank-you under her breath. She stopped and leaned against a trophy case in the school hallway. Wiping her eyes again, she gave him a tired smile. "I always get emotional when I think about Annabelle. I was sort of her honorary godmother. It's no wonder I had a hard time identifying her remains. If only you knew how pretty she was. . . ."

"But I do know," George reminded her. "My niece is her twin. I know exactly what you mean. Amelia's very beautiful."

Caroline nodded pensively. "You know, it's ironic. I used to worry about Annabelle spending so much time alone on that ranch in the middle of nowhere. Lon continued to go off fishing and hunting for days at a time." Frowning, she shook her head. "I just didn't understand his nonchalance. You see, for several years, we had a—a series of disappearances. Several young women in the area vanished without a trace. A few were even former students of mine. So, maybe I was more sensitive and worried about it than some people. But I couldn't help thinking about Annabelle, alone on that ranch, a perfect target for whoever was out there preying on young women." She shrugged. "And after all my concern, Annabelle ended up dying in a fire, started by her father's cigarette."

George stared at her. "How many girls disappeared? Did they ever find any of them?"

"At least a dozen or so in a period of about ten years," she said. "A while back, they discovered the partial remains of a young woman in a forest about twenty miles from here. They never found any of the others. And they never found the killer either."

"So he's still out there somewhere?" George asked.

"I think he's moved on to a different area," Caroline said, shuddering again. "Like a predator finding a new kill zone. Anyway, it's been about three years since the last girl disappeared. Her name was Sandra Hartman. She graduated from here just two months before her disappearance. I taught Sandra her sophomore year. She was supposed to meet some friends for a movie, but never showed up."

"You said this was three years ago?" George asked.

She nodded.

"Was this before or after the Schlessinger ranch burned down?"

"About a week before," she answered. "Why do you ask?"

"I'm not sure," George replied truthfully. It just seemed

strange that the girls stopped disappearing once Lon Schlessinger had smoked his last cigarette.

Karen glanced at her watch again. It had been almost twenty minutes now. She sat near the phone booth at one of the picnic tables in front of the diner. While waiting for George to call back, she'd gone into the restaurant and ordered a Diet Coke and a serving of fries to go. She'd come back out, sat down, and tried to eat. But she'd been too nervous; and after only a few fries, she'd tossed the bag out. Her soft-drink container was still on the table in front of her.

She couldn't stop thinking about Amelia's twin. If Annabelle was alive, it would explain so much.

Months ago, Shane had thought he'd spotted Amelia inside a strange car with a strange man at a stoplight in the University District. Amelia had had only the vaguest memory of it, after Shane had prompted her with a description of what he'd seen. Had he actually spotted Annabelle?

Karen remembered Amelia coming by her place the day before yesterday. She'd been acting so peculiar, and even looked a bit different. Hell, even Rufus had detected something wrong with her, and kept growling at her. Then she'd walked off with Koehler. Karen had figured the *other* Amelia had walked into her house that afternoon. She'd thought the *other* Amelia might have killed Koehler.

But there was no *other* Amelia. It was another person entirely.

How could Amelia—even with multiple personalities—be in two different places at one time?

She'd been in Port Angeles when Koehler had disappeared a hundred miles away in Cougar Mountain Park. And she'd been on a Booze Busters retreat in Port Townsend when her brother had died in Bellingham. The Faradays' next-door neighbor hadn't seen *Amelia* hosing down the dock around the time of Collin's death. No, she'd spotted *Annabelle,* washing away his blood after she'd bashed his skull in.

Karen shifted restlessly on the picnic table bench. She gazed at the darkening horizon, and then over the treetops in the direction of the Faradays' lake house.

Helene Sumner had seen Annabelle, and her boyfriend, Blade, at the house just days before Amelia's parents and aunt were brutally killed there. The Faradays would have opened the door to Annabelle, believing her to be their daughter. They may not have even lived long enough after that to realize their mistake. In Amelia's all-too-accurate dream, she remembered her Aunt Ina's last words before a bullet ripped through her chest: "Oh my God, honey, what have you done?"

Everything started to make sense, if Annabelle was indeed alive. She was the killer. But what was her motive? And what accounted for Amelia having these fragmented memories of her sister's violent actions?

An SUV pulled into the lot by Danny's Diner. Karen glanced at her watch again. She got to her feet and checked the phone inside the booth. Had she hung up the receiver improperly after her last conversation with George?

No, there was nothing wrong with the phone, except George's call hadn't come through on it yet.

"God, you're right!" a girl shrieked. "My cell phone isn't working. Shit! And I told Tiffany I was going to call her."

Karen saw three young teenage girls, and the haggard-looking mother of one of them, coming around the corner from the Danny's parking lot. All the girls were talking at once, and loudly, too. But Karen heard one of them over the others: "Look, there's a pay phone!"

Karen quickly ducked into the booth and closed the folding door. She picked up the receiver, but kept a hand over the cradle lever, pressing it down. "Oh, yeah? Really?" she said into the phone. "Well, I'm not surprised. . . ."

A gum-snapping girl with long brown hair stopped in front of the booth while her friends and their chaperone filed into the diner. She fished a credit card out of her little purse. What a 14-year-old was doing with a credit card was beyond Karen. She turned her back to the girl, and kept up her pretend conversation on the phone: "I had no idea. Well, she should take care of that right away."

After a few moments, Karen heard a clicking noise behind her. She glanced over her shoulder. The girl was tapping her credit card against the phone booth window. She glared at Karen, and then rolled her eyes.

Karen opened the door. "Hey, I have another important call to make after this," she said. "So, you may as well just buzz off, okay?"

"Bitch," the girl muttered. Then she swiveled around and flounced into the restaurant.

Suddenly, the phone rang. Karen's hand jerked away from the receiver cradle. "Yes? George?"

"Yeah, hi," he said. "Listen, I think you're right about Amelia's twin. There's every chance Annabelle is still alive. . . ."

She stood in Karen's kitchen, gazing at the housekeeper.

Outside, in the backyard, George McMillan's children played with Karen's dog. They hadn't noticed her yet.

"Amelia, everyone's been searching high and low for you, honey," the housekeeper said. She furtively glanced over her shoulder at the children, then took another step inside and closed the kitchen door behind her.

"Where's Karen?" she asked.

"She drove to the house in Lake Wenatchee, looking for

you," Jessie said. "She rented a car. Her own car's missing. Did you borrow her car, honey?"

"No, I didn't." Her eyes narrowed at Jessie. "Do you know if Karen has been to the lake house yet?"

Jessie nodded, and moved over to the cupboard. "She called about fifteen minutes ago from some diner up the road from there. You just missed her." Jessie pulled a container of lemonade mix from the cabinet. "I promised the kids I'd make them some lemonade. Would you like some, honey? Or maybe a nice cup of tea?"

"Don't bother yourself," she muttered.

"Sit down and take a load off, for goodness sake." She moved over to the refrigerator and took the ice tray out of the freezer. "I'll make enough lemonade for you, too. You have something cool to drink, and then we'll call your Uncle George. He's been worried about you, too."

She sat down at the breakfast table. "Where is Uncle George?"

"He had to go down to Oregon for some research thingy," Jessie said, retrieving four tall glasses and a pitcher from another cabinet. "He'll be back tonight, though. Karen, too. I guess we have to wait before we can reach her on her cell—something about bad phone reception around there."

Past Jessie's chatter, she heard the children outside, laughing. The dog let out a bark now and then. She glanced down at the purse in her lap. Inside, something caught the overhead kitchen light, and glistened.

The serrated-edged, brown-leather-handled hunting knife in her purse was a souvenir from the ranch. It had belonged to her father. He'd skinned his kill with it on hunting trips. He'd also used it on some of his women once he'd finished with them.

She remembered back when she was just a little girl, those furtive trips at night had seemed like such long ordeals. But in reality he'd done a quick job on the women they'd picked up together. The longest he'd gone on with one of them had been close to two hours. He'd dug their graves ahead of time, and driven them out to the preselected spot. She remembered those nights alone in the car, listening to the screams, waiting. He'd come back, covered with sweat, and often blood. He'd pull a piece of candy out of his pocket, and toss it to her. "That's a good girl," he'd say. "You're daddy's little helper." Then he'd pop open the trunk, get out the shovel, and promise to be back soon.

And he'd kept his promise. He'd always return within a half hour.

A few times, Uncle Duane came with them. Those nights always took longer. And he smelled bad in the car on the way home.

Her father always called it his *work*.

It wasn't until a few years after her mother died that her father began to take his work home with him. The longest he ever kept one of them in that fallout-shelter-turned-dungeon was eleven days and nights and that was Tracy Eileen Atkinson. There was something about her that he liked more than the others. For a while, she'd thought he'd never grow tired and bored with Tracy. But he did.

She'd snuck down into the basement and peeked in on her father as he finished Tracy off with his hunting knife. One quick stroke across the neck. She still remembered the startled look in Tracy's eyes, the thin crimson line across her throat that suddenly unleashed a torrent of blood.

That was when she first coveted her father's hunting knife. She was thirteen years old at the time.

She still hadn't tried it out on anyone, yet. Karen was going to be her very first kill with the old knife. She'd had it in her robe pocket when she'd *accidentally* stumbled into Karen's bedroom late last night. But the joke had been on her. She'd had no idea Karen had been sleeping with a gun beside her.

Two days before, she'd thought she had Karen cornered in the basement of that rest home. But Blade had botched it.

Returning to Karen's house this afternoon, she'd figured the third attempt would be the charm. But she hadn't figured on finding Karen gone, and the housekeeper with those two brats here in her place.

She stared at Jessie, hovering over the counter, her back to her. Outside, the children were howling, trying to get the dog to bark. She glanced inside her purse again.

No reason she still couldn't break in her father's old hunting knife, no reason at all.

"So honey, where have you been all day, for Pete's sake?" Jessie asked, pulling something else out of the cupboard. "Karen and your uncle have been calling just about everyone and asking if they've seen you. They didn't leave one turn unstoned as my Aunt Agnes used to say. . . ."

"I borrowed Shane's car and went for a long drive," she replied coolly. She studied the way the chubby housekeeper was bent over the counter, and how she had the glasses lined up. She couldn't see what Jessie was doing. Something was wrong.

Getting to her feet, she stepped up behind Jessie, and purposely bumped her in the arm, hard.

Jessie let out a little gasp, and a prescription bottle flew out of her hand. It rolled across the kitchen counter, and about a dozen light blue cylindrical tablets spilled out.

"Oops!" Jessie said, with a jittery laugh. "Look what you went and did. My arthritis medicine, I forgot to take it this morning."

She swiped the prescription bottle off the counter, and glanced at the label. "This is diazepam," she said, locking eyes with Jessie. "It's a sedative. And they're not yours. They're for the old man in the rest home, Karen's father. That was a silly mistake."

Jessie nodded and laughed again. "I'll say. I must be getting senile." She stirred the lemonade in the pitcher, and the ice cubes clinked against the glass.

She put the prescription bottle down. "The lemonade's ready, Jessie." She reached inside her purse again. "Why don't you call the kids in? And leave the dog outside, okay?"

"They have old yearbooks there at the high school library, right?"

"Yeah, I guess," George allowed.

Her back pressed against the phone booth's glass wall, Karen nervously tugged at the metal phone cord. "Could you get Annabelle's teacher to show you pictures of those girls who disappeared, and then make photocopies? You said she taught some of them. . . ."

"Yes," he answered tentatively. "But why do you want their pictures?"

Karen hesitated. She was thinking about one of Amelia's earliest memories: waiting alone in a car by a forest trail at night and hearing a woman scream. *When the screaming stops, then we can go home.*

"It might sound a little crazy," she said at last. "But I think if we showed pictures of those young women to Amelia, she might remember some of them."

"Karen, these girls were all abducted between Salem and Eugene," he pointed out. "I told you, the Schlessingers put Amelia up for adoption while they were still in Moses Lake. How do you expect her to remember things that happened in Salem when she's never even been here? It doesn't make sense."

"Maybe not," she said. "But I think Amelia has some sort of window into what's happening in her sister's world. She might even believe it's happening to her. I'm not sure I even understand it myself. But I have a feeling Mr. Schlessinger was somehow involved in the disappearance of these young women. If Annabelle knew about it, then Amelia might recognize one of those yearbook portraits. It might even trigger a memory. It could be the key that unlocks a lot of doors."

George sighed on the other end of the line. "I think I understood about ten percent of what you just said. But I have every confidence in you, Karen. I'll make the photocopies for you."

"Thanks, George," she said.

She didn't know how to explain it to him. She didn't understand it herself. How could Amelia have these premonitions, recollections, and sensations when all the while these things were happening to her sister, Annabelle? If Annabelle had indeed killed Amelia's family and Koehler, why did Amelia blame herself for those murders?

She'd told Karen that she'd felt the blood splatter on her face while shooting her parents and aunt. She said she'd used her dad's hunting rifle. "It felt like someone hitting me in the shoulder with a baseball bat every time I fired it."

Karen wondered how Amelia could feel those sensations.

Yet, it made sense somehow. During their first therapy session together, Amelia had described one of her early phantom pains—a severe burning sensation on the back of her wrist. She'd said it felt like someone was putting out a lit cigar on her. And just minutes ago, George had told her about Annabelle's bracelet. She'd worn it to hide an ugly burn mark on the back of her wrist from a childhood accident.

George obviously thought she was crazy to imagine Amelia might *recollect* those missing young women, because of her special connection with Annabelle. There was no easy way to explain. It was a phenomenon that had mystified Karen years before she'd even met Amelia, back when she'd been in graduate school. Trying to explain it was almost like solving an old riddle: *Why did the twin in Zurich have a fever and feel abdominal pains?*

"Karen, are you still there?" George asked.

"Um, yes, I'm here."

"So, you think Amelia and Annabelle's father was somehow involved in these disappearances," he said. "Well, I'm with you on that. Sure seems like an awfully weird coincidence to me. The first girl vanished about a year after Lon and his family moved here. And the last one disappeared a week before the fire that killed him. Plus, if what you say is true, and Annabelle is still alive out there killing people, well, it would explain some of her behavior, wouldn't it? The fruit doesn't fall far from the tree."

"Like father, like daughter," Karen said. "Another thing, if young women started to disappear after Lon moved to the Salem area, they must have *stopped* disappearing somewhere else."

"Moses Lake," George murmured.

"Caroline mentioned that in Moses Lake a neighbor man had molested Amelia."

"That's right," George said. "The cops later found out he was also responsible for abducting and murdering a waitress. Do you think Lon was somehow involved in that, too?"

"Maybe," Karen said into the phone. "It's worth checking out."

She thought about those memory fragments from Amelia's childhood. In one of them, Amelia's mother had her in the bathroom and she was asking the child, stripped to her underwear, "Did he touch you down there?" But Amelia had no memory of ever being molested.

"Can you ask Caroline if she knows whether or not this neighbor man was a Native American?" Her hand tight around the receiver, she listened to George murmuring to Annabelle's teacher.

After a moment, he got back on the line. "No, Caroline says Joy didn't mention anything about race, just that he was a neighbor."

"Then Caroline probably wouldn't know the name of the Moses Lake waitress who was murdered," Karen concluded.

She heard George talking to Annabelle's teacher again. Then he came back on the line. "Sorry. Joy didn't go into that much detail when she told Caroline the story."

But Karen wanted the details. The incident with the neighbor in Moses Lake had traumatized Amelia to the point that she had to be separated from her family. And yet, she had no clear memory of it or of the family she'd lost.

Lon Schlessinger had shot the neighbor dead. And this neighbor had apparently abducted and killed a local woman. Such a story would have been in the newspapers, at least, the local newspapers.

"Listen, George, I'm heading to the Wenatchee library," she said. "I want to find out more about this incident with the neighbor. Maybe there's something about it in the old Wenatchee papers."

"If it's any help," he said, "Amelia was officially adopted in April of '93, and she spent a few weeks in foster homes before that. So the incident with the neighbor couldn't have happened any time after February."

"Thanks. I'll start in February '93, and work backward until I find something. I'll keep my eyes peeled for young women missing-person cases in the area, too. I'll call you the minute I find something. I should be able to reach you on my cell once I'm out of these woods."

"Okay. Be careful," he said.

"Don't worry about me, I'm fine," Karen said.

"Be careful anyway. I keep thinking about Helene Sumner, and how she spotted Amelia at the lake house this morning. It could have been Annabelle, you know. And she could still be around there." George paused. "Watch out for yourself, Karen."

Karen had been right about Amelia. There was something wrong with her.

She stood too close, still clutching her purse and occasionally peeking inside it as if she were hiding some secret treasure in there. And then that strange smirk on her face, it was so unlike the Amelia she knew.

"Oh, let's give the kids a few more minutes outside with Rufus," Jessie said, forcing a chuckle. She wiped her hands on a dish towel. "They're having a blast, and that pooch hasn't seen this much attention since God knows when." She nervously gathered up the light blue pills from the kitchen counter. *Nice try, old girl*, she thought.

Karen had cautioned Jessie that Amelia might be dangerous, and said to call her immediately if she should happen to run into the 19-year-old. Jessie hadn't taken the warning too seriously. *Amelia, dangerous? That sweet thing?*

But then, suddenly, the young lady showed up in Karen's kitchen. No doorbell, no knocking, she just waltzed right into the house, bold as you please. Brazen as the guts of Jesse James, as her Aunt Agnes used to say. That was the first sign that something wasn't right.

So Jessie closed the kitchen door, to discourage Jody and little Steffie from coming inside, and to keep them out of harm's way.

The young woman in Karen's kitchen seemed too hardedged and cold. Though unable to put her finger on it, Jessie detected something *off* about her, the strange way she acted, looked, and talked. Then Jessie caught a glimpse of something glistening in her purse. It was a knife.

She remembered Karen's warning. She also remembered

where she'd last seen those light-blue pills that had made old Frank so dopey and tired. They were in the spice cabinet, beside the aspirin and Karen's vitamins. She thought she was being so clever with the lemonade routine. If Amelia was indeed dangerous, sedating her was one way to nip the situation in the bud and not do anyone harm. Jessie figured that once Amelia was down for the count, she could call Karen, and the police, if necessary.

But she'd been foiled even before slipping the stuff in her surprise guest's glass.

Well, it seemed like a good idea at the time.

Trying not to shake, Jessie dropped the diazepam tablets back inside the prescription bottle. She could hear Jody and Stephanie in the backyard, laughing, and barking along with Rufus.

Leaning against the counter, the young woman picked up one pill Jessie had missed. "Why were you trying to drug me, Jessie?" she asked. She handed her the tablet. "Did Karen warn you that I might be unstable?"

"What in the world are you talking about?" Jessie put the prescription bottle away, and then moved to the refrigerator. "That's just silly," she added, plucking a lemon from the shelf. She closed the refrigerator door, and reached for the knife rack.

"What do you think you're doing?" Suddenly the girl grabbed her by the wrist. She hit Jessie in the chest with her elbow. Whether or not it was an accident, it hurt like hell.

Jessie staggered back, and the lemon rolled across the floor. "Good Lord! I was just going to cut up a lemon for the lemonade!" She rubbed her chest and winced.

"It's a mix. You don't need to do that," she shot back. With a quick jerk, she released Jessie's wrist. "Now, go call the kids in, Jessie. They've been out there with that mutt long enough. I'd like to see my little cousins."

Trying to catch her breath, Jessie glanced toward the backyard.

Rufus started barking furiously. A second later, the front doorbell rang.

Jessie turned toward her. "Well, I—I better answer that before Rufus has the whole neighborhood over here," she said loudly, competing with all the yelps and barks. Jessie didn't wait for a response. She swiveled around and quickly headed for the front door, almost expecting the young woman to grab her.

Rufus was going crazy outside. Jessie could hear Jody talking to him. "What is it, boy? What's going on?" His voice, along with Rufus's barking, seemed to come from the side of the house now.

Jessie flung open the front door, and recognized Chad, a tall, stocky, soft-spoken man in his early thirties. He was one of Amelia's patients, and he looked like he was sorry he'd rung the bell. "Is Karen here?" he asked, over the dog's yelping.

Jessie could only guess how frazzled she appeared, and Rufus, straining at his leash, was leading the two children around from the side of the house toward the front stoop. Poor Chad looked as if he just wanted to flee. "Um, I have a five o'clock appointment with her," he explained, with an apprehensive look over his shoulder.

"Down, boy! Take it easy!" Jody chided Rufus.

"Down, boy!" Stephanie echoed.

A hand over her heart, Jessie stared at him. "Karen—she had to cancel her appointments today." She glanced back toward the kitchen. "Um, didn't you get her message, Chad?"

"Oh, nuts, I probably should have checked my answering machine," he replied. He bowed down toward Rufus. "Hey, there, pooch."

"Don't go away, okay?" Jessie said, distractedly. "Stay there. You too, kids. I'll be right back."

With trepidation, she headed down the hall toward the back of the house. She edged past the kitchen entryway and gazed into the empty room. The back door was wide open.

Jessie hurried to the door, and then looked out at the backyard: no one.

Biting her lip, she closed the kitchen door and locked the deadbolt. Then she tried the door to the basement. It was already locked. No one could have gone down there.

Right beside her on the kitchen wall, just inches from her head, the telephone rang. Jessie almost jumped out of her skin. She quickly snatched up the receiver. "Yes, hello?"

"Is this Karen?" a woman asked.

"No, this is her housekeeper," Jessie replied, again, her hand on her heart. She stepped out to the hallway as far as the phone cord would allow. She saw Chad, Rufus, and the children still at the front stoop. Chad was crouched down, petting the dog and talking to the kids.

Jessie sighed. "Karen isn't in," she said into the phone. "Can I help you?"

"I'm looking for Amelia Faraday. I'm her roommate, Rachel."

"Amelia isn't here right now. She—um, well, she just left."

"Do you know if she's coming back?"

I hope not, Jessie thought. But she merely cleared her throat and said. "I'm not really sure, hon. Is there something I can do for you?"

"Well, this is kind of an emergency," Rachel explained. "If you see her, please, tell her to call me *immediately.* I've got the police ringing the phone off the hook here. They're looking for her."

"Really?" Jessie murmured.

"It's pretty awful news," Rachel said. "It's about her boyfriend . . ."

"You mean Shane?" Jessie asked.

"Yeah, you know Shane Mitchell?"

"Yes, I do. Is he okay? What's happened?"

"He, um, well, he's dead," the girl explained, a little crack in her voice. "They found Shane in a canoe, drifting in Lake Washington by the 520 Bridge. It looks like he shot himself."

Meredith Marie Sterns was a pretty brunette who had disappeared the summer after graduating from East Marion High School in 1999. She had a dimpled smile and "Rachel" hair copied from Jennifer Aniston's hairstyle in *Friends*.

"Meredith spent most of that June backpacking around Europe with a friend," Caroline explained.

George stood over the Xerox machine, making a photocopy of Meredith's graduation portrait. They were the only ones in the high school's administration office; everybody else had gone home already. They had several old yearbooks piled on the secretary's desk beside the copier.

"I remember the Sterns were so worried that something might happen to Meredith while she was wandering around Europe," Caroline continued. "But it was less than a week after she'd returned home that it happened. She went with some girlfriends to see the Fourth of July fireworks at the park. I guess it was about twenty minutes before the fireworks were supposed to start when Meredith excused herself to go use the restroom. And she never came back. . . ."

George once again studied the photo of the girl with the Rachel hair. "She was so excited about going to Chicago in the fall," he heard Caroline say. "She'd been accepted into Northwestern. She was going to be a drama major."

Caroline had a story like that for every one of the missing young women. Part of George wanted to hurry up and just get the photocopies made. The sooner he hit the road, the sooner he'd be home with his kids. He was worried about them.

But he didn't rush through the task at hand, and he respectfully listened to Caroline's reminiscences for each missing girl. The stories broke his heart. Each one was somebody's daughter, sister, or fiancée. Each one had dreams and plans for her future. Each one had disappeared without a trace.

Twenty-two-year-old Nancy Rae Keller was an accomplished pianist who had performed in several concerts. She'd been earning some extra money as a waitress at a fancy restaurant called The Tides in Corvallis. The last person to see her alive was the restaurant manager. Nancy Rae had finished up her shift one Thursday night in March 2002 and headed out to her car. Nancy Rae's car had still been in the restaurant's parking lot on Friday morning. George couldn't see it in the black-and-white photo, but according to Caroline, "Nancy Rae had the most beautiful red hair."

The youngest to disappear was Leandra Bryant, nicknamed Leelee. The 15-year-old had been babysitting for two toddlers until 10:30 on a Saturday night in April, 2001. The children's father had offered to drive her home, but Leelee lived only two blocks away and insisted on walking. She should have been safe. But somewhere along those two blocks in a quiet, residential area of Salem, Leelee Bryant vanished.

The last among the missing young women was Sandra Hartman, the 18-year-old who had disappeared on her way to the mall to meet some friends for a movie.

George looked at the slightly grainy photocopy of Sandra's graduation portrait, and he saw a resemblance between the beautiful dark-haired senior and Amelia. It was the last photocopy he'd made. The Xerox machine still hummed for a moment before it wheezed and then switched off.

"Were any of these girls friends of Annabelle's?" he asked.

Caroline arranged the yearbooks by year. "No, only two of the girls were in school at the same time as Annabelle.

And I don't think either one of them ever had Annabelle over to their homes or anything. And, of course, I'm sure they never went out to the Schlessinger ranch."

George remembered Erin Gottlieb telling him that she hadn't set foot in the place. "That ranch in the middle of nowhere," she'd called it.

"You said the ranch house is still there?" he asked.

"Yes, but it's just a burnt-out shell now," Caroline replied. "There's hardly anything left of it. I don't think anyone's been out there in years."

George studied the photocopies again—all those pretty young women who had disappeared. "Could I ask you for one more favor, Caroline?"

She nodded. "Sure."

"Could you tell me how to get to the Schlessinger ranch?"

Chapter Nineteen

WENATCHEE – 23 MILES said the sign just past Leavenworth.

With a breathtaking view of the Cascade Mountains, the quaint Bavarian village was a big tourist attraction in central Washington, and one of the Route 2 landmarks Karen was supposed to look for on her way to the Wenatchee Public Library. The waitress at Danny's Diner had given her directions. Just to be sure, Karen telephoned the library on Douglas Street, and found out that, yes, they were open until 8:00 tonight; and yes, they had available both the *Wenatchee World* and the *Columbia Basin Herald*, which served Moses Lake. The microfiche files for both newspapers went back thirty years.

White-knuckled, Karen gripped the steering wheel and studied the winding, hilly highway ahead.

She realized now it was Amelia's twin in the hallway and basement of the convalescent home the day before yesterday. "Do it now," she'd heard Annabelle whisper. "Get her!"

Karen had heard the same hushed voice last night: "She's got a gun, for chrissakes . . . I can't . . . goddamn mutt . . ."

At the time, Karen had figured Amelia must have been talking in her sleep. But now, she knew it had been Annabelle, probably whispering to Blade.

If Annabelle had *accidentally* stumbled into her room last night to kill her, where had Amelia gone? Karen was positive *Amelia* had fallen asleep in the guest room last night. Some time later, perhaps before that predawn intrusion, a switch had been made. Karen wondered if Amelia had left on her own accord. Or had Annabelle—after so many years with her father—also become an expert at making young women vanish without a trace?

Her cell phone went off, and Karen realized she was finally out of that call-restricted area. Eyes on the road, she blindly reached inside her purse. She checked the caller ID: her home phone number. "Hello?" she said into the phone, a bit wary.

"Karen, it's me, Jessie. Thank God I didn't get that stupid 'Your call cannot be completed as dialed' recording again."

"You're still at the house," Karen said. "Is everything okay?"

"Hardly. I have terrible news." Her voice dropped to a whisper. "I still haven't told the kids. They're in the kitchen with Rufus. Shane is dead. That poor dear boy, can you imagine? It looks like he shot himself. . . ."

"Oh, my God," Karen murmured, the cell phone to her ear. "Are you sure? How did you find out?"

"Amelia's roommate told me. She called looking for Amelia. That's the other thing, Amelia showed up here quite unexpectedly, acting very strange. . . ."

A car horn blared. Karen suddenly realized she'd been drifting into the oncoming lane. A pickup truck barreled toward her. She jerked the wheel to one side. Tires screeched as she swerved back into her lane, and beyond, onto the shoulder off the highway. For a few, fleeting, gut-wrenching seconds, she thought the car would flip over.

"Good Lord, what's happening?" she heard Jessie ask.

Karen caught her breath, and veered back into her lane. "Nothing, I just need to get off this road, that's all." She saw a turnoff to an apple orchard ahead, and took it. Slowing down, she crawled over to a gravelly turnaround area for the one-lane road. Then she put the car in park. She listened while Jessie told her about the disturbing episode with Amelia, who "just wasn't acting like her sweet self."

Yes, Jessie said, she'd called the police after Amelia had made her hasty exit, and a patrolman had stopped by. He'd checked around the premises, and that was it. "He seemed to think I was a major kook," Jessie said. "I mean, Amelia never really threatened me or anything. But she had that knife in her purse, and it gave me the heebie-jeebies. Still, the worst thing she actually did was hit me in the chest when she grabbed my arm, and that might have been an accident. And here I was, trying to slip her some of those knockout pills, because you told me she was dangerous."

"Jessie, she is," Karen said. "She's very dangerous."

"I know, I believe you," Jessie replied. "But when I told this patrolman that the police were looking for her, he didn't know a thing about it."

Apparently, Amelia Faraday had not yet officially become a person of interest in Detective Koehler's disappearance.

"Anyway, we're still at your house," Jessie said, her voice a little shaky. "The cop said they'd call back here if he found out anything more. But I want to get these kids home."

"Have you talked to George, yet?" Karen asked.

"I thought I'd wait until we were safely at home before giving him the latest developments. I didn't want to worry him."

"Yeah, you're right," Karen sighed.

She stared out past the windshield at the starter trees in the orchard, lined up in a row. Their leaves fluttered in the breeze, and dusk loomed on the horizon. Her heart ached, and she wanted to cry for Shane, but there was no time.

She didn't for a minute believe he'd shot himself.

"Listen, Jess, please, be careful driving home," she said at last. "Make sure you aren't being followed. Keep an eye out for my car—and that black Cadillac."

"What black Cadillac?" Jessie repeated.

"The old black Cadillac with a broken antenna. It was following me around over the weekend. I told you—"

"Oh, Lord, honey, how do you expect me to keep track of all this stuff?" Jessie said, exasperated.

"Well, just watch out for it *now*, okay?"

"*I've seen it*, for Pete's sakes. A car matching that description was parked just down the block from George's house earlier today. It was still there when Jody and I left to pick up Steffie."

"Oh, my God," Karen murmured. "Listen, Jess, don't go back to George's. Better not stick around my place, either. Take the kids to a hotel, and make sure you're not being followed. Just hide out there for a while, order room service, and watch pay-per-view movies. I'll handle the bill. Call me once you get settled in, okay?"

"Well, all right," Jessie said. She sounded a bit perplexed. "I'm just not sure what hotel—"

Karen heard a beep, and checked the caller ID. She recognized the number: Amelia's cell phone.

"Jessie, I have another call," she said hurriedly. "Can you just get yourself and the children to a hotel? Any hotel, it doesn't matter: the Westin, the Marriott off Lake Union, anyplace. . . ."

"I hear you," Jessie replied.

"Thanks, Jess. Just make sure no one's following—"

"Yeah, I know," she cut in. "*Make sure no one's following us*. Will do. Take your call. I'll phone you in a bit." There was a click on the line.

Karen switched over to the other call. "Amelia? Is that you?"

"Hi, Karen," she murmured. "You must be so mad at me right now. I just listened to all the messages from you and Uncle George and Shane. I'm sorry. I didn't mean to worry you. It was awful of me to run away this morning."

Karen wasn't certain she was really talking to Amelia. It certainly sounded like her; and the call was coming from her cell phone. "Well, you, um, you couldn't have run very far," she said. "I just got off the phone with Jessie, and she said you paid her an unexpected visit at my house about a half hour ago."

"What?" she shot back, sounding stunned. "Karen, that's impossible. Why would Jessie say that? I'm nowhere near your house—or Seattle, even. I'm calling from Grand Coulee Dam."

The car engine was still running. Karen turned off the ignition, and listened to the motor die. "Grand Coulee Dam?" she repeated numbly.

"Yeah, I know, it's pretty crazy, huh? But I woke up from this horrible nightmare last night. In the dream, I was—I was attacking you with a knife, and you were screaming. . . ." She trailed off. "Anyway, I suddenly woke up, all sweaty. I was so scared that it might have really happened. I listened at your door, and heard you snoring. Did you know you snore?"

"No, I didn't," Karen said.

"Anyway, I figured you were okay. But I realized I had to get out of there before I hurt you, or somebody else. So I packed my things and snuck out of your house at around four o'clock this morning. I walked up to Fifteenth, and called a cab."

"You didn't take my car?" Karen asked.

"God, no. I'd never do that without asking you," she replied. "I had the taxi drive me to Shane's place. I borrowed *his* car, then drove to the house in Lake Wenatchee. I know it sounds nuts, but I just wanted to get as far away from everyone as I could. But when I went down to the house, I just couldn't make myself go in. So I climbed back inside Shane's car, and kept driving east."

"What time was this?" Karen asked.

"Oh, around eight-thirty or nine," she replied.

According to Helene Sumner, Amelia had been at the lake house at around just that same time. But she'd heard Amelia talking to someone, and laughing.

"Were you with anyone?" Karen asked.

"No, why?"

"Nothing, go ahead. You couldn't step inside the house, so you went on driving."

"That's right, so I ended up here at the Grand Coulee Dam. I've been here for the last few hours, Karen."

"What have you been doing there?" she asked.

"Well, I ate, I napped a little in the car, and I looked at the damn dam." She let out a skittish laugh, but then her tone suddenly turned serious. "Anyway, I've been here. I swear to God. This can't be another one of my blackouts. There's no way Jessie could have seen me in Seattle this afternoon. I'm at least four hours away. . . ."

Karen still couldn't help wondering if she had Amelia on the line or her twin, being very clever. "Amelia, do you remember our session the week before last, when you accidentally broke that cheap vase on the coffee table in my office?"

She listened to the dead silence on the other end of the line. There hadn't been a vase on her office coffee table. There had been no such occurrence. But Annabelle Schlessinger wouldn't have known that.

"Remember that session, Amelia?" she pressed. "Do you recall what we were discussing at the time?"

More silence.

"Amelia, are you still there?"

"Karen, I don't know what you're talking about," she

replied, at last. "Did I break a vase of yours? Oh, my God, is this something I blacked out?"

Closing her eyes, Karen smiled. "You know what? My mistake. That was someone else entirely. Never mind. Listen, I'm in Wenatchee right now—"

"What?"

"I'll explain when I see you," Karen said. "I can probably get to Grand Coulee Dam in about ninety minutes."

"Let me meet you there in Wenatchee instead, okay?" she asked. "I've kind of been-there-and-done-that here today, and I'd like to hit the road. I was about to head that way, anyway."

Karen hesitated. It made sense. They'd save at least an hour and a half traveling time back to Seattle if Amelia came to her. "Okay," she said finally. "Could you meet me at the Wenatchee Public Library on Douglas Street?"

"Sure, I know where that is," she said. "See you there in about two hours. I'm leaving right now. Oh, and if it's okay with you, I don't want to hang around Wenatchee too long, Karen. I'd like to be back in Seattle before nine tonight, and get the car back to Shane. I think he's kind of mad at me. He wasn't answering his cell phone earlier. Anyway, you don't mind if we meet up and then get a move on, do you?"

"No, that's fine, Amelia," she replied.

She couldn't tell her anything more, not right now.

"Then I'll see you soon, Karen."

"Drive safe," she said.

Before she headed out on the road again, Karen phoned Detective Jacqueline Peyton. After all the times she'd refused to pick up the policewoman's calls, Karen figured it probably served her right that she got Detective Peyton's voice mail. Karen waited for the beep.

"Hello, Detective, this is Karen Carlisle again," she said into the phone. "My housekeeper called the police about forty minutes ago. Amelia Faraday—or rather, someone pretending to be Amelia—was just at my house. I'm sure she's driving my Jetta. You have the plate number. I'm pretty sure she had something to do with Shane Mitchell's death, too. I hear the police found Shane in a canoe on Lake Washington, and they believe he shot himself. But it was this woman who looks like Amelia. She's dangerous. In fact, I think she killed Detective Koehler. I'm sorry I haven't been very cooperative in your investigation up to this point, but I can explain later. If you—"

The answering machine let out another beep, cutting her off. The connection went dead.

Karen realized she'd used up all her time.

Rural Route 17 outside Salem wound around a slightly scrawny forest area with several well-spaced dirt road turnoffs to farms and ranches. Old-fashioned mailboxes with the addresses on them stood at the edge of the long driveways. George couldn't see most of the farms and ranch houses from the car. They were too far down those winding private drives. The last vestige of daylight was fading. George switched on his headlights.

About three miles back, he'd passed a town of sorts. Sherry's Corner Food & Deli had a gas pump over to one side—along with a sign: RING FOR SERVICE! The store also advertised DVD rentals, fresh coffee, beer, and live bait. Across the street from them was a squat, beige brick storefront that had UPPER MARION COUNTY POLICE stenciled on the window. There was a patrol car parked in front of the place, along with an army recruiting sandwich-board poster by the entrance.

George imagined what it must have been like for Annabelle Schlessinger, living out here, alone a good deal of the time, according to her teacher. Small wonder Annabelle hadn't had any friends over to her father's ranch. There was nothing out here. Sherry's Corner was about as exciting as it got; even that was miles away.

George was beginning to think he'd passed the Schlessingers' place; the last driveway had been at least a mile back. But then the car's headlights swept across a driveway with a rusty, old, dented mailbox beside it. The address numbers and name on the mailbox were barely legible anymore: RR #17–14—SCHLESSINGER.

He turned down the bumpy, one-lane dirt road, which ceded to patches of crab grass and tree roots. There were also some fallen branches to navigate, along with old beer cans and other garbage. George figured the ranch must have attracted curious and bored high school kids who wanted to see where those two people had burned to death. So, maybe some of Annabelle's classmates had been to her home after all.

Taking a curve in the road, George saw the ranch house ahead, just as Caroline Cadwell had described it: a two-story, burnt-out shell. Wood planks boarded up the front door and windows. He noticed even more garbage littered around the blackened edifice—faded fast-food bags and more rusty beer cans. Over to one side stood a dilapidated barn, its door boarded up. Between it and what remained of the house were a stone well, covered with graffiti, and a tall wind pump creaking in the breeze.

George parked the car and switched the motor off. That squeaky wind pump was the only sound he heard now. He walked around the charred structure, kicking at the occasional pop bottle or beer can in his path. He tugged at a plank that was nailed over one of the windows. It didn't

budge. In the backyard, he noticed sporadic patches of wildflowers between one side of the barn and a wooded area.
They were the only bit of beauty and color on this drab, desolate place.

He wondered if the Schlessingers had buried some of
their dead ranch animals there. Wildflowers were supposed
to indicate a grave.

Or was something else buried out there?

The photocopies of the missing young women were
folded up and tucked inside George's sports jacket pocket.
He automatically touched the square bulge over his breast to
make sure they were still there.

Glancing toward the burnt house again, he saw the wood
panel over the back door was askew. George stepped up to
the door, and pulled at the plank. It moved easily. The lock
and handle on the soot-stained back door had been broken
off. He opened the door. From the threshold, he studied the
kitchen. It took a few moments for his eyes to adjust to the
darkness. But he could see the room had survived the fire.
The green linoleum floor was filthy and littered with garbage
from intruders. The only piece of furniture left was a broken
chair, lying on its side. The old stove still stood against the
grimy walls, but it had been stripped of the oven door and a
few of the dials. All the windows—covered up by the planks
outside—were broken. The curtains were in tatters. The
place was cold, with a stale, stuffy, acrid odor.

George wondered what the hell he expected to find here.
He touched that square bump in his sports jacket pocket
again.

The local fire and police departments had already been
through the place, along with a few scavengers. If they hadn't
uncovered anything, how did he expect to fare any better?

But those people had been looking for a cause of the fire,
while others had been scrounging for a piece of furniture or

a knickknack worth stealing. Still others had been seeking a cheap, morbid thrill, or a remote spot to get drunk.

George was pretty certain no one else had searched this place for evidence of the missing young women. He kept thinking about how it was just too much of a coincidence that they'd started to disappear when Lon Schlessinger had moved into this house, and that the last one had vanished a week before this place had turned to cinders.

George walked through the kitchen, and listened to the old, weakened floorboards groaning beneath him. The front hallway and living room hadn't fared as well as the kitchen. The walls were blistered and blackened. A huge section of the charred floor had collapsed. George could tell there was a basement to the house, but it was too dark to see anything. The stairway to the second floor had been destroyed. Only the black skeleton of a newel post and two steps remained. He had no way of going up to the second floor, where they'd found Annabelle's and Lon's remains.

Every time George breathed in, he smelled the soot and grime. He could even taste it now. He retreated back to the kitchen, and he found the door to the Schlessingers' basement. Opening it, he carefully started down the stairs. Halfway down, he heard a rustling noise that made him stop. A faint light seeped in from an uncovered small window that was broken. Below it was a shelf full of cheap planters holding brittle-looking vines of long-dead plants. Below that, there was a hose connection where a washer machine must have been. George listened again to the light rustling. He figured some rodents had made their home down there. He stopped and tucked his trouser cuffs inside his socks, and then continued down the stairs. Wire hangers dangled from an exposed pipe along the ceiling in what must have been the laundry room.

The next room was nearly pitch black, and had caught all

the debris from the living room floor collapsing above it. George took out his cell phone and switched it on. He used the little blue light to navigate through the cobwebs and the rubble. He saw an old-fashioned furnace over to one side, and directly ahead, a big, heavy-looking door. It looked like one of those old bomb shelters. He gave the door a tug, but it barely moved. Putting the phone back in his pocket, he yanked at the door again, this time with both hands. It squeaked open just a few more inches. He tried one more time, but the door didn't budge.

Switching on his cell phone again, he slipped it through the narrow opening and then glanced into the room. The blue light was just strong enough so he could see, past a haze of dust in the air, a cot and a bare metal bookcase against the wall. An old army blanket lay in a heap on the dirty floor. But he couldn't see anything else from where he stood at the doorway. The light wasn't strong enough. He couldn't even tell how big the room was.

Turning around, George made his way back through the darkness and debris until he reached the basement stairs. He hurried up to the kitchen, and then out the door. It felt good to breathe fresh air again. But he still had that awful sooty taste in his mouth. He ran to the car, popped open the hood, and took out the jack.

He needed to get a better look inside that little room in the basement. As much as he didn't want to think like someone who abducted and murdered young women, George could see that little room as a perfect dungeon. Maybe Lon liked to hold on to his toys for a while before he grew tired of them. What better place than that fallout shelter with the cot and a blanket?

Inside the house again, he headed back down the basement stairs with the jack. George switched on his cell phone once more as he weaved around the wreckage and maneuvered his way to the bomb shelter door. He had a tough time bracing the jack in a horizontal position, but finally got it to stick. He worked the lever, and listened to the heavy door creak open wider and wider. But then the lever started to resist and buckle, and no matter how hard George pushed, the door didn't move another inch.

The gap was a little over a foot wide. Stepping over the jack, George squeezed through the narrow opening. He prayed the jack wouldn't collapse on him. He imagined himself trapped in this tiny room, in this desolate house in the middle of nowhere.

He brushed against something with his foot, and heard a tinny, clanking noise. George directed the cell phone light toward the floor, and saw at least a dozen empty tin cans. He checked out the labels: most of them were for a cat food called Purrfect Kitty. There were a few empty cans of Del Monte brand sliced peaches, too. George also noticed a plastic bucket in the corner, tipped over on its side. There was nothing else in the tiny room, just the cot, the barren metal bookcase, and a discarded blanket. The only new discoveries he'd made were these lousy tin cans and a bucket, hardly worth all his painstaking effort to get inside the place for a better look

He seemed to be chasing after nothing. Hell, maybe it was indeed just a lousy coincidence those girls had started disappearing once the Schlessingers had moved here.

George poked at the blanket with his foot. Suddenly a rat scurried out from under the folds.

"Shit!" he hissed, dropping his cell phone. The light stayed on just long enough for him to see the rodent crawl out the gap in the doorway. Then everything went black.

George tried to catch his breath, but he couldn't. A panic swept through him. He thought he'd be able to see a very faint light through the doorway opening, but no. He couldn't see a damn thing, not even his hand in front of his face.

Standing there, paralyzed by the dark, he heard a strange

buckling noise. It sounded like the jack ready to give out. The big, heavy door made another creaking sound.

"Oh, Jesus," George whispered. He knew the phone had dropped somewhere near the bookcase. Blindly, he waved his hand around until he touched the metal shelf. He crouched down and started patting the floor. "Shit, where is it?" he muttered. "God, please . . ."

His hand brushed against the phone, and it slid across the floor. "Damn it," he growled. He anxiously felt around under the bookcase. Then something stung his finger. George snapped his hand back. "What the hell. . . ."

He wondered if it was another rat. But this was more like a pinprick.

Behind him, he heard the door giving out another yawn.

Shifting around, his knee touched something on the floor. George reached down and found the cell phone. He switched it off, and then on again. The light came on once more. "Thank God," he murmured.

He looked at his wounded index finger. It was bleeding.

Crouching down close to the floor, he used the cell phone light to check under the metal bookcase. He saw the pin sticking out on the back of something that looked like a name tag. He reached for it, carefully, so he wouldn't stab himself again. But he must have knocked it farther back against the wall. He had to squeeze most of his arm under the bookcase until his fingertips finally brushed against the badge, or whatever it was. Clasping it between his fingers, he slid his hand out from under the case.

He shined the light on it. "Oh, Jesus . . ."

It was the kind of name tag waitresses wear. This one was green with white indented lettering that said YOUR SERVER IS NANCY RAE.

George didn't need to look at the photocopies he'd made. He remembered Nancy Rae Keller, the talented pianist and part-time waitress, who had disappeared one Thursday night in March 2002 after finishing work at a Corvallis restaurant.

According to her former teacher, Nancy Rae had had beautiful red hair.

A loud groan emitted from the fallout shelter door. The jack buckled under the pressure.

George lunged toward the opening, slamming into the door just as the jack gave way. The device snapped out of place and flew into the pile of debris in the outside room. George was halfway through the opening when he felt the door move. It scraped against his leg, and he winced at the pain. But he didn't stop until he'd made it out on the other side of the big, heavy door. And all the while, he'd kept his cell phone and Nancy Rae's name tag firmly in his grasp.

He knew he'd hurt himself. No doubt his leg was bleeding. But that didn't matter right now. He'd gotten out.

And in a way, after five long years, so had Nancy Rae.

Chapter Twenty

The Schlessinger ranch—July 2004

She sat on her bed, painting her toenails—Sassy Scarlet. Her tabby, Neely, was curled up beside her. It was still pretty hot out, so she had the box fan in the window. A U2 song played softly on her boom box. Annabelle wore cutoffs and a sleeveless T-shirt. Her black hair was pulled back in a pony-tail.

She had a friend from school staying over tonight.

Annabelle hoped to chat a bit with Sandra. But she had to wait first, until her father finished with Sandra down in the basement. He'd been at her now for about a half hour.

At last, Annabelle heard him clearing the phlegm from his throat and lumbering up the stairs to the second floor. He passed her room without looking in, and continued on to his bedroom.

Annabelle shoved Neely off her bed, then got to her feet. From her bedroom, she peered into her parents' room. Her father couldn't see her, but in a darkened window across from her parents' double bed, she caught his reflection. He was wearing a T-shirt and work pants. He plopped down on the bed, then lit a cigarette. In a few minutes, he'd go take a shower and wash Sandra off.

Slipping on a pair of flip-flops, she snuck out of her room, and down the stairs. As she passed through the kitchen, she got a waft of her father's body odor, still lingering from when he'd passed through just minutes ago. He must have really worked up a sweat down in the basement. Annabelle paused for a moment, as she heard the pipes squeaking and the shower starting in the upstairs bathroom.

She got another dose of that musky stench as she started down the basement stairs. But at least it was cooler down in the cellar. In the laundry room, she grabbed a bath towel from on top of the dryer. Carrying it into the furnace room, she pulled on the string for the overhead light.

Annabelle listened to Sandra crying in the fallout shelter, but the sound was muffled. She laid the towel by the big, heavy door, then sat down on it. "Sandra? Can you hear me okay?"

There was a gasp, and then she cried out, "Who's there? Is somebody there?"

"It's me, Annabelle," she called to her. "Listen, I can't talk long—"

"Get me out of here! Please, please, you have to help me. . . ."

Why do they always say the same thing? she wondered, fanning at her toes and blowing on them so her nail polish dried faster. *Just like Gina, and all the others.* She let Sandra scream and beg for another minute, and then finally interrupted her. "Listen, I can't spring you out of there right now. It's just too dangerous. But I'll help you. I promise, you won't have to stay in there long—"

"No! You have to get me out of here *now*! Please, Annabelle, I want to go home, please!"

It was nice, the way Sandra called her by name. Anna-

belle leaned against the door. "Hey, Sandra? Please don't be
mad at me for this, okay? He forced me to do it. But I'll
make it up to you, I swear."

"I'm not mad at you," she said, her voice still full of
panic. "In fact, my parents will give you money if you help
me. I'm sure of it. They're rich. . . ."

Annabelle frowned. The offer of money was nice, sure.
But an offer of friendship would have been better. She had
this notion about killing her father and helping Sandra escape. Of course, then she'd have to go on the run. But she'd
already planned for that. For several months now, she'd
drawn money out of her father's account with forged checks
and the occasional trip with one of his credit cards to the
ATM at Sherry's Corner. So far, she'd stashed away over
three thousand dollars. There was also her mother's jewelry,
and a silver service that belonged to her grandparents. Annabelle figured she had about six or seven grand worth of crap
around the house that she could hock.

She imagined, after several days in captivity, Sandra would
bond with her. And if she helped Sandra escape, Sandra
would do the same for her. Like in *Thelma and Louise*, life
on the lam with her new best friend would be an adventure.
She and Sandra already looked alike. People would probably
mistake them for sisters, or even twins. That would be nice.

"Sandra, I left you something in there," she said. "That
stuff he used to knock you out, it's chloroform, and sometimes it burns your face. I knew he'd be using it tonight, so I
left you a little jar of Noxzema under that old rag in the corner. It'll help soothe the irritation. I left some chewing gum
there, too."

He always starved them for the first twenty-four hours.
The promise of food and water always made them more cooperative, especially after an initial bout with true hunger.
Some of them were probably even grateful to get the cat
food.

"Annabelle, I really, really want to go home. He hurt me. I'm in pain. . . ." She started crying again. "I miss my mom and dad. Please, please, help me. . . ."

Annabelle let her cry for a few moments. "I'll help you escape, Sandra," she said, finally. "But it's impossible to-night. Just hang in there, okay? And listen, if I get you out, I can't possibly stay here. You'll have to help me get away. Can you do that? Do you promise to help me make a clean break and go start somewhere else?"

"Yes, of course!" Sandra answered, almost too quickly. "I promise. I'll do anything you want. Just get me out of here! Please . . ."

"Sandra?" she said, her face pressed against the crack in the big door.

"Yes?"

"Earlier tonight, you asked me to go to the movie with you," Annabelle said. "Were you just inviting me out of po-liteness, because I was giving you a ride? Or did you really want to hang out with me? Because I'm not sure if I fit in with your friends—"

"Oh, no, I—I wanted you to come with us," Sandra replied. "I wasn't just being polite. I like you, Annabelle. You seem very nice." But the tone of her voice smacked of desperation, as if her life depended on giving the right an-swer.

And, of course, it did.

With a sigh, Annabelle got to her feet and gathered up the bath towel. "I need to go now," she said. "I don't want him to know we're in cahoots—"

"No, God, please, don't go. Annabelle, don't leave me here . . . please. . . ." Sandra started pounding on the other side of the door. .

Annabelle turned away. She reached up and pulled the string to the overhead light in the furnace room. Standing in the darkness, she listened to Sandra Hartman begging her to stay and talk just a little longer.

It felt kind of nice.

Wenatchee, Washington—three years later

SEARCH CONTINUES FOR MISSING MOSES LAKE WOMAN said the headline near the bottom of page 3 of the *Columbia Basin Herald* for October 21, 1992.

Karen had found it almost by accident. She'd been at the Wenatchee library for forty-five minutes now, scanning microfiche files, moving backward from February 1993. She was searching for a news story, but didn't quite know what kind of headline to expect, maybe something like *Child Snatcher Shot Dead* or *Dramatic Rescue Reveals Waitress-Killer*.

So far, she hadn't come up with anything, except a slight crick in her neck from all the tension. She tried not to rush through the files, but after scanning the headlines on the first five pages of every edition for two months, she started skipping days. Karen kept reminding herself that she wasn't in any hurry. Amelia was supposed to meet her here in an hour.

She hadn't heard back from Jessie, yet. Nor had George phoned with an update. Most surprising of all, Detective Peyton hadn't returned her call. And so far, she hadn't found a damn thing in the Moses Lake newspaper files, until now.

There was a photograph of the missing woman: a thin, pale-looking blonde with big eyes and short, curly hair. Karen read the caption: "Kristen Marquart, 22, was last seen leaving work at The Friendly Fajita on Broadway in Moses Lake last Wednesday night."

According to the article, Kristen's car was still in the restaurant parking lot the following day. Investigators determined the car had been tampered with, but they didn't say exactly how. Kristen, a graduate of Eastern Washington University, had been missing for a week when the article was written.

Karen saw the second-to-last paragraph, and grimaced. "Oh, God, here it is," she murmured to herself.

> Kristen Marquart's disappearance is the most recent in a rash of missing person cases in the Columbia Basin area, all young women. In August, Juliet Iverson, 20, vanished while picnicking with friends at Soap Lake. In March, Othello resident Lizbeth Strouss, 24, disappeared after finishing her night shift at a convenience store. Earlier in March, Eileen Sessions, 27, of Moses Lake vanished after dropping off her two children at day care. After 17 days, her remains were discovered near a hiking trail in Potholes State Park forest near the Potholes Reservation.

Four women had vanished in eight months, and the authorities didn't have any suspects. Karen had been hoping to find a story like this, and now that she'd found it, she felt horrible. These women weren't just part of some puzzle. They were real.

And it seemed even more likely now that Amelia's birth father was a monster.

Karen wondered if he'd abducted and killed any more young women before moving to Salem. Or had Kristen Marquart been the last?

Staring at the screen in front of her, Karen realized she must have scanned past the news story about Lon Schlessinger shooting the neighbor who had allegedly molested Amelia. That neighbor was also blamed for the murder of a waitress. Was the murdered waitress Kristen?

With a heavy sigh, Karen started to scan over the newspaper records again. This time, she wouldn't skip over any days. Her eyes were getting blurry from too much reading, too much driving, and too little sleep. But she kept searching for the story she'd missed.

Hunched in front of the warm, wheezing microfiche-viewing machine, she read every headline on the first few pages of every edition of the *Columbia Basin Herald* until she found a front-page headline on Monday, November 16:

CHILD ABDUCTION SPARKS SHOOTING DEATH

Dead Man Linked to Disappearance of Moses Lake Woman, Possibly Others

MOSES LAKE: The apparent abduction of a 4-year-old girl on Sunday led to a police standoff and the shooting death of a man, now linked to the disappearance of a Moses Lake woman in October.

Six hours after Lon Schlessinger, 34, reported his young daughter as missing, he led police to the house of a Gardenia Drive neighbor, Clay Spalding, 26. Police arrived at the scene at 5:45 P.M. to see the child escaping from a bedroom window in Spalding's ranch house. The girl was dressed in only her underwear. When Spalding began to chase after the terrified child, Schlessinger shot him with a Winchester hunting rifle. Spalding, an unemployed artist, was pronounced dead on arrival at Samaritan Hospital at 6:20.

Police found the child's clothes inside Spalding's home. They also made another startling discovery in the unkempt residence: a wallet full of identification and a locket, both belonging to Kristen Marquart, 22, a waitress and Moses Lake resident who has been missing since October 14.

Marquart was last seen leaving her place of employment, The Friendly Fajita, on Broadway in Moses Lake. Authorities are now reexamining the disappearance of three other young women in the Columbia Basin area for a possible connection to Spalding.

According to Miriam Getz, 70, who lived next door to Spalding for two years, her neighbor was "quiet and considerate, but very strange, something of a loner." She added: "He made people uncomfortable, and I think he enjoyed doing that."

Getz reported that the Schlessingers had asked if she'd seen their missing daughter at 11 A.M. on Sunday. She later spotted the child in Spalding's backyard, and immediately telephoned the Schlessinger house. In a 911 call to Moses Lake

Police, Lon Schlessenger said he intended to confront his Gardenia Drive
neighbor.

Lon Schlessinger shot Clay Spalding in front of four
Moses Lake policemen, and apparently, seconds later, the
panic-stricken little girl ran into her father's arms. If Lon
was in any kind of trouble for taking the law into his own
hands, there was no indication of it in the article. They tact-
fully avoided calling Amelia by name, but did mention:
*"Lon Schlessinger is a ranch foreman at G. L. Durlock, Inc.
in Grant Country. The Schlessingers have been Moses Lake
residents for five years. They have two children."*

There was a photograph of Clay Spalding on page two.
Karen remembered Amelia's description of her neighbor, the
nice Native American man with beautiful, long black hair.
He'd converted a backyard toolshed into a playhouse for her.
She'd eaten cookies in there at a little red plastic table.

The driver's license photo of Clay Spalding showed a
swarthy, handsome man with straight, near-shoulder-length
black hair and a slightly defiant look in his dark eyes. According to the article, two years before, Spalding had inher-
ited the ranch house on Gardenia Drive, along with a large
sum of money, from the home's previous owner. Prior to
moving to the Schlessingers' neighborhood, Spalding had
lived on the Potholes reservation.

Two paragraphs later, the article pointed out that of the
four recently reported missing women from the area, Eileen
Sessions was the only one confirmed dead. Her remains had
been discovered in a forest at Potholes State Park, not far
from the reservation.

Still, perhaps not to show too much bias against the al-
leged child snatcher, the article quoted Naomi Rankin, a
friend of Clay Spalding's, as well as a longtime Moses Lake
resident: "I've been very close to Clay for several years. He

was a brilliant artist and a lovely person. I don't think he was capable of hurting another human being, especially a child."

Karen wondered how Amelia could have only a vague, pleasant memory of this neighbor man, and not recall any of those nightmarish events from that October afternoon. "I liked him," Amelia had said, "but I don't think I was supposed to be around him."

"I don't get why we're supposed to stay in a hotel tonight," Jody said.

He sat in the front passenger seat with one foot up on the dashboard. Stephanie was in back, sorting through an old Bon Marché bag of kids' books, puzzles, and toys that had been on the Ping-Pong table in Karen's basement. The junk had originally belonged to Karen when she was a child. Jessie used to break out the bag of toys whenever Frank Junior or Sheila came to town and brought their kids to visit old Frank—anything to keep the children entertained for a while. She figured Stephanie would need something to while away the next few hours at the hotel.

There was a sci-fi convention in town, as well as an endodontists' convention, just her luck. All the hotels were full. But the clerk at the Edgewater Hotel had taken pity on her and found her a room at the Doubletree over by Southcenter Mall. Her timing was doubly awful, because of rush hour. They sat in bumper-to-bumper traffic on southbound I-5.

"I'd rather be in hell with my back broken," Jessie muttered, one hand on the steering wheel of George's car. She glanced in the rearview mirror again: no sign of Karen's Jetta or a black Cadillac. That was one consolation. If Karen was worried about them, they weren't in any danger right now. Nothing was going to happen to them in the middle of this traffic jam. Nobody was moving.

"Jessie, why do we gotta stay at a hotel?" Jody asked again.

"Oh, um, your dad thought it would be a good idea," she lied. "They—they're doing some work on the power on your block for the next few hours. We won't have any electricity, and rather than rough it, we're gonna live high on the hog at a nice hotel for the next few hours."

"They're waiting until *night* to screw around with the electricity?" Jody said. "That's kind of dumb. You'd think they'd do it during the day—when we don't need the electricity so much."

"So write to your city councilman," Jessie said. "There's stationery at the hotel, and there's also pay-per-view TV with new movies, *and* room service. You'll love it, Jody, I promise. With the room-service dinner, they give you these little bottles of ketchup and mustard. It's really neat. The best part of all is you don't have to do your homework while you're there."

She figured he wouldn't argue or ask questions about that.

"I hate mustard!" Stephanie announced from the back-seat.

"Well, you can just keep it for a souvenir, sweetie," Jessie replied. "They also have little bars of soap and little bottles of shampoo. And here's hoping they have an honor bar for dear old Jessie."

Once the kids were settled, she would treat herself to a glass of wine, or rather, *Karen* would treat her. That bizarre episode with Amelia had really shaken her up. She'd never seen Amelia act that way before, so creepy and smug, like a totally different person. And it was pretty darn unnerving to hear she was supposed to have been on the lookout for a black Cadillac today. That big, old beat-up car had been parked down the block from George's house since before Jody even got back from school. She wondered if anyone was sitting inside it, and if they were still there, waiting for her and the kids to come back.

"Are we gonna be at the hotel soon?" Stephanie asked.

"Well, unless I can shift this car into *leap*, we aren't going anywhere," Jessie muttered, eyeing the gridlock ahead. They weren't even past Safeco Field yet. "Hang in there, Steffie. We should be checking in to the hotel in about a half hour, tops."

"Y'know, we gotta go home first before we go anywhere else," Jody said quietly. "Steffie needs her inhaler."

"Oh, shhhh—" Jessie stifled herself. "Do you know the brand, honey? Can we pick another one up for her at a drug-store?"

"Can't," Jody said. "It's a subscription."

"Prescription, honey." She sighed. "Oh, Lord. . . ."

"She really needs it, too," Jody pointed out. "Mom used to say it was like asking for trouble if Steffie went anywhere without her inhaler. That's kind of a weird expression. Do you know what that means exactly? *Asking for trouble?*"

Jessie saw the sign for the West Seattle Bridge ahead, the exit for George's house. "Yes, I know exactly what it means," she said.

Biting her lip, she put on her turn signal, and started merging toward the West Seattle turnoff.

Sitting in the crummy little office across the street from Sherry's Corner Food & Deli, the sheriff had I Don't Have Time for This Shit written across her face.

She stared at George from behind a computer and a pile of paperwork on her big metal desk. Decked out in her brown sheriff's uniform, she was about forty-five, with short, dish-water-blond hair and a long, narrow, horselike face. Her lip-stick was on crooked. "Let me get this straight," she said. "You want me to go over to the old Schlessinger ranch and start digging up their backyard? And this is based on the fact that you were snooping down in their basement and found a name tag with 'Nancy Rae' printed on it?"

"Yes," George said, showing her the waitress badge again. "Nancy Rae Keller; she worked at a restaurant in Corvallis."

The cut on his leg from the fallout shelter door scraping him wasn't too serious. But it still stung like hell, and he'd torn his pants leg. He'd cleaned it up in the restroom in the sheriff's office.

George now sat in a metal chair with a green Naugahyde-covered cushioned seat and sturdy armrests. He imagined those armrests were used to keep a felon cuffed to the chair. But he couldn't see that happening around here much. One look at the place seemed to confirm that it wasn't exactly a hub of activity. A map of Marion County decorated the off-white wall, along with scores of police bulletins, many sun-faded, dusty, and starting to curl at the edges.

Yet, the sheriff acted as if she was in the middle of a major crime bust, and he was taking up her time.

"Nancy Rae has been missing for five years now," George pointed out. "She's one of several missing-person cases in the area, all young women."

"I'm well acquainted with those old missing-person cases," the sheriff said. She waved at the four ugly metal file cabinets behind her. "I have all of the files there . . . somewhere. I also have all this *here*," she said, slapping at a pile of papers on her desk. "And it needs to be processed and filed. Now, I can't just drop everything and go on an archaeological dig with you in the Schlessingers' backyard. First of all, you're lucky I don't charge you with trespassing, Mr. McMillan. That ranch is private property."

"Well, I don't think I'd be the first one to trespass there," George replied, at the risk of incurring her wrath. "The place is pretty trashed. I saw a lot of beer cans and garbage."

"Yes," the sheriff nodded. "For a while there, certain morbid teenagers hung out there to get drunk, but we put a stop to it. That waitress tag probably belonged to one of them."

"I doubt it. If you knew where I found it—"

"All right, so you want to go out there now and start digging?" she cut in. "Based on what—a *hunch*? And some tidbit you read in a book of amazing facts about wildflowers indicating grave sites? We can't do that, Mr. McMillan. First, we'd have to call a judge for a search warrant, which we'd be damn lucky to get by noon tomorrow. We'd also have to notify the current property owner. The ranch was bought by some chemical company in Boise eighteen months ago. A fence was supposed to go up around the place last year, but it didn't happen . . ."

She stopped to look at her deputy, who ambled through the doorway. The skinny, dark-haired young man wore a brown uniform and had a goofy-looking buzz cut. Walking around the counter, he carried a small bag and a can of Diet Coke.

"Twenty minutes for a lousy roast beef sandwich?" the sheriff asked him. "What did Sherry have to do? Kill the cow?"

The beleaguered deputy set the bag and soda on her desktop. "They were out of potato salad, so I got you chips," he muttered.

"Fine, fine, thanks, Tyler," she grumbled. The sheriff tapped a pile of folders on the corner of her desk. "File these, and then clock out. I don't want the county paying you overtime tonight. That's just more paperwork for me. I get more done without you here, anyway."

Sighing, he collected the files and stepped toward the metal cabinets behind her.

The sheriff opened up the can of Diet Coke. "If you're serious about this, Mr. McMillan, we can't just start digging over at the Schlessinger ranch. We need to go through the proper procedures. That'll take time. Now, I see you there, tapping your foot, and if you're anxious to get going on this, you have a long wait ahead."

George squirmed in the chair. What had made him think

he could get back to his kids tonight? If the cops actually followed his tip and found some bodies at the Schlessinger ranch, they'd want him to stick around. Hell, it might take days before they even uncovered anything.

"I'll tell you what," the sheriff said, reaching into the carry-out bag. "You leave Nancy Rae's name tag with me, along with a number where I can get ahold of you. I won't charge you with trespassing. And I'll pass your tip onto the state police in the morning."

George sighed. At least that freed him up to go home. But it meant waiting for confirmation that Lon Schlessinger was responsible for the disappearance of all those women. George also wondered if the sheriff even took him seriously enough to bother contacting the state police.

"Listen," she said, obviously reading his hesitation. "The last of those missing-person cases was over three years ago. . . ."

Behind her, the deputy stopped filing and glanced over his shoulder. "I went to school with Sandra Hartman," he said. "She was the last one—"

"Yes, Tyler, I know," the sheriff said, dismissing him. She unwrapped her sandwich. "You've already told me all about it. I'm not talking to you right now."

The deputy sneered at her back. Shaking his head, he resumed his menial task.

The sheriff rolled her eyes, then turned to George. "Anyway, my point is, it's an old case. If the late Lon Schlessinger is somehow involved, and there are indeed bodies buried on his property, nothing about that will change between now and tomorrow morning. I can assure you, Lon will still be dead. And on the off-off-off chance some bodies are buried on his ranch, they won't be going anywhere, either."

Frowning, she peeled the wheat bread back and inspected her sandwich. "It can wait until morning, Mr. McMillan," she said distractedly. "So please, quit tapping your foot. Leave the name tag and your phone number. And let me eat my lousy dinner in peace."

Ten minutes later, George was parked across the street at Sherry's Corner Food & Deli. He'd left his rental on the far side of the lot, behind a Winnebago so the car couldn't be seen from the precinct office. He was surprised the Food & Deli had shovels for sale, but then it made sense, considering the neighborhood. George bought some Neosporin for his leg, as well as a shovel and pick. He felt like a smuggler carrying them out of the store in full view of the sheriff's office across the street. He quickly loaded the tools into the trunk of his car.

Shutting the trunk, he peeked around the back of the Winnebago. George saw the deputy come out of the police station. He headed across the road again for another trip into Sherry's Corner.

"Tyler?" George said, moving toward the store entrance. "Deputy?"

The young man stopped to stare at him. "Hey, you're still around," he said, half smiling. "So the bitch didn't scare you away?"

"No, she didn't," George said. "Listen, deputy, how would you like to help solve Sandra Hartman's disappearance, and maybe make your boss look like an idiot in the process?"

"Well, last I heard, dear," the old woman said. "They sent Amelia to live with Joy's relatives up in Canada someplace."

Miriam Getz was petite with thick, cat's-eye glasses and short curled hair that was light brown with a pinkish hue, obviously from a bad dye job. She wore a string of pearls and pearl earrings with her lavender sweat suit.

After making a few calls, Karen had found out Clay Spalding's former next-door neighbor was still alive. But the 84-year-old Miriam was no longer living in Moses Lake. She now resided in New Horizons, a rest home in East Wenatchee, just a fifteen-minute drive from the library.

New Horizons wasn't on a par with Sandpoint View, but it was pleasant and certainly clean enough. Karen had caught Miriam in the corner of the TV lounge, working on her crossword puzzle. There were about a dozen other residents in the room, watching *The Russians Are Coming, the Russians Are Coming* with the volume a bit too loud. Over where Miriam sat, it was a bit quieter, but her cronies still burst into laughter every few moments.

Sitting down beside her, Karen had explained that she was Amelia Schlessinger's therapist, and she needed to find out more about Amelia's childhood. Miriam had heard about Joy Schlessinger's suicide shortly after the family had moved to Salem. But she hadn't known Lon had died, too, more recently.

"What about Annabelle?" Miriam asked, putting aside her crossword puzzle.

"I'm pretty sure she's still alive," Karen told her. "But I don't know her like I know Amelia. I'm trying to help Amelia remember certain things from her childhood, especially that incident with Clay Spalding fourteen years ago."

Miriam shook her head. "Gracious, I'd think she'd be better off not recalling any of it."

Karen gave her a sad look. "Well, she isn't, Mrs. Getz— Miriam," she said quietly. "I think she might need to know. I've read some of the newspaper accounts of what happened. It sounds like you know more about it than anyone."

The old woman nodded. "I suppose I do."

"I was counting on that, Miriam," she said. "So, can you tell me about Clay?"

She frowned a bit, then shrugged. "Well, he was this In-

dian who, excuse me, *Native American*, who used to work
for my neighbor, Isadora Ferris. She was elderly. . . ." Miriam
let out a sad laugh. "Listen to me, I'm probably older now
than she was then. But she was a frail thing with Parkinson's.
Anyway when Izzy passed away, she left the house to Clay,
along with several thousand dollars. And believe you me,
that didn't go over well with the neighborhood. It didn't help
matters either that Clay let the place go to pot, and after he'd
kept it so beautiful while he was working for Izzy, too. It was
a sweet, little one-level ranch house. I never could figure out
why he didn't take better care of it. Sometimes, he even put
these odd *art* pieces of his on the front lawn, usually some
weird concoction made out of tin cans and wire hangers and
Lord knows what else. It could look really junky out there."

She sighed. "But to be fair, he was a nice, quiet neighbor.
He even shoveled my walk for me one winter. And he was
very sweet to those twins, too, especially Amelia. He didn't
get along with Lon or Joy. But for some reason, that one little girl liked him."

Karen nodded. "That's the impression I got, too. Amelia
told me about a little playhouse he had in his backyard. It's
one of the only things she remembers about him."

Miriam sighed, and fidgeted with her pearl necklace.
"Yes, well, he *seemed* harmless enough, at least I thought so,
until that day."

"Can you tell me what happened?" Karen asked. "Do you
remember?"

"As if it was yesterday," Miriam said. "Around eleven
o'clock that Sunday morning, Joy phoned me, asking if I'd
seen Amelia. Well, Amelia or Annabelle, I couldn't tell the
difference, but I hadn't seen either one. I guess Lon had gone
searching for her over at Clay's house earlier, and Clay even
let him look through the place. Apparently, Amelia wasn't
there. But wouldn't you know? Around five o'clock, I looked
out my kitchen window and spotted that little girl in Clay's

backyard. She was all by herself, bundled up in a jacket. I saw her come out of that playhouse and duck in Clay's kitchen door. So I immediately called Joy. Then Lon got on the line. He asked me to come over and tell him *exactly* what I saw. Well, once I told him, Lon announced he was driving to the police station. He said he'd bring an armed police officer back to Clay's house. Then off he went, and he took Annabelle with him."

Miriam removed her glasses and rubbed the bridge of her nose. "Well, about twenty minutes later, Lon was back, with Annabelle. The child was hysterical, squirming and shrieking to raise the dead. Lon had his hand over her mouth most of the time. He said he didn't even make it to the police station, because Annabelle starting pitching such a fit. None of us could figure out what was wrong with her." Miriam put her glasses back on. "But do you know what I think it was?"

Karen just shook her head.

"It didn't occur to me at the time, but I think Annabelle must have somehow known her twin sister was in distress. You know how some twins have a certain—*thing* between them?"

"Twin telepathy," Karen said, nodding.

Miriam nodded, and patted Karen's knee. "That's what I think it was. Anyway, poor Annabelle was carrying on so badly, they locked her in her room."

Karen squinted at her. "The child was upset, and their way of handling it was to lock her in her room?"

"My sentiments exactly," Miriam whispered. "But Lon ruled the roost in that household, and he's the one who locked Annabelle in the twins' bedroom. Then he fetched his hunting rifle and called up the police. He told them he was headed over to Clay's house to confront him and get his little girl back. All the while, Annabelle was screaming and crying behind that locked door. My heart just broke for her."

Miriam clicked her tongue, and shook her head. "I told

Lon I didn't think the gun was necessary. I kept saying, 'Let
the police handle it, for goodness sake!' I was so worried
Amelia would get hurt. But Lon couldn't be stopped, and out
the door he went. I followed him down the block. Joy stayed
behind. Lon was almost at Clay's house when I heard the
sirens. Two police cars came speeding up the block. Then,
over all that noise, I heard screams.

"I turned toward Clay's house and saw that pitiful little
girl climbing out a side window and crying for help." Miriam
closed her eyes and put a liver-spotted hand over her mouth.
"All she had on was her *underwear.* I just get sick when I
think about it. After that, everything happened so fast: the
sirens, tires screeching, all the policemen shouting, and that
poor, sweet child running across the yard, practically naked.
And this was November, mind you. Clay came out the front
door, and he started to run after Amelia. That's when Lon
shot him. I remember how in midstride, Clay suddenly flopped
back and fell on the ground."

Miriam let out a long sigh. "Then Lon threw his rifle down,
and Amelia ran into his arms. She was hysterical, crying, but
Lon kept rocking her and telling her, 'You're safe now, baby.'"

"And Clay Spalding was dead," Karen murmured.

Miriam nodded. "I think he died in the ambulance on the
way to Samaritan Hospital."

"What about Amelia?" Karen asked. "I understand she
was never really the same after that day. I hear her parents
had a very hard time with her."

"Well, it might have been more gradual than that," Miriam
said. "I know she was giving Lon and Joy some problems
even before that Sunday. So Lord knows how long Clay had
been—*pawing* at that poor little girl. I heard stories later that
he had Polaroid snapshots of Amelia, *undressed.*" She shook
her head. "Anyway, if she had problems before that day,
well, you're right, they just got worse and worse after that.
She tried to run away several times. I remember once, talk-

ing in the front yard to Joy and the twins, and a pickup truck came speeding up the block, like a bat out of you-know-where. I said to Joy something about how they could kill somebody, driving that fast. And before we knew it, Amelia broke away and ran into the street smack dab in front of that pickup—*on purpose*. The driver almost had an accident, swerving to avoid her. Four years old, and she was trying to kill herself. Can you imagine? Lon and Joy kept her home most of the time after that, and they didn't take visitors. I hardly saw her. Then I heard they sent her to stay with Joy's relatives, a cousin, I think."

Karen imagined Lon's solution to Amelia's problems was to lock the tormented girl in her room most of the time.

"What about the sister?" she asked.

"Annabelle? Oh, she was very well behaved. I don't think they had any problem with her." Miriam rubbed her chin. "No, the only time I ever saw her kick up a fuss was that afternoon before the shooting. And then later, I remember noticing her in her bedroom window, looking out and crying. I guess she'd seen the whole awful thing. But she didn't act up or anything after that, not like her sister."

Karen reached over and put her hand on Miriam's bony arm. "Did Lon run into any legal trouble for the shooting?" She winced a little. "I mean, even if it seemed justified, some people might say he took the law into his own hands."

Miriam frowned. "Well, I know there were some concerns. But Lon cooperated with the police a hundred percent."

"Did a doctor ever examine Amelia to determine whether or not she'd actually been molested?"

With a pained look on her careworn face, Miriam shrugged. "I really don't know. But they found her clothes in Clay's bedroom. And in the kitchen drawer, they found a wallet and a necklace belonging to a woman who had been missing for nearly a month, a waitress."

"Kristen Marquart," Karen interjected. "I read about her."

Miriam nodded, then shuddered a bit. "You can just imagine what it was like for me to realize I'd been living next door to a serial killer for two years."

"Did they ever find Kristen's body?"

Miriam fiddled with her necklace again. "No, I don't think so."

"And did they ever really connect Clay with any of the other disappearances?"

"Well, they found whatever was left of one poor woman near the reservation where he used to live. That was enough for me. Oh, this girlfriend of Clay's raised a big fuss. . . ."

Karen nodded. She'd already left a voice mail for Clay's friend, Naomi Rankin, who still lived in Moses Lake. But Naomi hadn't phoned back yet.

"She insisted he was totally innocent, and incapable of hurting anyone. But she didn't see what I saw that day. No, she certainly did not."

"Then you believe Clay murdered those young women," Karen murmured.

Miriam glanced at Karen over the rims of her cat's-eye glasses. "Well, dear, the girls stopped disappearing after Clay was shot dead. So what do you think?"

"I have to go to the bathroom," Stephanie announced. "Real bad."

"Well, hold on a little longer, honey," Jessie said, with a glance in the rearview mirror. "We're almost there. The last few blocks are always the worst."

Driving up the cul-de-sac toward George's house, Jessie kept looking for that beat-up black Cadillac with the broken antenna. She didn't see it. She didn't spot Karen's Jetta either. Nothing looked unusual or out of place as she pulled into the driveway: no strange cars, no smashed windows, no one lurking around the house.

Approaching the front door with the children, Jessie didn't notice anything wrong with the door handle. To be on the safe side, she would have left the kids in the car while she ducked into the house for the damn inhaler. But Steffie had to go to the bathroom. She was all fidgety and squirming as Jessie unlocked the door. At least the door was still locked. That was a good sign.

"Now, let me go in first," Jessie announced, reaching for the light switch.

But Stephanie darted past her through the doorway, and made a beeline for the bathroom off the kitchen. Jessie had left the light on in there.

"I gotta go, too," Jody said, heading toward the facilities by his bedroom.

Rolling her eyes, Jessie turned and saw the door open to the front closet, with the light on. Had she left it like that?

She remembered setting the alarm code before hurrying out of the house earlier. It should have started beeping when they came through the front door. Something was wrong. "Steffie? Jody?" she called.

Starting toward the kitchen, Jessie glanced around the living room, and stopped dead. "Oh, no," she murmured. She felt this awful sensation in the pit of her stomach. For a few seconds, she couldn't move.

The drawers to the antique cabinet were left open. One drawer was taken out completely and dumped on the floor.

She heard a toilet flush. Continuing toward the kitchen, Jessie saw that someone had been through the dining room breakfront, too. More open drawers, a few of them dumped out and scattered on the floor. The silver candlesticks on the dining room table were missing. All Jessie could think about was getting the children out of there, and then calling the police from a neighbor's house.

"Kids, we need to leave!" she called nervously.

"What?" Jody called back. "What's going on?"

Jessie turned and saw him coming from the bedroom hallway. But Jody suddenly stopped in his tracks. His mouth open, he gaped at Jessie and shook his head.

She realized he was looking at something behind her. She heard a whimpering sound, and recognized Steffie's cry. Jessie swiveled around, and for a moment, her heart stopped.

Stephanie stood trembling in the kitchen doorway. Tears streamed down her face. She'd wet herself.

Standing behind her was a young man with black hair and sunglasses. He wore a shiny black suit, and held a gun to Stephanie's head.

Chapter Twenty-one

"Holy crap, I think I found something," the deputy said. He stopped digging for a moment and gaped down into the hole.

George hadn't had much difficulty persuading Tyler to follow him out to the Schlessinger ranch. The deputy had had a little crush on Sandra Hartman back in high school, and for a while, he'd obsessed over her sudden disappearance. And George had been right about Tyler's hatred for his boss. He'd suggested that if they found a body buried on the ranch, Tyler could say he'd gotten suspicious and followed George out there while off duty. And yes, wouldn't the sheriff look stupid after that?

Tyler had a flashlight in his car, and they'd set it on a tree stump so it shined in the general direction of the wildflowers. They'd chosen a patch, and started in. George had worked the pick, and Tyler had manned the shovel. While they'd worked, the deputy had gone on and on about how much he couldn't stand that ballbuster boss of his. They hadn't even dug two feet down when Tyler had noticed the bones.

George grabbed the flashlight from the stump, and directed it into the pit. He figured Lon must have been lazy and careless about disposing of his victims' bodies, because the grave was way too shallow.

And the bones were way too small.

"It's a fucking cat," Tyler grumbled. He leaned on the shovel, and glanced at the other wildflower patches. "You were right about these pretty little buds indicating a grave. But I bet this is a boneyard for fucking cats. Ranchers and farmers often have a mess of cats to keep mice and rats away."

"Well, let's try one more," George said, putting the flashlight back on the tree stump. He grabbed the pick again. "Just to be sure, okay? I mean, if it's another cat, it won't take us long to find it."

"I think we're wasting our time here," the deputy said. "And I don't want to miss *American Idol* tonight."

"Just another fifteen minutes," George said, swinging the pick into a new section of wildflowers. "Just think, you might help solve Sandra Hartman's disappearance. What was she like, anyway?"

They dug for twenty minutes, while Tyler talked about what a knockout Sandra had been. Then George got a call on his cell phone. He checked the caller ID. It was home. He dropped the pick, and clicked on the phone. "Jessie, is that you?" he asked.

"Yes. Hello, George," she said.

He could tell immediately that something was wrong. "What's going on?" he asked warily.

"Oh, we have a situation here," she said. "Y'see, my sister's sick, very sick, and I need to go see her. She lives in Denver. Anyway, how soon can you come home?"

"Um, it'll take at least two and a half hours," he said. "Jessie, I'm so sorry about your sister—"

"Well, we had a family emergency here, too, George," she

said stiffly. "Steffie had a bad asthma attack. I called the doctor. She's fine now. She's resting. But she's asking for her daddy."

He could tell from Jessie's tone, it was more serious than she let on.

"If it's worse than that, Jessie, please, tell me," he said. "I'd rather know now."

"No. But I need you to hurry home."

"Well, could you put Steffie on the phone? I'd like to talk to her."

"Um, I can't, George. Like I said, she's resting. Just come home as soon as you can, okay?"

"I will, Jessie, thanks. I'm leaving now."

"Be careful," she said. Then there was a click and the line went dead.

He hit the disconnect button. "I've got to go," he murmured. "A family emergency up in Seattle, my daughter needs me."

Tyler leaned on his shovel. "How are you getting back there?"

Wringing his dirty hands, George shrugged. "On the way down here, I flew to Portland and then rented a car."

"It would be faster for you if you took a charter from McNary Field here in Salem," Tyler suggested. "You'd zip home in no time at all. The airport's not too far from here. Want to follow me out there?"

George hesitated. "Thanks, but could you give me directions instead?" He glanced down at the new crater they'd dug. It was at least three feet deep

The deputy gave him a wary look and chuckled. "Holy crap, you want me to keep digging?"

"Just ten more minutes, please," George said. "If it was a cat, we would have found it by now. Something else is down there."

Tyler took a moment, then nodded. "Okay, I'll keep at it," he sighed. "So, let me tell you how to get to McNary Field from here."

The man with the sunglasses took the receiver away from Jessie's face and hung up the phone.

"Good job," he said, with a tiny smirk.

While holding the phone for her, he'd kept the other extension—George's cordless—to his own ear. He clicked that off, and then set it on the kitchen counter.

Jessie was tied to a kitchen chair, her wrists bound together behind her with duct tape.

She'd been tied up like that for the last twenty minutes now. Their intruder had forced Jody to strap her into the chair. He'd used Jody's little sister as a negotiating tool, and the 11-year-old boy had been very cooperative.

"That's right," he'd told Jody, one hand over Steffie's mouth. The other held the gun to her head. "Now, wind the tape around fatso's stomach and the chair back. Strap her in real tight. Huh, you might need a few yards to get around all that blubber. . . ."

Shooting him a look, Jody hesitated.

"Just do what he says, honey," Jessie whispered. She was worried Steffie would have an asthma attack right there. The little girl trembled and quietly wept while the intruder tickled her earlobe with the revolver barrel.

Jessie sat there helpless as he made Jody wrap the tape around her ankles, fixing them to the chair's front legs. He tested Jody's work, pulling at each adhesion.

Then he took the children into their bedrooms. Cringing, Jessie listened to him barking instructions to Jody on how to tie up his sister. She heard Steffie whimpering the whole time, and Jody telling her to be brave. Jessie prayed and prayed that the next sound she heard wouldn't be a gunshot.

"That's right, put the tape over her mouth," the man said at one point.

Jessie listened to Steffie's muffled whining.

"C'mon, your turn," the man growled to Jody. "Take me to your room."

For the next few minutes, it was deathly quiet. Then suddenly, Jody let out a loud cry. It sent a jolt through Jessie's heart. "What are you doing to him?" she cried.

She waited anxiously for the next sound. Finally, she heard Jody's stifled moaning. At least he was still alive.

"There's no reason to hurt the children!" she called. "We're not stopping you. Please, just take whatever you want and leave!"

A few long moments passed before the young man ambled back into the kitchen with the cordless phone from George's study. "Oh, I'm not leaving for a while," he announced. "In fact, we're all going to wait here for their daddy to come home."

Then he'd forced her to make the call to George.

Jessie couldn't figure out why he wanted George to rush home. But she realized this wasn't an ordinary robbery. This was something much worse.

She stared up at that pale, young man with the jet-black hair and those tiny bangs over his forehead. Jessie wished she could see his eyes behind those dark glasses. "Listen, what's your name, anyway?"

He didn't respond. But he seemed to be studying her behind the sunglasses.

"Well, you heard George tell me that he won't be here for another two and a half hours," Jessie continued. "Since we're stuck here together that long, I should at least know you by name, *any* name. What should I call you?"

"Call me Your Majesty," he replied, deadpan.

"Well, Your Majesty, I want to compliment you on the

way you dress," Jessie said. "That's a very snappy suit. It shows you're serious and have a lot of self-respect. I think you're also smart enough, and compassionate enough, to care about those kids. You must know they're scared,and very uncomfortable."

"They're fine, hog-tied on their beds."

Jessie sighed. "The little one has asthma. If she has an attack, we won't be able to hear her. You've taped up her mouth. She could suffocate." Jessie's voice started to shake. "And she's wet herself. I'm sure you saw that. You have a heart. I know you do. If you'd just let me change her clothes and wash her up. Then the two children and I, we'd sit quietly on the sofa together. You could still keep our wrists and ankles tied. . . ."

"You talk too fucking much," he said coolly. "Would it help shut you up if I tied a plastic bag over your head?"

Jessie stared at him, and didn't say another thing.

George was driving down Rural Route 17 about a mile away from Sherry's Corner Food & Deli when he saw the patrol car in the distance. The red strobe lights on the roof flashed and glowed in the darkness ahead. He heard the siren's wail.

"Oh, no," he muttered. If that was the sheriff on her way to the Schlessinger ranch, he didn't have time to talk with her or answer questions. He couldn't stop for anything. He needed to get back to Seattle. He could tell from talking with Jessie earlier that he hadn't gotten the full story about the situation at home. Something was terribly wrong.

He watched the cop car, speeding toward him. The flashers were getting brighter.

Tyler must have found a body. Why else would the sheriff be speeding toward the ranch? Well, they could carry on without him.

George saw a mailbox and the driveway to a farm on his right. Switching off his headlights, he made the turn. He navigated down the dark, narrow, gravel road that wound behind some trees. Then he slowly turned the car around. The sound of the police siren grew louder, closer. Hands on the steering wheel, George watched the police car speed by.

His cell phone rang. The deputy had given him his cell number earlier. George recognized it. "Tyler?" he said.

"I found another skeleton," the deputy said. "It wasn't a cat this time. You were right. There are human remains out here." He let out a sigh. "Jesus, I still can't believe it. This could be what's left of Sandra Hartman right here in front of me."

"Did you call the sheriff and tell her?" George asked, though he already knew the answer.

"Yeah, she's on her way," Tyler answered. "She wants you to come back and show us exactly where you found the waitress's name tag. The state police are on their way, too. This place is going to be like Grand Central Station in about an hour."

George winced. "Listen, Tyler, do me a favor. Pretend you couldn't get ahold of me. I can't stick around. I need to get home to my kids. It's an emergency."

There was no response on the other end.

"Tyler?"

"Okay, but I don't think she'll believe me."

"Thanks." George switched his headlights on again, and started back onto Rural Route 17. He didn't see the police flashers in his rearview mirror. The sheriff's car had sped down the road, out of sight.

"Could you do me another favor?" George asked. "Don't tell them where I'm going, okay?"

"Well, I can't guarantee they'll figure it out, but I'll try to stall them."

"Good. Thanks. And hey, don't let that creep of a sheriff

grab any credit for finding those bodies. You're the one who did it."

"Okay," he said, with a dazed laugh. "Jesus. I'm really blown away. I still can't believe it. I'm standing here, looking down at this skeleton, and it could be Sandra."

His eyes on the dark road ahead, George didn't say anything for a moment. He was thinking that Sandra had been the last young woman to vanish. And Annabelle was still alive.

"I wouldn't expect to find Sandra Hartman's corpse out there on the ranch," George said finally. "You're more likely to find her buried in Arbor Heights Cemetery—beside Lon Schlessinger."

The Schlessinger ranch—July 2004

"Sandra, can you hear me?"

She leapt up from the cot. Hobbling toward the big, bulky door, she accidentally kicked a few empty tin cans. She'd been living on Purrfect Kitty cat food, canned sliced peaches, and water for the last several days and nights. As long as she'd cooperated with him, she'd gotten food.

"Annabelle?" she cried, leaning against the door. "Is that you?"

"I'm getting you out of here *now*," Annabelle called. There was a knocking sound, and then a loud clank, as if something metal had dropped to the concrete floor.

It was the same noise Sandra had become accustomed to hearing before *he* came in to beat her or screw her, or whatever he had an itch to do to her that particular night. "Assume the position!" he'd call, before opening that big door. She had to kneel by the cot, her back to him, and her arms at her sides. Then he'd start in on her.

But this was Annabelle. For several days now, Annabelle Schlessinger had promised to help her escape. Each time, she'd said the same thing. "If I spring you out of here, you have to help me get away and start someplace new, okay?" Annabelle had kept telling her to be patient and hang in there. It would only be another day or two.

They'd always talked through the closed, bolted door. But now that thick, cumbersome door squeaked open. Sandra felt her whole body trembling. She couldn't wait to get out of there. She didn't even think to grab her shoes. She just started pushing at the door.

Annabelle stood and blocked the door opening for a moment. Her hair was cut short and dyed blonde. "Do I look different?" she asked with a hopeful smile.

Sandra balked.

"I told you, I'm getting out, too," Annabelle said.

"Well, you—you look great!" Sandra gasped, not sure what to say. "Let's go, okay? All right?"

Annabelle grabbed her hand and led her toward the basement stairs. "C'mon, we just need to get some stuff out of my room. . . ."

Sandra's legs buckled as she raced up the stairs with Annabelle. She hadn't run for days; she hadn't even been able to walk more than a few steps without turning around in that cramped, filthy cell. She stumbled on the stairs, but quickly got up again and kept moving.

At the top step, she noticed the kitchen door directly ahead. It had a window in it. She could see outside. It was night.

Annabelle started to run past the door. Sandra stopped abruptly. "Wait!" she whispered. "I thought we were getting out of here."

"I told you," Annabelle said, tugging at her arm. "I need to get some stuff in my room first."

"But he might come back. Please, for God's sake. . . ."

"He might come back?" Annabelle repeated, laughing. "He's upstairs, out cold. He had too much to drink, as usual. He passed out on the bed."

Sandra tried to pull away, but Annabelle wouldn't let her go. "What if he wakes up?" she asked, tears in her eyes. "Please, Annabelle, I just want to get the hell out of here!"

"Would you relax?" Annabelle said, dragging her into the kitchen. "I know what I'm doing. I gave him the same stuff he used on you the other night, chloroform. Believe me, he won't wake up. I told you I'd do this right, Sandra. We're *walking* out of here in ten minutes."

As Annabelle led her through the kitchen, Sandra noticed the telephone on the wall. "Why don't we just call the police? Everyone must be looking for me."

Annabelle swiveled around. "We can't involve the police, stupid!" she hissed. "Goddammit, don't you remember? I'm the one who set you up, the same way I set up Gina and all the others. I'm as guilty as he is." She grabbed a lock of her recently dyed blond hair. "Why do you think I went to all this trouble to look different? I need to get away and start new someplace else. You promised you'd help me. . . ."

"I will," Sandra said, flustered.

"I stole a car yesterday, and stashed it behind some bushes near the end of the driveway," Annabelle said, leading her to the front hallway. "The thing's an ugly piece of crap, an old Tempo. I just moved it a few minutes ago—our *getaway car*. It's parked outside the front door right now."

They started up the stairs to the second floor. "I've secretly been taking money out of my father's account for months," Annabelle explained. "Plus I've got some of my mother's jewelry. I can hock that." She paused at the top of the stairs. "Oh, speaking of jewelry . . ." She took off her bracelet.

Catching her breath, Sandra gazed at the ugly mark it had covered on the back of Annabelle's wrist.

"I want you to have this," Annabelle said, slipping the wide, silver bracelet onto Sandra's wrist. She did it in an almost ceremonial way. "It means we're one and the same."

Baffled, Sandra stared down at the bracelet.

Annabelle was pulling her down the hallway. "C'mon, take a look at him," she said. "He's totally unconscious."

"Can't we just *go*?" Sandra pleaded. "Please, I want to get out of here."

"No, I need to say good-bye to him," Annabelle insisted. She dragged her into the master bedroom.

Her father lay on the bed, his jeans unfastened in front and a T-shirt riding high on his exposed, hairy beer gut. It rose up and down as he breathed heavily in his sleep. Sandra could see the red marks on his face from the chloroform.

Annabelle stared at him, and her grip on Sandra's arm tightened. "I hope you wake up in time to feel the flames," she whispered to her unconscious father. She shook with rage. "I hope you'll be in terrible, terrible pain, you fucking scumbag."

Then she spit in his face.

Sandra winced. "Annabelle, please, you're hurting me. . . ."

The talon-like grip on her arm loosened, and then Annabelle released her. She wiped the tears from her eyes and took a few deep breaths. "I better give him one more dose of this stuff," she said, reaching for a bottle and rag on the bureau.

"What did you just say about *flames*?" Sandra asked numbly.

But Annabelle didn't answer. Her face pinched up and turned away from her work, she soaked the rag with chloroform.

Sandra rubbed her arm and, once again, frowned at the silver bracelet on her wrist.

When she looked up, she saw Annabelle coming at her. Before Sandra knew what was happening, Annabelle shoved her against the wall and stuffed the rag in her face.

Sandra's head slammed back against the wall. Dazed, she fought and struggled to push Annabelle away, but the other girl was stronger. The fumes were too much. She tried not to breathe in, but it was no good. She couldn't move. She felt paralyzed.

"You promised," she heard Annabelle say. "You're going to help me get away and start new someplace else."

After that, Sandra didn't hear anything.

Sandra Hartman didn't feel anything either, not even later when the flames burned her body beyond recognition. She never regained consciousness during the fire. She never felt the horrible, excruciating pain.

But Lon did.

Chapter Twenty-two

Amelia still hadn't shown up yet. And she wasn't answering her cell phone.

Standing on the steps outside the Wenatchee Public Library, Karen felt the cold night wind cut through her. She glanced at her wristwatch: 7:00.

She couldn't have missed Amelia. She'd been at the rest home for no more than a half hour. The trip had been worthwhile, too. Miriam Getz had given her a better idea about the incident that had traumatized Amelia as a child. Still, it didn't make sense that Amelia clung to such sweet memories of this neighbor man who had obviously been trying to molest her. The only people who didn't believe that Clay Spalding was pure evil were Amelia and Clay's friend Naomi Rankin.

Karen had left Naomi a second voice mail, but still no response.

However, the person she was most concerned about right now was Jessie. It had been at least ninety minutes since she'd spoken with her. How long did it take to find a stupid hotel room, anyway? Jessie certainly should have called her by now to say that she and George's kids were all right. Something must have happened. And Karen had no way of getting in touch with her, because Jessie didn't own a cell phone.

She took out her phone and punched in George's number. Maybe Jessie had gotten in touch with him instead.

She caught George in his car on his way to the Salem airport. He told her about the graves at the Schlessinger ranch.

The wind kicked up, and Karen shuddered on the library steps. "Well, there were four missing-person cases in Moses Lake in 1992," she said into the phone. "The last one was a few months before the Schlessingers moved to Salem. I'm still trying to dig up more information about that incident with the neighbor molesting Amelia. So far, it seems pretty much the way Annabelle's teacher described it to you. In the meantime, I'm standing in front of the library here, freezing my butt off, waiting for Amelia."

"Are you *sure* it's Amelia?" George asked.

"Almost positive," Karen said. "She borrowed Shane's car and drove out to Grand Coulee Dam early this morning. God knows why Grand Coulee Dam. But she's on her way here now. If all goes well, we should be back in Seattle before ten." She sighed. "Anyway, I'm worried about Jessie and the kids. Have you heard from her?"

"Yeah, that's why I'm trying to get home. Jessie called a little while ago. I think something's wrong at the house."

"What do you mean?"

"Steffie had an asthma attack. She's supposed to be okay now. But I'm not sure Jessie's telling me the whole story."

"She called from your house?" Karen asked.

"Yeah—"

"And Jessie didn't say anything to you about running into Amelia at my place this afternoon?"

"But I thought you said Amelia's been at Grand Coulee Dam all day."

"She has been." Karen told him about Jessie's brush with *Annabelle* that afternoon, and how Jessie had noticed Blade's Cadillac parked outside George's house earlier in the day. "Jessie didn't tell you any of this?" Karen asked.

"No, she didn't say anything—"

"Did she mention that Shane is dead?"

"Oh, no," George murmured. "God, no, she didn't. . . ."

"The police think he shot himself," she said sadly.

"Jesus, Karen, what's going on?"

"I told Jessie to take the kids and check in at a hotel," she explained. "It doesn't make any sense that she'd go back to your house. George, something's wrong."

"Well, maybe she just got a little mixed up with everything that's happening," he said. "Plus, Jessie has a family emergency of her own, too. She has to take off for Denver tonight. Her sister's very sick. It sounds serious."

For a moment, Karen couldn't say anything.

"George," she whispered, at last, "I'm sorry, but Jessie doesn't have a sister."

"I've called ahead and chartered a plane," George said. "I should be at the Salem airport in about five minutes. I'll call you when I land in Seattle. That should be at around eight-thirty. Can you stick around until then, Jessie?"

"Yes, that's fine," she said into the phone the young man held to her ear. He listened in on George's cordless. Jessie was still strapped to the chair, with her hands taped behind her. She'd lost some of the feeling in her arms.

"Any updates on your sister?" George asked.

"No. I was just about to call them," she replied.

"Is it your sister Estelle, the one with Alzheimer's?"

Jessie hesitated. He somehow knew this was a setup. "Yes, it's Estelle," she said, going along with the fake name

George had picked. "I'm really worried the old girl won't last the night," she said carefully.

"I'm sorry to hear that, Jessie," he replied. "Well, I'll be there soon, unless you want me to send someone else over there to take over."

His Majesty shook his head at her.

"No, I—I can hold down the fort until you get here."

"Could I talk to Steffie? Or is she still asleep?"

"Sorry, George, she's still napping." Jessie glanced up at the young man. Behind him, through the living room window's sheer drapes, she could see someone walking up the McMillans' driveway. Jessie couldn't tell who it was. The person was too far away. With his back to the living room, the man in the dark glasses hadn't noticed yet.

"What about Jody?" George was saying on the other end of the line. "Could you put him on the phone for a second?"

Jessie's throat went dry. "Um, I—I'm sorry, George, he's in the bathroom. He just stepped in the shower." She watched the woman approaching the front door now. It was George's neighbor from across the street, a sixty-something divorcée named Sally Bidwell. She was thin with short silver hair and wore a black pantsuit. She'd been out of town at the time of George's wife's death, but had been over twice this week to see if they needed anything. George had told Jessie that Mrs. Bidwell had an extra key to the house in case Jessie ever got locked out.

As she came closer to the house, Mrs. Bidwell stopped and stood on her tiptoes so she could peek into the living room window.

Jessie tried not to stare at her. She didn't want His Majesty to see they had a visitor.

"Well, it looks like I struck out again," George said. "But they're both doing okay, Jess?"

"Yes, George," she said. "For now, they're okay."

"Thank you, Jessie. I'll get there as soon as I can."

The man started pushing the phone harder against her face. "Hurry up," he mouthed.

"Okay, George," she said. "Good-bye."

The man in the sunglasses quickly hung up the phone, then clicked off the cordless. " 'For now, they're okay?' What's that shit? Was that your way of telling him something's wrong?"

Jessie just helplessly shook her head at him. She glanced toward the living room window again, but didn't see Mrs. Bidwell.

Suddenly, the doorbell rang.

The young man quickly snatched his revolver from the kitchen counter and crept over toward the front door. The doorbell rang again.

Jessie heard a muffled cry coming from Jody's room.

His back pressed against the wall, the man waited. He had the gun drawn. He seemed very calm and cool, or maybe it was just because Jessie couldn't read his expression behind those sunglasses.

Outside, Mrs. Bidwell backed away from the door. Craning her neck, she stood on her tiptoes again and tried to get another look into the living room window. Squirming in the chair, Jessie wondered if Mrs. Bidwell could see her though the sheer drapes. She held her breath and watched the young man reach over for the door handle.

Mrs. Bidwell lingered on the front stoop, trying to peek inside the house.

Because the Lake Wenatchee shootings had been such big news, the McMillans had endured their share of snoops this week. Jessie had seen a few driving down the cul-de-sac to catch a glimpse of the house, and others actually came right up to the house and tried to peek into the windows. In contrast, there were also several nice neighbors who had stopped by with flowers, casseroles, and condolences, Mrs. Bidwell among them. But she'd always struck Jessie as a bit over-solicitous and meddling.

At this point, Jessie wasn't sure if she wanted Mrs. Bidwell to see anything or not. She figured George would know how to handle this. But she didn't trust Mrs. Bidwell.

Finally, the woman shrugged her shoulders and turned around.

Jessie let out a sigh.

The man in the sunglasses moved over to the edge of the living room window, and he peered outside.

Through the sheer curtains, Jessie watched Mrs. Bidwell walk back up the driveway. But then she stopped and glanced inside the car for a moment. She turned toward the house again.

The man ducked back, and the sheer curtain fluttered.

Mrs. Bidwell stared at the window for a few moments. Then she took another few steps toward the house again. Pausing for a moment, she reached into her purse. Then she continued down the driveway past the front walkway, toward the back door. Jessie couldn't see her through the living room window anymore.

The man darted back into the kitchen. Swiping a dish-towel off the counter, he turned toward Jessie and grabbed her by the hair. Jessie struggled as he stuffed the dishtowel in her mouth. Helplessly, she watched him scurry over to the back door.

The neighbor knocked a few times. And then Jessie heard the door lock being manipulated. Mrs. Bidwell was using the spare key. Jessie wanted to scream out a warning, but she couldn't.

The kitchen door opened. "Hello?" Mrs. Bidwell called, stepping into the kitchen. "George? Anyone home?"

The young man waited on the other side of the door with his gun ready. Mrs. Bidwell couldn't see him, but she spotted Jessie, bound and gagged in the chair. All Jessie could do was shake her head at the woman.

For a moment, Mrs. Bidwell stood there, paralyzed, gaping at Jessie.

The man with sunglasses tucked his gun in the waist of his pants. Mrs. Bidwell swiveled around. She let out a gasp, then bolted toward the door. But he slammed it shut in front of her. He grabbed her and slapped his hand over her mouth. Arms flailing, the thin woman tried to fight him off, but he was too big for her. She struggled and kicked, but he didn't let go. All the while he held onto her, he hardly changed his expression. There was just the hint of a smirk on his face as he carried out his task—like a robot, not a trace of emotion.

He took his hand away from Mrs. Bidwell's mouth for only a few seconds as he reached for his revolver again. She screamed, until he clubbed her over the head with his gun.

The woman let out a feeble cry. She was stunned, but still conscious. She started to squirm as the man with the dark glasses dragged her into the living room. He threw her on the couch. Mrs. Bidwell let out another gasp, as if she'd gotten the wind knocked out of her.

The young man grabbed a sofa pillow and put it over her face.

Then he fired his gun into the pillow.

Jessie watched in horror as the woman's body twitched and convulsed with spasms. Then she slumped across the couch, suddenly still. Feathers from the pillow floated in the air around her. Jessie caught a glimpse of Mrs. Bidwell's face—her open eyes and the huge, gaping hole in her left cheek. Then the young man gave the corpse a forceful shove. The woman rolled over on her face. A bloodstain started to bloom beneath her on the beige sofa.

The young man seemed annoyed as he moved away from

the body. Frowning, he brushed the pillow feathers off his shiny black suit. He straightened his tie, readjusted his sunglasses, and then headed for the kitchen sink. Turning on the cold water, he ran his hand under the stream.

"Fucking bitch bit me," he grumbled.

Tears in her eyes, Jessie stared at Mrs. Bidwell's corpse. For the last forty minutes, Jessie had been hoping against hope the young man would just take whatever else he wanted and then leave. But now she knew that wasn't going to happen.

Now she knew he wasn't going to leave this house until he'd killed her and the children.

"Oh God, George, you're walking into a trap."

"I know," he said.

It was one of the only things George was sure about.

At this point, he figured either Annabelle or Blade, or both of them, were holding Jessie and his children hostage at his home. And they wanted him there, too.

"Karen, I really have no choice," he said into the phone. He kept his eyes on the road. He'd just passed a sign indicating McNary Field was straight ahead. He knew he was close to the airport because he saw a Best Western and a Holiday Inn Express just up the road. "I have a feeling they're keeping the kids alive so Jessie will cooperate with them," he said. "And obviously they're using Jessie to talk me into coming home. I'm hoping no one will get hurt as long as they're still trying to lure me there. I have about ninety minutes to figure out a strategy. I'm not calling the police, at least not yet. Maybe when I get to Seattle. We'll see."

He let out a nervous sigh. "Karen, if you could keep digging into Annabelle's past, maybe you can figure out what the hell she wants, why she's doing this. You know psychology. Why is she killing everyone close to Amelia? If I could figure out what Annabelle's after, that would help me when I walk into the house ninety minutes from now."

Tears stung his eyes, and George felt his throat closing up. "I might be able to bargain with her, give her what she wants, or at least figure out where she's most vulnerable. Maybe I can get my kids and Jessie out of there alive."

"I'll do what I can, George," she said. "Amelia should be here any minute now. Maybe we can get her to intervene and talk to her sister. Maybe that's all we'll need. Whatever this is, it's between the sisters."

"I think you're right," George murmured.

He suddenly realized he'd just passed a turn sign for the airport. "Karen, listen, thank you. I've got to go."

"Okay, call me when you get to Seattle. Take care, George."

He clicked off the cell phone, and turned the car around in an Arby's parking lot. He backtracked and found another sign for the airport. In the distance, he heard police sirens, which seemed to become louder as he got closer to the airport. George saw an intersection ahead, where traffic was at a standstill. Two cop cars with their flashers on sailed through the junction and turned onto the airport drive.

As traffic started up again, George made a left through the intersection, and then took a right to the airport on Aviation Loop. He had a bad feeling in his gut. He could see the two patrol cars, parked in front of the terminal's main entrance, their flashers still swirling.

He wondered if Tyler had caved and told the sheriff where he was headed.

George pulled into the lot and parked. Overhead, a plane was landing. George's ears got a blast of the engine's roar as he climbed out of the car. The night air had a chill to it. He clutched the lapels of his sports jacket up under his chin, and spied the two police vehicles in the distance.

A maroon minivan with RESIDENCE INN written on the

side door had pulled up behind the squad cars. The driver, wearing a blazer the same color as the minivan, had gotten out of the car to talk to one of the cops. After a few moments, he stepped away from the cop car, waved, then ducked back into his minivan. He drove through the parking lot toward the main road.

George waved him down. "Are you with the Residence Inn?" he called. It was a stupid question, but still, the guy stopped.

The driver rolled down his window. He was in his early twenties with wavy black hair and a touch of acne. He nodded at George. "Yes, sir, are you headed there?"

"No, I'm meeting someone who needs a room for the night," George lied. "Do you know if they have any vacancies?"

The driver reached into his maroon blazer and pulled out a card for the Residence Inn. "Call that number, and they'll take care of you."

"Much obliged," George said. Then he nodded toward the police cars. "What's the hubbub about, do you know?"

The young man nodded. "They got a tip from some guy about a bunch of dead bodies buried at a farm outside of town."

"A bunch of dead bodies?" George repeated.

He nodded. "Yeah, they've dug up three so far, and they think there are a lot more." With his thumb, he pointed to the patrol cars. "One of those cops is a buddy of mine. He said this is going to be big. So, better book your pal's room with us pretty quick. Once all the news people get here—and that'll be soon—all the hotels will fill up."

"Thanks, I'll get on that." George nodded toward the cop cars again. "So what are they doing here? Are they the welcoming committee for the news people?"

The driver shook his head. "No, they're looking for the

dude who tipped off the county police about the stiffs, some Seattle guy. They want to hold him for questioning. They think he's trying to blow town."

"Imagine that," George murmured. He tucked the Residence Inn business card in his pocket. "Well, thanks for the help. Have a nice night."

The minivan drove off, and George ducked back into his car. He thought he was going to be sick. What the hell was he going to do now? He had to get home to his kids. He didn't even want to think about how scared Jody and Steffie probably were right now, and what was being done to them.

He couldn't afford to stick around the airport any longer. No doubt, those cops had a description of his car, maybe even the license plate number.

George backed out of the parking space. He watched the two squad cars in his rearview mirror as he merged onto the airport drive. They didn't move, thank God.

He started driving, not even sure where he was headed. He just needed to get away from this airport and the police. It would take him an hour to make it to Portland by freeway. But he'd probably be detained at the Portland airport if he tried to book a flight or a charter. He couldn't *drive* all the way back to Seattle. That would take at least four hours, and he ran the risk of some cop spotting his car. They'd be looking for him all along I-5.

"Do you even know where the hell you're going?" he cried out loud. His hands, white-knuckled, gripped the wheel.

He took a few deep, calming breaths. George caught a glimpse of the street name as he went through an intersection: Waverly Drive. He realized he was close to Willamette University. The traffic became heavier as he headed into a commercial area full of bars, restaurants, and coffee shops.

George saw a sign: ATOMIC CYBER CAFÉ. He also noticed a parking space, and immediately pulled into it.

The Internet café was dimly lit and about half full of college kids slouched in front of the computer screens. "Can I get Internet access here?" George asked the barista behind the counter.

The young man had a small square of beard hair under his lower lip, and glasses. He wore a red apron. "You bet," he nodded. "The first half hour is free with a beverage. All I need is a driver's license for a deposit."

"Thanks." George slapped a five-dollar bill and his license on the counter. "Just a regular coffee, please, or whatever you've got that's quick."

A few moments later, George tried not to spill his coffee as he hurried over toward the free terminals. There were a few by a nicely dressed, uptight-looking man in his fifties, who gave George a narrow glance. Sitting down near him, George realized the guy was looking at porn. George ignored him. He switched on the terminal, and connected to the Internet. He brought up Google, and then typed in Salem, Oregon, Charter Helicopter.

He got two results: both businesses in Jefferson, Oregon. He pulled out his cell and called the first place, Coupland Aeronautic, Inc. He wasn't sure if anyone would be answering at 7:20 on a Monday night. His chances of actually chartering a helicopter at the last minute like this were probably nil.

A woman picked up: "Coupland, this is Kate."

"Hi. I'm in Salem, and I need to get to Seattle as soon as possible. Could I charter a helicopter for tonight?" he asked.

"You're in Salem, that's about a half hour away," the woman said. George could hear her fingers clicking on a keyboard. "If you can get here by eight o'clock, we'll have you in Seattle at eight-fifty tonight. Does that sound good to you?"

"That sounds great to me," George replied.

* * *

"Hello, Naomi, this is Karen Carlisle calling again. . . ."

Karen sat in her rental, parked across from the Wenatchee library. Though she got clearer phone reception outside, Karen had ducked inside the car to avoid the cold. It had also started drizzling. From the driver's seat, she had an ideal view of everyone coming and going at the library. She was still waiting for Amelia. It had been well over two hours since they'd last talked, and still no answer on her cell.

Naomi Rankin wasn't picking up either. This was Karen's third message in ninety minutes for Clay Spalding's friend. She now understood how telemarketers felt pestering a total stranger. In the last two messages Karen had tried to sound friendly and professional. She hadn't mentioned Clay or the Schlessingers. She'd just left her name and phone number, and said it was extremely urgent that Naomi call her back.

Though she didn't want to say too much on the answering machine, Karen decided to start explaining herself for message number three. "I'm sorry to keep calling," she said. "But I'm a friend of Amelia Schlessinger's. I'm hoping that name is familiar to you. I understand, years ago, you and Amelia had a mutual friend. If I could talk with you for just a few minutes, I—"

There was an abrupt click on the line. "Listen, if you call here one more time, I'll get the cops on your ass."

"Naomi?" Karen asked meekly.

"I don't have to talk to you," the woman growled. "Shit, I thought I'd heard the last from you assholes fifteen years ago. Get a life, okay?"

"Please, don't hang up," Karen said. "I'm not calling to harass you—"

"Yeah, I'll bet you aren't," she muttered. "I've heard it all. There's nothing new you can tell me. So piss off."

"Naomi, wait! You want to hear something *new*?" Karen had a hunch this would get her to listen. "Right now, the police are digging up corpses at the old Schlessinger ranch outside Salem. Young women started disappearing in the Salem area back in 1993, when Lon Schlessinger moved there from Moses Lake. Isn't that about the same time women *stopped* disappearing around Moses Lake?"

There was a silence on the other end of the line.

"Naomi?"

"Who are you?" she murmured.

"I'm a friend of Amelia's, and she doesn't recall much about her childhood in Moses Lake. But she does remember a Native American man—a neighbor who was very kind to her. You and Amelia seem to be the only ones from around there who don't think Clay was a monster."

"So, I'm not totally alone. Amelia, of all people. . . ."

"I read about what happened. Naomi. And from the way you reacted to my call, I get the impression people must have harassed you for defending Clay in the newspapers."

"And on local TV, too," Naomi said. "For a while there, I averaged about eight threatening calls a night. I also got my share of hateful stares at work and around town. If you really want people to hate you, just speak up for someone who's been labeled a serial killer and a child molester. For years, I still received those creepy calls, even after I changed my number. I didn't let them list me in the phone book until about three years ago." She sighed. "I'm sorry about earlier. I wasn't sure who you were when you left those first two messages. I thought it was some sort of scam or a telemarketer. But then you mentioned the name Schlessinger, and I just got sick to my stomach. It was a real blast from the past." She paused. "So, they found bodies on the Schlessingers' property."

"That's right," Karen said. "Lon's been dead for three years. His ranch house burned down with him in it."

"You know, I always knew Clay was framed for that woman's disappearance," Naomi said. "Now it all starts to make sense. Lon killed those women. You've read the newspaper account of it, so you know the story. He was in Clay's house earlier that day, hours before he shot Clay. He could have planted that waitress's wallet and necklace while he was there looking for his runaway kid. God, all this time I thought the cops had planted that stuff. I knew for a fact Clay couldn't have abducted that waitress. He and I were together the night Kristen Marquart went missing."

"Did you tell that to the police?"

"Of course. I practically screamed it from the rooftops. But no one believed me. I was in love with Clay for several months. So no one really took me seriously and, after a while, I just made them angry. A lot of people in that neighborhood already had a negative opinion of Clay, anyway. He didn't quite fit in on Gardenia Drive."

"Because he wasn't white?" Karen asked.

"Oh, I guess that might have had a little something to do with it," she admitted. "But Clay carried around a chip on his shoulder after inheriting that house. He felt everyone still regarded him as Izzy's yardman. I think he did things to piss people off. He stopped mowing the lawn, and let the place go just to prove he wasn't a yardman any more."

"I heard from his neighbor that he used to display some of his art on the front lawn, too," Karen said.

"Who did you talk to?" Naomi asked. "The old lady?"

"Miriam Getz."

"Yeah, she had it out for him. She and two of Lon's cop friends were the main *witnesses* who said Clay was trying to molest Amelia that day."

"Well, I don't think she was lying to me, Naomi," Karen said delicately. "Outside of the art displays and letting his lawn 'going to pot,' as she put it, Miriam didn't seem to have any problem with Clay as a neighbor. But her mind changed when she saw what happened that day."

"She might not have been *lying* about what she saw,"

Naomi pointed out. "But she sure jumped to the wrong conclusion."

"Well, she saw a little girl in her underwear, crawling out of Clay's window, screaming for help," Karen said. "I've tried to figure out how *not* to jump to the same conclusion Miriam did. I'm thinking along the same lines as you, Naomi. Lon Schlessinger was pure evil. He must have set Clay up. I think you're right about him planting the wallet and the locket. But this incident with Amelia . . ."

"Lon used to beat her and her twin," Naomi said. "Did you know that?"

"No, but I'm not very surprised."

"He hated Clay from the word go. I don't know if it was because Clay was Native American, or because of his long hair, or the artwork on the front lawn. But Lon despised Clay. Maybe that's why the little girls turned to Clay when their dad started abusing them. They knew they had an ally with Clay. God knows, they couldn't go to their mother. She was totally clueless. Amelia ran away to Clay's house several times, more than her twin. I remember Clay saying Lon had Annabelle on a tighter leash, and she was afraid of him. She was a lot more obedient and likely to give in to her father's demands. Clay used to teach art to the kids on the reservation, and he knew about children. He said Amelia was a little rebel. That's why she and Clay got along so well. They both had that defiant streak."

"And as the more rebellious of the twins, Amelia probably got more severe and frequent beatings," Karen said.

"Right," Naomi said. "I saw some of the bruises on that little girl. It was revolting."

"Why didn't you report it to the police?"

"Clay tried. One time, when Amelia was over there, he touched her back and noticed her cringing. He asked her if anything was wrong, and she said, 'I think I was a bad girl again.' Then she showed him her back, and it was all black and blue and purple. Clay could hardly keep from going over to the Schlessingers' and kicking the shit out of that son of a bitch. I talked to him on the phone, and got him to calm down. I told him to take a few Polaroids of the bruises and then we could go to the police. Well, he did that, only he reported it to some cop who was a fishing buddy of Lon's. Clay didn't know. This cop didn't do a damn thing except ask Clay how he'd gotten the little girl to take off her blouse. They twisted it around. After Clay was shot, these stories circulated that he had photos of the little Schlessinger girl naked. But those were pictures of her bruised back, which he'd tried to give to the cops."

"Oh, my God," Karen murmured.

"So, weeks later, that Sunday morning Amelia went missing, Lon came over to Clay's looking for her. Clay let him come in and look around. But he also took that opportunity to tell Lon that if he found one more mark on Amelia, he'd kill him. Anyway, after Lon left, Clay called me. He said it was obvious Amelia had run away again, and he thought she might show up at his house eventually. He wanted me to come over. He also figured if Amelia had any new bruises, *I* should take the Polaroids, and then we'd call the state police, a lawyer, or child protective services."

Naomi let out a long sigh. "I was at work when he called me that Sunday. They needed me there to work the register at the goddamn Safeway. I remember Clay asking me, 'You mean, you can't take a few hours off to help a child who might be in trouble?' Then he hung up. That was the last thing he ever said to me."

Naomi started to cry. "I was still at work when someone at the store told me Clay had been shot because they'd caught him trying to molest a neighbor's little girl. I couldn't believe it, and I still don't. Clay never would have hurt Amelia.

I might not have been there to see how it happened. But I know they have it wrong. There's a difference between what people saw that day and what's true. I'm certain of that."

"I agree with you," Karen said. "Do you think it's possible Amelia was in her underwear because she wanted to show Clay some new bruises?"

"I wondered that, too," Naomi said. "But they'd have said in the newspaper that she'd recently been beaten and then, no doubt, used it as more evidence against Clay. Besides, I don't think Clay would have let her take off a stitch of clothing after that cop made those innuendos about the Polaroids."

"Well, maybe Amelia was napping—" Karen started to say. But a click on the line interrupted her.

"I'm sorry. Just a sec," Naomi said. "Let me see who this is."

She clicked off, and while Karen waited, she figured even if they came up with a reason why Amelia had been in her underwear, they still couldn't explain why she'd run screaming from Clay's house and into her abusive, sadistic father's arms.

Naomi clicked back on the line. "Are you still there?"

"Yes."

"Listen, there's a crisis at work, and I need to go over there, to the same Safeway. I'm a manager there now. How's that for progress?"

"Well, congratulations," Karen said, with a weak laugh. "Thank you for talking to me, Naomi."

"If you're ever able to figure out what really happened that day, let me know, okay? You have my number. Sorry I wasn't more help."

"But you have been, believe me," Karen said. "Amelia's still in trouble. And you have helped her, Naomi. You have."

"Well, thanks. Take care."

Karen clicked off the line. She sat in the front seat of the car and watched the raindrops sliding down her windshield.

Across the street, a woman stepped out of the library, put up her umbrella, then headed down the sidewalk. She disappeared around a corner.

Karen glanced at the library doors again and then at her watch: 7:50.

"Damn it," Karen murmured. "She should have been here at least an hour ago."

Amelia was once again missing.

The car window was open. Amelia felt the cold wind whipping through her hair and an occasional raindrop on her face. She was driving Karen's Jetta, on her way to Wenatchee. She felt tense, but excited, too. She thought about how she'd finally get to use her father's hunting knife slitting that bitch, Karen Carlisle's, throat.

Amelia woke up with start, and in total blackness. She'd been having these horrible dreams all night. This was the latest, her gleefully planning Karen's murder.

Earlier, she'd had a nightmare in which she'd put a gun in Shane's mouth and pulled the trigger. They'd been in rowboat on a lake somewhere. She'd washed Shane's blood off her face and hands with lake water. It had seemed so real. But Amelia kept telling herself these were just nightmares. She was still asleep in the spare bedroom at Karen's house.

But why was it so dark? And what had happened to the sound machine? She didn't hear the waves and those seagulls. In fact, she couldn't hear anything.

A panic swept through her. She didn't remember the bed feeling this hard, or the scratchy blanket. It smelled musty, like a basement.

Something had happened in the middle of the night.

Amelia had thought she'd dreamt that, too. She'd seen herself at night in Karen's backyard with a strange-looking, pale man with jet-black hair. They'd lifted a decorative stone from the garden, uncovering where Karen hid the house key. Then they'd snuck into the house. The next part, Amelia figured *must* have been a dream, because she and the man had been in Karen's spare bedroom, standing over *herself* in the bed. She'd watched herself sleeping. Bending over the bed, the man had put a damp cloth over her face. It had burned. For a moment, she'd felt as if she were suffocating.

Had it all really happened? It must have, because she was no longer in Karen's guest room. This dark, dank room was in a totally different place far away from all sounds and light.

Amelia sat up and blindly groped around for a light. Her hand brushed against a lamp beside her, and she switched it on. Someone had taken away the lampshade, and the bare lightbulb was blinding. It took Amelia a moment to recognize the secondhand lamp from the guest room in the lake house. Sitting up on a cot with an army blanket over her, she glanced around the gray little room. There were a few boxes shoved against the wall, a stack of old records and board games, some old paint cans, and a broken hard-back chair.

Amelia ran a hand through her hair, and realized most of it had been chopped off. They must have cut her hair, very short, while she'd been asleep, but why? She touched her nose and lips. They still burned from whatever was on that cloth the man put over her mouth. She had no idea how long ago that was. She looked around for a clock or a mirror. But there wasn't one on the makeshift nightstand beside her. Someone had turned over a box to hold the lamp without a shade.

But they'd left her an opened can of Del Monte sliced peaches, a pack of chewing gum, and a small jar of Noxzema.

Amelia stared across the room at the big, bulky door. It was closed.

She knew where she was. This place had always given her

the creeps. For years, she'd been afraid of somehow getting trapped here.

She was in the family cabin by Lake Wenatchee in the basement fallout shelter.

And yet, somehow, at this very moment, she could still feel the motion of Karen's car, and a cold breeze through the open window kissing her face.

And she knew Karen was going to die.

Chapter Twenty-three

She wandered up and down the aisles at the Wenatchee library, searching for Amelia. Karen figured she might have missed her somehow. But she'd already walked around outside the building in the cold rain searching for Shane's car. She'd seen plenty of vacant parking spots, and no sign of the VW Golf. She'd already explored the reference, periodicals, and nonfiction sections with no luck. Now, as she zigzagged around the shelves of books in the fiction section, Karen heard an announcement over the PA system saying that the library was closing in five minutes. Above her, every other row of overhead lights went off.

Karen was filled with a lost, hopeless feeling. She kept thinking about how Amelia was the only one who could get through to her sister, Annabelle. She might even know Annabelle's next move.

After four months with Amelia in therapy, Karen still didn't have a handle on her. What kind of therapist was she anyway? Even with all she'd uncovered about Amelia's childhood, Karen still felt as if she didn't really know her. It baffled her that little Amelia had fled from Clay's house the way she had that day. Besides her twin, he'd been her only friend, and she'd run away from him, screaming.

"The Wenatchee Public Library is now closing," a woman announced over the public address system. "We will be open again tomorrow at 10 A.M. Please exit through the front doors. Thank you and have a nice evening."

Slump-shouldered, Karen wandered toward the front of the library. She wasn't sure about what to do, except maybe call the state police. She could give them a description of Amelia, and Shane's car, and then ask them to look for a motorist in trouble on Highway 2, somewhere between Grand Coulee Dam and Wenatchee.

A little blond girl, who apparently didn't want to leave the library, was screaming and crying as her father dragged her toward the exit. Karen held the door open for him. He nodded at her, muttered "Thank you," then finally scooped the screaming, squirming kid into her arms. Karen watched them walk down the library steps. She thought about how Lon Schlessinger had handled that same situation by throwing the hysterical child in her room and locking the door.

She remembered what Miriam had told her about Lon taking Annabelle with him on his aborted trip to the police station that Sunday afternoon fifteen years ago: "He said he didn't even make it to the police station, because Annabelle started pitching a fit. None of us could figure out what was wrong with her."

Karen hiked up the collar to her trench coat and started down the library steps. She could still hear that little girl screaming as her father carried her to their car, halfway down the block. Karen suddenly stopped dead. The rain was stronger now, but she didn't move. "Oh, my God," she whispered. "He never went to the police station. He went and switched the twins."

It was exactly as Naomi Rankin had said: "There's a difference between what people saw that day and what's true. I'm certain of that."

Annabelle had been the cooperative twin, the one their father had had on a tight leash. She'd pretended to be her sister that afternoon.

It was a skill she would hone later as a young adult.

Ignoring the rain, Karen stood on the sidewalk. Behind her, the lights inside the library went off. All she could think about was Amelia, struggling in her father's arms as she'd been smuggled out of Clay's house, dressed in her sister's clothes. Karen could almost hear her screams, until her father had clasped his hand over her mouth and locked her in her room. And from her bedroom window, Amelia might have seen everything that had happened down the block at her friend Clay's house. She might have even seen her father gun him down.

No wonder they'd found it necessary to get rid of the child after that. She'd been too rebellious. She'd seen too much.

No wonder Amelia had blocked out all memory of her family—a demented, violent, serial-killer father, an ineffectual mother, and the twin sister who had betrayed her.

Karen suddenly realized her cell phone was ringing. She grabbed it and checked the caller ID. She didn't recognize the number, but the area code was local: 509. "Hello?" she said into the phone.

"Karen, it's Amelia. . . ."

"Oh, thank God," Karen said. "Where have you been?"

"I'm sorry. Are you still waiting for me at the library in Wenatchee?"

"Yes. Didn't you get any of my calls?"

"No. Something must be wrong with the frequency, because I tried to phone you several times, but it didn't answer. It didn't even go to voice mail."

"Where are you, honey?" Karen asked.

"Well, I feel like such a lamebrain. I decided to try a different way back, and ended up getting lost. I totally overshot Wenatchee, and then Shane's car broke down. It's been a nightmare. . . ."

"Where are you now? I'll come pick you up."

"Well, I ended up getting a tow from this garage my dad used to go to near Lake Wenatchee. They were about to close, so I asked one of the guys there to give me a lift to this little restaurant near our lake house."

"You mean Danny's Diner?" Karen asked.

"Yeah. How do you know about Danny's Diner?"

"I was there earlier today," Karen said. She started walking toward her car. "I'll explain when I see you. Listen, this is important, okay? Have you had a—premonition about something happening at George's house?"

There was silence on the other end.

Karen stopped in her tracks. "Amelia?"

"Um, I'm not sure what you mean."

"Have you had any feeling that something's wrong at George's house, something with Jessie or the children?"

"No. Why are you asking?" There was a little panic in her voice. "Karen, are they okay?"

"Um, for now, I think they're all right." Karen hurried toward her car. "I'll be at the diner in about thirty minutes. And please, please, don't go anywhere, Amelia. I need your help with something, and it's very important. We have a lot to talk about, too."

"Does it have anything to do with why you're in Wenatchee?"

"Sort of," Karen said, climbing inside her car. She shut the door and started up the ignition. "I'll explain when I get there. I promise."

She switched on the wipers and headlights. She didn't hear anything on the other end of the line. "Amelia?"

"If you were at Danny's Diner, you must have gone to the

lake house," she said. "Were you looking for evidence that I was there the night everyone was killed?"

"Amelia, I *know* you weren't at the lake house that night." Karen pulled out of the parking spot, and started down the road. The highway on-ramp was two blocks ahead. "Stop blaming yourself for that, and for a lot of other things," she said, "even things dating back to your early childhood."

"My God, you found out about my real parents, didn't you? Are they still alive?"

Karen didn't answer. It wasn't something she wanted to tell her over the phone.

"Karen, please. For God's sake, don't make me wait. Alive or dead, I'm not going to fall apart if you tell me now. I don't even remember them. I'd just like to know. Are they alive?"

"No, honey, I'm sorry. They're both dead."

"Were they dead when the Faradays adopted me?"

"No, they were alive at the time. Amelia, I'll explain it all when I get there."

"Do you know why they gave me up?"

"I have a pretty good idea, now," Karen admitted. "But I'd rather not talk about it over the phone. Besides, I'm just about to get on the freeway. I need to hang up. Just stay there and wait for me. We have a long drive back to Seattle. I'll tell you everything then."

"Karen?" she said, a sudden urgency in her tone.

"What is it?"

"Earlier just now, you asked if I had any premonitions about something happening at Uncle George's house. . . ."

"Yes?" Karen said, her grip tightening on the steering wheel.

"Well, I've had this awful feeling most of the night that someone's in danger. But it's not Uncle George, or my cousins, or Jessie. I keep thinking something bad is going to happen to *you*, Karen. Please, be careful. Okay?"

"Well, I—I will be. Thanks," Karen managed to say. She swallowed hard, and then started onto the highway on-ramp. "Just stay put and I'll see you soon."

"All right," she said. "Good-bye, Karen."

Standing in the booth outside Danny's Diner, Annabelle hung up the phone and started laughing. She loved screwing with Karen's head like that, warning her of the danger ahead. And yet Karen was rushing here, probably speeding all the way to her demise.

It was unfolding perfectly, even better than she'd planned. Looking back now, if she'd killed Karen in the basement of that rest home—or in her bed last night—her death just wouldn't have had the proper impact. It was important for Amelia to see Karen, her therapist, her confidante, her last remaining friend, dead. It was important for Amelia to realize that she had no one left but the twin sister she'd forgotten she had.

Amelia had run away by herself that Sunday morning in November nearly fifteen years ago. She hadn't said a thing to her about it. Amelia had just disappeared, leaving her alone to deal with their angry father. And when he was riled, it never mattered who had misbehaved, he lashed out at whoever happened to be around at the time. The only way she and Amelia had survived up to that point had been by sticking together and being there for each other. They had their own secret language. They could read each other's thoughts. They protected each other. And it wasn't just because they loved each other. No, it was more than that. Whenever Amelia got a beating, Annabelle felt it, too, and vice versa. Amelia only made things worse for *both* of them when she incurred their father's wrath, which she frequently did. Their father may have beaten Amelia more often and more brutally, but Annabelle still felt every punch, slap, and kick.

One of the worst sessions had been after their dad had gone out to punish a bad woman. It had been one of those nights Uncle Duane had come along to help their father with his "work." They'd brought Amelia. Apparently, she'd done everything they'd told her to do. But as soon as they'd put the bad woman to sleep in the car, Amelia had started screaming and crying. She'd even tried to jump out of the car. Their father and Uncle Duane had been furious with her. She'd almost ruined everything. It had been a night of agony for both twins. Amelia had bruises all up and down her back. But Annabelle had felt every blow, too. The next day, Annabelle couldn't get out of bed, she ached so much. But even with all her pain, Amelia had snuck off to that Indian's house. She didn't tell Clay *why* she'd been beaten. She only showed him the marks on her back. "Clay took pitchers of me," Amelia later told her. Annabelle never got to see the "pitchers," but after that, they weren't allowed to go anywhere near Clay's house.

Weeks later, on that chilly Sunday morning in November when Amelia ran away, Annabelle knew where she'd gone. So did their father. But he didn't find Amelia hiding over at Clay's. However, Annabelle knew her sister was there, hiding from both Clay and their father. Even though Amelia hadn't told her about her plans to run away, and even though they would both get in trouble for it, Annabelle kept silent. She didn't want to betray her sister.

Sure enough, a few hours later, Mrs. Getz called from down the block, saying she'd spotted Amelia in Clay's backyard. Their father asked the old woman to come over, and tell him exactly what she'd seen. Annabelle got scared when her father announced he was taking her with him to the police station. She thought she and her sister might end up in jail or something.

But once Annabelle climbed into the car with her father, he told her, "You'll have to be your sister for a while. It's pretend."

She'd been only four years old at the time, but Annabelle remembered everything about that day. She recalled feeling relieved the police weren't going to arrest her or Amelia. Her father drove around the block, and parked in back of old Mrs. Getz's house. They cut through her yard. He kept telling Annabelle if she said one word, cried, or even coughed, he'd smack her.

They crept through the bushes and into Clay's backyard, past the little playhouse that Amelia loved. The windows at Clay's house were too high for her to see, but her father got a look inside. At the risk of making him mad, Annabelle kept tugging at his shirtsleeve. "Is she in there?" Annabelle whispered.

With a sigh, her father finally lifted her up to the edge of the window so she could see. Inside, Amelia sat at Clay's kitchen table, eating a cookie and drinking orange juice. Clay was on the telephone. He hung up the receiver, then moved over to the table. "C'mon, pumpkin," she heard him say, his voice a bit muffled through the glass. "I want you to lie down and take a nap. I need to talk to some people. They're going to help you. They'll make sure he won't ever hurt you again."

Annabelle kept waiting for Amelia to say, "What about my sister? Can you make sure my sister doesn't get hurt, too?"

But Amelia didn't say anything. She just finished her cookie.

Annabelle's father set her back down on the ground. Crouching along the side of the house, they moved over to another window that Clay had just opened a bit.

Annabelle tugged at her father's sleeve again. She wanted to know what was happening. "Stop that," he hissed. "Want me to crack your face?"

She kept very still and said nothing for several minutes.

"Goddamn redskin, he doesn't know who he's dealing

with," her father muttered, almost to himself. "Well, I've already planted something in there for you, Cochise, and it'll fix you, but good. Smug, uppity son of a bitch."

He turned to Annabelle. "Take off your clothes," he whispered.

Aghast, she just shook her head. It was cold out. And besides, she didn't want anyone to see her naked.

"Do it!" her father hissed. "You can leave your underpants on if you want. I need to put your clothes on Amelia, so Mrs. Getz thinks she's you. I told you, you're going to be Amelia for a little while."

Her father explained how she would have to sit and wait on the bed in Clay's house until she heard a police siren getting close. That was her cue to climb out this window and start screaming.

Trembling, Annabelle nodded obediently and started to undress.

Her father pushed the window up, then gave her a boost to the ledge. She crawled into the bedroom. Gasping, Amelia sat up in Clay's bed. Annabelle put her fingers over her lips and shushed her. She could hear Clay on the phone in the kitchen: "Yes . . . I've been on hold for five minutes now. Is there anyone in that office? Yes . . . yes . . . I know it's Sunday, but I have a situation here . . ."

When their father climbed through the window, Amelia recoiled. She looked like she was about to scream. Within seconds, he was on her, stuffing a handkerchief in her mouth. She struggled as he started to undress her. "C'mon, help me put your clothes on her," he whispered to Annabelle.

"Well, all I'm getting are these damn recordings," Clay was telling someone on the phone in his kitchen. He sounded so frustrated. "But I don't want to leave a message, damn it. . . . No, I need to talk with a person. . . ."

Annabelle wanted so much to put on Amelia's clothes, but her father had insisted she run outside in her *underwear*.

Humiliating as that might be, it was better than a beating. She helped her father smuggle Amelia out the bedroom window. Then she crawled into Clay's bed and waited. It seemed like forever.

"Fine. Screw you," she heard Clay say in the kitchen. "I'll get someone else to help me."

Finally, she heard the sirens in the distance. Clay called to her, thinking she was Amelia. "Are you okay in there, pumpkin? You asleep?"

She didn't answer. She listened to the sirens getting louder and louder. Shaking, Annabelle moved to the window. She hadn't even gone outside yet, and already she was cold. Peering over the ledge, she thought she might hurt herself crawling out there.

Clay came to the bedroom doorway. "Amelia?"

Wincing, Annabelle jumped out the window and hit the ground. She could hardly breathe, and yet, somehow, she forced out a scream. She saw the police cars with their lights flashing. They pulled up in front of Clay's house. Then she saw her father marching toward the front door with his hunting rifle.

Annabelle let out another shriek and started running toward the police cars, until she heard the loud bang.

She swiveled around at the edge of the front yard. Clay must have come out the front door to chase after her. But now he lay sprawled on the ground, with blood all over his shirt and his long black hair in his face.

At first, Annabelle was horrified. But then she thought about how her twin sister had abandoned her, and run to this man for protection. He was going to help Amelia, and didn't even mention helping *her*.

Suddenly, she liked that he was dead. It felt good.

After that, things between her and Amelia were never quite the same. Amelia was different, withdrawn, and acting crazy most of the time. Her parents finally sent her away to live with another family.

Then they moved to the ranch in Salem, without Amelia.

While Annabelle endured her father's abuse and those awful nights she was forced to help him with his *work*, she still picked up snippets of her twin sister's experiences in a series of foster homes. Amelia wasn't very happy, but her life was easy in comparison to Annabelle's plight. Then something happened to Annabelle that was worse than her father's most severe beating, worse than those long, lonely nights in the car, listening to those women scream and beg.

What happened was Amelia had decided to forget about her.

Annabelle never really forgave her for that.

She knew her sister was adopted by the Faradays. She still had a glimpse into Amelia's sweet, privileged life with them, but she didn't get to be a part of it. As far as her lucky sister was concerned, she didn't exist, and never had.

After her mother had killed herself, her father and Uncle Duane kept grilling Annabelle about where Amelia was. They knew she'd had a special connection with her twin. Though Annabelle knew her sister's last name was now Faraday, she didn't tell them a thing. She somehow sensed they wanted Amelia dead. And Annabelle was still very protective of her sister, even though she didn't deserve it.

Later, Annabelle figured it out. Her father and Uncle Duane had planned to do away with Amelia shortly after Clay had been killed. In a rare moment of clarity, Annabelle's mother intervened. She persuaded her husband to put the problem child into foster care.

When she was a teenager, Annabelle found some documents tucked away in her father's desk drawer. Shortly before the move to Salem, her mother and father had signed papers completely relinquishing parenthood of Amelia.

But once her mother was dead, Annabelle's father and her uncle were desperate to track down Amelia. They wanted to kill her, because of what she knew and what she might tell. They had no idea Amelia had forgotten all about them.

Stupid Duane had killed those people at the adoption place and gotten himself killed for nothing.

She didn't talk about Amelia with anyone until later in high school. Annabelle thought it might make her more interesting to people if she'd had a twin who died. But it didn't make her popular. And all the while, she had a window into her sister's life. Annabelle had her nose pressed up against that window. She knew Amelia Faraday had a kid brother and parents who loved her. She lived in a beautiful house with a dock and a lake in the backyard. They had a weekend home, not far from another lake.

The closest Amelia Faraday ever came to true misery and pain was when Annabelle experienced it firsthand. Even then, Amelia had no idea where the sensations and visions came from.

It hurt Annabelle to be disregarded like that. It hurt more than all the physical pain and horror she'd endured growing up on that ranch with her awful father.

Now Amelia was beginning to feel some of that pain firsthand. First her brother, then her parents and her aunt, her boyfriend. One by one, the people Amelia loved weren't there anymore. Within an hour, her therapist—along with her uncle and her cousins—would all be dead, too.

Amelia would have nobody, except the sister she'd chosen to forget.

Huddled inside the phone booth in front of Danny's Diner, Annabelle listened to the rain beating on the roof. She made another call. It rang twice before he picked up. "Yeah?"

"Hi, babe. How's everything there?"

"Fine," he said, "except we got one down."

Annabelle frowned a bit. "Already? Was it one of the kids?"

"No, a snoopy old bitch of a neighbor. But I have it under control. I asked the housekeeper, and she said the lady lived alone. So nobody's going to come looking for her. In fact, I'm tempted to check across the street and see if she has anything in the house worth taking. Bet she has a shitload of jewelry."

"Now, don't get greedy," Annabelle said. "Stay put. I don't want any of the other neighbors to see you going over there. They might call the cops. You could screw this whole thing up. You've collected a car full of crap from Uncle George's. That's enough. What's the latest on Uncle George, anyway?"

"The last time he talked to fatso, he said to expect him around nine o'clock."

"Good. Well, be careful, babe. I got these vibes from Karen that they suspect something. So, if you get nervous, or things don't seem right to you, then just abort. Shoot the maid and the kids, and get the hell out of there. We'll worry about the uncle later."

"I won't get nervous," he said.

"Well, once you've finished them all off, hurry here, baby. I need you."

"Huh," he grunted. "You just want me to help you escape."

"Well, you promised," she said. "You're going to help me get away, and we'll start new someplace else. See you at the lake house around midnight."

Annabelle hung up the phone, and stepped out of the booth. She walked through the cool night rain back to Karen's car in the parking lot of Danny's Diner. She glanced over the swaying treetops in the general direction of the lake house.

Once she'd killed Karen, she'd wait for Blade. He was in

love with her—at least he thought he was. He would be easy to kill.

She had a two-gallon tote container of gasoline in the trunk of Karen's car. That would be enough to set the lake house on fire. The cops would find two burnt bodies in there, Karen and Blade. She knew what she was doing. She'd pulled it off without a hitch three years ago. Funny, she'd pretty much told Sandra the same thing she'd told Blade moments ago: "You're going to help me get away, and we'll start new someplace else."

When she'd said *we*, Blade had probably thought she'd meant her and him.

But she wasn't thinking of him at all.

His hands taut on the steering wheel, George studied the road ahead. He'd made it to the city of Jefferson in less than twenty minutes. Speeding along I-5, he'd kept his eyes peeled for patrol cars.

While in the cybercafé, he'd checked MapQuest for directions to Coupland Aeronautics, so he knew the helicopter place was only about a mile ahead in this industrial area. George passed several warehouses, a railroad and container yard, and a chemical plant.

He'd just talked with Karen, who was on her way to meet Amelia at the restaurant near the Lake Wenatchee house. Apparently, Amelia didn't have any premonitions about the kids or Jessie being in trouble—not yet, at least. Karen said she'd call again from the pay phone when she got to the restaurant. George couldn't help remembering the last time someone had promised to call him from that place. It had been Ina, the day of her murder.

Although he wanted to phone Jessie again, he decided to wait until he was ready to board the helicopter. The more he thought about how scared Jody and Steffie had to be, the harder he pressed on the accelerator. George started to pass a truck in front of him, but as he veered into the oncoming lane, he saw an SUV barreling toward him. Its horn blared. George swerved back into his own lane behind the truck, again. He got ready to try once more, but noticed the truck's right turn signal blinking. It slowed down to a crawl to pull into a Chevron plant. George tried to go around it again, but another truck nearly ran into him. Its horn continued to wail, even after George swung back into his lane.

Catching his breath, he waited for the trucker in front of him to make the damn turn. Then he saw a clear road ahead, and he pushed harder on the gas.

George passed Donahue Drive, one of the last major intersections before the helicopter pad, at least, according to MapQuest. And then he noticed the flashing light in his rearview mirror. "Oh, shit," he murmured, releasing his foot from the accelerator. "God, no, please. . . ."

The cop car was descending on him. He could hear the siren now.

"Please, God."

George's stomach was in knots as he slowly pulled over to the road's shoulder. The lights in his rearview mirror were blinding now. For a moment, the bright strobes illuminated the inside of his car. And then the policeman passed him.

George sagged forward against the wheel. He took a deep breath, and pressed on. But he couldn't stop trembling. He watched the squad car take a right turn ahead. He hoped the cop wasn't headed to Coupland Aeronautics.

For the next few blocks, he drove at the 35-miles-per-hour speed limit. Then he noticed the airfield ahead to his left. Two helicopters were parked on the airstrip. George didn't see a cop car anywhere near the place. Yet his hands still shook on the wheel as he went beyond the tall chain-link fence and followed the signs to customer parking. He didn't think he'd breathe right or stop shaking until he saw his kids and knew they were safe.

He was just pulling into one of the parking spots when someone trotted out of the trailer office. George rolled down his window and saw that it was a woman in her midthirties, wearing a gray jumpsuit. She was pretty with dark brown hair, pulled back in a ponytail. "Mr. McMillan?" she said, approaching his car.

George nodded a few more times than necessary. He was waiting for her to say something like, "I'm afraid the Salem Police are looking for you. . . ."

Instead, she leaned toward his car window and smiled. "Hi, I'm Kate. You spoke with me earlier. If you need to park for more than twenty-four hours, go ahead and take a spot where that green sign is."

George glanced over his shoulder and saw a green sign on a light post: LONG-TERM PARKING. He looked back up at the woman and nodded again. He was still shaking, and he could tell she'd noticed.

"They charge twelve bucks a day for long-term parking," she said. "It'll be added to your bill. And speaking of paperwork, it's all ready for you. Just come on into the office. We'll get it signed, and we'll be our way to Seattle. I'll be your pilot tonight, Mr. McMillan. Do you have any luggage for your trip?"

He shook his head. "No, I don't. But thanks."

"Okeydoke," she said. "Then I'll see you in the office." She turned and trotted back toward the trailer.

George tried to take a few calming breaths as he maneuvered over to the long-term parking area. It just dawned on him that this was a rental, and he'd have to somehow get it back to the rent-a-car company. But that didn't matter right now. He was just relieved he'd be on his way to Seattle soon, with no one detaining him. No delays.

Still, he couldn't stop trembling, even after he'd parked the rental and locked it. Standing beside the car, he took out his cell phone and dialed home once more. He just needed to hear Jessie assure him again that Steffie and Jody were all right.

George listened to the ring tones, four of them so far. Something was wrong. Why wasn't Jessie picking up? He'd figured they were checking his caller ID. They must have known his cell phone number by now. If they were trying to lure him there using Jessie and the kids, they would have had her pick up by now.

The machine clicked on. Hi, you've reached the McMillans. Sorry we're not here to take your call. But if you'd like to leave a message for George, Ina, Jody or Stephanie, just talk to us after the beep!

It was Ina's voice on the recording. He still hadn't changed it.

The beep sounded. George kept wondering why no one was picking up. "Hello, Jessie?" he said into the machine. "Um, it's George. I'm on my way. I should be there around nine o'clock. I just wanted to touch base with you. Are you there, Jessie? Jody? Steffie? Well, I guess you're not there. I'll see you guys soon, okay?"

He clicked off the line. Then he punched his home phone number again. Another four ring tones went by while George gazed out at the two helicopters on the airstrip. One of them was waiting for him. Ina's recorded message came back on.

George quickly clicked off the cell phone. He had a horrible feeling in his gut. No one was picking up at his house—just the voice of someone already dead.

Chapter Twenty-four

At Danny's Diner, the burgers and sandwiches were served in red plastic baskets, lined with paper. Desserts came from a rotating display case near the cash register. The walls were decorated with neon beer signs, mounted fish plaques, and another sign by the counter that said:

Our Credit Manager is HELEN WAITE. *If you want to pay on credit . . .*

GO TO HELEN WAITE!

The dinner crowd was dwindling in the cozy, homey little restaurant. Karen noticed a family of four in a booth, an older couple at one of the tables, and two trucker types, both at the counter with a few stools between them.

And Amelia was nowhere to be seen.

The waitress, a chubby blonde with a Farrah Fawcett hairdo left over from the seventies, told Karen she could sit anywhere. So Karen plopped down at a window table and prayed that Amelia just happened to be in the restroom.

She waited three minutes, then got up and checked the ladies' room. No one.

This was crazy. Amelia had called from here thirty minutes ago. She'd been stranded, without a car. Karen had practically begged her to stay put, too. And now she was gone. How could someone just vanish like that?

But then, that sort of thing had happened a lot, back when Amelia and Annabelle's father had been alive.

With a nervous sigh, Karen sat back down at the table. She decided to give Amelia three more minutes. Then she'd call her from the phone booth outside. Of course, if Amelia was anywhere in the vicinity, her cell phone wouldn't work. So it was probably pointless.

Karen glanced at her wristwatch. George would touch down in Seattle in less than an hour. They were counting on Amelia to somehow intercede with her sister.

Had she somehow already met up with Annabelle?

Karen looked out the rain-beaded window. Against the darkness, she saw only her own reflection. She looked haggard and worried. The blond waitress came by for Karen's drink order. Karen noticed her name tag: YOUR SERVER IS CONNIE.

"Could I have a Diet Coke, please?" Karen said. "Also, Connie, I was supposed to meet someone here. Have you seen a very pretty, 19-year-old girl with shoulder-length black hair? She should have been here about a half hour ago."

Connie shook her head. "Nope, sorry, I haven't noticed anyone like that tonight, hon—been here since four. I'll get your Diet Coke in a jiff." She sauntered toward the kitchen.

Digging out her cell phone, Karen checked the last caller. She left her trench coat on her chair, then hurried outside. Ducking into the phone booth, she checked the number over the receiver. It was a match. Amelia had been here.

As she stepped out of the booth, Karen saw someone walking along the roadside. Coming from the direction of the lake house, she seemed to emerge from the darkness.

"Amelia?" Karen called to her.

Although it was still drizzling lightly, she dawdled. Her black hair was in wet tangles, and the navy-blue rain jacket was too big on her. The sleeves came down to her fingers. She seemed lost in thought. It was another few moments before she appeared to notice Karen, and then she waved and ran toward her.

"Amelia, what are you doing out here?" Karen asked. "You'll catch your death."

She gave Karen a hug. Her cheek felt cold. "I'm sorry. Were you waiting long?"

"Not very," Karen said. Pulling away, she held her at arm's length and looked at her. Karen noticed she wasn't wearing any makeup. "What were you doing, honey? Why didn't you wait in the diner?"

She let out a long sigh, and tugged at a strand of her hair. "Oh, I decided to walk down to the cabin. But I only got halfway there before I chickened out and turned back. I keep thinking it would be good therapy for me to go there and see it."

"I don't think that's such a great idea," Karen replied. "You'd only get upset if you went there now. It would be pointless." She put an arm around her. "C'mon, let's get you some coffee, something to warm you up."

As she ushered her into the restaurant and back toward the window table, Karen heard the blond waitress call out to someone: "Well, hi there, Frenchie!"

The two of them sat down. "We should make our orders to go," Karen said. "I'd like to get on the road soon. . . ."

"Frenchie?" the waitress chirped again.

Karen looked up and realized she was approaching their table. "Well, Frenchie, aren't you going to say hi?" the waitress asked.

Karen stared across the table. "Amelia?"

Still tugging at a wet strand of hair, she looked up at the

waitress. "Oh, hi . . . Connie," she said, obviously reading the name tag.

"When you walked in just now, you acted like you didn't know me," the waitress said.

She smiled up at her. "Oh, I'm sorry. I'm kind of spacey today. How are you?"

"I can't complain," the waitress replied. "Who'll listen?"

"Did you just call her 'Frenchie'?" Karen asked.

The waitress nodded. "I don't even have to give this one a menu. She always orders the same thing, the French dip. Every time she comes in here with her folks, she . . ." The waitress trailed off, and a pained look passed across her face. She shook her head. "Oh, hon, I'm so sorry. All of us here felt terrible when we heard about it. . . ."

"Thanks, Connie," she murmured, her head down.

"I'll get your drink order, hon," Connie said. "The usual? Sprite?"

She nodded. "Thanks very much." She waited until the waitress retreated toward the kitchen, then she leaned across the table to Karen. "I can tell she's embarrassed. Could you excuse me for a minute, Karen?"

Getting to her feet, she walked over to the counter. She murmured something to the waitress, who was at the soda machine. Connie put down the glass of soda, then came around the counter and gave her a hug. After a moment, the tall, white-haired cook ambled out from the kitchen and quietly spoke to her, too. He shook her hand, but she leaned in and kissed him on the cheek. He blushed a bit.

Finally, she came back to the table. "They're so sweet," she whispered. "They're getting our drinks to go, and are refusing to take any money, not even a tip. Listen, I need to use the bathroom, and then we can get going, okay?"

Karen watched her walk toward the restrooms.

Five minutes later, they stepped out of Danny's Diner,

carrying their drinks, along with two pieces of pie that the waitress insisted they have for free.

"God, Karen," she said, stopping to look back at the tacky, little chalet-style restaurant. She had tears in her eyes. "Aren't those people nice? It makes me sad to think I'm probably never coming back here."

Karen just patted her arm, and said nothing.

They headed to the rental car, and Karen unlocked the door for her.

She hesitated before climbing inside. "Karen, I know you're in a hurry to get to Seattle, and we have a lot to talk about," she said. "But could we go by the lake house first?"

She grimaced. "Oh, Amelia, like I said, I don't think you should go in there—"

"Please, Karen, I feel I need to do it for closure. On top of that, there are some things of mine in that house, and I don't want to have to come back here." She sighed. "I really don't think I could go in there on my own, or with anyone else for that matter. You're the only one. C'mon, it's just a five-minute drive. Can't we just do this, and get it over with?

Karen stared at her for a moment, then she took a deep breath and nodded. "All right, Amelia. We'll swing by, if that's what you really want. Hurry up, get in."

She climbed into the passenger seat, and set their drinks in the cup holders.

Karen got behind the wheel, then handed her the carryout bag. Starting up the car, she backed out of the parking space. Karen paused before shifting gears, and turned toward her. "Are you sure you want to go?" she asked. "Honey, you should know, there are still bloodstains. And everything's covered with dusting powder for fingerprints. It's not going to be pleasant."

She nodded glumly. "I figured as much. But I still want to go, Karen. And I want you there with me. Like I said, I need to have closure."

"Okay," Karen murmured.

Then she pulled onto the dark, winding road toward the beach house.

The big monster of a door wouldn't budge.

Amelia had tugged and tugged at the handle, but it was no use. Someone must have jammed the lock on the outside.

Panic-stricken, she couldn't get a normal breath. And she was shivering in the cold, windowless little room. Amelia kept the itchy blanket wrapped around her. Under that, she still had on her T-shirt and flannel pajama bottoms from last night. Her bare feet were freezing and filthy from walking on the dirty concrete floor.

She'd already searched every inch of the place, looking for a wrench, a crowbar, or *anything* to pry the door open. At the same time, she realized it would probably take a jackhammer to penetrate the damn thing.

During her search, she uncovered a watercolor she'd painted of the lake house back when she was ten. It was pretty godawful. No wonder the thing had ended up in the fallout shelter behind some boxes. Her parents had framed it, but the glass in the frame was now cracked. Amelia slipped the watercolor out of the frame, and saw a sheet of black cardboard backing it. With that behind the glass, it was almost like a mirror—a cracked mirror.

Amelia looked at her reflection, and the close-shorn haircut someone had given her while she'd slept. She could see the skin irritation around her nose and mouth.

"Why is this happening?" she whispered, tears welling in her eyes. "Who's doing this to me?"

Whoever it was, they were probably coming back for her. They'd left her food, a light, and a blanket. They wouldn't have done that if they weren't coming back. They wouldn't have left her anything if they expected her to die in this gloomy little crypt.

Her hands shaking, Amelia slipped a piece of broken glass out of the frame. It was about eight inches long, and very sharp along the edge. If someone did come down here, she would be ready for them.

For some reason, she thought of Karen Carlisle. The last thing Amelia remembered was falling asleep in Karen's spare bedroom, while Karen sat in that rocker in the corner. Had Karen decided that she was so dangerous she had to be locked up? Had Karen shorn her hair like a convict and then stuck her in this makeshift little prison?

Amelia couldn't think of any other explanation. Maybe that was why she had this sudden, inexplicable contempt for her therapist and friend. She was as close to Karen as she'd been to the family she'd just lost. Amelia remembered having had this same loathing for her brother, Collin, before his *accident,* and for her parents and Aunt Ina the night they'd died in this house.

All she could think about was slitting Karen's throat.

Wrapped up in the blanket, she sat down on the edge of the cot and stared at the jagged piece of glass. She told herself that she could never hurt Karen. Amelia started to cry.

But she didn't let go of the glass.

She stared at Karen and shook her head. "How could I feel things from this twin I didn't even know I had?" she asked. "How could I have forgotten all about her?"

Karen took her eyes off the road for a second. "Well, you have to consider, you were four years old when you last saw her." She searched for the little inlet off Holden Trail, but she couldn't see much beyond the headlight beams in front of her. It was a treacherous drive at night with no guardrail along the side of the road, nothing to stop the car from tumbling downhill if she overshot her lane.

They were both silent for a moment. The windshield wipers squeaked, and rain tapped on the roof. Karen wasn't sure what to tell her. There was so much to explain. She'd decided Amelia didn't need to know about her father just yet. That could wait. But she had to understand what was happening now. It was very likely they'd need her to talk to her twin sister, and reason with her.

"A lot of bad things happened to you, Amelia," she went on. "I think you made yourself forget most of it. That's how you were able to survive. But your twin didn't forget you. She still has you on her frequency. I think she's had a very hard life, too. You must have experienced some of it second-hand with those phantom pains and the nightmares."

"So you're saying this twin sister killed my parents, and Aunt Ina and Collin?" she asked, incredulous. "And I was on her *frequency*?"

Karen nodded. "Yes, I'm sorry, Amelia. But I think you were picking up those violent sensations and images from her. That's why you blamed yourself for everything she was doing."

She shook her head. "I'm still blown away. Why is she doing this?"

Karen sighed. "I don't know for sure. Obviously, she has a grudge against you or something. Maybe she resents that you've ended up having a better life."

"Or maybe she feels I abandoned her."

"Well, whatever her reasons are, Amelia, you need to remember it's not your fault."

"So her name's Annabelle," she murmured. "My God, all this time I thought I had a split personality or something. "

"No, you've just been picking up on the things she was doing. You didn't know it, but you have a window into her world." Karen saw a turnaround on the left. "Isn't this it?" she asked.

"Um, yeah," she said distractedly.

Karen pulled into a small alcove, but she didn't switch off the ignition. "Listen, before we go down there, I need to ask you again, Amelia. Are you picking up any kind of *feeling* that something's wrong at your Uncle George's house? Do you sense that George, your cousins, or Jessie are in any kind of trouble?"

She looked back at Karen and shook her head. "Why do you keep asking that? *Are* they in trouble?"

"Your Uncle George is worried, and so am I." Karen glanced at her wristwatch. George would be landing in Seattle within a half hour.

She turned off the ignition. "Listen, Amelia, on our way back, I want to stop by Danny's again and phone your uncle. Then I might have you call his house. If Annabelle is there, we'll need you to talk to her."

She let out a stunned little laugh. "Karen, I don't understand any of this. Are you saying my sister's at Uncle George's house?"

Karen nodded. "We think it's possible. Are you sure you're not sensing something? You've always known ahead of time what your sister's planning. You're not feeling anything?"

She shook her head. "Nothing about Jody or Steffie. Right now, I just feel this very strong need to go to the lake house. Please, Karen." She opened the car door. "Don't worry about the trail at night. Just hold on to my hand. I know it by heart by now."

Karen got out of the car and paused at the top of the trail. In the darkness, she could barely see the path through the trees and shrubs. But she was thinking about something else that didn't seem right. She'd figured Amelia would have been far more concerned right now about the safety of her only surviving family members. Instead, she was bent on visiting the lake house one more time for *closure*. Karen was waiting for George's plane to land before calling and consulting him on their next move. But Amelia didn't know any of that. It didn't make sense that a final trip to the lake house was such a priority.

There had been a moment back at the diner, when she hadn't recognized the waitress. A tiny alarm had gone off in Karen's gut, then.

She thought about all the other people Annabelle must have duped before killing them. Did the Faradays, George's wife, or Shane ever realize before their violent deaths that they were staring at Amelia's twin?

"C'mon, Karen." She smiled and held out her hand. "I'll lead the way."

Karen hesitated, but then grabbed her hand. Engulfed in darkness, she started to follow her down the trail. She took cautious little steps in the direction she was being pulled. Around her, she heard raindrops pattering on leaves, and branches rustling in the gentle wind.

She thought about her dad's old revolver in her purse. "Amelia, remember what we were talking about in your last session?" she said, hating the nervous little wiggle that crept into her voice. She cleared her throat. "Um, you were telling me how you really resented Shane sometimes, and for no apparent reason. Remember that?"

She paused. "No, Karen, I don't. I don't recall saying anything like that."

In the dark, Karen couldn't see her face, or her expression. Did *Annabelle* know she was being tested again? Or was this *Amelia*, quite understandably, not remembering a conversation that had never happened?

"Actually, it's weird you should mention Shane, right after you asked about those premonitions," she went on. "I can't help thinking something might have happened to him. And I—I feel I've caused it somehow. What do you make of that? Do you suppose I just feel guilty, because I borrowed his car without asking him?" She started moving again, pulling Karen's hand. "Anyway, I'm worried about him, Karen. He's not answering his cell, and he hasn't returned any of my calls."

Karen could hear the vulnerability in her voice, and it sounded so much like Amelia. She wondered how she was going to tell her that Shane was dead. There was so much Amelia still didn't know.

Karen continued down the slope with her, blindly following her lead. She could only make out shapes in the murky blackness around her, and every step seemed precarious. She had to put all her trust in her guide.

"Careful, Karen," she heard her say. Her grip tightened. "It's a little slippery here. And there's a big ditch on your right."

Karen felt the wet ground and gravel under her shoes. She told herself: If this is Annabelle, she could have so easily killed you by now.

"We're almost there, Karen. Thank you for doing this." She steered her around a curve in the trail. "So, about Shane, do you think he's okay? You don't suppose this—*Annabelle*—has gotten to him, do you?"

"I—I can't say for sure," Karen replied, feeling horrible. She couldn't tell her the truth right now. It was too much.

"There's a railing and some flagstones coming up, and then we're out of the woods."

With her foot, Karen tapped around the dirt and gravel until she felt the flat flagstones beneath her. She held on to the wooden railing with her free hand. She could now see Amelia's silhouette and, in front of them, a clearing, and the Faradays' lake house.

They started up the stone pathway to the house.

The terrain had flattened out, but she still held onto

Karen's hand. "Y'know, when we go back to Danny's Diner, I'm calling Shane again." Her voice had a little tremor to it. "And then let's try to track down this twin sister I didn't know I had. We need to stop her before she hurts someone else."

"We will, Amelia," Karen said.

"My God, look at this," she muttered, stopping to stare at the front door. The strips of yellow police tape fluttered in the wind.

"Are you sure you want to go in?" Karen asked gently.

"Yes, it's something I've got to do," she said. Letting go of Karen's hand, she stepped toward the door. "We keep a key hidden up here."

Karen watched her reach up and pat along the top of the doorway frame. The sleeve of her oversized rain jacket slipped down her bare arm. Karen saw an ugly scar on the back of her wrist. She stifled a gasp.

Amelia had remembered the pain. But Annabelle still carried the scar.

"Here it is," she announced, the key in her hand. "I was afraid the police might have found it and taken it." She brushed aside some of the loose yellow tape, and put the key in the lock. "My, God, it's not even locked. . . ."

Karen couldn't move. She just stared at her, and tried to get a breath.

Annabelle opened the door, then turned toward Karen. "Do you want to lead the way this time?"

Karen shook her head. She waited until Annabelle stepped inside the house, then she reached inside her purse for the revolver. She came to the doorway, and saw the 19-year-old standing in the middle of the living room.

"Oh, my God, Karen, look at the blood," she cried. Annabelle was a very good actress. She recoiled, then opened her bag and frantically dug into it. "God, I think I'm going to be sick."

Karen already had the revolver out—and pointed at her. "Stop it, Annabelle," she said.

But Annabelle pulled something out of her purse.

"Hold it right there!" Karen yelled.

Annabelle froze. Karen still couldn't see what was in her hand.

For a moment, there was dead silence, and then a faint murmuring sound. It came from the basement, and yet seemed so far away, too. "Karen? Is someone there? Karen! Help me!"

Karen recognized Amelia's voice.

She didn't see the blackjack in Annabelle's hand, the same deadly little leather-covered club her father had used on Tracy Atkinson and several others when he'd knocked them unconscious.

All at once, Annabelle swiveled around.

Karen didn't even realize what was happening. She was still thinking about Amelia, downstairs somewhere. She saw Annabelle swinging her arm toward her. Then she felt the awful pain on the side of her head. She didn't even have time to raise the gun.

Karen crumpled onto the floor just inches away from the bloodstains left by Ina McMillan.

"Hi, you've reached the McMillans," Ina said on the recording. "Sorry we're not here to take your call. But if you'd like to leave a message for George, Ina, Jody, or Stephanie, just talk to us after the beep!"

The beep sounded, and then George's voice came over the answering machine. "Jessie?" he said anxiously. There was a lot of noise in the background—car horns honking, a whistle blowing, and people talking. "Is anyone there? Hello . . ."

"Let's keep Daddy in the dark a little longer," said the young man in the sunglasses. "It just means he'll be all that more anxious to get here."

Jessie didn't say anything. She stared at him with dread. She couldn't feel her arms anymore, and it was hard to get a normal breath. But she was more worried about the children. She hadn't heard a peep from Stephanie's room in almost an hour. Jody had let out a few muffled coughs about ten minutes ago, but not another sound. She wondered if they could hear their father's voice right now.

"I can't figure out why you're not picking up," George said on the machine. "I'm thinking maybe Steffie had another asthma attack, and you had to go to the hospital. Um, Jessie or Jody, if you get this, call me on my cell as soon as you can. Let me know what's happening. It's 9:15, and I'm at the airport. The line for taxicabs is nuts. I'll try to get there soon. It might take another half hour. Jessie, thanks for waiting around. I know you need to fly out to Denver tonight. You might need some money. I don't think you know about the safe in the house, but I certainly have more than enough in there to pay for your ticket. When I get home, I'll make sure you're covered. . . ."

The young man chuckled. "Jackpot," he whispered. He snatched the cordless from the counter. "Make him tell you where this safe is, and then get the combination." He reached for the kitchen phone.

"I think this machine's about to cut me off," George was saying. "See you soon—I hope." He clicked off, and the recording beep sounded.

"Shit," the young man muttered. He put down the cordless, and hung up the kitchen phone. "Well, we'll have to call Daddy back in a little while." He smirked at Jessie. "So, it sounds like you don't know anything about this safe, huh?"

Wide-eyed, she just shook her head at him.

George clicked off his cell phone. He nodded to the eleven-year-old. "Thanks, Brad," he said, over all the noise from the cop show on TV. "You can turn that down now."

He stood in the Reeces' family room, an open area with a

vaulted ceiling right off the kitchen and breakfast nook. He looked out the sliding glass door at the Reeces' back lawn. Amid the trees and tall hedges at the far end of the yard was a little pathway Brad and Jody used to go back and forth to each other's houses. George couldn't see his house from here. The bushes were too tall.

Jody's best friend since first grade, Brad was a slightly beefy red-haired boy with thick glasses. He wore jeans and a T-shirt advertising *My Name Is Earl*, his and Jody's favorite TV show. He had the tough, surly look of a wrestler, but he was very sweet. Lucky, too, it turned out.

George's helicopter pilot had radioed ahead for a taxi, and a cab had been waiting for him when they'd touched down at Boeing Field. George had tried to phone his neighbor across the street, Sally Bidwell. He'd thought about using her house as a sort of command post and holding area—a safe haven for the kids and Jessie, if he could get them out of the house. But Mrs. Bidwell hadn't picked up her phone. So George had tried the Reeces, and gotten Brad. His parents had gone out for the night, and he was home alone. In fact, he'd tried calling Jody earlier in the evening to invite him over for pizza, but no one had picked up. He'd thought about cutting through the backyards, knocking on the McMillans' back door, and inviting Jody in person. But at the very last minute, he'd decided against it. Lucky.

Jody's friend had certainly come through in a pinch, too. Brad had already scurried around the house and come up with everything George had figured he might need: a crowbar, a screwdriver, and a sharp serrated-edge kitchen knife. The items were laid out on the Reeces' breakfast table.

George put his cell phone back in the pocket of his sports jacket.

Brad aimed the remote control at the TV and hit mute. "Do you think you ought to put some of that black stuff on your face, too, Mr. M?" he asked.

"That's not a bad idea, Brad," he said. "But I think I'm okay without it."

He glanced over at the mute TV. George wasn't sure if, over the phone, the cop show had sounded like an airport taxi stand. He wasn't even sure if his message had gotten through to anyone. He could only hope it had. He hoped his fabrication about a safe full of money in the house would keep whoever was there preoccupied. They'd wait for him now. He'd made it clear that no one else had the combination. And they'd need to keep his children alive if they wanted his cooperation. It might even prompt them to have Jessie phone him back.

He knew Annabelle Schlessinger—or her friend—hadn't broken into his home for money. But he also knew that a 19-year-old on the lam wasn't about to pass up the chance for a safeload of cash.

If they thought he was still at the airport, they wouldn't be expecting him within the next five minutes.

His hand shaking, George slid open the glass door.

"You sure you don't want me to come with?" Brad asked anxiously.

"No, thanks, I really need you here," George said. His stomach was full of knots as he collected the crowbar, screwdriver, and knife from the kitchen table. He slipped the knife and screwdriver into the side pocket of his sports jacket. "If I can get Jody, Steffie, and Jessie out of there, I'll send them over to you, Brad. Then you can call the cops." He'd already told Brad this, but it merited repeating. "And if in twenty minutes, you don't see any of us—"

"Then I call the cops, and get them to haul ass over to your place—9203 Larkdale," Brad interjected.

George nodded, then he mussed Brad's red hair. "You know, Jody's very lucky to have you for a friend," he said. "You and he will be talking about this night for a long time."

He stepped outside.

"Good luck, Mr. M," Brad whispered, standing in the doorway.

George gave him a nod, then ran to the hedges bordering the Reeces' backyard. Weaving through the bushes and trees, he saw the back of his house. It had been nearly twenty hours since he'd left home to catch a flight to Portland and drive to Salem. Now, that seemed like days ago. He was beyond tired, running on his wits and pure adrenaline. And he still couldn't stop shaking.

He noticed lights were on in the kitchen and living room and master bedroom. The kids' rooms were dark. George couldn't see anyone, or anything else. From the edge of the yard, he crept up toward the house, to Jody's bedroom window. But it was too high to see inside.

Grabbing a plastic patio chair, George pushed it against the side of the house, then he stepped onto the seat. It was a little wobbly, and he clung to the window ledge as he peered into the bedroom. He saw his son in the darkness, curled up on the bed, hog-tied with his hands and feet behind him. Duct tape covered his mouth. His eyes were closed. George was overwhelmed with rage and frustration. But at least Jody was breathing.

Two windows down, he looked in on Stephanie, tied up on her bed in the same fashion, like a little animal. She was trembling. He could see the tears on her cheeks. The piece of duct tape over her mouth seemed too big for her little face.

He kept telling himself, *at least they're alive*.

Their backyard sloped a bit, and the kitchen was closer to ground level. George didn't need the patio chair to look inside the window. He heard the TV going, a small portable they kept at the end of the kitchen counter. Suddenly, someone walked right past the window, and George quickly ducked down. He waited a moment, then straightened up and peeked over the window ledge.

The intruder in his kitchen was a young man with pale

skin and very black hair. He wore sunglasses and a black suit. He'd probably seen *Reservoir Dogs* one too many times. He looked like a cocky son of a bitch. He turned down the TV and said something to Jessie.

George could see her, tied to a kitchen chair. At least she didn't have any tape over her mouth.

The creep in the sunglasses grabbed the cordless phone from the kitchen counter. It looked like there was a gun on the counter, too, but George wasn't sure. Beyond the kitchen, he had a glimpse into the living room, where someone was sprawled facedown on the blood-soaked sofa. It looked like his neighbor, Mrs. Bidwell.

"Oh, my God," George murmured, horrified.

The young man picked up the receiver from the kitchen wall phone, and started dialing. He held the phone to Jessie's face, and then he switched on the cordless from the study so he could listen in.

All at once, George's cell phone went off.

"Shit!" he muttered, ducking down again. He quickly dug the cell phone out of his jacket pocket and switched it off. Crouched down against the house, he gazed at a patch of lawn illuminated by the light pouring out the kitchen window. He watched a shadow looming in that silhouette. He knew the young man was standing at the window directly above him, looking out. For a few seconds, George didn't move. Finally, the shadow moved away. "Couldn't have been anything," he heard the young man say. "You sure you don't know where this safe is? I've just about turned the master bedroom upside down."

George dared to peek over the window ledge again. Jessie was shaking her head. "You heard him on the phone earlier. I don't know a thing about it."

"It's screwy he's not answering his cell," the guy muttered. Then he said something else, but he moved too far away from the window for George to hear.

George glanced at the patio chair that he'd left beneath Stephanie's bedroom window. He decided to try getting Jody out first. Jody would be faster, and less panicked than Steffie.

Crouched against the house, George caught his breath. He'd expected to see someone looking exactly like Amelia in there. But it appeared as if the man in the sunglasses was running the show by himself.

George wondered where Annabelle Schlessinger was.

Her head throbbing, Karen regained consciousness. She lay facedown on the dirty living room floor of the Faradays' beach house. Her hands were tied behind her with some kind of cord. She could still hear Amelia's muffled cries for help coming from the basement. But she didn't hear the rain anymore. Karen wondered how much time had gone by.

A shadow passed over her, and she squinted up at Annabelle. Karen almost didn't recognize her. Her hair was cut in a short shag style. She'd also changed into a black sweater and jeans. In her hand she held the revolver that had belonged to Karen's father.

Karen realized she must have been unconscious for at least a half hour. Annabelle couldn't have cut her hair and changed clothes in much less time than that. Thirty minutes. George was already at his house by now.

"Is Blade here?" Karen asked warily.

A tiny smile flickered across Annabelle's face. "You know about Blade? Well, I'm impressed." She shook her head. "No, Blade's in Seattle, running an errand for me. In fact, I'm pretty sure he's finished and on his way here now."

Karen was thinking of George, Jessie, and the children. They could already be dead right now. Tears welled up in her eyes. Then she heard Amelia's muted cries again.

"Where have you got her?" she asked. "In the basement? Do they—do they have a storage room down there?"

"They have a fallout shelter," Annabelle replied, still standing over her.

Karen shuddered. George had told her about his discovery in the fallout shelter at the Schlessinger ranch. "I'd have thought you wouldn't want to be anything like your father," Karen muttered, her face still against the carpet. "And here you are, Annabelle, following in his footsteps."

"Not exactly," she replied. "I have no intention of killing Amelia. I don't want that at all. But my sister will learn what it's like to be abandoned and totally alone. She has that coming to her."

Karen suddenly felt Annabelle's foot on her neck. Some dirt from Annabelle's shoe trickled into her ear. Annabelle started to apply a bit of pressure on her neck and the side of her face. "In just a little while, Amelia will have no friends or family left," she said. "You see, Blade's been at *Uncle George's* house. So Amelia's uncle, her little cousins, and your maid too, I'm afraid, they're all—poof, gone. You're going to be on the casualty list, too, Karen, very soon. Then Amelia will have no one, except me—the sister she forgot she had. But you know something, Karen? I'll forgive her for deserting me. I'll stick by her, the way she should have stuck by me."

"For God's sake, how could Amelia have *stuck by* you?" Karen countered. She felt even more weight pressing against her neck. "Your parents gave her up. They sent her away."

"Yes, but she didn't have to fucking *forget* me," Annabelle shot back.

Karen felt more weight pressing against her neck. She could hardly breathe.

"We could have still been there for each other," Annabelle said. "We were for a little while, after they put her in foster care. I could still sense what she was going through, and I knew she picked up on my feelings, too. We might not have talked, or seen each other. But we still *shared*. I didn't feel so alone—until her life got better. Then she turned her back on me, Karen. It was like screaming in one end of a phone, with no one listening. I knew she was there, but she cut me out of her life. All I could offer Amelia was pain, so she decided to forget about me."

"What would you have done if you were her?" Karen asked, barely able to get the words out. "Can you really blame her?"

To her amazement, the pressure on the side of her neck and face eased up. Annabelle stepped back. "Go ahead, I'm listening," she said.

Karen swallowed hard and caught her breath. "Amelia was four years old at the time," she said. "She didn't make a conscious decision to forget you, Annabelle. She was just trying to survive. Didn't you do some pretty awful things to survive, yourself?"

Annabelle stared down at her for a moment. "Well, thank you, Karen," she said finally, with a trace of condescension. "Knowing that makes it easier for me to forgive Amelia. After tonight, the police will be looking for her. Me, too, I guess, since I have her face. I've already cut her hair." She patted her own new, short hairstyle. "Like it? I bought us some coloring, too, Auburn Sunset, it's called. Blade got Amelia and me fake ID's, too. I posed for both of us in a wig. Blade thinks he's running away with us, but I'm leaving him behind. It's going to be just Amelia and me, the way it always should have been." She let out a sigh. "You know, my parents used to tell people they'd sent Amelia to live with relatives in Winnipeg. Isn't that funny? Because I think Amelia and I will end up in Canada someplace."

Karen rolled over on her side, and stared up at her. "Your plan is flawed, Annabelle," she said carefully. "You know that, don't you? Amelia will never get over this . . . *genocide* of her adopted family and friends. She won't forgive you for it. She'll never understand."

"That's why I need you to talk to her for me, Karen. You'll make her understand."

Annabelle grabbed her arm, almost breaking it as she pulled her up to a standing position. Karen tried to keep from stumbling. She was dizzy, and her head ached.

"One last counseling session," Annabelle said. "You've done family counseling before, I'm sure. It's all about understanding, forgiveness, and moving on."

Pressing the gun to Karen's back, Annabelle prodded her into the kitchen, and then to the basement door.

With the screwdriver, George pried off the bedroom window screen. He stepped down from the patio seat, and carefully set the screen against the house. Then he grabbed the crowbar, and boosted himself back up again. The window wasn't locked, but he still had to prod the crowbar along the sill to get the damn thing to move. It resisted, making a loud creaking sound.

Jody suddenly squirmed on the bed and rolled over on his side. His eyes lit up when he saw his father. But George couldn't help worrying. That little bit of noise could have given him away. Any minute now, he expected Annabelle's friend to appear in Jody's doorway with a gun in his hand. He'd just seen what that lowlife had done to Mrs. Bidwell.

His heart racing, George worked quickly. He pulled the window open, stopping only for a moment as it squeaked again. The patio chair beneath him moved, and he almost lost his balance. Grabbing hold of the ledge, George pulled himself up. He climbed through the opening, then into Jody's bedroom. He could hear the TV more clearly now. And he could hear Jessie, too.

"Would it kill you to go in there and take the tape off their mouths for just a few minutes?" she was saying. "Lord, it's been over two hours. . . ."

"Get off my fucking back," the man retorted. "Want to join your friend over there on the couch? Now, you need to give their daddy another call, and find out where this safe is . . ."

George crept to Jody's bed. He leaned over and whispered in his ear. "Don't make a sound, okay?" He carefully peeled the tape off his son's mouth. Jody gasped, then took several deep breaths.

Taking the kitchen knife, George cut at the tape around his wrists and ankles. With his shaky hands, he was so afraid he might nick him, but he didn't. Once free, Jody threw his arms around him. George could feel that he'd sweated through his shirt.

He whispered in Jody's ear again. "I want you to jump out the window and run to Brad's house. He's waiting for you."

Jody shook his head. "I'm not leaving you guys. . . ." He climbed off the bed. But his legs must have fallen asleep, because they suddenly buckled underneath him. George caught him before he tripped, and then he helped his son to the window. "I'll be okay, Dad," Jody whispered. But he still leaned on him. "Don't ask me to run out on you guys. I want to help. . . ."

George hesitated. "All right, you wait outside here. I'll lower Steffie down to you in a few minutes. Then take her to Brad's. I'll get Jessie out, and we'll meet you there. Understand?"

Jody nodded. "I love you, Dad."

Giving him a kiss on the forehead, George helped him out the window, and then down to the patio chair. From there, Jody hopped to the ground. But his legs gave out on him again, and he stumbled, like a paratrooper landing. Jody seemed to roll with it. He quickly pulled himself up and nodded at his father again.

Moving to the bedroom door, George peeked toward the kitchen. The young man stood in front of Jessie, holding both phones again, one to his own ear, one to Jessie's. "George, this is Jessie," she was saying into the kitchen extension. "Are you there? Pick up . . ."

George darted down the hall to Stephanie's room. He saw that she'd wet herself, and it incensed him. He just wanted to kill that smug bastard for doing this to his children. He took a few breaths, then moved toward Steffie's bed. She seemed to be sleeping.

As George started to bend over her, Stephanie suddenly gaped up at him and tried to cry out. "Quiet, sweetie," he whispered in her ear. "Please, hush. I'm going to cut you loose and take you into Jody's room. But you mustn't make a sound."

George paused for a moment. Jessie had stopped talking. He heard footsteps. The young man was coming toward the children's bedrooms.

Creeping back to Stephanie's door, George stood with his back to the wall. He had the knife ready.

It sounded like the man had stepped into Jody's room, but George wasn't sure. He glanced over at Stephanie and put his finger over his lips.

Wide-eyed, she stared at him and suddenly became very still. Then a shadow swept over her. She knew enough to look away from her father—and at the man standing in her doorway.

George remained perfectly still.

The shadow moved away, and the footsteps retreated. The young man was headed toward the living room now. George heard a click, like a door opening or closing.

He hurried back to Stephanie. He gingerly cut the tape around her little wrists and ankles, and then lifted her off the bed. It seemed cruel, but he kept the tape over her mouth for now. He couldn't risk her crying out again as he smuggled her into Jody's room. Carrying her out to the hallway, he stroked her hair.

He didn't hear anyone talking in the kitchen. Peering around the corner, he saw only Jessie. Tied to the kitchen chair, she struggled with the tape binding her wrists in back of her, but to no avail. George wondered where the hell the man with the sunglasses had gone.

Ducking into Jody's room, he carried Steffie to the window. He looked outside, and his heart sank. Jody wasn't there.

Whimpering, Stephanie clung to him. He couldn't drop her out the window. It was too high for her, and she was terrified.

Suddenly, the kitchen door slammed.

George swiveled around. He skulked back to Jody's bedroom doorway and glanced toward the kitchen again. For a moment, he couldn't breathe. It was as if someone had just punched him in the gut.

He saw the young man holding Jody up by his back collar. Blood trickled from a gash on the corner of Jody's forehead. He seemed dazed, barely able to stand. The young man pressed a gun to his ear.

George was paralyzed.

Even with those dark glasses on, it was obvious the man was staring right at him. "Hi, Daddy," he said. "Look who was trying to run away. I think I heard his skull crack when I hit the little bastard." He smirked. "So, do I get a reward for finding him?"

A flat-edged shovel was wedged under the handle of the fallout shelter door.

That big, heavy door muffled Amelia's voice. "Who's out there? Karen? Please, somebody . . ."

With her hands tied behind her, Karen stood in the Faradays' cold, clammy cellar. Among the clutter, there was a washer and dryer pushed against the wall, a bicycle, and some boating equipment. Karen noticed a drain in the middle of the concrete floor, and cobwebs on the exposed pipes running along the low ceiling.

Annabelle kicked the shovel aside, and it hit the floor with a loud clang. On the other side of the door, Amelia suddenly fell silent.

Karen felt woozy from the blow to her head earlier, but she fought the nausea and dizziness. She furtively pulled at the cord around her wrists while Annabelle was busy with the door. The hinges groaned as she opened it.

Amelia stood by a cot in the grimy little room. Her hair had been cut in a short shag style identical to her sister's. Despite the blanket wrapped around her, she was trembling. She wore the same T-shirt and flannel pajama bottoms she'd had on last night. In her hand, she held a jagged piece of glass. Dumbstruck, she stared at Annabelle.

For a moment, neither one said a thing.

"Are you going to pretend you don't know me?" Annabelle asked finally.

Amelia slowly shook her head. Clearly, she couldn't comprehend what she was seeing. She didn't move.

Karen kept tugging at the cord around her wrists. The skin there started to chafe and burn.

"Tell her who I am, Karen!" Annabelle barked. She suddenly grabbed Karen's arm and jerked her forward.

"Amelia. . . . honey, this is your twin sister, Annabelle," she said carefully. "You haven't seen her since you were four, not since before the Faradays adopted you. Do you—do you recall telling me that you often talked into the mirror when you were a little girl? You—"

"You have to remember me," Annabelle cut in, her voice choked with emotion. "Just look at me, Amelia. I'm your sister, your *real* sister. Those others, they weren't your real family."

Amelia stared at her. "My God, *you* killed them, didn't you?" she whispered.

Annabelle let go of Karen's arm. "I did it to bring us closer together," she said. "You needed to feel what it's like to have absolutely no one. That's what happened to me after you left, after you forgot about me. You need to feel that *firsthand*, so we can be the same again."

Karen edged back from her again. She kept pulling at the binding around her wrists. She felt it loosening.

"You killed my parents," Amelia whispered, squinting at her twin, "and Collin and Aunt Ina. . . ." She still had the piece of glass in her shaky grasp, as if ready to strike. "I *felt* it when you killed them. I thought it was me. . . ."

"I'm closer to you than any of them ever were," Annabelle said. "And we can be sisters again, Amelia. We'll be there for each other. You really don't have a choice. There's no one left."

"My God," Amelia whispered, tears in her eyes. "You shot Shane, too. In a boat. I saw it. I thought it was a nightmare. Oh, Jesus, he's dead, isn't he?"

Annabelle nodded. "I had to. It makes us closer. My boyfriend will die tonight, too. It's one more thing we'll share. We don't need them if we have each other. Don't you see?"

Suddenly, she grabbed Karen again, and yanked her toward the fallout shelter doorway. Karen stumbled onto the dirty, concrete floor. Annabelle pulled her up by her hair.

"Stop that!" Amelia cried. "Stop hurting her!"

"Karen, make her understand!"

Trembling, she knelt in the doorway. She frantically tugged at the cord around her wrist. She could almost squeeze her hand past the knot. "Your sister wants you to start someplace new with her. She killed that police detective. The police think you did it. They'll probably blame you for my death, too. Annabelle's making it so you have no one else to turn to except her."

Annabelle rolled back her sleeve and pressed the revolver to Karen's head. "And I'll look after you, Amelia, I promise," she said. "I've forgiven you for turning your back on me. You'll forgive me, too. You'll have to. I'm the only family or friend you have left."

Tears streaming down her face, Amelia stared at her twin sister. "That mark on the back of your wrist," she murmured. "I felt it when that happened. Someone burned you. . . ."

"Our father put a lit cigar out on me. You felt it, too?" Amelia nodded.

"See?" Annabelle said, with a tiny smile. "We feel each other's pain."

Karen tried not to squirm as the cord scraped a layer of skin off her knuckles. Still, at last her hands were free. But she kept both hands clasped in back of her. The cord dangled off one wrist.

"Please, Annabelle, put the gun down," Amelia said, finally. "You don't have to do this. Let her go. Karen's my friend."

"I know she's your friend," Annabelle whispered, nodding. "That's exactly why she has to die."

"Wait. Look at me," Amelia said, imploring her. "Do you *really* feel what I'm feeling right now?"

Annabelle nodded.

"Okay," she said. Then she slashed the piece of glass across her own hand.

Annabelle let out a shriek. The gun flew out of her grasp.

It happened so fast, Karen wasn't sure if Annabelle had dropped the gun in a moment of panic or if she had actually felt the glass, too. Karen only knew that the revolver dropped on the floor right in front of her. She dove on it.

All at once, Annabelle was on top of her, frantically clawing at her, struggling to retrieve the weapon. Karen fought back. She wouldn't let go of the revolver. With her elbow, she smacked Annabelle on the side of her head, but the young woman was relentless. She tugged at the revolver and scratched at Karen's hands. Suddenly the gun went off.

An earsplitting shot echoed in the tiny gray room.

* * *

Jody went limp and fell to the kitchen floor at the man's feet.

George quickly put Stephanie down and started toward his son.

"No way!" the man said in a loud voice, glaring at him from behind the dark glasses. He had his .45 trained on Jody's crumpled body. "First you show me the safe, then you can tend to the kiddies."

Crouching down, George carefully pried the duct tape from Stephanie's mouth. He watched her eyes tear up with the pain. Once he pulled the tape off, she gasped for air, and then started crying. She threw her arms around his neck. "Daddy, Daddy . . ." was all she could say.

The young man grabbed Jody by the collar, then dragged him across the kitchen floor as if he were a bag of laundry. Then he dumped him at Jessie's feet. George could see Jody was still breathing. But he was afraid his son might have a concussion.

"We need to get him to a doctor," Jessie said.

"Shut the fuck up!" the man snapped. He turned to George, and pointed the gun at him. "I want to see where this safe is," he said. "C'mon, show me, and bring the little brat with you."

"It's in the living room," George lied. He took one more look at Jody, still breathing, but not moving a muscle. The blood from the gash on his forehead had trickled down to his jaw.

"*Where* in the living room?" the man pressed. "I've been all over this dump."

"Around this corner," George said, shielding Stephanie's eyes from the sight of Mrs. Bidwell's corpse on the sofa. Steffie cried softly. Her whole body was trembling. George patted her on the back. "When I say *go*, run as fast as you can out the front door," he whispered. "When I say *go*. Okay, honey?"

She sniffed, then nodded her head.

"Good girl," George said under his breath.

"So where is it, man?"

George nodded to an antique oval mirror on the living room wall. It was 24 by 18 inches, with a very ornate, pounded-tin frame.

"The mirror?" the young man said. "Shit, I already looked behind there, asshole."

"Well, then you weren't looking very carefully," George replied.

"Show me."

George patted Steffie on the back again. "I need to put you down for a minute, sweetie," he said, setting her on her feet. "Be a good girl, and remember what I told you."

Stephanie clung to his leg.

Swallowing hard, George reached for the mirror on the wall. "The money's not in the wall, it's in the back of the mirror," he lied. He glanced back at the man with the sunglasses, and then lifted the mirror off the wall. It was lighter than it looked, only a few pounds. "There's about six thousand dollars back here, sort of an emergency fund. It's yours. Just take it and *go*. Do you hear me? Just *go!*"

All at once, Stephanie scurried toward the front door.

The young man turned his gun on her.

He didn't see that behind the mirror frame, there was nothing. He didn't see George swinging the mirror at him with all his might.

A shot rang out. The young man howled in pain as George hit him in the face with the mirror. There was an explosion of glass.

Squeezing his eyes shut, George turned his head away for a second.

When he opened his eyes again, Stephanie was gone, and the front door was open. The .45 lay on the carpet amid shards of reflective glass.

In a stupor, the young man stared at George. His sunglasses had been knocked off his face. His eyes were listless. Blood dripped from several little bits of broken mirrored glass embedded in his face. One large piece was stuck in his neck. In a daze, he pried it out. Blood gushed from the fatal wound, cascading down the front of his white shirt, tie, and the shiny black jacket.

He remained standing, looking stunned.

George heard the sirens from police cars coming up the street. He realized Jody's friend, Brad, must have called the police. The searchlights and beams from the red strobes poured through the windows. For a few seconds, the same light danced off the mirrored fragments in the young man's face.

Then he collapsed dead on the floor.

Through the sheer window curtains, George could see four police cars pulling in front of the house. One policeman ran across the yard and scooped up Stephanie.

George started toward the kitchen, and stopped dead.

His forehead still bleeding, Jody stood near the kitchen counter with a tired smile on his face. He staggered toward his father, and threw his arms around him.

Dazed, George embraced his son. He glanced over at Jessie, a bit unsteady on her feet, slowly making her way into the living room. George realized Jody must have untied her. He kissed the top of Jody's head. "God, you—you sure had me fooled," he murmured. "I thought you were practically dead."

"Me, too," Jody said, with a weak laugh.

"We still need to get you to a doctor," George said. With an arm around his son, George dug the cell phone out of his pocket. He checked for messages. There were two Jessie had left on the home phone and two more from that sheriff in Salem. No one else.

"Are you calling Karen?" Jessie asked.

He nodded. "It's been nearly two hours."

It rang and rang. No one picked up. It didn't even go to her voice mail.

Jessie gave him an apprehensive look. He just shook his head at her.

When he'd last talked to Karen, she'd been on her way to meet Amelia at the restaurant near the lake house.

George stayed on the line. He didn't want to hang up just yet, not even as the three of them started toward the front door.

Jessie paused for a moment and looked down at something on the carpet amid the mirrored fragments. Frowning, she kicked it out of her way and then moved on.

The bent, broken sunglasses skittered across the floor.

Chapter Twenty-five

Breathless, Karen ran along the water's edge.

Her head was still throbbing, and her lungs burned, but she pressed on toward Helene Sumner's house. She could see the lights on inside her cottage farther up the beach.

She'd left Annabelle Schlessinger in that grimy, little fall-out shelter with a bullet in her stomach. Annabelle's black knit top had been soaked with blood by the time Amelia had staggered back down to the cellar with several dishtowels from the kitchen. They'd managed to move Annabelle to the cot, and pulled off her blood-sodden sweater. Karen had told her to lie still and keep the towels pressed against the wound.

But Annabelle wouldn't stop screaming and squirming. Her shrill cries echoed off the walls of the little gray chamber. Her legs were curled up toward her stomach as if some shifting in her organs had locked them there. Pale and trembling, she seemed very afraid. "Don't let me die in here!" she cried several times. She'd lost a lot of blood, and Karen noticed her breathing was shallow. She wasn't sure about her chances. At the same time, she couldn't help wondering if

Annabelle was stronger than she let on. Was it an act to throw them off guard?

Karen remembered something Naomi Rankin had told her about Annabelle always being the weaker twin. Amelia was the stronger one.

The cut across the palm of Amelia's hand wasn't too deep. Karen wrapped a wet dishtowel around her hand to slow the bleeding. Amelia admitted the searing pain in her stomach—exactly where her sister had been shot—was far more severe.

She promised to look after her twin sister. "Helene Sumner's house is closer than Danny's Diner," she told Karen, catching her breath as they paused in the fallout shelter's doorway. "You're better off calling the paramedics from there."

Furtively, Karen tried to pass the revolver to her, but Amelia shook her head. "I won't need it," Amelia whispered. "She won't try anything."

"How can you be so sure?"

"Because," she said with a pale smile, "I can *feel* it, Karen."

"Just the same," Karen murmured. "I'll leave this upstairs on the kitchen counter. You haven't been through the living room yet, have you?"

Amelia shook her head. "No, why?"

"Don't go in there if you can help it," Karen said. "I'll explain later."

Coiled up on the bed, Annabelle let out another shriek. "Hurry, goddamn it! I'm bleeding to death!"

"Watch her like a hawk," Karen whispered, giving Amelia's shoulder a pat. She raced up the basement stairs. She left the revolver on the kitchen counter, and then ran out of the lake house.

That had been only five minutes ago, and yet it seemed like forever.

Helene's dog started barking as Karen banged on the

front door of her cottage. "Ms. Sumner!" Karen cried. "Ms. Sumner, I need to use your phone! Please! It's an emergency!"

The old woman answered the door with a robe on and a rifle in her hand. It took her a moment before she seemed to recognize Karen from that afternoon. She held her collie by the collar while Karen, frazzled and out of breath, asked if she could use her phone to call the police. "There's been a shooting at the Faradays' cabin," she explained. "Somebody's hurt."

"My goodness," Helene murmured. She pulled her dog aside and cleared the doorway. "C'mon, Abby, move it. Come in, come in. I thought I heard a shot about fifteen minutes ago. The phone's right there in the kitchen. . . ."

Helene's kitchen had a huge old-fashioned stove, a blue Formica-top breakfast table with three mismatched chairs, and the only working telephone in about a mile. It was a yellow, wall-mounted phone with a dial instead of a touch-tone pad. Karen called the police on it.

The 911 operator said they'd be at the Faradays' house with the paramedics in fifteen minutes.

"Is it Amelia who was hurt?" Helene asked, once Karen hung up.

With a hand still on the receiver, Karen shook her head. "No, it's—a relative of Amelia's. Could I make another call? It's long distance, but I'll pay you back."

Helene nodded. "Go ahead."

Karen dialed George's cell phone number. She nervously tugged at the phone cord and counted the ring tones. On the fourth ring, he picked up: "Hello?"

"George, it's Karen," she said, the words rushing out. "Is everyone okay there?"

"Yes, yes, we're all fine," he said, sounding just as anxious as she was. "Thank God you called. I've been so worried. How are you? How's Amelia?"

Relieved, Karen just wanted to sink down in one of the chairs at Helene's breakfast table. But there was no time. She quickly explained to George what had happened. "I'm not sure if Annabelle's going to pull through," she said.

"Well, her boyfriend didn't make it," George remarked. "Just a second . . ."

Karen heard him talking with someone on the other end. Then he got back on the line. "We're here at the West Seattle police station," he said. "My house is a mess. We can't go back there tonight, and Jessie says all the hotels in town are booked. She thought you wouldn't mind putting up Jody, Steffie, and me for the night."

"Not at all," she said. "There's plenty of room. Please, make yourselves comfortable. Jessie has a key."

"Thanks. Think you and Amelia will make it home tonight?"

"It might be a few hours, yet," Karen said, still catching her breath. "We'll have a lot to explain to the police here."

"I'm probably in for the long haul myself," George said. "Salem's finest have quite a few questions for me. If I make it to your house before you and Amelia, I'll wait up for you."

"That would be really nice, George," she said with a little smile. "Listen, I should get back to Amelia and her sister."

"Please, be careful, Karen," he said.

"See you later—at my house."

She hung up, and then started to dig into her purse. "Thank you, Ms. Sumner. Do you think five dollars will cover it?"

Frowning, Helene shook her head. "Put your money away, for goodness sakes. Do you need any medical supplies? I have some bandages and hydrogen peroxide. . . ."

"I think we're okay," Karen replied, heading for the door.

"What exactly happened?" she asked. "Did I just hear you say something about Amelia's *sister*?"

"I'll explain it to you later, okay?" Karen said, still frazzled. She opened the door. "I really need to get back. Thank you again, Ms. Sumner."

But Karen stopped abruptly. In the distance, she heard a strange pop—like a firecracker going off. Helene's dog let out a yelp. The old woman put a hand over her heart. "My goodness, there it is again."

Karen gazed at her and blinked.

"That's the same sound as before," Helene explained.

"Oh, no," Karen whispered. She turned and started in the direction of the Faradays' house. At first, she just took a few cautious steps, but then she started moving faster.

"I wouldn't go back there!" Helene called. She held on to her dog's collar to keep her from chasing after Karen. "Miss, I wouldn't go there! That was a gunshot! Wait for the police!"

But Karen didn't stop. She didn't hear her. She was thinking about Amelia.

And she was running for her life.

Ten minutes before Frank Carlisle's old revolver was fired for a second time that night, Amelia had been standing in the doorway of the fallout shelter. She'd watched over her twin sister, curled up on the cot with a bloody dishtowel on her stomach. Shivering in just her bra and jeans, Annabelle looked so vulnerable. There were patches of blood smeared on her exposed pale, creamy skin. Her every breath seemed like a struggle. "I'm cold," she whispered, her teeth chattering.

"I know, I'm cold too," Amelia replied, wincing as she clutched her own stomach. The cut on her hand was starting to sting, too. She wondered if her sister also felt it.

Amelia had bled all over that itchy old blanket when she'd slashed the palm of her own hand. She knew there were extra blankets up in the bedrooms. She'd told Karen earlier she didn't think Annabelle would try anything. But she wasn't so sure anymore. She noticed the large piece of glass still on the floor beside Annabelle's shoes. Amelia and Karen had removed her brown suede flats in an effort to make her more comfortable.

Amelia quickly retrieved the shard of glass. "I'll get you a clean blanket," she said, finally.

"Thanks," Annabelle whispered. It seemed like an effort as she lifted her head to look at her.

Amelia backed away from the fallout shelter, but then she hesitated. She had a bad feeling about leaving Annabelle unguarded. She didn't know if it was her own intuition or if she'd read her sister's thoughts. But suddenly she didn't trust her.

"I'm sorry," Amelia murmured, with one hand on the thick, heavy door. She pushed it shut.

"Amelia, no!" her sister cried, her voice muffled.

Amelia set down the piece of glass. Then she grabbed a square-edged, short-handled shovel from the floor, and propped it under the door handle. "I'll be right back," she called to her sister. She had a déjà vu sense about this moment, about talking to someone locked in a bomb shelter. Amelia didn't remember ever experiencing this before—certainly not here in the basement of the lake house. She wondered if something similar had ever happened to Annabelle.

Ascending the basement stairs, she felt slightly winded and dizzy. Between the pain in her gut, the slash across her hand, and everything else, it was a wonder she hadn't fainted yet. In the kitchen, Amelia went to the sink, and slurped some cold water from the faucet. She splashed her face, and felt a little better. Then she grabbed the revolver off the counter.

Annabelle's purse, a large leather satchel, sat on the

kitchen table. Amelia peeked inside it to make sure her sister didn't keep a gun of her own in there.

Annabelle didn't have a revolver, but she had a blackjack and a hunting knife. Amelia glanced around the kitchen for a place to hide them. She finally stashed them in the refrigerator inside the crisper drawer. She dumped the purse's remaining contents onto the tabletop to make sure she hadn't missed anything. Amid the junk, she noticed Annabelle's wallet: her lipstick and compact; several loose bills, some twenties among them; chewing gum; and a beautiful black onyx ring.

It was Shane's ring. He'd loved it. That ring had belonged to his grandfather.

Amelia felt a pang in her gut, and she started to cry. Clutching the ring in her wounded hand, she wandered toward the living room. She'd forgotten Karen's warning not to go beyond the kitchen. She hadn't been prepared to see all the dried blood on the wall behind the rocking chair. Another large bloodstain marred the carpet. In both cases, she knew whose blood she was looking at, because she'd seen it happen through her sister's eyes. She'd seen Annabelle murder her mom and dad, and Ina, as well as Collin, and Shane.

Amelia tearfully gazed at Shane's ring again, then she kissed it and tucked it inside the pocket of her flannel pajama bottoms.

Now the only thing she held was the revolver.

Her sister knew about guns. But Amelia didn't. She'd never really fired a gun before. She'd only experienced it secondhand.

Amelia forced herself to go halfway up the stairs, until she saw the bloodstains on the wall by where Annabelle had shot her mother. Almost in a trance, she walked back down the steps and out the front door.

She needed a practice shot. She didn't want to screw it up

when she did it for real. Though barefoot, and dressed in only her pink T-shirt and flannel pajama bottoms, Amelia barely felt the cool night air whipping at her. She didn't even notice that the ground was wet and cold, and hundreds of stars were out tonight. All she thought about was showing Annabelle that she could kill, too. She picked out a target— a pine tree about thirty feet from the house. Aiming the revolver at a branch, she squeezed the trigger. On the branch, there was a small explosion of bark, wood, and pine needles. She felt a jolt in her hand, and the sound made her jump.

But she hadn't dropped the gun.

The shot still echoed across the lake.

She could do this, Amelia told herself. It was easy.

She turned around and headed back inside the house. She would tell Karen and the police that Annabelle had suddenly attacked her. They'd believe her, too. Amelia couldn't help smiling a tiny bit. She was already thinking like her sister.

With the gun in her hand, she passed through the living room, and then into the kitchen. Once again, she glanced over at Annabelle's purse and its contents strewn on the kitchen table. She wondered if she'd missed anything, perhaps some jewelry belonging to her mother or Ina.

All at once, she started to feel faint again. She couldn't get a decent breath, and she was deathly cold. The only thing keeping her going was her anger. Amelia tried to ignore the signals, the strange feeling that her sister was already slipping away.

She didn't notice anything familiar amid the debris from Annabelle's purse. She opened up the wallet, and saw some fake ID's and credit cards that were obviously not hers. Amelia didn't recognize any of the names on the cards.

She found a photograph in the wallet, creased and worn as if it had been carried around for a long, long time. It was a picture of two identical, dark-haired little girls in overalls, holding hands and smiling at the camera. The color was so faded, and the images nearly washed out. But Amelia remembered those overalls were a very pretty shade of green.

She remembered, and she started to cry again.

Karen ran as fast as she could.

Somewhere along the way, she'd stumbled over a tree root and hit the ground hard. She'd banged her knee, but dragged herself up and relentlessly pressed on toward the sound of that gunshot. Her throat had gone dry, and it hurt every time she tried to breathe. Still, she didn't slow down.

She kept hoping to hear the police sirens. But there was nothing except Helene's dog barking in the distance. She couldn't even see the Faradays' house yet.

Karen kept wondering who had fired the gun. At this point, it could have been either Amelia or Annabelle. And at this point, she was probably already too late.

All of a sudden, she stumbled again and hit the damp sand. It knocked the wind out of her. Pulling herself up once more, her hand brushed against a piece of weathered driftwood. It was almost the size of a baseball ball—with a few rounded-off knobs where branches had once been. Karen picked it up off the ground, and then caught her breath for a moment. She wondered if this piece of wood was anything like the plank Annabelle had used to bash in Collin Faraday's skull.

Clutching the makeshift club tightly in her fist, Karen hurried toward the Faradays' house. She could see it in the distance now. The lights were on in the living room and the front hall. As she came closer, Karen could see the open front door and the silhouette of someone sitting on the front step. "Amelia?" she called.

Shivering and pale, she'd thrown a blanket over her shoulders. Even closer, Karen recognized the flannel pajama bottoms. She noticed the bloodstained dishtowel wrapped around her hand.

But Karen abruptly stopped when she saw the revolver in her other hand. "Amelia, did you—did you fire the gun?"

Tears in her eyes, she nodded.

"Did Annabelle attack you?" Karen asked.

"No. I didn't fire it at anybody," she replied with a tremor in her voice. "Annabelle—she's dead. I left her alone for a few minutes, and when I went back down there, she was dead." She let out a little cry. "I never had a chance to talk with her—to understand. . . ."

Karen sat down beside her on the front stoop. She didn't know what to say. She just gently patted her back and let her cry.

Hearing a noise behind them, Karen glanced over her shoulder. She didn't see anyone in the doorway, but she noticed some drops of blood on the floor. There was a trail leading out to the front stoop, and it wasn't old, dried blood, either. It was fresh.

Earlier, they'd managed to suppress the bleeding from the cut across Amelia's palm. Mystified, Karen glanced at the dishtowel around her hand. Then she glanced down toward the stoop at the small puddle of blood. Another drop hit the puddle. And it wasn't coming from Amelia's hand.

It wasn't coming from Amelia at all.

Karen gasped. She noticed that nearly all the color had drained from the 19-year-old's face, and sweat beaded on her forehead. But she was smirking. And she had the gun aimed at Karen. Even with a bullet in her gut, and sitting in a puddle of her own blood, Annabelle was still smiling.

At that moment, Karen figured she was as good as dead.

A shadow suddenly passed over them both. Karen glanced back in time to see Amelia in the doorway. Amelia raised the square-edged, short-handled shovel, and brought the flat end of it crashing down on her sister's head. It made a hollow ping as it cracked against her skull. Annabelle let out a cry, and the gun went off. A spray of dirt exploded from the ground near Karen's feet.

Annabelle lurched forward and toppled onto the ground. The revolver flew out of her grasp. Stunned, she rolled over on her back. The blanket fell aside, exposing the gaping wound in her stomach, and two blood-soaked dishtowels.

Amelia warily stood over Annabelle, as if her sister were a wounded rabid dog. She kept the shovel in her hands, ready to strike her again if necessary. She was shivering in just her oversized T-shirt and nothing else.

Karen gaped up at her. In the distance, she heard the police sirens.

"I left her alone for a few minutes," Amelia said, catching her breath. "I thought about killing her, and then suddenly, I started to remember everything. I felt sorry for her. So I went down there again, bringing her a blanket, and she clubbed me in the head with her shoe."

Sprawled out on the ground in front of them, Annabelle laughed. But then she started to cough, and blood sprayed out of her mouth. She coughed again, and more blood spewed out. Suddenly, she couldn't seem to get a breath. A look of panic swept over her ashen face. She seemed to be choking on her own blood.

Karen started to get to her feet. But Amelia moved more quickly. She tossed aside the shovel, and hurried to her sister's side. She held Annabelle's head in her lap.

Annabelle reached up and touched Amelia's cheek. Her every gasp was a death rattle.

Amelia gently smoothed back her sister's hair. "It's okay, Annie," she whispered.

Karen watched, and didn't say a word as Annabelle Schlessinger struggled for her last few breaths. Amelia's twin listlessly stared up at the starry sky. Then her jaw slowly dropped and one last breath escaped from her mouth.

Amelia kept stroking her hair for another minute. "There now, Annie," she whispered. "There now. . . ."

The wail of the sirens became louder and louder. The headlights and red strobes illuminated the forest behind the lake house.

Amelia didn't have any tears in her eyes when she covered her twin sister's face with the blanket. She finally stood up, and then wandered over to Karen. She wrapped her arms around her and dropped her head on Karen's shoulder.

"I don't feel the pain anymore," she whispered.

Epilogue

Karen opened her eyes as the squad car turned down her street. To her amazement, there were no TV news vans or police cars parked in front of her house, no reporters or on-lookers. All was quiet on her block at 6:40 that morning.

Both she and Amelia had nodded off intermittently in the back seat of the patrol car for the last forty-five minutes. This was their fourth ride in the back of a police car since leaving the Lake Wenatchee house so many hours ago.

It had been during that first trip—to the Wenatchee Police Station—that Karen told Amelia about her biological father and mother, and about something Amelia had wanted to know for a long, long time. The cops and the ambulance only used their sirens when other vehicles or pedestrians were around, but their red flashers remained on for the whole trip. "Back when we had our very first session, you men-tioned something to me," Karen said during one of those quiet periods. Amelia clutched her hand. The ambulance, carrying Amelia's dead twin was in front of them, and the red strobe illuminated the back of the police car. "You men-

tioned that when some of those other therapists tried to hypnotize you for information about your childhood, what you
wanted most of all was to remember the name of that nice
neighbor, the one with the playhouse."

Amelia nodded. "Yes, I still feel that way."

"His name was Clay Spalding," Karen said, smiling.
"And he was a good man."

Two policemen from Moses Lake came to the downtown
Wenatchee station at around midnight. Karen made certain
to set the record straight with them about Clay. She knew
Naomi Rankin had always held her head high at work and
around town. She'd never been ashamed of her friendship
with Clay. And now, people in town would understand why.

A doctor was called in to patch up both Amelia and Karen.
Amelia didn't need stitches in her hand, but the doctor ban-
daged it up. Karen received an ice pack for the bump forming on her head, where Annabelle had hit her with the
blackjack. They both got a dose of Tylenol, too.

Between the two of them, they drank about a gallon of
bad coffee in the police station while answering scores of
questions over and over again. The Wenatchee station was
surrounded by reporters, TV news crews, and spectators.
The precinct had become a hub of activity with e-mails, faxes
and phone calls coming in and going out to Moses Lake,
Salem, Seattle, and Issaquah.

There was a TV on in the officers' lounge. It was tuned to
CNN. They'd made the national news. Karen and Amelia
caught a brief clip of George being interviewed. He stood by
the West Seattle Police Station's main entrance. He looked
tired and haggard, but still handsome. Off-camera reporters
held microphones in front of him. "No, I don't think I'm a
hero or anything," he said, shaking his head. "My friend,
Jessie Shriver, my son, Jody, and my daughter, Stephanie—
they're the real heroes. And I want to thank Jody's friend

Brad Reece for all his help. He was really there for us. And
most of all," George went on, "I want to thank Karen Carlisle. She's a friend of my dear niece, Amelia Faraday. More
than anyone, Karen helped save my family."

By dawn, Karen heard that Salem police and local FBI,
working through the night at the old Schlessinger ranch, had
so far excavated seven bodies from shallow graves on the
property. They planned to continue digging through the day.
They were also reexamining missing-person cases, all young
women in the Salem and Moses Lake areas, as well as in
Pasco, where Duane Lee Savitt lived until his death in 1993.

Exhausted, yet wired from so much coffee, Karen and
Amelia were taken by helicopter to Issaquah. Once they
landed, they had another trip in the back of a cop car to
Cougar Mountain Wildland Park, where Karen pointed out
for the police the path she'd used in her fruitless search for
Detective Russ Koehler's body.

With Karen's assistance, and in the light of dawn, the
local police had better luck than she'd had two nights before.
They found Koehler's picked-over, half-buried corpse in less
than an hour.

Karen suggested they check to determine if he'd been
shot with the same gun used to kill Shane. She had no doubt
that Annabelle had pulled the trigger each time.

Someone had tipped off the press about the Cougar
Mountain Park expedition; so the place was swarmed with
TV cameras and news vans by the time Karen and Amelia
were whisked out of there.

That had been forty-five minutes ago, and Karen had expected more of the same as they approached her house.

"I shouldn't jinx it by saying this," she murmured, waking
up from her nap in the back seat of the police car. "But I
can't believe there aren't any reporters here."

"Well, the newspeople got to sleep sometime, I guess,"

replied the cop behind the wheel. "Enjoy the peace and quiet while you can."

Amelia was practically sleepwalking as they started up the front walkway together. Karen kept an arm around her, almost holding her up. Before they even reached the front stoop, Jessie opened the door and Rufus scurried out. Whining, he excitedly nudged Karen's leg with his snout over and over. She petted him and scratched him behind the ears. Amelia petted him, too. His tail wagging, Rufus seemed to lap it up. Only twenty-four hours before, he'd growled and bared his teeth at her twin. Somehow he knew the difference. He let out a happy yelp.

"Hush, Rufus!" Jessie whispered. She wore a blue sweat suit, part of the limited wardrobe she still kept at the house from the days when she'd looked after Karen's father. Considering what she'd been through the night before, Jessie looked surprisingly rested and fresh.

"Well, you two are a sight for these sore ones," she whispered, waving them in. Then she put her finger to her lips. "The kids are asleep in the second guest room. George got in at three this morning. He tried to wait up for you, but conked out on the living room sofa."

She gave Karen a long hug. "Oh, sweetie, thank God you're okay," she said, patting her back. "Did you girls get anything to eat?"

"Doughnuts," Karen murmured. "I think we need sleep more than anything."

"Your dad caught you on the Channel Five Sunrise News in the lounge at the rest home," Jessie said. "He phoned here just a few minutes ago. You might want to call him before you hit the sheets, let him know you're all right."

Jessie broke away and led Amelia inside the house. "Poor thing, you're asleep on your feet, just like a horse. I changed the sheets in the guest room for you. There's even a sound machine in there. You can sleep as long as you want. I'll try to keep the kids quiet."

From the doorway, Karen watched Jessie and Amelia go up the stairs. With a sigh, she sat down on the front stoop, and pulled her cell phone out of her purse. She had Sandpoint View Convalescent Home on her speed dial. When they answered at the front desk, Karen asked to be connected to the lounge. She recognized the voice of the nurse on duty there.

"Hi, Lugene, it's Karen," she said quietly. "Is my dad there in the TV room?"

"He sure is, Karen. We've been seeing you on the news. You'll have to give out autographs next time you're here. How are you doing? Are you okay?"

"Yeah, but I'm pooped."

"Well, I'll get Frank. I know he's eager to talk to you. By the way, it looks like it's one of his good days, Karen."

While Karen waited for her father to get on the line, Rufus wandered over and set his head on her knee.

"Is this my girl?" her father said on the other end. "My famous daughter?"

"Hi, Poppy," she replied, patting Rufus's head. "I understand you saw me on the news."

"Are you all right? Are you home yet?"

"I'm sitting on the front step right now with Rufus. I'm pretty tuckered out."

"Jessie said that good-looking fellow who was on the news is staying there with his kids. Sounds like you have a full house there. It's been a while since that's happened."

Karen smiled wistfully. "You're right, Poppy. It's been a long time."

"Must feel good," he said. "Well, I should skedaddle. I have to get dressed. I don't like going to breakfast in my

bathrobe like some of these folks here. We're having blue-
berry pancakes this morning. They make very tasty blue-
berry pancakes here. Get some sleep now, honey. Okay?"

"Okay, Poppy. Have a good breakfast, and I'll see you
soon."

"My angel," he said, before hanging up.

Karen waited until Rufus trotted inside, then she quietly
closed and locked the front door after him. She heard the
shower running upstairs, and knew it was Amelia. Though
she felt grimy, Karen wasn't certain which she needed more,
a bed or a bath.

Peeking into the darkened living room, she saw George
curled up on her sofa. His shoes were off, and the sports coat
he must have used to cover himself had slid down past his
hip. Karen went to the hall closet and retrieved her dad's old
robe, the one she still used to cover herself when napping on
that same couch. She tiptoed into the living room and gently
draped the robe over George. With his slight beard-stubble
and that sweet, peaceful expression, he looked so handsome
while he slept.

Then his eyes opened, and he took hold of her hand. "I
tried to wait up," he said with a sleepy smile. "Are you okay,
Karen?"

Hovering over him, she nodded. "Fine, just tired."

He squinted at her. "Jody has a bump on his forehead in
the exact same place as you do. Sure you're okay?" He
squeezed her hand.

She nodded again.

"Jessie says you and I need to go out to dinner soon and
discuss how much overtime we owe her for yesterday and
today. I think we should, don't you?"

Karen smiled and nodded once more.

He brought her hand to his face, and then kissed it.
"Thank you for my family, Karen."

* * *

"Karen?" Amelia called from the guest room.

She was just emerging from the bathroom. A waft of steam drifted out the doorway after her. Karen wore her terry-cloth robe and had a towel wrapped around her head. She'd decided to shower before turning in, and was glad now that she had. It felt as if she'd washed away everything from the last twenty-four grueling hours.

Jessie had ducked into Karen's dad's bedroom for a cat-nap. She planned to go shopping in an hour so she could fix breakfast for everybody—bacon, eggs and waffles, the works.

Karen had thought she was the only one still awake in the house.

"Karen, is that you?" Amelia called softly.

The guest room door was ajar. Karen pushed it open and looked in on Amelia.

The shades were drawn, and the sound machine was on. Amelia sat up in bed, wearing one of Karen's T-shirts. Her dark hair was in tangles from her shower twenty minutes before.

"Can't you sleep?" Karen asked, padding into the room. She sat down on the edge of the bed.

"I was just lying here, thinking," Amelia whispered over the sounds of waves and seagulls. "It'll be nice to spend some time later today with Uncle George, and Jody and Steffie. Ever since Collin died, I haven't been able to really look them in the eyes. As much as I tried and you tried, I couldn't quite get over the feeling that I'd killed him. Now I know the truth. After so many months, it'll be good to look my uncle and cousins in the eyes again."

Karen reached over and smoothed back Amelia's tangled hair.

Amelia glanced at a black onyx ring on the night table. Beside it was a worn, faded photo of two identical, dark-haired little girls in overalls. They were smiling and holding hands in the picture.

Amelia sighed. "I realize now what Annabelle went through, and how much she must have suffered." She shrugged and shook her head. "But I—I can't cry for her. . . ."

Amelia wrapped her arms around Karen, then rested her head on her shoulder.

"It's okay," Karen said, holding her. She knew the tears would come later.

And she would be there to help her through it.

More Books From Your Favorite Thriller Authors

More Nail-Biting Suspense From Your Favorite Thriller Authors

re Thrilling Suspense From ur Favorite Thriller Authors

If Angels Fall by Rick Mofina	0-7860-1061-4	$6.99US/$8.99CAN
Cold Fear by Rick Mofina	0-7860-1266-8	$6.99US/$8.99CAN
Blood of Others by Rick Mofina	0-7860-1267-6	$6.99US/$9.99CAN
No Way Back by Rick Mofina	0-7860-1525-X	$6.99US/$9.99CAN
Dark of the Moon by P.J. Parrish	0-7860-1054-1	$6.99US/$8.99CAN
Dead of Winter by P.J. Parrish	0-7860-1189-0	$6.99US/$8.99CAN
Paint It Black by P.J. Parrish	0-7860-1419-9	$6.99US/$9.99CAN
Thick Than Water by P.J. Parrish	0-7860-1420-2	$6.99US/$9.99CAN

Available Wherever Books Are Sold!

Visit our website at **www.kensingtonbooks.com**